PRAISE FOR MATT JOHNSON

Longlisted for the CWA John Creasey (New Blood) Dagger

'Terse, tense and vivid writing. Matt Johnson is a brilliant new name in the world of thrillers. And he's going to be a big name' Peter James

'Utterly compelling and dripping with authenticity. This summer's must-read thriller' J S Law, author of Tenacity

'From the first page to the last, an authentic, magnetic and completely absorbing read' Sir Ranulph Fiennes

'Out of terrible personal circumstances, Matt Johnson has written a barnstormer of a book in *Wicked Game* – one that fans of Chris Ryan, Andy McNab and Peter James will drool over. His first-hand experience of police work and counter-terrorist operations gives this page-turner a chilling authenticity that few others in the genre can hope to rival. But despite his police pedigree, Johnson also gets inside the terrorists' heads to give them credible motivation. Nothing is clear-cut in a labyrinthine plot, which is gripping and which – despite thrills and spills aplenty – never falls short of believable. The ending is neatly tied up, but leaves the reader eager to follow lead character Robert Finlay's further adventures' David Young, author of *Stasi Child*

'The magic mix of jeopardy, emotion and action. I could not put it down' Louise Voss

'Matt Johnson shows he's been there, done it and worn the T-shirt in his first novel. Entertaining and gripping throughout, it is authentic writing at its very best. His ability to overlap reality with the fictional characters, from both a soldier's and cop's perspective is uncanny. Top-quality entertainment from a first-class writer' D.N. Ex-22 SAS Regiment

'A book by an ex-cop and -soldier has the potential to go wrong and fall flat due to it being all about inside knowledge that is tough to decipher by the public. This book isn't like that. It is a genuine page-turner, very well written, and just flows from one scenario to the next. It is clear the author lived through these times and this is evident in knowledge and description. Excellent' Ian Patrick

'A former SAS officer finds himself a target of a terrorist cell years after he has left the forces, creating a fast-moving storyline. I was so gripped that I could not put it down. I loved the main protagonist, Robert Finlay, but I particularly loved his feisty wife, Jenny. I'll be looking out for the sequel' Segnalibro

'The writing is direct: facts and histories stated, not left for the reader to pick over: there isn't time to stop and sift the finer aspects of motivation – to do so would only slow the plot. Events cascade, ruthless killers spill into the open, and the agencies who should be tackling them are far less united and coherent than one might expect … You'll enjoy this book if you're into thriller and action: even if you think you're not, the pace of the writing will carry you away. Robert Finlay's not a man who gives up easily' Blue Book Balloon

'From the first page through to the last, the reader is completely hooked and drawn in by the writing and the descriptions; this is such an absorbing and thrilling read. The authenticity of the writing, and the knowledge of what happens in particular situations raises this above other thrillers. *Wicked Game* really does give you flash, bang, wallop, and, like bullets, no words are wasted, but hit the target every time. Matt Johnson is a new name in thriller writing and with his brilliant writing we have a new star' Library Thing

'A real cracker of a book and I have no hesitation to give it five stars. I look forward to reading more books from this gifted writer' Bookworm

'Finlay is an older male who is settled down with a wife and child and is feeling his age a little. He's not some fit, handsome superhero. He's an ordinary man, who has made career choices that have put him in extraordinary situations, which in turn have led him down a path where he has to face difficult decisions. It's this normality about Finlay that appealed to me and kept me reading. The believability of the story. The authenticity' Rebecca Bradley

'An action thriller of the highest order that deserves to be read widely. It is hard to believe such an accomplished work is a debut' Never Imitate

'Despite having read hundreds of thrillers, it's rare to find one with this level of authenticity and with some real passion behind the writing ... I would describe *Wicked Game* as a thriller with a heart, and the story behind it and Matt's own experiences are what makes it beat' Book Addict Shaun

'A gripping and quite frantic story of espionage, misplaced loyalties, revenge, retribution and double-crossing. With twists and turns, and red herrings at every corner, *Wicked Game* is an impressive debut' Random Things through my Letterbox

'The case is so intriguing, full of red herrings and twists, highlighting years of service by Finlay and his team, the trail of potential enemies left behind. This is in some ways a spy novel, with tantalising glimpses of M15 and Home Office interference. Above all else, though, *Wicked Game* is a tense, exciting thriller that presents Finlay's gigantic effort to keep his family safe, trying to rediscover physical and military skills long put to rest, and facing seemingly insurmountable odds. The ending is stunning!' For Winter Nights

'Talk about a kick-ass novel! From the very first page, I was shocked into holding my breath. It reads like an action movie, but with all the bubbling tension in between, some of it so quiet and subtle that Matt lulls you into a sense of false security. Then BANG, he thumps you, shocks you, jolts you into submission, before doing it all again' The Book Trail

'This book oozes authenticity ... when barely a week goes by without us hearing about terrorist attacks somewhere in the world, on behalf of some cause or other, it reminded me of the thanks and respect these men like Matt Johnson – some of whom pay a heavy toll; some of whom pay the ultimate price – are due from us' Crime Worm

'The sheer dogged determination of Robert Finlay provides one hell of an exhilarating ride, as he dodges bullets, explosives, and the shadows of his past, in this *Wicked Game* of cat and mouse. Expect nothing less than a thrilling journey, where secrets and revenge are delivered with guts and precision and the stakes are as high as they get – Finlay gives new meaning to the SAS motto of "Who dares, wins"' Little Bookness Lane

'It's the first-hand experience of terrible events that really gives *Wicked Game* an unshakeable feeling of authenticity, which is woven deep into the fabric of the story' Espresso Coco

'I've always been a fan of thrillers, with the build-up of tension, the action-packed heroics and insane bravery. *Wicked Game* is a stonkingly accessible British thriller, with its roots firmly set in recent UK history and a strong sense of authenticity running through it' Northern Crime

‘The story itself is a complex web that the police, security services and Finlay himself are all trying to untangle. It is never clear who can be trusted and what agendas they are trying to move forward, except for Finlay, whose fight for survival we follow most intimately through his own thoughts. The tension takes hold early on and never lets up as the danger gets closer to home and Finlay realises that only he can secure his family’s safety as he is forced to face his past up close and personal’ Live Many Lives

‘Matt Johnson has a very real talent and gift for thriller writing. *Wicked Game* cracks along at a great pace, with plenty of gripping and original plot twists and turns, and a finale that wouldn’t be out of place in a book with a protagonist called Reacher’ Mumbling about…

‘This is a breathtaking debut novel that will have you on the edge of your seat’ Thrillers, Chillers & Killers

‘*Wicked Game* builds the tension in an intelligent and emotional way, has many layers to both time, place and sense of character, and is basically a top notch “thriller” that has a dark heart and an emotional soul. It is not a book that will be read and then forgotten – this one will stay with you. Excellent, thought-provoking, clever and beautifully written’ Liz Loves Books

‘With his first-hand real-life experience Johnson has an understanding of what was going on in the minds of his friends, superiors and even terrorists. This is translated into excellent psychological portraits of the main characters. Facts mixed with fiction and unclear boundaries between both are bases for moving authentic narration and brilliant storytelling’ Crime Review

'*Wicked Game* is an absolutely brilliant new thriller, and the plot is fast-paced, twisted and exciting. Finlay is a man who is prepared to break all the rules to protect his family, but he is also very human and likable. I can't praise Matt Johnson and *Wicked Game* too highly' Promoting Crime Fiction

'On every page, tension is carefully built, as a portentous revelation is offered or a memory smothered. Johnson litters his tale with the plotting equivalent of incendiaries: cops we don't quite trust, a career that came abruptly to an end, a secret needing to be kept ... Gripping stuff' New Welsh Review

'Matt Johnson delivers characters that feel pain, emotion and fear. There are some pretty sit-on-the-edge-of-your-seat moments because you know certain events are unstoppable and you can't avoid watching them unfold. A cracking book right to the end' From Dusk till Dawn

'Fall headlong into a gripping and absolutely cracking story, featuring an ex-SAS, turned Met police officer, battling for his life ... Johnson turns his knowledge into the most fabulous and readable story that just zings along with authenticity and exhilarating attitude. I'm excited to be in at the start of what promises to be a fabulous new series, and honestly can't wait for the next!' Love Reading

Deadly Game

ABOUT THE AUTHOR

Matt Johnson served as a soldier and Metropolitan Police officer for twenty-five years. Blown off his feet at the London Baltic Exchange bombing in 1992, and one of the first police officers on the scene of the 1982 Regent's Park bombing, Matt was also at the Libyan People's Bureau shooting in 1984 where he escorted his mortally wounded friend and colleague, Yvonne Fletcher, to hospital. Hidden wounds took their toll. In 1999, Matt was discharged from the police with Post Traumatic Stress Disorder. While undergoing treatment, he was encouraged by his counsellor to write about his career and his experience of murders, shootings and terrorism. One evening, Matt sat at his computer and started to weave these notes into a work of fiction that he described as having a tremendously cathartic effect on his own condition. His bestselling thriller, *Wicked Game*, which was longlisted for the CWA John Creasey Dagger, was the result.

Follow Matt on:
www.mattjohnsonauthor.com

Or Twitter:
@Matt_Johnson_UK

Deadly Game

Matt Johnson

Orenda Books
16 Carson Road
West Dulwich
London SE21 8HU
www.orendabooks.co.uk

First published by Orenda Books in 2017

A catalogue record for this book is available from the British Library.

ISBN 978-1-910633-66-3
eISBN 978-1-910633-67-0

Typeset in Arno by MacGuru Ltd
Printed and bound by CPI Group (UK) Ltd, Croydon CR0 4YY

SALES & DISTRIBUTION

In the UK and elsewhere in Europe:
Turnaround Publisher Services
Unit 3, Olympia Trading Estate
Coburg Road,
Wood Green
London
N22 6TZ
www.turnaround-uk.com

In the USA and Canada:
Trafalgar Square Publishing
Independent Publishers Group
814 North Franklin Street
Chicago, IL 60610
USA
www.ipgbook.com

In Australia and New Zealand:
Affirm Press
28 Thistlethwaite Street
South Melbourne VIC 3205
Australia
www.affirmpress.com.au

For details of other territories, please contact *info@orendabooks.co.uk*

For Hannah, a special daughter and friend.

And for Harley.

To appreciate harmony, we must know war.
To value freedom, we must know slavery.
To find peace, we must vanquish the Devil at his chosen game.

Prologue

1999. Romania

The wind can kill.

Relia Stanga recalled her father's words clearly as she huddled against the stone garden wall for shelter.

Winter was around the corner. The east wind was beginning to turn cold. Soon, she would need to take a chance and wait inside the house for the factory bus to arrive. In a few short weeks the winds from the east would bring snow and then, as Father had warned, it would be certain death to wait in the street for the six o'clock pick-up.

One day, she prayed, summers would no longer be spent cutting and gathering wood to see them through to the following spring. One day, there would be food on the table every single day and she would not have to rely on mother for hand-me-down clothes.

One day ... with luck, she would find a new life.

For now, Relia contented herself with wrapping her mother's woollen coat tight around her slim figure, lifting the collar and making herself as small and as tight as possible.

The wall provided the only protection from where she could see the approach of the bus. Miss the bus, no ride. Miss the ride, no job. Miss the job, go hungry.

Home for Relia was a small village on the north-east edge of Romania, near the border with Moldova. She was now seventeen and had spent the previous day with the men, cutting logs. Huge piles were now stacked in the village stores and in shelters people had built in the yards at the rear of their houses. Most of the harvest had been sold. Father and her brother had left at first light to deliver the last of the summer maize crop. With the income, they would buy salted meats that would be eaten once a week with potatoes and root soup.

On their return from the market, the men would be drunk. It was their release. They would meet friends, gossip, moan about the harvest, play cards and drink. Sorrows would be drowned with home-distilled *țuică*. Relia's father made his own from a family recipe using apples and plums. The women said it was the work of the devil, for the rage it sometimes brought out in the men.

Father was a hard-working man, a good man. But the drink would release his pent-up frustrations and anger. Mother would always bear the brunt of his wrath. The children just kept out of the way. This was the way of men; they had to vent their rage, and using the women stopped them from killing each other. This was the way of things, as it always had been.

But now, Relia had a plan.

Every month or so, the factory would host men from the city. Men from Brasov and Bucharest. Men who wore suits, drove Mercedes cars and talked of incredible adventures.

A friend who was a house servant to the wife of the factory owner told her the men came looking for girls. Relia could barely contain her excitement on learning these girls secured work in places in the city, in kitchens or waiting on tables. They had jobs, proper jobs, and they made enough money to keep some for themselves and send the rest home for their families.

The men would choose the best-looking girls. To each they would give a small, yellow ticket. It was their approval to ride in the warm van on its way to the city – their passport to a better life. The men were due today.

Beneath her worn clothing, Relia was possessed of unusual beauty, and yet they had not noticed her. She was determined that would change. She was slim, pale skinned, and was blessed with shiny, raven-black hair that a woman in the village had recently cut into a neat bob. She had bought a little make-up, and her friend, the servant, had loaned her a dress that would show off her figure. The next time the men came to the factory, Relia was to help serve their drinks.

The bus arrived. It was late, as always, and, as he always did, the driver drove fast to get the workers to the factory by seven o'clock. Relia snoozed on the journey. She didn't mind the potholes, the tight bends, the heavy braking or the driver swearing. The bus was warm. For nearly forty minutes she could drift into a world where there was no cold, no hunger.

When they arrived at the factory gates, Relia looked across to the owner's house. On the drive she saw his car – a big four-wheel drive. Then she saw the Mercedes, a black one, and behind it, a black van. The city men had arrived.

She checked her pocket, fearing she may have forgotten the powder and lipstick. It was there. As the factory gate opened, she saw her friend. There was a smile, then a wink. Today was the day. Today she was to have her chance.

✝

The day on the factory line passed slowly. Relia was a glue mixer. The factory made shoes. Leather imported from Mongolia was cut, shaped and stitched together by hand. Relia helped make the adhesive that would bind the upper parts of the shoe to the sole. It was easy work. Day after day she simply poured ingredients into containers in the prescribed measures and mixed them for the correct amount of time and at the right temperature. It was the heat of the glue room that made the job sought after in the winter and hated in the summer.

Due to the constituents of the glue, all the workers in the glue section smelled of fish, a fact that earned them the nickname *pesti*. Relia knew that as soon as she finished, she would have to sneak over to the owner's house, use her friend's bath and clean herself. Only then would she be ready to serve the city men and, hopefully, her freshly scrubbed skin and hair would be perfumed well enough to mask the fishy smell.

During the day, four girls were interviewed by the city men. Three of them were selected for employment, given their tickets and instructed to send messages to their families that they would not be home that night. In fact, they might never be home again. With one exception, Relia could not recall selected girls having ever returned to the villages. Who could blame them? With a new life in the city, money in their purses and, probably, husbands, there was no reason to come back to such a lowly life. Some would write, many would send small amounts of money, but none came back to the poverty of the villages.

The one that had returned had been the wife of one of the city men. She had spoken of having made her fortune, of the bright lights and excitement of the city, of girls marrying American soldiers and of the opportunities available to those willing to leave the villages. As she spoke, she held the young factory girls spellbound. The older women weren't convinced. 'If it sounds too good to be true, it probably is,' they would mutter. But the young women wanted their chance and it was them the city men came to see.

✠

That evening, Relia avoided the queue for the homeward-bound bus and crept slowly around the back of the factory. Here, she knew she could find the gate to the owner's house. It was locked, as always. The owners thought all the workers were thieves.

At the arranged time, six o'clock, her friend Elisabeta was waiting.

Elisabeta unlocked the gate from the inside and the two girls then scurried along the concrete path towards the house. In the half-light from the windows of the house she could see the garden was green and luxurious, nothing like the sun-parched yards of the village. It was the first time she had seen behind the high walls into this secret place. Only the owners and selected house staff were allowed such a privilege. Relia had heard the stories and now, with her own eyes, she could see it was as beautiful as they said. To one side there was even a swing and a fountain.

Relia paused for a moment to stare. It was just like she had seen in the well-thumbed magazines that sometimes appeared in the factory for the workers to look at during their breaks.

Voices came from the house – male voices – laughter.

'Hurry,' her friend whispered. 'We mustn't be seen here.'

Relia understood. If they were caught, it would be assumed they were stealing. They would be dismissed if they were lucky, jailed if the owner called the police. The *politia locale* were good men, in the main, but they would always believe a respected factory owner over a poor village girl.

Elisabeta stopped as they reached the small door that led to the servants' quarters. She pressed a single finger to her lips then gently opened the door.

The first thing that struck Relia was the heat. Even in this part of the house, it was warm and comfortable. In the village they could only afford to heat one room. Here, there were radiators in all the rooms, and even in the corridors.

That evening, Relia enjoyed the longest, hottest bath she had ever experienced. She scrubbed her hands, her feet, her face, all the while sniffing herself to check the smell of fish was fading. She washed her hair four times before she was satisfied the aroma was gone.

Elisabeta sprayed her sparingly with a body perfume. Relia would have liked a little more but her friend was insistent. The owner's wife gave it to all the female staff so they wouldn't carry their body odours into the main rooms. There was one spray-can each per month, and they were expected to make it last.

When Relia saw the dress Elisabeta had prepared for her, she nearly wept. It was thin, silk-like and hugged her figure. Although blue, it was such a dark shade as to almost appear black. The design was sleeveless and reminded Relia of pictures she had seen of film stars like Marilyn Monroe. It was sexy.

The dress was a colour all the household staff wore to serve dinner. But for Relia it had a different purpose. Skin tight, it emphasised her curves and suggested hidden treasures. On this night, it was to lure the city men.

At eight o'clock, the head girl sounded the brass gong in the hallway to signal dinner was prepared. Elisabeta served at table and had arranged that Relia would support her. The girl who normally filled that role had agreed to hide in her room for the evening. Elisabeta was sure her absence would not be noticed, especially when the men saw Relia.

The plan worked. The men fell silent the moment they set eyes on the new girl in the dark-blue dress. Smiling, the owner asked who she was, and while Elisabeta explained, the oldest of the city men beckoned Relia closer. . When the owner had grunted his approval, the old man immediately asked Relia if she would take up a chance to be his personal assistant in Brasov.

Relia nodded and then backed away as the men negotiated a price to secure her services. She heard the figure of two thousand lei being argued over, before the owner and the elder city man shook hands. The deal was done. There was much laughter and the men returned to eating and drinking.

That evening, as the chosen girls waited for the city men's van to be made ready, they wrote letters to their families. The factory owner's wife had suggested it, and even helped them with the wording.

'Are you excited?' one of the girls asked Relia, as the owner's wife collected their envelopes and left the room.

But Relia didn't answer. The owner's wife had left the door ajar and, through the gap, Relia could now see her dropping the little stack of letters into one of the sacks they used for rubbish in the factory.

'Relia?' asked her companion, a tiny frown knitting her brow.

Relia shook herself and smiled, but a gnawing sense of worry remained.

'Yes,' she replied. Then, trying to sound more certain: 'Yes, I can't wait.'

Chapter 1

Metropolitan Police Headquarters, New Scotland Yard, Central London, October 2001

Dawn was breaking over the capital.

Grahamslaw watched the circle of moisture form on the glass. It was early and, despite the double glazing, the cold autumn air had penetrated to the inner surface. His warm breath created a small, clouded patch that grew with every successive exhalation.

Twelve floors down, traffic was starting to build up into unbroken lines. Most were delivery vehicles that, by now, would have completed their allotted tasks and were heading back to their depots. There were one or two private cars, but not many, and very few of those drivers would be heading to the underground car park below the building in which he stood. That was almost exclusively reserved for operational transport and the few luxury cars the Met retained for the exclusive use of the most senior ranks. From the black, box-like shapes discharging heavy grey exhaust fumes, it looked to the anti-terrorist detective like most of the snaking, weaving lines were formed by taxis.

The Anti-Terrorist Commander checked his watch. Ten past six. Toni Fellowes was late, but that wasn't a real cause for concern. Provided the MI5 officer turned up within the next twenty minutes he would have plenty of time to get to his next meeting. For now, he was determined to enjoy what were probably the only moments of tranquillity he would experience that day.

A noise from the corridor caused him to turn towards the door. Squad members were starting to arrive for work. The skeleton night team would be pleased to see the first arrivals. A quick handover briefing and they would be on their way to their homes and some welcome sleep.

Turning towards the desk – a large, oak affair that had followed him up the ranks and through a plethora of different offices – he cast an eye over the report that lay waiting to be read by Ms Fellowes. Time for one last check through. Swinging his large chair around, he sat and began to read.

Metropolitan Police

To: Director T Dept, MI5
From: Commander SO13, Anti-Terrorist Squad
Cc. Commissioner, Assistant Commissioner 'SO'
Date: 29th September 2001

Re: Operation Hastings – Executive Summary

Sir,
This interim report deals with the recent attacks on serving police officers in London, their aftermath and the conclusions I have reached through my investigations.

In recent weeks, four Metropolitan police officers and one MI5 officer were killed on duty as a result of terrorist action.

These were:

1. Inspector Robert Bridges (attached Marylebone Police Station)
2. PC John Evans (attached Hackney Police Station)
3. PC Roderick Skinner (attached Barkingside Police Station)
4. PC Giles Duncan (attached Marylebone Police Station)
5. Nial Monaghan, MI5

Inspector Bridges and PC Duncan were killed as a result of an improvised explosive device (IED) planted by suspects 1, 3 and 4 listed below. PC Skinner was shot dead outside his home address by suspects 1 and 3. PC Evans was shot by suspect 2 during a street check of a suspect vehicle, which, it transpired, was carrying equipment and material intended for use in terror attacks in the capital. Suspect 2 was shot and killed by the armed response crew that responded to this incident.

Attempts were also made by suspects 1 and 3 to murder Inspectors

David Heathcote and Robert Finlay, Sergeant Michael Holbrook (all attached Stoke Newington) and PC Kevin Jones (attached Hornchurch).

Results of investigation – summary

Investigations carried out by SO13 determined these murders and attempts were not the result of random attacks on uniformed police officers doing their duty. Early on in the enquiry it was established that Inspectors Bridges and Finlay, and PCs Skinner and Jones all formerly served in the army together as members of 22 Special Air Service Regiment (SAS).

During the course of the attacks, SO13 were able to identify five suspects:

1. Declan Costello, born Ireland, now deceased
2. Seamus McGlinty, born Ireland, now deceased
3. Dominic McGlinty, born Ireland, now in custody and remanded at HMP Belmarsh
4. Michael Hewitson, born Kentish Town, now in custody and remanded at HMP Belmarsh
5. Richard Webb, alias Selahattin Yildrim, born Ireland, now deceased

Enquiries have now established that, following attacks on Inspector Bridges and PC Skinner, an approach was made by MI5 officer, Nial Monaghan, to involve Inspector Finlay and PC Jones in a plan to intercept and terminate the attacks on other former soldiers.

Monaghan was known to both Finlay and Jones as their former Commanding Officer at the time these officers were all serving in the SAS in the 1980s. Finlay and Jones were persuaded to assist Monaghan in what they believed to be an attempt to identify those responsible for murdering their former military colleagues and to prevent further murders.

The activities of the suspects and the resulting incidents can be summarised as follows:

1. Street search of lorry by police patrol car led to the unplanned shooting of PC Evans.
2. Planned IED attack targeted and killed Inspector Bridges, with the collateral death of PC Duncan.
3. Planned shooting of PC Skinner.
4. IED attack on a car due to be carrying Inspector Finlay resulted in serious injury to Inspector Heathcote and Sgt Holbrook.
5. IED car bomb attack at home of Inspector Finlay caused injury to Explosives Ordnance Disposal Officer, Rupert Reid.

And following the approach made by Mr Monaghan to Finlay and Jones and their involvement in his plan:

6. Shooting attempt on the life of PC Jones, resulting in serious injury to the officer and the death of Declan Costello.
7. Attempt on the life of Inspector Finlay, together with his wife, resulting in the death of Richard Webb.
8. IED car explosion causing the death of Nial Monaghan.

Result of subsequent enquiries

In attempting to establish a motive for these attacks, several lines of enquiry were pursued, including surveillance of officers Finlay and Jones. It was established that these two officers were making their own efforts to identify the terrorists and were likely to be in possession of relevant information as to motive.

It was further established that Finlay and Jones had secured access to unlawfully held firearms, explosives and equipment in order to pursue their efforts.

With the authority of the Home Secretary, a decision was made to allow Finlay and Jones to continue, under surveillance, in the hope they would lead the enquiry team to the attackers and enable arrests to be made.

Motive

In 1980, while serving with the SAS in Northern Ireland, Robert Finlay was attacked by four armed men. In the resulting firefight, Finlay killed three men, one of whom was the brother of Richard Webb.

It has now been established, beyond reasonable doubt, that the reason for the attack on Inspector Finlay was a result of a personal sense of grievance and a desire for revenge on the part of Richard Webb.

Correspondence found in the possession of Nial Monaghan reveals the attacks on the other former SAS soldiers appear to be due to a desire on Monaghan's part for revenge, he having formed the belief his wife committed suicide following the revelation of affairs with men serving under Monaghan's command. Our evidence is that Monaghan and Webb were co-operating on this murderous campaign.

There appears to have been no separate motive in the murders of PCs Evans and Duncan, who appear to have been killed because they were in the wrong place at the wrong time.

Since the deaths of both Monaghan and Webb, the attacks have ceased. This tends to corroborate the preceding evaluation.

In conclusion

Dominic McGlinty and Michael Hewitson are awaiting trial on charges of conspiracy to murder and to cause explosions.

Following the decision of the Home Secretary to allow Finlay and Jones to operate in an armed unsupervised role, a report was submitted to the Crown Prosecution Service as to whether either officer should be charged with any offence. The decision was made (with Home Secretary and DPP authority) that no criminal action would be taken against either officer.

Inspector Finlay, together with his family, is currently being provided with secure accommodation by MI5 and is expected to return to work soon.

PC Jones has made a good recovery from his injury, has declined the offer of secure accommodation and is also expected to return to full police duties in the near future.

Media interest

While some speculation has appeared in the press with regards to the attacks on Metropolitan officers, no mention has been made or theory attributed to the involvement of former armed services personnel.

The Metropolitan Police Press Bureau has ensured all arrests resulting from this operation have been credited to police enquiries. Deaths of suspects have been attributed to self-inflicted injuries (Webb) and lawful police action.

Full report

My understanding is that Director 'T' has tasked MI5 officer Antonia Fellowes to act as support officer to the Finlay family and PC Jones and to complete a final confidential report to the Home Secretary on the activities of Monaghan and Webb.

Respectfully submitted,

William Grahamslaw
Commander, SO13
Anti-Terrorist Squad
Specialist Operations Directorate
New Scotland Yard

Chapter 2

Just as Grahamslaw reached for his pen to sign the report he sensed he had company.

He looked up and saw Toni Fellowes standing in the doorway. 'May I join you?' she asked.

Without speaking, the Commander indicated his visitor should use the seat on the other side of the desk. The MI5 officer looked smart and business-like: a dark-blue trouser-suit complemented by matching shoes – low heels, she always wore low heels – and a white blouse. Under her left arm she was carrying a stiff, buff-coloured folder. Given her next port of call would be the Home Office, she gave the appearance of being well prepared.

'Apologies for my lateness, Commander. Is that the Hastings report?' Fellowes closed the door behind her and sat down.

'Hot off the press, you might say. Taken me the best part of a week to finish, it has.' Grahamslaw quickly signed the final page, tapped the pages together neatly and slid them across the desk. It wasn't, he mused, a particularly lengthy or complicated report, just that the previous few weeks had easily been the busiest of his police career. Demands on anti-terror policing had increased manyfold since the New York attacks on September 11th. Finding the time to complete a report hadn't been easy.

As Fellowes flicked through the document, his gaze returned to the window.

He was pleased the Director of Public Prosecutions had seen fit to take no further action against Finlay and Jones. They had faced a situation most would find beyond imagination. Their former Commanding Officer had played a game with the two former soldiers – leading them a merry dance in order to draw them in, mislead and then kill them. That they had managed to turn the tables on him was to their immense credit. What troubled the Commander now was whether there was really a need to continue the investigation. The decision to appoint an MI5 liaison officer to look after both PC Jones and the Finlay family was well founded and Toni Fellowes had handled the responsibility with her usual professionalism. But as to whether there was a point in continuing to dig, he had serious doubts. From his limited experience of the murky world of the men in suits, he had learned that such things were often best left alone.

But now, with his report signed, the enquiry was effectively out of his hands.

After her brief flick through the document Fellowes slipped it back into the buff folder.

'I thought you'd want to read it now … just to check it over, perhaps?' he said.

She shook her head. 'No time. I'm hoping the Security Service contribution will simply be a rubber stamp to your conclusions.'

He smiled, broadly. 'Let's hope so, Toni. This wasn't the kind of thing that happens every week, was it?'

'It wasn't. Do you mind if I ask what your plans for Jones and Finlay are, now the Home Secretary has approved the decision not to prosecute?'

'With Jones it should be fairly straightforward. He's making a decent recovery from his injuries and he told me he wants nothing more than to get back to being a normal cop. For Finlay, things are more complicated, as you know.'

'I spoke to his Chief Superintendent.'

'Let me guess,' said Grahamslaw, 'not keen on having him back?'

'He's a realist. Finlay is something of a pariah, now. Too many people know both his background and about the attacks on him.'

'The Met rumour mill always did work quickly.'

'I spoke to Hereford as well. They've had calls – people checking up on him, some of them former members of the regiment who were being nosy.'

'He won't be easy to place … and he's too young to retire.'

'And his skill set isn't what you might describe as easily transferrable.'

Grahamslaw shrugged. 'You sound like you're building up to something. If it's a position with the Security Service, I can tell you now, he won't go for it.'

'I know. He's made that more than clear when I've talked it over with him. I was thinking of something closer to home.'

'Here at the Yard, you mean?'

'Yes, exactly. Easy commute from the safe house and somewhere we can keep an eye on him.'

'But doing what? He has no detective experience and he's not the kind of man to slip easily into some kind of administrative role.'

Fellowes paused for a moment. 'Is it too late in his career to be taught to do detective duty?'

'Depends what you have in mind. Junior CID courses are normally for DCs ... but I'm sure I could swing something, if needed.'

'How about your new trafficking squad? It's undermanned and underfunded.'

'Max Youldon's team, you mean?'

'That's right. I thought he might do well working with Nina Brasov.'

Grahamslaw pondered the idea. 'It might work. Brasov is damn good ... Finlay would learn a lot from her. She's been doing some undercover work lately that takes her away from the office, though.'

'I could have a word at the Home Office, if that would help?'

'To what end?'

'Your budget. A little help with the cost of running the squad.'

'You're suggesting, if I put Finlay on that squad, the Whitehall mandarins might be more sympathetic to our requests for more funding?' The Commander laughed. 'I'm not so green as I am cabbage-looking, you know.'

Fellowes smiled, her expression open and betraying no guile.

He returned her gaze, maintaining a friendly exterior, but he wasn't fooled. It was his guess Toni Fellowes was using him to help get Finlay placed so she could concentrate on the work that would have been building up in the aftermath of 9/11.

'OK, I agree,' Grahamslaw said. He grinned, almost imperceptibly, and this time to himself. He hoped Finlay would prove agreeable to the offer. The first step would be to get him up to the Yard to talk about it. And if a little plan he had in mind proved successful, that might happen sooner rather than later.

Chapter 3

MI5 safe house, West London

The transition from the disturbed world of my subconscious to self-awareness was brutal.

As I woke, I found the bed beneath me was wet, soaked in sweat, my skin dripping. Although I was hot, I shivered, my heart pounding, my chest heaving with huge, deep breaths.

My senses returned, and with them awareness … familiarity. I recognised where I was. Home.

Our *new* home. And I was alone.

I'd been dreaming again, one of a number of disturbing nightmares that now regularly troubled my sleep and ended with me waking, like this, gripped by panic. And although the scenes varied, they were always very similar. Sometimes I would be fighting with my fellow policemen, desperate to alert them to some form of danger. In other scenarios, the strength in my limbs would be overcome by gravity and the unnatural, weighty resistance of the air around me. Time and again, these dreams would feature people from my past – ghostly memories returning to haunt me. Most nights I would lie on a bath towel in anticipation of the moment when my dreams would wake me. It helped to absorb the sweat and saved on bed sheets.

I lay quietly for a few moments, waiting for my body to wind down from its imaginary exercise. My eyes, accustomed to the dark, allowed me to pick out the now familiar window of our bedroom. I say ours, although it was no longer shared.

Jenny had recently taken to sleeping in the spare room. Twice, while asleep beside her, I had struck out and hurt her. I hated sleeping alone, we both did. But, for the sake of our health and her safety, it became unavoidable.

We were now resident in West London. Home was a big, Edwardian place in a quiet side street. It had four bedrooms – all with high ceilings and decorative plasterwork – and a wonderful modern kitchen and living room. Jenny loved it. It came fully furnished, so the bulk of our furniture had been put into storage. All there was for us to do was look after the garden and keep the place fairly tidy. As I whiled away the days thinking about what had happened and deciding on when to return to work, I found the distraction of that garden very therapeutic.

For the first three weeks in our new home, a combined team from MI5 and Special Branch had kept guard. While it was in some ways uncomfortable – you could never relax, knowing someone was the other side of the door – it did give me an interesting insight into how the Royal Family and senior politicians must feel to have people like me shadowing their every move. The Royals seemed used to it; we found it a struggle.

Jenny and I had been debriefed by an efficient yet considerate MI5 officer called Toni Fellowes. Toni had been appointed as our family liaison officer and had now become something of a friend. She and Jenny seemed to get on particularly well.

As Toni and I got to know each other, we had, inevitably, compared backgrounds. She was also ex-services, having been a Lieutenant in the Royal Navy, seconded to the Special Boat Squadron, before her skills with language and computers had seen her recruited by the Security Service.

Having gained her trust, and become easier with her company, I probed Toni for information on Richard Webb, the man who had tried to kill us. Toni appreciated that, even though Monaghan was dead, I still had questions outstanding: Had Webb been acting alone or were there others? Was there a cell that might still have me as a target? And what about Monaghan, my old boss? What part had he played in the conspiracy to kill my former colleagues? Was he actually MI5?

It was early days, though. Toni was helpful but what she could tell me was limited. She made no promises but explained that initial analysis by SO13 suggested Webb had been acting outside any terrorist command structure in order to pursue his own deadly agenda. Monaghan really had been MI5, it was just his wife's affairs had eaten away at him to such an extent, he decided upon revenge. He had got it into his mind that his late wife had been sleeping around and, as a result, he had decided to deal with all her supposed lovers. The two men had then linked up to pursue their deadly agenda. Monaghan had needed a team to take on the attacks; Webb wanted to find me. Now, with both of them dead, Toni explained the threat to my family had almost certainly disappeared.

I remembered her words exactly, so important were they to me and my family. It may have been something or nothing, but Toni's use of the word 'almost' troubled me greatly.

And the dreams continued.

Chapter 4

I was now awake and alert. Experience had taught me a return to sleep would be impossible. I lay still and, as I often did these days, I worried about the future.

In the period since the attacks, I'd been doing a lot of thinking: about how I could get back to work, what role I could find, that kind of thing. I knew it wasn't going to be easy.

A meeting with Bob Sinclair, my Chief Superintendent at Stoke Newington, hadn't gone well. It might have best been described as a 'full and frank' discussion. He pulled no punches and, as reasonably as he could, he explained to me I had become something of a problem.

To his mind, the best thing for me was a move away from the front-line to an office job at Scotland Yard, maybe as a staff officer to one of the senior ranks. Intelligence work was also a possibility. He did his best to put a positive spin on my predicament, explaining there were a myriad of non-operational jobs in the Met – projects and departments where you could spend a whole career moving from one role to another, never wearing a uniform or going on the streets again. He was sure I would find something to suit me.

I saw his point: colleagues thinking of me as a bullet magnet wouldn't exactly make me sought-after on any shifts. So, even though I didn't like what he was saying, I understood it. A job sat behind a desk didn't appeal to me, though. It suited some; the kind that liked to be tied to a career structure and a pension but had lost the taste for front-line policing. As one desk job came to an end, they would simply apply for another. We called such people 'plastics'. In time, they were policemen in name only. No way was I going to become a plastic.

☩

Having spent the afternoon in the garden, I was still turning these questions over in my mind as I left home late that night to drive the familiar route back into the Hertfordshire countryside. It had now been some time since we had moved away from our old home and I needed to return to collect a few items I was anxious should remain secret.

In a hide concealed within the old oak tree at the end of the garden of our cottage, lay an Armalite rifle and a Heckler & Koch MP5. Disassembled but complete, they needed to be moved somewhere more secure before somebody found them and I ended up in even more difficulty.

In the aftermath of the firefight in which Richard Webb had tried to kill us, the Anti-Terrorist forensic people had seized my old pistol, the Beretta trophy weapon I had kept since my time in Northern Ireland. I had been sad to see it go; it was like parting with an old friend.

A lot of the guys from Hereford had trophy weapons they were supposed to hand in to the Quartermaster but had 'forgotten' to do so. Small arms and ammunition, knives and other weapons would be dropped by both enemy and friendly combatants during skirmishes. It was said that, during the Gulf War, more small arms seized from enemy soldiers were secretly brought into the UK by returning soldiers than there were weapons taken into the war in the first place. Stories like that have a habit of becoming exaggerated, but I wondered if some might be true.

I approached the cottage from the north, across the fields behind the back garden. I didn't expect the place to still be under surveillance – human or electronic – but I wasn't about to take any chances. To protect my clothes, I'd pulled on an old RAF boiler suit I had picked up in an army surplus store. Cheap and cheerful, it didn't exactly flatter my figure, but it would do the job. I was planning a long crawl through the fields and hedges to reach the garden of our former home.

Progress across the fields was slow. There was only a little light from a half-moon, and, for much of the time, I had to feel my way. I made best use of the firm areas adjacent to the hedges and the additional cover this also provided. At about four hundred yards short of my target, I started to belly crawl. Within a very short distance, I was breathing hard and my elbows were starting to bruise. I had known it wasn't going to be easy and promised myself that soon I would start making an effort to get fit again. It was months since I had done any running and my lack of fitness made hard work of what should have been a simple job.

I lost count of the number of times I stopped to gain my breath. Eventually, after about an hour, I reached the end of the garden and sat back against the old oak tree. Here, I was well hidden and able to rest, my heart rate dropping gradually as I recovered from the exertion. I waited for several minutes, listening and watching. All was quiet.

Hidden by the trees surrounding me, I eased myself to my feet and quickly located the loose bark that concealed the hide. In the dark, I had to feel for what lay within. I was careful, moving very slowly, cautious for any sign things were not as I had left them many weeks previously.

I'd wrapped the component parts in oiled paper. Five small packages contained bolt carriers, stocks, grips, magazines; and then a final box held the two firing mechanisms. There was some body armour, a veil, gas mask and fire-resistant coveralls. With everything safely stored in my bag, I was just about to replace the bark when my hand touched something unexpected.

It was paper. An envelope.

For a few moments, I stood immobile, my arm still inside the tree trunk, contemplating the implications of what I held in my hand.

Certainly, the envelope wasn't mine. Jenny knew about the hide but she hadn't mentioned anything.

At first, I thought it had to be some kind of trap, or somehow linked to the attempt to kill me. But that just didn't make sense. It would have been much easier to set up a wire to trigger an IED the moment I removed the bark. No, it was a sealed envelope, pure and simple. Inside, there would be a message. What it said and from whom it came would have to wait until I got back to the car and had a chance to read it.

I sat down and looked at the envelope, weighed it in my hand and sniffed it. It appeared to be white, and seemed to only contain paper, maybe one sheet. In the darkness, I couldn't tell if there was anything written on it or even whether it was addressed to me.

I slipped it into my thigh pocket and made sure the Velcro tab was secure. Having found the mysterious note, I didn't plan to lose it.

One thing was certain. The hide was compromised and whoever left the note had guessed I would be back to recover my kit. The writer wanted to make a point. And if that was the case, then I figured they wouldn't be watching the fields looking for me. I hoped my assumption was correct as, after just fifty yards crawling away from the garden on my stomach, I tired of the effort. I stood up, picked up my things and walked quickly back towards my car. I was done with scrabbling about in the dirt.

I checked the car and then stashed the disassembled weapons and kit safely in the boot. The envelope sat on the passenger seat, calling to me to open it.

For several miles I kept a close eye on my rearview mirror. Finally, convinced I wasn't being followed, I pulled over and switched on the interior light.

The envelope had just one word on it, 'Finlay', handwritten, in biro. I didn't recognise the handwriting.

My hands were shaking as I peeled it open. There was a single sheet of paper inside.

When you are ready, call me.

It was signed *Bill G.*

Grahamslaw.

From the moment I had appeared on Commander Grahamslaw's radar, he had been telling me my days as a uniformed cop were numbered. Resist it as much as I tried, I couldn't dispute his logic.

I took a deep breath and thought. My next step would be crucial. Telephoning Grahamslaw wouldn't be enough. I would go to see him. But first, I had another little job to take care of.

The next spot I would choose to hide my kit best not be known to anyone, especially not the Commander of the Met Anti-Terrorist Squad.

I had just the place.

Chapter 5

Toni Fellowes hated the journey in to work.

Every working day, she would make the ten-minute walk to North Harrow tube station to join the other commuters. Ignoring her fellow travellers, she would bury her head in a book to try and remove herself from the discomfort of the journey. Toni enjoyed reading, it took her to dream places away from the confines of her routine. But sometimes she wasn't really paying attention to the words on the page; instead she was thinking, planning.

Not that there was really much point in planning. Without exception, her ideas had been dashed on the altar of reality. Every crowded and uncomfortable tube ride seemed to serve as a reminder of her failure to convert thought into action. With Christmas not far away she knew, once again, she would most likely start a new year in the same line of work. Yet, she would still promise herself that her situation was only temporary.

It wasn't that she didn't enjoy the challenge of working for the Security Service; it was more a case of needing a new challenge, or a change ... something to stop the routine.

Things had been very different nine years previously – on 23rd November 1992 to be precise, the day she had first been approached to join MI5. At the time, having only just passed out from Dartmouth as a Royal Navy officer, an ability with languages had seen her assigned as a temporary Liaison Officer to the SBS, the Special Boat Service.

At the time, the SBS had been working on an operation with the Met firearms branch to ambush a large drugs shipment that was being brought into London on a three-hundred-ton, South-American-registered supply vessel labelled 'Foxtrot Five'. As the crew were known to be Spanish speaking, Toni had been brought on to the operation to help the SBS take control of the ship's bridge.

In the event, when the assault on the ship took place, the whole crew were absent ashore. They were picked up by local police and Toni's translation skills were never utilised. But she had experienced the adrenalin rush of the assault; she had been able, albeit temporarily, to wear the kit of the 'men in black' and – most notably – she had succeeded in getting noticed by MI5.

Two weeks after returning to Plymouth, her Commanding Officer had called her into his office with the news she had been selected for an interview in London. The CO had immediately surmised it was with one or other of the intelligence services and warned her what to expect. He was aware that MI5, in particular, was looking to recruit candidates from red-brick universities rather than the Oxbridge officer class it had traditionally focussed on. Toni had read modern languages at Sussex. Fluent in French and Spanish, and with a working knowledge of Russian, in the opinion of the CO, she was ideal MI5 material.

The first interview took place in a nondescript office block behind Tottenham Court Road in London. Much to her amusement, the taxi driver who picked her up at Paddington recognised the address and even wished her luck if she became a spy.

Inside, the offices were austere, bland; the magnolia emulsion that decorated the walls peeling and in need of repair. There was just the one interviewer, Kate – a tall woman in her late thirties who looked to be dressed more for a day's shopping in Harrods than conducting interviews. Kate was the typical Roedean type, the kind Toni had seen many times in Brighton while she had been at university. For an hour, they had talked about Toni's school life, her reasons for joining the navy and about all manner of other subjects, including her opinions on political matters and terrorism. Several times during the interview Kate unexpectedly switched languages – using both Spanish and Russian. Toni's responses in the former were fluent, in the latter, slow but correct.

At the end of the interview Kate pushed a form across the desk and asked Toni to sign it. The heading read *Official Secrets Act*. After completing this formality, they undertook a short tour of the building. Most doors were closed but those rooms Kate showed Toni around were, without exception, cluttered and untidy. Her guide apologised for the conditions and was at pains to stress it was the nature of the work that was interesting and not the cramped working environment which, apparently, had always left a lot to be desired.

Toni was enthralled by the whole experience. The secrecy, the kudos, the very thought of knowing she might become an MI5 officer, all excited her.

During the following week back in Plymouth, she repeatedly checked her correspondence tray for any indication as to the result of the interview. One day, a brown envelope appeared. She had been invited to sit the Civil Service Selection Board; she would undertake a two-day series of tests, which involved verbal and numerical reasoning, written and management exercises, and, finally, interviews with another MI5 officer and a psychologist.

A month after the brown envelope arrived, Toni heard from her parents that they had just been visited by a 'very nice man' who had asked a lot of questions about her school life and political interests. It was part of the vetting process. Two weeks later, Toni attended the selection test. The interview went well and, a little under four months from the day she had boarded the 'Foxtrot Five', she walked into the MI5 training office in Grosvenor Street, Mayfair with five other successful candidates to start the Security Service induction course.

☩

Nine years later, and Toni was now a team leader in 'T' department, T2E section. In that time, she had moved department six times, been promoted three times and moved office eight times. Her current role was working with the Met Special Branch and, as such, she was now based in a rather bland office on the eighteenth floor of New Scotland Yard. With twelve months now under her belt here, this was the longest she had been at the same desk.

She reported through her line manager, Dave Batey, to Director 'T', or 'Dirt' as he was affectionately known. Dirt had given her an assignment which had, at first, appeared to be something of a burden. She was to resettle and liaise with the family of a police officer who had been the subject of a personal terrorist attack. And that was how she had met Robert Finlay, a cop who had kept his army service secret for nearly twenty years, until forced to take extraordinary steps to protect himself and his family from harm.

As things had turned out, the responsibility had given her a great deal of pleasure. Although he was currently experiencing some emotional difficulties following the attacks on his family, Robert Finlay was unlike any cop she had ever met. Unorthodox and possessing skills that enabled him to solve problems in ways many police officers would deem unacceptable, he was, in many ways unique. He was a survivor, but he was also a problem. The career that had given him such an interesting pedigree was now his curse. To many, he was persona non grata – an outcast, a difficulty for supervisors and perceived as a threat by many of his peers.

Working with Finlay, an idea had come to Toni about how to overcome this particular challenge – a thought that had niggled at the back of her mind, refusing to go away. So, when she got wind of Commander Grahamslaw's decision to create a small team to look at slave-trafficking in the capital city, the timing couldn't have been more perfect.

Jenny – Finlay's wife – was a fighter, a determined personality who seemed to be the glue that held the family together. Their daughter,

Becky, well ... she was a delight, pure and simple; the kind of child who would make any woman want kids of her own. They seemed a solid family unit, if a little out of the ordinary.

But, just recently there had been problems. Jenny had reported her husband was suffering flashbacks and nightmares. On several occasions Robert had woken from a violent dream, soaked in sweat. During quieter moments, when she and Toni had been able to talk, she confided that she and Robert had been forced to start sleeping in separate rooms.

There were also times when he seemed to drift into a world of his own, deep in thought and unaware of his surroundings. Often he was agitated, short-tempered and impatient, even paranoid – continually checking his car for IEDs. Not that this latter behaviour surprised Toni. Having had a bomb placed under your car once, it would be a long time before a person would be able to feel comfortable getting into a vehicle.

Keen to be helpful, Toni had spoken to a police-appointed psychiatrist about Jenny's concerns. He explained post-traumatic stress to Toni, its symptoms and its causes. It appeared that Robert Finlay was a classic case. The psychiatrist had recommended Finlay make an appointment with him, so they could talk about beginning a course of treatment. But, he warned, Finlay would first need to accept there was something wrong and would have to agree to being helped. The psychiatrist had also suggested getting Finlay away from the work environment for a period – perhaps for a holiday; something that would give him a chance to relax. Toni had passed this suggestion on to Jenny.

If Robert accepted the idea of a holiday, she had the perfect trip in mind.

Chapter 6

As Toni left the tube train at St James's Park, she began to plan her day.

First on the 'to do' list was to dictate an update to be added to Commander Grahamslaw's Operation Hastings report. After that, Director 'T' wanted a full report on Nial Monaghan. Until he derailed and started organising the deaths of ex-SAS soldiers worldwide, Colonel Monaghan had been a team leader in T5E/3 department, responsible for the study of Middle Eastern terrorist logistics. He had also assumed administrative responsibility for ROSE – a now defunct department that had looked after the relocation and placement of retiring field agents and certain former special-forces soldiers. The Director, she had been told, was anxious to bring matters to a close as soon as possible. It was her job to see that happened.

A lot of people were making the short walk from the tube station towards the entrance to New Scotland Yard. After the 9/11 attacks, security had become exceptionally tight. Inside the main entrance, armed SO19 officers now stood guard, and, in the adjacent streets, officers from the Diplomatic Protection Group made regular patrols. The crowd from St James's Park underground station became a scrum as it entered the revolving door to New Scotland Yard, and the queue for security checks at reception was a test of patience. With everyone in a hurry to get to their desks, the long delays were incredibly frustrating.

Waiting patiently in line, Toni took the opportunity to look at the Eternal Flame and to read the Book of Remembrance, which listed, in date order, the names of officers killed on duty. The book had recently been absent while the names of the four officers killed in the preceding weeks were added to it.

She was especially pleased Rod Skinner's name had now been placed in the book. Skinner was one of Finlay's former colleagues and had been at home at the time he was shot. At great personal risk, he had bravely saved the life of a young boy.

The Police Federation had argued that, by saving the boy before himself, PC Skinner had placed himself on duty. There had been some resistance from the official channels, mainly due to the financial implications and the increased benefits such a decision would accrue to his widow. But in the end, the Federation prevailed. Skinner was named in the book and his widow received her full pension. There was even talk of a posthumous decoration.

Today, the Remembrance Book page detailed a number of officers whose deaths had occurred in circumstances ranging from a collision with a lorry while on motorcycle training through to a WPC who had been stabbed while attempting to detain a man during the course of a house search. One entry listed the death of an Explosives Officer who had been killed in 1981 when he had been attempting to defuse a bomb. They were all sad reminders of the price some paid to keep the streets safe.

With security checks complete, Toni headed for the lift and the eighteenth floor. Access to the Security Service offices was very limited, so she was the only person who pressed '18'.

Once in the Security Service corridor, all directions were restricted by solid doors that only opened in response to a digital security code or through a CCTV and buzzer-entry system controlled from the inside. If the occupants didn't like the look of you or weren't expecting a visit, you didn't get in.

Toni tapped in the code, waited for the door to release and pushed the door open. Nell, her assistant, was already at her desk. Slipping off her coat, Toni slung her handbag beneath her workstation and headed straight to the small room at the rear of the office where they kept the kettle. She needed a coffee.

'How did the meeting go?'

Toni turned to see Nell standing close behind her. 'OK … I think.'

'Did he say yes, then?'

Steam emerged from the spout as Toni tipped a second spoon of granules into the least-stained mug she could find. 'I think so. He agreed it was a good idea.'

Nell was standing too close. It was something she did – invading your personal space. But Toni was used to it now. Nell had peculiar traits but, as a researcher, she was second to none. Questionable social skills were a small price to pay for her expertise in the world of digitised information.

'Good,' said Nell, as she returned to her workstation. 'The Finlay file you requested is on your desk.'

Toni added milk to the coffee, walked over to her desk and turned on the PC. She sipped at the hot drink, felt the caffeine beginning to do its job, and picked up the thin file. It looked old, as if it had been stored for many years without being previously referenced. It bore the Ministry of Defence logo.

As she read, she made notes in a Word document she labelled 'Finlay'.

Grammar school in Pinner – near where she lived herself. Joined Royal Artillery aged eighteen and selected for 22SAS. In 1980, shot in the foot during a firefight in Northern Ireland shortly before playing a support role at the Iranian Embassy siege.

All very interesting, she thought, if a little lacking in detail. After that it wasn't clear what Finlay had been posted to. There was a gap in the record that perplexed her; she made a note to ask Nell to look into it.

Toni had to admit, she was surprised by the file. She knew from personal experience that the Armed Forces would grind to a halt if it weren't for records and documents. From your first walk-in through the door of a recruiting office to the day you left or died, every part of your military life was documented. Every posting, every interview, every inoculation, every course, every precise detail was written down and recorded by an officer or clerk.

As she studied the documents further, she realised, in Finlay's case, over three years' worth of records was missing. They only resumed at a point just before he left the army in 1985 to join the Metropolitan Police. The Met's records confirmed he had served as a PC in Camden, a sergeant at Barnet and then moved to Royalty Protection, where he had sat the Inspector examination and been promoted in situ. Then, it appeared he had become bored and had asked for a transfer back into uniform.

And then, Monaghan had come looking for him.

+

By the time the day ended, Toni's contribution to the report on Operation Hastings was almost complete. But there was one element by which she wasn't convinced: Monaghan's motive for attacking Finlay and Jones. Grahamslaw thought it was an angry husband's mistaken belief. Toni wasn't so sure. And she disliked uncertainty.

To that end, she logged on to the service network and placed a formal request on 'the system' – the intelligence services database that facilitated access to relevant files. She needed more information on Monaghan, and also on Webb – the Irishman he had enlisted to help him. Hopefully, someone with the necessary level of security clearance would approve the application. While she was there, she also ordered a full forensic analysis of Monaghan's home. She prided herself on being thorough. To her mind, Dirt would expect nothing less.

Chapter 7

Grahamslaw's letter had the effect he clearly wanted: I thought about little else for the rest of the day. Jenny seemed aware I was distracted and, by and large, she left me to mull things over in my own sweet way. I guessed she trusted me to work something out. In the end, I telephoned the Commander's office and made an appointment to see him the following day.

London tube journeys had changed since the terror attacks in New York. Many of the larger, better-known rail stations now had armed police on point duty outside and there were often police patrols on the trains themselves. At St James's Park, where I left the train, there was a small team of officers with a sniffer dog checking every passenger who came through the barriers.

At New Scotland Yard I made my way through the security checks, took the lift to the fourteenth floor and soon found myself wandering along the hallowed corridors of the Anti-Terrorist Squad. I turned in several directions, trying to get my bearings as I studied the nameplates on the huge number of doors – some closed, some open, but none the correct room. Most of the offices were occupied and on several occasions, unsympathetic faces lifted to glance in my direction before returning to a computer screen or conversation.

Eventually I found an open-plan room with a plate bearing the name 'SO13' on the open door. Inside there were, perhaps, thirty detectives, all working industriously at their desks. To one side a small meeting seemed to be taking place, with a PowerPoint presentation holding the attention of everyone present.

For a moment, nobody saw or spoke to me. Then, two young male detectives dressed in matching white shirts, suit trousers and departmental ties stepped quickly away from their desks and ushered me back out into the corridor.

'Who are you, mate?' the first one asked.

I explained, adding I was there to see their Commander.

The mention of Grahamslaw's name caused an exchange of glances. Much of the Anti-Terrorist Squad's work is highly confidential – internal eyes only and often very secret. The two detectives were clearly concerned I may have seen or heard something I shouldn't have. They instructed me to wait while one of them left to check out my claim.

Within a minute he returned, with Grahamslaw just behind him.

'Follow me, Inspector,' said the Commander. The greeting was formal, austere. No handshake, no warmth. I did as I was told.

We crossed the large room to an internal office on the far side. The smaller office had glass walls, no doubt so the Chief could keep an eye on his Indians.

'Shut the door, Finlay,' Grahamslaw said, his tone no more mellow, and sat opposite me, behind the desk.

Again, I did as I was told, without question, and stood for a moment, wondering what was about to unfold.

The Commander seemed to relax. 'OK, Finlay, sit down and take it easy. I won't be smiling – for reasons which will become clear; but you can relax, we can't be heard in this office. I'm glad you could make it.'

'I got your note,' I said.

'Took you longer than I expected. You'll forgive me if we don't discuss the other bits and pieces that were sitting there waiting for you?'

'Certainly. But rest assured, that has been taken care of.'

Grahamslaw ignored this, and for a moment studied my face, which clearly bore a puzzled expression.

'I won't beat about the bush, Finlay; here's why you're here: there are many in my department who feel Kevin Jones and you should have been arrested. There are even several people who think you've been spared due to political interference; that you led the department a merry song and dance, and, if not totally hung out to dry, you still should not be allowed to get away with it. That said, I will tell you, the majority understand the predicament the two of you faced. However, I do have to respect the … shall we call it "spectrum of views" … and I can't be seen to be too sympathetic towards you.'

Grahamslaw doodled on a small pad as he spoke, his eyes moving between me and the windows that separated us from the larger room. 'Fact is Finlay, your options are limited. The rumour mill on division means coppers are either scared of you or scared of working with you. Royalty won't have you back with this kind of history and you are not the kind of bloke to settle in a desk job.'

'I haven't thought about much else the last two days,' I answered. 'I wondered … well, surveillance maybe?'

Grahamslaw laughed, slapping his knee hard as he rocked his chair. 'I don't think so. Remember how easily your wife sneaked up on you and Kevin at Harlow Common and how he got that black eye? Somehow I think you're a little too old for that game now.'

I smiled. He was right. When Kevin and I had met to talk over how we were going to react to the attacks on our old friends, Jenny had crept up on us before either of us had seen her.

'Any ideas?' I asked.

'I've talked your situation over with MI5—'

'Not a chance,' I interrupted. 'I don't have the brains for them and as to field work…'

Before I could finish, Grahamslaw held up his hand to stop me in mid-sentence. 'No, not a job. Just to ask them whether the personal threat to you and your mates is at an end. They tell me that, barring any unexpected developments, they're confident it died with Monaghan and Webb.'

'That's what they've told me and Jenny. I hope they're right.'

'I think they are. No, what I have in mind for you is a job working for me. The Commissioner has seen fit to widen the Specialist Ops portfolio to include the links between organised crime and people trafficking. Alternatively, we've been given funds for a small team to travel to Kenya to look into the death of a British girl thirteen years ago.'

'Thirteen years?'

'Yes; you might have seen it in the newspapers. At the time it was thought the victim had been killed by lions. We've brought in two of our best to look into it and they could use someone with your particular skills to go with them.'

'Sounds interesting,' I said. 'Likely to take long?'

'The Kenya enquiry? Not sure, but my guess is just a few months. The trafficking team is likely to be long term, though.'

I was interested – genuinely so. Kenya was a place I had always wanted to visit but, with it being a short-term assignment, my guess was Jenny would prefer I took the more secure, long-term option.

'Think about both, Finlay,' Grahamslaw concluded. 'And get back to me with a decision as soon as you can.'

I promised I would.

Chapter 8

Best-laid plans.

Toni wondered how Grahamslaw had come up with the Kenya enquiry as an alternative idea. Three phone calls later and she had things back on track. Nell had done well to spot the other gig was on offer, and before Finlay had even had the time to consider his answer, Toni had nipped the opportunity in the bud. He would be joining the slave-trafficking squad. Having him heading off to Kenya didn't fit with her plans – or the promises she'd made to Jenny, for that matter.

It wasn't the first time Toni had had cause to be grateful to her researcher. Nell Mahoney was very special – an unusual young woman with an interesting background. And her entry into the ranks of MI5 had been anything but straightforward.

An Oxford classics graduate, Nell had been uncertain as to her career plans so had chosen to continue her academic studies, achieving high grades in both her master's degree and doctorate. She was still only in her mid-twenties when the security services found her, something that had come about when she was caught hacking into Government computer systems.

In fact, that wasn't quite accurate – Nell hadn't actually been caught by the authorities. She had been reported by a fellow student, who had noticed what her acquaintance had been looking at. And looking is all Nell had been doing.

When MI5 opened a PF – a personal file – on Nell, it was followed by an interview. The purpose at the time wasn't recruitment, it was investigation. Miles Grantham, the officer who called on her, had realised, from the moment they started talking, that the subject of his enquiry was rather unusual. Nell was autistic, a woman with Asperger syndrome.

Miles' first clue came when he noticed how clumsy Nell was – spilling the tea she made for them – and how she struggled to look him in the eye as they talked. Nell was also unusually intense and had incredible recollection. Miles' suspicions were heightened further by her focus on her interests and her inability to recognise hacking into Government computer systems as wrong.

Familiar with the syndrome, having been a teacher before joining MI5, Miles asked Nell to demonstrate how she had hacked into the protected network at the Cabinet Office. He wasn't surprised that Nell had been pleased to show him, but he was amazed at how quickly she was able to do it, the dexterity with which she navigated past the firewalls, checks and system queries, and the confidence with which she approached what should have been virtually impossible challenges. The Government network was supposed to have been impregnable, yet here in Oxford was a young woman who made hacking into it look like child's play.

When asked why she did it, 'Knowledge,' was Nell's one word response. She simply wanted to learn.

While aware his job was to investigate and report on Nell, Miles had warmed to his suspect. He deliberately slowed the progress of his enquiry to allow himself time to build a better picture of her. He spoke to Nell's parents. They lived near Oxford and were pretty ordinary folk – middle class, not especially gifted or intelligent, and neither were graduates. They had noticed Nell was unusual at a very early age. She was quick to learn to speak, but soon developed her own vocabulary and was intolerant of others who couldn't follow her. She also became incredibly task-focussed. When they bought her building blocks, her parents were amazed to find her creating copies of the box cover pictures within minutes of first seeing the toy. They also recalled how an aunt had given Nell a road atlas as a present. Within a day she had memorised a list, in alphabetical order, of all the towns and villages in Oxfordshire.

Nell was different – special, was her parent's description. At school she had been bullied and had struggled to relate to her peers. Yet she had ended up top of the class and had been the only child to win a scholarship to Oxford.

As an adult Nell had developed strategies to overcome many of the empathy challenges that had caused her to be picked on as a teenager. She referred to herself as an 'aspie', or 'homo superior' and had an incredible memory for jokes. Her delivery was appalling, but she managed to make people laugh, which seemed to give her immense pleasure.

Eventually, and with her parents' agreement, Miles formulated a plan. Instead of prosecuting Nell, MI5 recruited her.

After completion of her initial course, Nell was assigned to 'G' department and posted to GCHQ in Cheltenham. Her job, not surprisingly, was to root out hackers. She was the classic poacher turned gamekeeper.

Away from the supportive home environment, however, Nell had struggled to adjust to life on her own in Cheltenham. Within a few short months, she had asked for a move closer to home. In March 2001, her file had appeared in Toni's in-tray. The application was approved; Nell had moved back in with her parents and Toni acquired a new assistant. The service still kept an eye on Nell, though. Given her predisposition to curiosity, a watching brief was maintained by GCHQ on her internet activity, particularly with regard to her personal social media use and for any indication she might be returning to her old habits.

They knew, for example, that every Friday, after dinner with her parents, Nell would retire to her room and then switch on her computer. Friday was 'Slashdot' forum night. Nell would tap in her username – Pixie22 – and then search out some of her favourite members. The site labelled itself as 'News for Nerds', but Nell and a few of the regular contributors spent a lot of time talking about taking the forum and their ideas in a new direction.

Lots of the users were autistic to varying degrees. Many of them were also highly gifted. Toni had smiled at one particular report describing how they often joked they had been born on the wrong planet or, possibly, they were an evolutionary step in man's development. Either way, Nell and her friends knew they were different. The new direction they were talking about was going to be a website especially designed for them. One of the more innovative and outspoken contributors had even suggested a name, 'Wrong World'. Nell apparently thought it an excellent idea.

Every so often, Toni would receive a supplementary update from the monitoring team in Cheltenham. So far, they had reported no cause for concern. But they still watched.

Each morning since her transfer to London, Nell had travelled by train to Paddington and then used the tube to get to St James's Park. Every evening she would make the return journey home. The same routine that bored Toni was comforting to Nell. And as a researcher, she was the best Toni had ever worked with.

Which was the reason Toni was now experiencing frustration at the slow speed at which the Monaghan enquiry was progressing. Her instincts told her there was more to the story than met the eye, but Nell had been unable to discover anything. She had worked her way through MI5 files, records and databases. She had even hacked into Ministry of Defence systems. Nothing. Monaghan's military record was deleted. The only clue was the fact that even someone as good as Nell couldn't find anything.

'It's impossible,' Nell exclaimed, as her hands whirred across the keys of her laptop. 'No way can they hide every trace of deletion.'

Eventually, just one avenue of enquiry seemed left. Nell offered to hack into the MI6 system. She had been confident she could do it, but Toni had to balance their need against the shit that would fly if they got caught.

She decided against it, hoping her request for official access would soon pay dividends. If not, a hack remained a possibility.

Chapter 9

'I can't thank you enough,' said Jenny.

Toni smiled as she sipped at the coffee Finlay's wife had just made. 'A job at Scotland Yard should be just the ticket,' she replied.

The two women were both stood at the bedroom window. In the garden, they could see Finlay digging near the small shed.

'I'm serious,' said Jenny. 'Things have become a real struggle lately.'

'He's still not sleeping well?'

Jenny shook her head. 'It's not just that. I'm really regretting moving into the spare room. Since I did that, he's become even more distant, and every time I try to raise the subject, he manages to steer the conversation onto something else. It's like he just doesn't want to talk to me.'

'He'll come around, I'm sure.'

'Well, I hope so. I just despair of what to do.'

Toni leaned forward, her nose touching the cold glass. 'What exactly is he doing out there?'

Jenny threw up her hands. 'God knows. He says he finds it relaxing,'

Toni paused for a moment before continuing. 'I may have an idea,' she said, quietly. 'You remember I said I'd speak to a specialist?'

'Did you have any luck?'

'I found a consultant at Barts Hospital who was very helpful. When I told him about Robert's behaviour, he asked me about other symptoms – moodiness, irritability, that kind of thing.'

'Oh, he's irritable alright. Add to that the periods of silence and it's like walking on eggshells. Half the time I wonder if he's the same man I married.'

'That fits with what the consultant said. Post-traumatic stress was his suggested diagnosis.'

Jenny turned away, her face screwed up. 'Just as you guessed, then? I googled it like you suggested … came up with *combat stress*.'

'It's more common than we realised, it seems. The consultant told me anyone can get it, not just soldiers. Exposure to any kind of a traumatic event can trigger it; the kind of thing you and Robert went through could easily be a cause.'

'So, why don't I have the same problem? Why am I just fine?'

'I think he feels responsible. It's not just the violence of what happened. It's because he believes it was being secretive about his history that caused it ... and I also think there's some underlying anger towards Monaghan.'

Jenny let out a deep breath. 'So ... what's your idea then? At the moment, things are so desperate I'm up for trying anything.'

'Not really my idea, as such, but I can do the arranging. Apparently, what Robert needs is some time alone to relax – a holiday, that kind of thing. Time to unwind and get his thoughts in order.'

'Alone?' Jenny retorted. 'What, without me and Becky, you mean?'

'Yes. To give—'

'No. I said from the very start we're in this together. I'm not sending him off somewhere on his own.'

'He wouldn't be on his own,' Toni replied, calmly. Jenny looked confused as she continued. 'He'd be monitored. I can make the arrangements. We have a small budget to cater for such things, and, if he showed any signs of being in difficulties, we would whisk him home, pronto.'

'I ... I'm not keen. I hated it when he was on Royalty Protection. He was always away. It was like leading separate lives.'

'This would be different. This would be for just a week – to give him the time to get things back into perspective ... and we'd set things up for you to keep in regular touch by telephone. It would soon pass and, you never know, he might come home a new man.'

'I don't know ... do you think it might work? Could a week be enough?'

Toni returned to the window. 'I hope so, I really do. You did say you'd do anything ...'

'Now you're quoting me.'

'I just meant ...'

'I know what you meant, Toni. I'm just struggling with the idea. Where exactly would you send him?'

'Egypt; we have an arrangement with a hotel on the Red Sea.'

'Egypt?' Jenny exclaimed. 'Are you serious? I thought you meant the Norfolk Broads or something … somewhere nearer home, certainly.'

Toni saw a tear on Jenny's cheek. 'It's difficult, I know, but the consultant said something to me about the healing effects of the sun. He'd not get that here in the UK.'

'And for just a week, you say?'

'Just a week. It's a great hotel and with great beaches. There's a dive school next door, he could even do some snorkelling.'

A smile flickered across Jenny's lips as she wiped her face. 'He might … he might. He once said he regretted never learning to dive.'

'So, will you think about it … maybe run it past him?'

'I will … think about it. No promises though.'

Chapter 10

'Egypt?' I asked.

'That's the idea, yes.' Jenny replied, smiling.

The smile was forced, I could tell. Normally, her face was animated: laughing, frowning, scowling, showing surprise or compassion. Only when she was sleeping or thinking hard, like now, did her expression stay still. Something wasn't right and, if I knew Jenny, she wouldn't have easily accepted the idea of me travelling alone. I finished the potato I was chewing on. It was hot, and the time it took for me to swallow allowed me a few moments to think. Toni Fellowes had somehow persuaded her I needed a holiday; on my own, and to Egypt of all places.

They'd been watching me through the bedroom window; and as they'd watched, it now appeared a plan had been hatched. I had known they were there and, as I had been hiding the weapons I'd recovered from the cottage, I was thankful that, despite a brief discussion on what I was doing, they hadn't popped down into the garden. Prior to recovering the contents of my old hide, I had spent some time pottering about in the garden of the safe house. I'd managed to excavate a small, dry cavity beneath a collapsed Anderson shelter, partially hidden behind an ancient wooden shed. As a temporary home for the kit, it was fine. Nobody would expect to find it so close to me, not even Grahamslaw. At least, that was what I hoped. The first chance I got, I would arrange to move everything to the hide Kevin had made near his place.

I had mixed feelings about the suggestion of a break. Certainly, if Jenny had raised even the slightest doubt or objection I would have knocked the idea on the head.

'Who came up with that one?' I asked.

'I'm not sure, really. It sort of developed as we talked. I share things with Toni, you know that; and she notices things. She's no fool; she was straight on to it as soon as I started sleeping in the spare room.'

'Saw the bed had been slept in, I guess.'

Stood at the sink with her back to me, Jenny continued washing the dishes as we chatted. 'Yes. And then she asked about ... well, let's just say she's concerned about you, like I am. And she's told me about an arrangement they have to sort out recuperation trips for people who are stressed.'

'Stressed?' I said. 'Is that what she called it?'

Jenny stopped what she was doing, pulled a chair up next to me and sat down. I stopped eating.

'I know what *it* is, Robert. And I know it takes time ... to get better ... to make a full recovery.'

I could feel my heart starting to race. It was one of those moments, the 'we need to talk' point our conversations always seemed to reach recently. The urge to stand up and walk away was becoming irresistible.

Jenny placed her hand on my arm. 'Apparently there's a dive school next to the hotel. You always did say you fancied scuba diving.'

I glanced up at the ceiling. 'That was years ago. I was just a kid who loved Jacques Cousteau. I'm nearly fifty now.'

'Are you saying you wouldn't take up the offer if it was there?'

'No. It's just ...'

'It's just … excuses. The way I see it, we've got nothing to lose. Living here, we're virtually under house arrest. I'll get a week to take Becky to see my mother; you get a week to rest and relax. What could be wrong with that? And when you come back, well, then you can start that new job and we'll have a brighter future to look forward to. Now … what do you say?'

The way Jenny put it, I had little basis for argument. And the way she looked at me … well, I could tell she cared. It was a free trip and, yes, I had always wanted to learn to dive. She was also right about one thing – I did feel in need of some time to relax and unwind.

I nodded, at the same time feeling my eyes well up. I leaned across the table, took Jenny's hand in mine and squeezed it tight.

Chapter 11

Once I'd made the decision, the arrangements were put into place surprisingly quickly.

I called Bill Grahamslaw to apprise him of developments, only to find he knew all about them. In fact, it was clear he and Toni Fellowes had been closely monitoring my situation. Sadly, the chance of a few weeks in Kenya had blown out. Something to do with my relevant experience, it seemed. I was disappointed, but not overly so. The job on the slave-trafficking unit sounded exciting and I readily settled on the offer. We agreed I would start on the Monday after my return from Egypt.

Not everything went entirely to plan, though. Toni's assertion MI5 would cover the full cost of the trip turned out to be mistaken. The Whitehall mandarins baulked at the prospect of paying for me to learn to scuba dive. Hotel and flights were covered but spending money and entertainment was going to be down to me. By the time the news filtered through to me, the flight was booked and I'd set my heart on doing a PADI diver course, so I agreed to pay for it myself.

My new Commander had some additional advice. Inevitably, he

pointed out, I would meet up with fellow Brits at the resort, and, as was the norm in such conversations, the subject of what I did for a living would come up.

'Say you're a cop and it acts as a lead into all kind of things from "what do I say if I'm caught speeding" through to "do you know my mate's uncle who's a detective",' he said, dryly.

I wasn't too bothered by that kind of thing, but Grahamslaw pointed out that the recent London attacks on police officers followed by the 9/11 incidents had put the police uppermost in many people's minds. Uncomfortable questions might be asked, and memories I was trying to put behind me might be raked up.

I was persuaded. We even agreed on what I would say if asked. I was to be a driving instructor. Plain, simple, not too interesting and easy enough to talk about if pushed.

For the plane journey, Jenny gave me a book. Ever since finding out about my past she had been reading books about the SAS. This was one we had been lent by Toni, who had suggested I might like to read it during the trip; it was called *Cyclone* and was written by an author called Chas Collins. Jenny had already read it and, as we headed to the airport, I saw she had popped it into my carry-on bag.

I promised to look at it on the plane.

Chapter 12

The first time you pull on a dive mask, place the compressed air regulator in your mouth, lower your body into the water and then breath is, for many, a life-changing event.

One day into my holiday, after a trouble-free flight, a short evening walk around the resort and a reasonable night's sleep, I had my first such experience – under the guidance of my charismatic South African instructor. I was hooked.

As I inhaled, the air came through with a reassuring hiss; as I breathed out, bubbles danced gently over my cheeks. The heavy tank and weights seemed as nothing in the water. It was a new world, one I immediately wished I had experienced when much younger.

Catherine, the instructor, had been allocated a group who had failed to show. I was, therefore, her only pupil. My initial training took place in the hotel pool, surrounded by a mixture of Eastern Europeans and Russians in permanent party mode.

Bikini-clad women adorned the pool-side loungers sporting oiled bodies and expensive-looking jewellery. Their male companions were lively, noisy and seemed to spend most of their time at the bar. They also liked to show off; several times, as I went through my underwater drills, I experienced the human equivalent of depth charges as one of them leapt into the water to cool off.

Apart from Catherine and the dive-school staff, there seemed to be no other English speakers. That surprised me a little, given what Toni had said about the hotel being used as a recuperation venue, but I soon forgot about it as I began to enjoy myself.

On the third evening, Catherine invited me to join her for a beer. We sat chatting with the dive staff at the pool bar. Thankfully, on this particular evening, the other guests seemed to be engaged elsewhere and the customary loud music had been turned down. I ordered cold beers for the two of us and enjoyed listening as the instructors regaled us with tales of sea creatures spotted on the reefs and amusing stories of customers' diving skills. The small group seemed very relaxed and had no problem with my being amongst them. One of them – an older man called Mike – was the senior instructor. Catherine informed me Mike had been a navy diver before moving out to Sharm to help start up the dive school.

Catherine and I were teased a bit as it seemed the last time she had a one-to-one with a learner diver they had started a relationship. She explained that they were still in touch and most evenings she would talk on the phone to him at his home in Rome. She was hoping to join him for Christmas if the dive school would give her the time off.

As we chatted, I mentioned the other hotel guests, and Catherine explained the men were in business and the women were mostly their trophy brides – 'arm candy' was the expression she used.

There was one notable exception, she said: Marica – a Romanian girl in her early twenties, who was having private lessons. She was very beautiful, Catherine commented, and many of the men seemed in awe of her. But she was accompanied at all times by a man who seemed to be more of a minder than a husband or boyfriend. The girl spoke quite good English, it was said, and, unlike the others, seemed well educated. Mike was her instructor.

Mike stood up to get in a round of beers. Even though it was evening, the air was warm and comfortable. Nobody seemed to be in a rush to head off to bed. Then, exactly as Grahamslaw had predicted, the subject of my work came up. One of the dive staff asked me what I did back home.

I lied; the convincing, easy lie I had prepared. I said I was a driving instructor. It caused some mirth as it transpired Catherine had still to pass her test, having failed it three times. And, just as predicted, those present soon lost interest in my very normal and unexciting background.

As Mike was returning from the bar with our beers, I had my first sight of the Romanian girl.

Marica appeared near the entrance to the bar area with an older man. Catherine was right; she was stunning. Slim, with short, jet-black hair, she wore a tight, cream-coloured jumper with stretch-fit blue jeans and flat shoes. The man with her was also casually dressed, in jeans and a loose-fitting shirt. I recognised his demeanour immediately. He was a bodyguard.

He waved to Mike, beckoning him over, and, as he did, I could see him scanning the bar, checking and assessing those present. He was weighing up any danger, looking for a threat, his manner sharp, attentive and professional. As he looked in my direction, I avoided his eyes. You can tell a lot from a man's eyes. If this man was as skilled and as experienced as he appeared, I was aware he might see something in mine I would prefer he didn't.

When Mike returned to our group he wasn't happy. 'She wants to do an advanced course to follow the open-water,' he said to Catherine.

She shrugged as she reached for her beer. 'Is she up to it?'

'Yes, but I really need to have her with someone else – a buddy.'

Catherine hardly paused for breath before turning to me. 'How about you, Robert?'

I was confused. It showed, so Mike explained. The Romanian girl was due to finish her basic training at the same time as me. She wanted to add on another two days' instruction to do the advanced course. Mike was committed elsewhere but she was a prestige customer at the hotel and he had been told to give her whatever she needed. Catherine was the only spare instructor, but she was assigned to me for the week.

'How do you fancy doing the advanced course, free of charge, of course?' Mike offered. 'We'd just need you to be a dive buddy to the Romanian girl; Catherine will teach the both of you.'

'Does the minder go everywhere with her?' I asked.

'Everywhere except bed, the head ... and under the water,' Mike laughed.

I agreed. The chance to have extra diving instruction free of charge made it a no-brainer for me. 'If the rest of my course goes smoothly and I pass the basics, count me in,' I said.

✠

The following day was our first away from the pool. And, from the moment Catherine gave me the signal to descend into the warm sea, an unrivalled grin decorated my face. Any fear I had of being many feet below the surface quickly dissipated as I experienced the sensation of weightlessness for the first time. It was as though I was flying, the reefs passing gently below me as we swam. All manner of brightly coloured fish darted through the complex coral. I was transfixed.

That evening, when I called home, I struggled for superlatives to describe it to Jenny. It wasn't a long phone call, just enough to touch base and have a quick chat. She was moved to comment that I sounded more upbeat than I had in a long time. In a slightly secretive tone, she also mentioned having a surprise for me for when I arrived home. Despite my efforts, she wouldn't be drawn on what it was.

The next couple of days diving saw me progress from complete ignorance to becoming only just competent. I wasn't the most natural of divers. My comical attempts to stop myself floating to the surface when I was supposed to be descending frustrated me, yet seemed to amuse Catherine no end.

On the day I passed the basic course, I swam over to Catherine and threw my arms around her. My sheer exuberance was such, if it hadn't been for our masks and regulators, I swear I would have kissed her.

I was now definitely up for doing the advanced course. As I enjoyed another evening beer at the bar, Catherine headed to the dive-school office to make the arrangements. The next day, I would get to meet Marica and her bodyguard.

Chapter 13

MI5 office, New Scotland Yard

'I don't agree with this,' Nell said, angrily.

'It's my call, Nell. Now, will you please just get on with what I asked you to do?'

Nell returned to her workstation. What had started off as a difficult morning didn't look to be getting any easier. Toni turned back to her desk, attempting to ignore the disapproval emanating from her assistant, whose behaviour was making it almost impossible to concentrate on the task at hand – the buff file that contained the personal details of a new addition to the team. A young man called Stuart Anderson would be joining them very soon.

As the muttering became quieter, Toni said a silent thank-you that a difficult situation now seemed to be over. In her peripheral vision, she noticed Nell lean across and adjust the books she kept as reference material on her desk. One appeared to be slightly out of line. Nell straightened it then sat back as her outburst of temper gave way to normality. It looked as if the moment had passed.

Toni relaxed. Many aspects of Nell's personality and condition made day-to-day interactions with her difficult. But when focussed on a research project these challenges became strengths. Others found exhausting the repetitive nature of continued searches and the total concentration required to glean documents for key information. To Nell, though, such tasks were second nature and hugely satisfying. She established routines, applied herself to the job and completely ignored the world around her. Often, she would forget to eat; and woe betide anyone who interrupted her train of thought.

Abruptly, Nell stood up again and walked across to Toni. She braced herself; it seemed she wasn't out of the woods just yet.

'Toni, I think it is utterly reprehensible – using Robert Finlay in this way. It's obvious what you're doing. You made sure he took the Collins book with him, knowing full well he might bump into the author and get chatting to him. It's obvious ... you plan to pump Finlay for intelligence when he gets back, don't you?'

'It was too good a chance to miss, Nell. The publishers of that book are staying at the hotel and the CIA need to know where Collins got his information from to write it. He wouldn't tell anyone normally, but he might get talking to a former mate, mightn't he?'

'But he's not a field agent, and he's in your care because of recent traumatic events. Your cavalier treatment of him is ... unconscionable.'

Good word, thought Toni, and so typical of Nell. But enough was enough. It was time to dead-end this.

She swung around on her chair, aware her temper was rising. But Nell was standing so close it was impossible to stand. Her legs were locked straight, feet astride, hands on hips. She looked angry.

Toni looked her assistant in the face and, for a moment, stayed silent. 'Do you mind?' she then asked.

A look of confusion crossed Nell's face.

'You're in my personal space, Nell.'

For a moment, Nell seemed uncertain as to what to do. She didn't move, didn't react.

Toni decided to leave it. 'What precisely is bothering you, Nell?'

'Like I said, I think what you are doing is reprehensible, and I want no part of it ... it's unpalatable.'

'Are you referring to sending Finlay to Egypt or creating him a cover story?'

'Sending him, of course. Finlay shouldn't need a cover if he is simply going to recuperate. If he is getting into something more convoluted then he should do so knowingly. I think you are seeking to trick a vulnerable man, merely because it is convenient for you.'

Toni pushed her seat backwards, avoiding having to crane her neck to look her assistant in the eye. 'Nell, I think things are not quite so black and white here as you might like...'

'But he has no training, no relevant field experience, and, from what you've said, is reluctant to even consider working for MI5, let alone embroil himself in a covert operation. This stinks and you know it.'

Toni breathed deeply and counted to five. This wasn't going to be easy. 'Look Nell,' she lowered her voice, slowed down. This was no time to lose tempers. 'You need to understand a few things before you start to judge. For a start, he does have field experience. He did undercover work in Northern Ireland when he was in the army. And he is trained – he did courses; the same kind of preparation I've done.'

'But at that time he knew what he was doing, he was properly briefed. This time he hasn't a clue.'

'That's as may be, Nell. But what you might not appreciate, as we sit here in this nice cosy office, is ignorance can be a distinct advantage. One of the most frequent ways undercover people give themselves away is body language. They see their target and show signs of recognising them – make eye contact or something similar. Someone sees that and they're blown. Finlay is a clean skin and has no idea who he is mixing with. Not knowing will protect him. He's been told to avoid the potential embarrassment of admitting he's a cop by saying he's a driving instructor. Your job is to make sure his story is verifiable.'

'But that's exactly my point. By creating him a cover, that's a de facto admission he is *undercover*. He's not ... he's just a cop having a holiday.'

'...Who might just meet someone who spills things to him that wouldn't be told to any of us. Don't you get that?'

Nell stepped back, just slightly. A first indication she was coming around. 'So what happens when they get suspicious of him?' she asked.

'They won't ... because you'll make sure of it. And if he gets into any scrapes then, believe me, Robert Finlay can look after himself.'

'And when he gets back, will you tell him?'

Toni scrunched up her face. 'I've thought about that, and the answer is ... possibly. At the moment I plan to debrief him carefully and learn what I can without alerting him.'

'You want him to work for MI5 don't you?' asked Nell, her tone now more inquisitive than accusatory.

'Yes, you know I do. He'd be good, especially if he recovers well. I'd be lying if I said I'm prepared to give up on the idea just because he's going through some post-trauma issues.'

'He won't.'

'Won't what?'

'Won't join MI5. He made that quite clear during the Hastings debrief.'

Toni kept calm, her voice reassuring. She was winning the argument. 'He says that now, yes. But Finlay is working for us without even realising it. If I handle it right – break it to him retrospectively, as it were – I think he might be persuaded. He thinks he's not up to it. If I can show him he's been doing it already ... well, you never know.'

'I don't believe his objection is based upon competence. I think he wants family life, plain and simple.'

'Trust me, Nell. Men like Finlay live for excitement. He might crave the comfort of the nest at this moment in time, but it won't be long before he wants back in the thick of it.'

'But, it's against regulations. Article thirty-four, para—'

'Enough!' Toni exclaimed.

'But, it clearly says—'

'I know what the regulations say, Nell, so don't you go lecturing me on them. This is one of those situations that require us to think outside the box, to use our imaginations to solve challenging problems...'

'To use people, you mean? Like you're using Robert Finlay?'

'Using people is what we do, Nell. This is the Security Service, not the Boy Scouts. Just remember, it's my call and my responsibility. For now, your job is to provide the cover story details I have requested ... and I would very much appreciate it if you got on with it. How far have you got?'

'Not far. I hadn't really started.'

'I thought as much. Now just tell me how you're going to do what I asked?"

'OK ... OK. I can create a self-employed record with the tax office, a new National Insurance number, certification and registration records. He'll be a genuine driving instructor before midday today.'

'Thank you, Nell. Midday it is.'

As her assistant moved away, Toni wilted back into her seat. Nell could be an uncompromising character and exhausting to manage at times, especially when the bit was between her teeth. But Toni did allow herself a small smile. Nell's cover story would be good ... and who knows what Finlay might learn.

Chapter 14

I had enjoyed the best night's sleep I'd had in a long time.

It was seven-thirty, and I was catching a minibus to head out of town to a jetty where we were to board one of the dive-school boats. Apart from Catherine and the driver, I was the only passenger. There was no sign of the Romanians.

'They're meeting us at the boat,' Catherine explained.

She was right. As we pulled up at the wooden jetty, I saw a black Mercedes parked near the water's edge. The boot was open to reveal scuba gear. Standing at the edge of the landing stage was Marica, the Romanian girl. She was wearing a thin, blue dress and flip-flops, and stood with her back to us, looking out to sea. There was no sign of her bodyguard.

'Wait here, Robert,' said Catherine.

I did as she asked, watching as the two women chatted for a moment. Catherine pointed back to the bus. I waved. Marica smiled. It was a warm smile; she seemed friendly, relaxed. Perhaps this wasn't going to be too bad after all, I thought, especially if the minder was not around.

But a few seconds later, a familiar, muscular figure appeared from the rear deck of the boat. I guessed he had been making a few checks before allowing us on board. It's what I would have done.

Our ride for the day was called *Orchid*. She was a twenty-six-metre, custom-made vessel with eight crew and five cabins. On this day she would be carrying just five passengers: four divers and the bodyguard. As I stepped aboard, Catherine explained a fourth diver was joining us for safety reasons. He was below decks sleeping, having spent the night on the boat.

It was time for introductions. As I had hoped when she first smiled at me on the jetty, Marica turned out to be absolutely charming and her command of the English language was excellent. Catherine left us to get to know each other as she went to supervise the loading of the dive equipment.

The bodyguard, who I discovered was called Petre, stayed in the background. Not surprisingly, Marica talked about the dive course we had both just completed and the wonders to be seen beneath the surface of the Red Sea. She was at least as hooked as me, and, given her youth, I guessed she would enjoy the allure of scuba diving for many years to come. One of the crew brought us some *t'aamiyya* for breakfast. It was traditional – hot and wrapped in pita bread to make it easier to eat by hand.

As we ate, I found myself warming to the young Romanian. Although she was clearly from a wealthy background and well educated, Marica was modest and friendly. I learned she was soon to be married and that her husband-to-be had sent her on this trip because he was a keen diver himself. He had booked them a honeymoon in the Maldives, where he wanted his new bride to experience the wonders of the Indian Ocean.

I also learned that Marica's father was a businessman who had a part-share in the hotel where we were both staying – me in a standard room; Marica in the penthouse suite. She was a lucky girl, who it seemed had not been spoiled by her privileged upbringing.

The boat cast off within a few minutes and Catherine joined us. We chatted about many things over the next hour. As the sun warmed us and I took in the views across the sea, I felt very relaxed.

Soon it was time for Catherine to brief us on our first dive – explaining the lessons to be covered and the sights to be seen on the reef we were about to explore. We were to do a drift dive – an exercise where the boat would drop us off and then, after the current had swept us gently along the reef, pick us up at the spot where we should emerge.

When the time came to do the pre-dive safety checks, I used the mnemonic Catherine had taught me to help remember what to check – Buoyancy vest, Weights, Releases, Air and Final check. Marica wasn't familiar with it and when I started saying 'Bruce – Willis – Ruins – All – Films' out loud, she collapsed in a fit of laughter. It was contagious and I found that soon, I too was joining in.

My ability to laugh came as something of a surprise. When the threat to my family had been exposed, I seemed to have lost my good humour. Now, on a holiday at the Red Sea, alone with two people I had only just met, the knack was returning. I smiled to myself. It was a small thing, but significant.

Perhaps Toni and Jenny had a point.

☩

I was on the top deck, after the dive, enjoying the sun and the views, when Catherine appeared behind me and disturbed my thoughts. Marica, who had been on the lower deck, was just behind her.

Catherine explained we were due to complete our wreck and deep-dive training. The crew had suggested we head out to the *SS Thistlegorm*, a freight vessel sunk by German bombers in the Straits of Gubal during WWII. The shipwreck lay at a depth we could manage and was, apparently, a highlight of any dive trip to the Red Sea.

As we listened to our guide, Marica seemed to sense my interest. 'This will be a special dive for you Robert?' she asked, as Catherine finished her short talk.

'Sounds fascinating,' I replied.

'No, I mean very special. It is a grave of soldiers. This will have special meaning for you, I guess?'

Marica had my attention. 'Why do you say that?'

She smiled, again with warmth. 'Petre says you were a soldier. He says he can tell. Something about the way you move, the way you check the dive gear ... he says one can always tell another.'

I smiled. Petre was no fool. 'Yes. A long time ago. I didn't realise it still showed.'

'Petre doesn't speak good English, but with my blessing he asked if this evening you would join us to eat. He would wish to talk with you.'

'I'm not sure. It was a long time ago.'

For the first time, other than to check my dive gear, Marica touched me. Her hand gently resting on my forearm, she looked me straight in the eye. She was very, very pretty. 'Please ... for me, Robert. Tell me you will come.'

'Could Catherine join us?' I asked.

I had always been a sucker for a pretty face and when Marica agreed to my request, I accepted her invitation.

Chapter 15

We arrived at the site of the *Thistlegorm* later that morning.

Ryan, the safety diver, was already kitted up and dived down to hook the *Orchid* to the wreck. There were about six similar boats in the area, all dropping off and picking up divers. Unlike the mill-pond calm near to Sharm, here the sea was quite choppy; it was a struggle to keep our balance on the rear deck as we prepared to enter the water. Catherine went first, indicated where we would find the anchor line to descend, and then I jumped in after her.

As soon as I hit the water I felt the sensation of tranquillity return. All external noise was eliminated, other than the gentle sound of my breath and the bubbles exiting my mouthpiece. I had never meditated, but I figured this was about as close to that experience as I had ever been.

Feeling a tug on my right arm, I turned to see Marica reaching for the anchor line I was now holding. Even with her face covered by a mask and regulator, I could see she was smiling broadly.

Following Catherine, we released the stored air in our buoyancy vests and started the descent down the anchor line. Beneath us the water was a little murky, with perhaps a fifteen-metre field of visibility. Soon, though, a huge, dark shadow began to take form. It was the wreck.

We continued to descend, the shape of the *Thistlegorm* gradually growing in size and resolution as we approached her. Now far from the surface, the effect of the waves faded and all was peaceful. With Catherine leading, the four of us traversed the ship's superstructure.

For half an hour, we floated past decaying steam engines, military vehicles and broken-off parts of the ship. We closed in on hatches and portholes that gave us a tempting view of the ship's interior, and I wondered what treasures would be revealed in the later dive, when we were to be shown inside the wreck. It was a humbling experience, knowing such an incredible sight marked the grave of so many men.

I felt sorry for poor Petre. On the surface, he could do his job to the best of his ability, but here, beneath the waves, his charge was in the care of professionals with other skills. I knew he wouldn't be comfortable until he saw Marica on the surface.

The dive went all too quickly. My breathing control was improving slowly but, as usual, I was the first to signal I was low on air. My depth gauge showed we were at nearly thirty metres. I looked upwards at the equivalent of several swimming pool depths of water. I felt I should be a little scared – certainly in awe – but I wasn't. The whole experience was relaxing.

I signalled to Catherine my time was up and, as I did, I noticed something odd. From the air tank on her back I could see a trickle of tiny bubbles heading towards the surface. I had been behind her for most of the dive and hadn't noticed it before. As I watched for a moment, the trickle of air became a steady stream. To my side, a rapid movement in the water caught my eye. Ryan was moving quickly past me, swimming towards Catherine.

I watched, uncertain what was happening. Ryan took hold of our instructor's arm and pointed towards his own air tank. He made twirling movements with his finger and then indicated Catherine's tank. It dawned on me. She had a leaking seal. At the point where the regulator attaches to the tank a rubber O-ring prevents air leaks. It looked like the seal had blown.

I was close enough to see the alarm on Catherine's face as she checked her gauges to ascertain how much air she had lost. As she did so, there was a rush of air from the blown seal.

I remembered there was a drill for this we had learned in the pool. Now, I saw Ryan giving us a live demonstration. He took hold of Catherine's buoyancy vest as she spat out her own regulator and reached for the bright yellow spare attached to his tank. Catherine placed the spare in her mouth and I saw the reassuring sign of her exhaling. She was safe, but now our two guides were linked to Ryan's tank and we were thirty metres beneath the surface.

Catherine gave me an 'OK' signal and then a thumbs-up to indicate we should surface. By this time Marica was with me. She touched my left shoulder, imitated the thumbs-up and turned to head back to the anchor line. I waited for a moment, unsure as to whether I should be helping our guides, but they waved me away. I trusted they would be fine and started after Marica.

We found the anchor line easily enough and started the ascent. I stayed just behind and below Marica as I glanced back to where Ryan and Catherine were following. They seemed to have things under control: the air leak from Catherine's tank had stopped, presumably as the supply was exhausted, and she was swimming gently alongside Ryan as he held onto the anchor rope.

I forgot it was necessary to make a three-minute decompression stop to allow absorbed nitrogen to escape from our bodies; but, fortunately, Marica remembered. At a depth of five metres I bumped into her as she waited. Above, I could see the boat bobbing about on the waves.

The sea looked rougher than when we had entered the water. Foam and air spread in patterns around the ladder onto the rear deck and I could see the propeller was spinning quite fast. I couldn't decide if the boat was under power or if the current was causing the spin, but I didn't relish the prospect of colliding with it.

Below us, the two guides had also made it to the decompression stop. It looked like we were all going to be fine.

Chapter 16

After three minutes, Marica signalled it was time to surface and started the ascent to the steel ladder. The boat was rocking. I could see the ladder was now swinging through the water as the boat dipped heavily forward and rocked violently in the swell.

As Marica approached the ladder, the end of the heavy steel moved away from her with the current. And then the boat rocked back, sending the bottom rung crashing violently into her head. I watched, powerless, as her mask went flying. Immediately, there was a cloud of blood in the water.

For a second it seemed surreal. Our instructors were below and linked to one tank. My companion was clearly hurt. I was the only one left who could help. On the boat they would be unaware of the struggle in the depths beneath them. I waved frantically to the two guides and screamed into my mouthpiece. It was a natural reaction, but pointless. Under the water they would not hear me.

Marica started to sink. As her face dropped clear of the cloud of blood I could see she was unconscious. I had to make a quick decision. I swam towards her but she was sinking too fast. I tried in vain to follow, but I was too buoyant. I swiftly let the remaining air out of my buoyancy vest as I struggled to see where she was headed. It was impossible. I couldn't descend fast enough. My mind raced.

Then I caught sight of Catherine. She had pulled away from Ryan and was heading towards me with something in her hand. It was a lead weight. She took hold of my vest, pulled a valve to release more air and shoved the weight into one of the side pockets.

It worked. I began to descend, and quickly. Some five or so metres below me, I could see Marica slowly drifting away into the depths.

I've heard stories of people kissing under water, of divers exchanging air to survive – one breathing into the other; one inhaling as the other exhaled. I had thought it a romantic fantasy, an idea, not a reality.

That day beneath the Red Sea, I pressed my lips to a woman as I had never done before. Marica was drowning and sinking, her mouthpiece hanging uselessly to one side. I wrapped my arms around her, took a deep breath from my own regulator and then kissed her. With our lips sealed I breathed out and at the same time undid my weight belt. As it fell away from me, I felt the sudden expansion of air in my lungs and vest as we rushed towards the surface.

Somehow, perhaps with the combination of decreasing pressure and my breathing into her, Marica exhaled. There was an awful taste of bile and seawater but I kept my mouth firmly attached to hers. Such was the rate of our ascent we burst through the surface within seconds.

Ryan was still in the water, waiting for us. On the dive deck of the boat I caught a glimpse of Catherine struggling up the ladder in the swell. Ryan wasn't a big man but his strength surprised me as he grabbed both Marica and me.

Marica was coughing violently and struggling to breathe. With her mask lost, her dark hair now hung across her face. Blood was streaming freely from her nose and mouth.

In the swell, it was a struggle to stay upright; in the pitching waves I tried in vain to find my own regulator so I would at least be able to breath. But it seemed every attempt I made was met with a mouthful of salt water. Soon, I began to weaken and I felt my grip on Marica fade. I was coughing, almost uncontrollably, and starting to taste blood in my mouth. From behind, I felt strong hands on my arm. Marica was pulled away from me.

For several moments, I lay still, my face to the sky, the waves breaking over me. I needed to gather my strength for the final push towards the boat. I could hear shouting, alarmed, panicky voices, confused and fearful. Rescuers, I hoped. Next moment, my regulator was pushed forcibly into my face and I felt a rush of air as the purge button was pressed to clear it of water. I opened my mouth and clamped onto the mouthpiece at the same moment as my right arm was pushed through a lifebelt. I hung on tight.

A voice shouted, '*Prenez*. Hold.' It was Petre. He was in the water.

As I breathed, the feelings of panic subsided. Marica and Ryan were being towed towards the boat. Petre stayed with me, holding me tight to the lifebelt as we waited for the others to be pulled onto the deck by the crew. He was still wearing his shirt and trousers.

Within a few minutes, the rope between us and the boat became taut. Petre pushed me onto the same ladder that had struck Marica and wrapped his arms around me as I made the arduous climb onto the rear deck. I made slow progress. The combination of swallowing salt water, exhaustion and adrenalin made my legs shake badly and I struggled to keep a grip. But with each step, Petre took the weight of my air tank and helped me stay on the wet ladder. I was acutely aware he had no air supply and nothing on his feet but still he held me.

It was as he lifted me I first caught sight of a tattoo on his forearm. In the water the pattern wasn't clear but even through my daze, I recognised the words at the base. '*Legio Patria Nostra*'. The motto of the French Foreign Legion.

I made the final step and rolled forward onto the deck, a melee of hands unclipping and removing my vest, tank and fins. I lay still for several minutes, my eyes closed, gathering my breath as strength gradually returned to my body.

There was a voice above me. 'You saved her, Robert.' It was Catherine.

I tried to speak, but my mouth was salty and dry. I made a 'drink' gesture with my hand and within a few moments someone prised open my fingers and squeezed a plastic water bottle into them. My throat was raw and the first mouthful stung. I spat it out and drank again. The second attempt tasted less salty, the third better still. By the fourth, I had drained the bottle and could speak.

'Is she OK?' I spluttered, as Catherine helped me to my feet.

'Petre is taking care of her. She's got a nasty cut on her head, probably concussed, but he seems pretty confident she'll be fine.'

For a few seconds I felt light-headed. 'How about you and Ryan?'

'We're both fine.' Catherine smiled warmly. 'For someone so bad at buoyancy you did really well.'

I smiled back. 'Thanks. Not an everyday intro to diving, eh?'

'No, and Petre was brilliant too. He got Marica out of the water and then went back for you. He's even bandaged Marica's head; seems to be good at first aid as well.'

I thought back to my initial impression on meeting Petre: the way he carried himself; his job as Marica's bodyguard and the tattoo I had just seen on his arm. 'I would imagine Petre is a pretty resourceful bloke, Catherine.'

'Well, he's bloody strong,' she replied, her South African accent coming through clearly. 'You should have seen him lift you up the ladder with all your kit still on.'

I hadn't seen Petre lift me, but I had felt it. I'd felt the strength in his shoulders and arms and the sense of relief my route to safety was in his hands. 'Tell him thanks,' I said.

'Tell him yourself.' Catherine indicated over my shoulder. As I turned, Petre was now stood just behind me, his open hand extended.

'My English is not good, Robert.' He spoke slowly, the accent East European, I guessed. 'I just wish to say thank you for save Marica.'

I took the hand that was offered and, once again, I felt the strength of the grip.

✠

Later that evening, alone in the bar with a cold beer for company, I sat and thought about that handshake and the knowing look in Petre's eyes. There was something in that gaze – a kinship, something that soldiers have, something I figured he also saw in me.

I'd phoned Jenny as soon as I reached the hotel, simply wanting to hear her voice. I lied about the events of the day, though, and told her what a relaxing time I'd been having. It seemed the right thing to do. Marica was in hospital overnight for observation and Petre was at her side. Ryan and Catherine had kept me company for an hour before heading off to their digs.

The hotel was quiet now, but I was too restless to sleep. I also doubted if I would be able to focus on the Chas Collins book.

There was nothing for it. I ordered another beer.

Chapter 17

Sleep proved elusive that night; in the end, I threw off the bed covers in disgust and tried making a brew. Unfortunately, Egyptian tea didn't quite cut it for me and the only milk available was UHT from a tiny plastic container. I took one sip and decided to head out for a walk.

The hotel and dive school were only a short distance from the beach.

Wearing just a T-shirt, shorts and sandals, I wandered across the sand and settled down on one of the loungers overlooking the sea.

Although the beach was devoid of tourists, there were local people busying to and fro, preparing for the day. Beachfront restaurants were being cleaned, pavements swept and wagons unloaded. In the east, the sun was rising higher over Saudi Arabia, its rays turning the dusky Arabian sands to gold. Dawn was my favourite time of day and, for once, I was grateful for the effects of the insomnia.

The break of day brought back memories. Half-light is a soldier's friend. Before the invention of light-intensifying technology, most attacks would take place at dawn. Soldiers had long ago learned from animals – in the half-light it was harder to see the hunter coming.

Which is probably how Petre managed to get so close to me. 'You rise early, Mr Finlay,' he said, in a quiet voice.

I turned my body slightly to see the stocky bodyguard just feet away. He seemed to be sharing the view over the gentle surf. 'You surprised me, Petre,' I answered.

'Perhaps,' he shrugged. 'Perhaps not? Perhaps your skills are old, Mr Finlay, but you still have them.'

I was curious. As Petre sat down on a lounger just to my left, I caught another glimpse of the Legion tattoo on his arm. He noticed my glance.

'You recognise?' he asked. 'You also served *Legion étrangère*?'

I looked at Petre's suntanned face. I guessed him to be in his mid-thirties. His hair was cut very short, his eyes bright blue and alert. If he had been in the Legion in his early twenties then there was every chance he might be acquainted with men I knew. At that time a lot of soldiers had left the British Army following government cutbacks and restructuring. The Legion parachute unit had been a popular destination.

Several of the lads from the SAS squadrons had made the move rather than face civvy street. The Legion was well known for accepting trained soldiers from other countries who were in need of a regular wage or were running away from some kind of problem. It saved a fortune in training costs.

'*Legio Patria Nostra*' was the motto of the 3rd Foreign Infantry Regiment, which was almost certain to have been where Petre served.

'Not me, Petre,' I answered. 'Short time British Army.' I also smiled to myself, amused by how I had dropped into Brit-speak, the stilted English we often use when talking to foreigners.

'I guess. You move like soldier.'

'Your tattoo gave you away, Petre.'

Petre glanced at his arm and laughed. 'I was young man. We drink too much, do crazy things. Some stay with us always.'

'How is Marica?' I asked.

Petre nodded. 'She is good, hospital take good care of her. Bit of headache and bruise, but she will be fine. I wait with her through night. First thing she say this morning is to find you. She would like to see you.'

'Are they keeping her in?'

'Just for one day. Concussion and checks. I take you to see her, OK?'

I had a mostly free day. After the near disaster on the boat, Catherine had asked me to join her at a debrief with the manager of the dive school. After what had happened, it wasn't likely I'd be told I'd passed the advanced diving course, so I wondered if they were simply looking to cover their arses in case anyone should make a claim.

To allow enough time, I suggested to Petre we meet outside the hotel at about ten. He agreed.

After my visitor had headed off, I stayed at the beach for nearly an hour, enjoying the sea and the sky. It was still before seven when I started the walk back to the hotel.

Word of my exploits had spread quickly amongst the East European guests. As I walked into the breakfast room, I was aware of faces turning to look at me. On previous mornings I had been ignored; just another lone, male diver. Today it was different; the two dozen men and women gathered around the self-service counter and at their tables all became quiet.

It was pretty obvious I was the cause of the reaction, but I was unsure exactly why; were they friendly or hostile? I didn't have to wait long to find out. As I continued walking towards the self-service area, two overweight men stood up from their seats and approached me. Both were in brightly coloured shirts, shorts and sandals.

I was tense for a moment until I saw their broad smiles.

Hands were extended. We shook; they both then hugged me and uttered words in a tongue I didn't understand. I was able to work out the sentiment, though. More men came over to pat me on the back. There were more handshakes and then a woman who spoke English approached. She was a little older than Marica, but looked similar: slim with long black hair. Her blue dress looked to be silk and oozed wealth.

'I am sorry if we surprise you, sir. My friends wish to say their thanks,' she said.

'You're friends of Marica?' I asked.

'Yes, friends. The men here, they work for her father in Romania. It is said that you saved her from death under the sea. Today, you are a hero.'

I smiled, feeling more than a little embarrassed by the attention. But as the English-speaking woman talked, I also noticed the reverence in which she seemed to be held by the others. The men gave her space; the women remained seated or at the breakfast bar.

'Not a hero. Just right place, right time, that's all,' I replied. I wasn't quite sure how to extricate myself from this unexpected reception. In the event, my unease seemed to be noticed. My new friend said something to the men and they all started to return to their seats. One shook my hand again and several gave me a thumbs-up signal.

'Please understand, Mr Finlay—'

'You know my name?' I interrupted.

'Yes, of course. I hope that does not trouble you. We are always careful about who Marica mixes with. We asked the dive school about you before it was agreed for you and Marica to be together. As I was saying, please understand our thanks. Marica is a very special person – not just the daughter of our employer, but a girl we love with all our hearts.'

'As you know my name, do you mind if I ask yours?'

'Anca. I am Anca Cristea; Marica is my sister-in-law.'

We shook hands. For someone so slim, I was surprised at the strength in her grip. There was a short round of applause from the others. I did my best to acknowledge them before heading to the breakfast bar. I was hungry.

I chose waffles with honey, loaded a second plate with eggs and bacon, and found a seat by a window overlooking the pool. It was only then I realised that Ryan, the safety diver, was sitting at a table near me.

Ryan said nothing. As our eyes met, he just winked. I smiled and started my breakfast. We both knew my rescue of Marica had been a fluke. As a novice diver, I had no idea of the risks and had acted on instinct. Marica had been very lucky I had reached her. If Catherine hadn't emptied the air from my buoyancy vest and put extra weight in it, I would never have worked out how to re-descend quickly enough. It was a team effort: Ryan helped Catherine, Catherine helped me and I helped Marica. Then Petre helped all of us.

I took my time over breakfast and then went back to my room for a rest. The Collins book was by the side of the bed. I picked it up, found my place and within two pages felt my eyelids start to close.

Chapter 18

An hour and a half later, I stirred. Checking my watch, I confirmed I had enough time for a quick shower before I was to be picked up and taken to the hospital.

I found Petre waiting outside the hotel in a chauffeured Mercedes. As I approached, the driver opened a rear door for me and I climbed in. Petre sat in the front with him. The soft leather seats were cool, the air conditioning quietly keeping the interior at a pleasant temperature. I had ditched the T-shirt and shorts in favour of a light-blue denim shirt and jeans.

It was a comfortable ride to the hospital. The more I learned about my fellow Romanian hotel residents, the more I began to understand that not all East Europeans are poor. These people had money to spend. This was demonstrated when, fifteen minutes later, we approached what I quickly realised was no run-of-the-mill facility. The drive, gardens and exterior were beautifully cared for. It was clean, free of litter and had an air of peace and comfort about it.

Our driver pulled up outside reception and, as I followed Petre in through the glass doors, I was struck by how much the hospital waiting area, with its ochre marble floor and sumptuous seating, resembled the lobby of a luxury hotel. Spacious, opulent and quiet, it had little in common with most of the hospitals back home. This was private medicine at its most luxurious.

A uniformed porter led us to the second floor. As the lift was occupied, we opted for the ornate, spiral staircase. A short walk along a landing and we arrived at a solid-looking wooden door. Petre knocked.

The door was opened and Anca appeared. Behind her I could see three more women sat around a bed, laughing and chatting.

Marica was sitting up in bed and greeted me with a warm smile. Apart from a bandage around her head, she looked intact and healthy. I was invited to sit close to her. Over the next few minutes, I once again suffered the awkward plaudits of her friends who, despite their limited command of English, seemed determined to embarrass me.

Marica explained that, as she was soon to be married, Anca was her chaperone while Petre provided protection. Petre worked for Marica's father, who ran an import/export business near Bucharest. It seemed her father had heard what had happened and was keen I should be told how grateful he was.

After about ten minutes chatting, Anca declared that her charge was beginning to tire and it was time she had some more rest. As I made to leave, Marica handed me a sealed envelope.

'For you,' she said.

I opened it. Inside was a small, white card bearing embossed silver writing, in what I guessed was Romanian.

Seeing my puzzled look, Marica explained. 'It's a wedding invitation. Please say you will come, Robert.'

'I'm not sure.'

'You have a wife, perhaps? She will come too?'

Put on the spot, there was no way I could refuse. 'Of course,' I replied. 'I'm sure she would love to.'

'Please, everybody,' Marica demanded, waving the others towards the door. 'Leave Robert with me a moment, alone.'

They obeyed without question, even Anca.

Only once we were by ourselves and the door closed, did Marica speak again. 'I will always be grateful to you, Robert.'

'Right time, right place Marica. I did nothing anyone else wouldn't have done in the circumstances.'

'Possibly. But for me, it was you. You risked your life for me. I will always remember that kiss, Robert. I remember we were coming up near the boat, then the next thing I knew you were kissing me in the water. I was weak, it seemed a dream. Then I was on the boat and Petre was tending to my head wound. Only then did I learn what had happened. But ... I remember that kiss ... in the water.'

'I had to get you breathing.'

'I know, I know. But it was special. Promise me you will tell no one of that kiss ... no one.'

I made the promise. There was no need for anyone else to know. I guessed the fiancé might be the jealous kind, so I was happy to stay silent.

'And now, let me sleep,' she said, and took my hand.

As I made to leave she smiled again. It was such a pretty smile. One that, many years previously, would have been enough to seduce me.

I said goodbye to everyone and travelled alone back to the hotel. Petre had work to do and I had a meeting with the dive school to get to, a bill to pay for my tuition and a suitcase to pack.

I also wondered how much a flight to Bucharest was going to set Jenny and me back.

Chapter 19

MI5 office, New Scotland Yard

The paperwork on Toni's desk was building up.

In the aftermath of 9/11, all priorities had changed. Although the accepted remit of MI6 had been limited to foreign soil, while MI5 concentrated on domestic security, this was being transformed; overlap was now commonplace. For Toni and many other MI5 officers, the effect was a massive shift in focus from Irish terrorism to Al Q'aeda and the large number of suspected operatives and sympathisers who were now domiciled in the UK.

So, in addition to the paperwork, she was spending one evening each week learning Arabic. All her fellow pupils were Secret Service officers. Their tutor was an Iraqi-born MI6 agent. Not surprisingly, the officers compared notes about their work. All reported frustrations at being unable to recruit agents and informants from within the Arab and Moslem communities. They all had heavy workloads and they were all feeling the strain. Many were talking of moving on to pastures new.

Toni was one of them.

One job had been causing her a particular headache. Someone in northern England was providing information to two French journalists who were writing a book that was, allegedly, going to include a chapter on an MI6 Gaddafi operation.

That suspicion stemmed back to February the previous year, when *The Sunday Times* had published an article claiming MI6 had worked with Al Q'aeda on a plan to assassinate Colonel Gaddafi. It was an embarrassing revelation for MI6. It was thought that the French reporters were going to expose the fact British taxpayers' money had been used to indirectly fund an organisation hell-bent on attacking Western interests; specifically, the group that had been behind the New York attacks on September 11th.

The source of the *Sunday Times* article was known to be a

Manchester-based Al Q'aeda operative called Al-Liby, who had been given political asylum in Britain. In May 2000, Al-Liby had gone underground following a raid on his home in which a 'Manual for Jihad' had been found. Finding Al-Liby and confirming if he was the journalists' source was now Toni's responsibility; that was if he was still in the UK. If not, she would be forced to pass the case to MI6. And that was something she would prefer not to do.

It was a similar story with the Chad Collins book, *Cyclone*. Cristea Publishing – based in Romania, of all places – was a relatively new publishing house and was still something of a mystery. Toni knew it was making waves in the literary world and had signed several well-known authors. Intelligence Services had paid little heed – nobody had thought it worthy of a personal file; until *Cyclone* appeared on the shelves and the CIA saw what it contained. That had put the cat amongst the pigeons, and now finding Chas Collins was a priority. He was a ghost – an expert in remaining off the Security Service radar. As Toni saw it, anyone who could get close to the author and learn his sources was likely to see their career benefit.

Now, with Robert Finlay due home from Egypt, she had learned enough to suggest the decision to send him there had been the right one. Even though the intelligence report that Chas Collins was going to be holidaying in Egypt had proved wrong, there was good news from the dive school: Finlay had saved Cristea Publishing's owner's daughter from drowning and had, as a result, been invited to her wedding in Romania. Toni now had a second – and probably better – chance to engineer a meeting between the author and Finlay.

Babysitting the Finlay family had, at first, been an unwelcome addition to her growing workload, but she had grown to like them and now it had produced a most unlikely outcome. She allowed herself a smile at a good week's work, despite the frustrations around finishing the Hastings report.

Debriefing Finlay, however, would also provide an opportunity to secure answers to those frustrating questions – in particular, about the gap in his military file. It was a question that had prompted her to go through his army disciplinary record that very day. There was only one entry: an admonishment for inaccurate recording of expenses.

Yet something still niggled her. It would be easy enough to finish the report and agree with the findings but, on her initial MI5 course, her instructor had impressed upon his students something that had become indelibly engraved on her brain: 'Assumption is the mother of all fuck-ups.'

It was a piece of advice she now followed. Until every question was answered to her satisfaction, the file would remain open.

Chapter 20

I decided to use the final morning in the hotel for a decent rest and to make a real attempt to finish my book. It was another warm Egyptian day. In the sheltered area near to the pool, I stripped off down to my shorts.

Despite some of the personal and self-promotional stuff, which I skimmed through, the bulk of the Collins' book was fascinating. It was an eyewitness account of the author's experiences during the Afghan-Russian war of the 1980s. As I had been in Pakistan at the time, training Mujahideen fighters to use anti-aircraft missiles, it was especially interesting. The author was certainly well informed. It seemed likely I had served with him, although, from the blurred photographs and descriptions, I wasn't able to work out who he was.

I was still reading when Anca distracted me. I hadn't heard her approach and was only aware of her presence when a shadow appeared on the pages.

'What are you reading that keeps you so preoccupied, Robert?' she asked.

I lifted the book to show her the cover. She threw her head back and laughed. I figured she didn't share my taste.

'You like this book, *Cyclone*?'

'So far, so good.'

Anca laughed again. 'My father-in-law will be very pleased to hear this. Look inside the cover at the name of the publishers.'

I did as she asked. 'Cristea Publishing Company, London,' I read out loud.

'If you remember, my name is Anca Cristea. My husband's father started the company. He has many businesses; this is one of them.'

I smiled. It was a fascinating coincidence.

'Marica has invited you to her wedding?' she continued.

'Yes, I hope to be able to make it, if I can get time off from work.'

'What do you do Robert? Are you still a soldier?'

It was my turn to laugh. 'No, my soldiering days are long behind me. These days I work for myself. Nothing glamorous: I work for small businesses – doing the books, paperwork, that sort of thing.' As I spoke, I realised my answer had started to stray from the one I had given the dive staff. Fortunately, I remembered in time. 'And I teach people to drive cars,' I added.

'Yes, as you say, not glamorous. Anyway, I think you will have a nice surprise at the wedding.'

'You think?'

'Yes, Chas Collins, the author of your book, will be there. Maybe he will autograph it for you?' Anca laughed again, a cheeky laugh I would have attributed more to a teenager than to someone who looked so elegant.

I smiled back. 'Perhaps he will.'

'Will you be flying home today?' Anca asked.

'Yes, I leave for the airport at lunch time.'

She extended her hand. I stood, placed the book on the lounger and we shook hands. Again, I noticed her grip was surprisingly strong. Her hands were also harder and the skin less smooth than I had expected. The strength extended to her forearms; under her thin, blue dress, the muscular development was clear and defined.

'I look forward to seeing you again, Robert. Please enjoy your flight.'

As quietly and quickly as Anca had appeared, she was gone.

I watched her descend the steps from the pool area into the hotel foyer. She moved elegantly, the material of the dress accentuating her figure. A nice lady, I thought. No doubt from a good family. I had noticed a large wedding ring shining on her finger. The Cristea son who had married her had secured himself a very good catch.

It was time to settle the bills that MI5 weren't covering. The hotel bar service was reasonable and cheap. The dive-school account was likely to be a different matter, however. With the cost of the course, equipment hire and Catherine as guide, I knew I was going to be stung for quite a bit. It had been worth it, though. I felt so much more relaxed than the tense man who had arrived at the resort a week earlier.

Armed with my credit card, I made my way to settle up. But an embarrassing surprise awaited me: at both the hotel and the dive school, I found my bills had been paid in full. Neither would tell me by whom, but it wasn't too hard to work out.

In the dive-school equipment area, I found Catherine cleaning and filling air cylinders. She winked at me when I asked who had paid. 'It's not every day we have a hero here, Robert.'

There was no point in arguing. But I was left with mixed feelings: relief at not heading home with a large credit card bill and slight guilt I didn't feel worthy of the gesture.

I returned to my room, squeezed the last few items into my suitcase and then boarded the small bus that would drop me at the airport. Two hours later, with the Collins book nearly finished, I was on the plane home.

Chapter 21

London Embankment

Toni Fellowes was in a hurry.

Although it wasn't a long walk to the MI6 building, the weather had taken a turn for the worse. With no waterproof coat or umbrella, she now found herself dodging from shop canopies to bus shelters, and from trees to doorways in an attempt to avoid the rain.

MI6 HQ, the Secret Intelligence Service building at Vauxhall Cross, was a place people like Toni didn't get to visit very often. Even with her level of security clearance, Toni was only allowed access under escort. Shaking herself dry, she was compelled to wait in reception until a junior MI6 clerk arrived to see her through the metal detectors, security doors, CCTV and fingerprint access points. The clerk took her security pass, disappeared into a nearby office for a few minutes and then, after returning the pass, led the way.

Howard Green, her contact and host, was waiting in his office. It helped they were on friendly terms. Several times, outside work, they had enjoyed lunch or dinner together. At one point, Toni had hoped the relationship might develop beyond work, but then Howard had mentioned he was married. For her, that had ended the possibility of anything more than friendship between them, although Howard had persisted in his attempt to persuade her otherwise. Eventually, though, he took the hint, and now when they met he was always cordial, even if she occasionally caught him staring at her legs.

No longer a field agent, Howard now managed, supervised and organised the people that did the spying. He was a conduit between information provider and information recipient, running a network of agents who might contribute nothing, but who just might secure intelligence that would reveal activities the UK Government needed to know about. As such, his level of security clearance was high.

Howard had requested the get-together, supposedly to discuss a mutual interest. Toni thought it perfect timing as she needed to secure authority to view the high-clearance personal files relevant to the Hastings report. She hoped that some bargaining might see them both leave the meeting happy.

As the clerk closed the door, Toni was a little surprised when Howard kissed her cheek in welcome. If the act had been intended to lower her guard it wouldn't work, she thought. But her curiosity was aroused. Her host continued more formally, explaining his current role. He was now responsible for operations in Eastern Europe – specifically Romania and Moldova. He was investigating links between criminal gangs, gun running and the terror groups that purchased weapons through these sources. Toni kept a straight face but, as soon as she heard the word 'Romania', she had a feeling she knew where the conversation was leading.

She feigned surprise, however, when he said, 'Tell me about Robert Finlay.'

'That's why you asked me here?' she said, stalling as she considered how best to answer the questions that would inevitably follow.

'Yes, his name has come up on my radar. What do you know of him?'

'Do you mind if I ask why MI6 have an interest in him?'

'You first, Toni,' Howard smiled. 'I can see the question surprised you. I am prepared to explain, but tell me about him first. I've read the digital copy of his PF; and I know the hard copy is booked out to you. I'm hoping you can tell me more than my version shows.'

Again, Toni hesitated. Most of the essential background on Finlay was in his PF – his personal file. There wasn't much more she could, or wanted, to add. And considering Finlay was what she wanted to ask Howard Green about, it was possibly a fortuitous coincidence, possibly not. She decided to maintain an air of cooperation.

Summarising what she could recall of Finlay's family history, schooling, education and army and police careers, Toni went through as much as she was prepared to say, including a run-down on the recent attacks on Finlay and his former colleagues, and ending with SO13's conclusions about the motives behind the attacks.

Howard listened intently, occasionally jotting a note on a small pad that sat on his desk. Toni noticed how he nodded as he listened. If he had read the file, he would know most of what she was saying.

Just as she was finishing, Howard waved his hand, as if a little bored. 'So you are babysitting him because of the attacks?' he asked.

'We are. And Dirt has asked me to confirm the SO13 conclusions before we declare the enquiry complete.'

'What are your personal thoughts on Finlay, Toni?'

'He's a nice man. Loyal. But he has a lack of emotion about him. It's like things just don't get to him. You get the feeling he has seen too much in his life and some of it is bottled up inside somewhere.'

'You like him?'

'Why do you ask?'

Howard smiled. 'All in good time, Toni. Do you *like* him?'

'Yes, I do, very much.' Toni was surprised by her own frankness and how quickly she answered the question.

'Have you recruited him?'

'No ... I haven't.'

'Tell me what he was doing in Egypt this past week ...'

'Is that why you're asking?'

'Yes. His presence there is my reason for meeting you now. I'm willing to think it is just a coincidence, but Finlay has met up with some very interesting people.' Howard pulled a small, buff file from a drawer in his desk as he spoke.

He's lying, Toni thought. Nobody in this profession truly believes in coincidence. 'His reason for going there is the fulfilment of a dream from his childhood,' she explained. 'That much I can tell you. I think Egypt might even have been my idea. He needed a holiday and I suggested it to him.'

Howard flicked open the file. 'Ever heard of the Cristea family?'

He handed Toni a photograph of a young woman standing next to a swimming pool. To one side of her there was a tough-looking man with short hair and behind them stood Finlay, dressed rather shabbily in an old T-shirt and shorts. There was no mistaking him.

'No, I haven't,' she lied.

Howard snorted, just gently. 'The woman is Marica Cristea. The man is her bodyguard. Marica is a member of an interesting Romanian family … I find it very difficult to believe you are not aware of them.'

'Why so?'

'Cristea Publishing. You have read the security briefing on the *Cyclone* book, I presume?'

Toni recognised the hint of sarcasm in Howard's tone. 'Ah … yes, of course … *that* Cristea family.'

'Indeed.' Howard flicked at the file, impatiently. 'Look, Toni. I'm going to be up front with you here, and, trust me, it would be best for you if we are straight with each other.'

'In what way?'

'By being honest about why you chose that particular resort for your man to take his break in. So … a straight question to which I expect a straight answer: Were you trying to get your man close to the *Cyclone* author so you could learn the sources of his information?'

'I'm not sure I follow?' Toni answered, doing her best to sound innocent.

Howard huffed. 'Does Finlay work for you?'

'Definitely not. I'm just tasked with investigating the attacks on him and his old friends and getting his family resettled.'

'So why, when I google Robert Finlay, does a search reveal him to be a driving instructor? Is that normal for a cop on an innocent holiday?'

Toni stayed silent. She was rumbled. Silently, she handed back the photograph; she could see her hand was trembling.

Howard saw it too. A smug grin crossed his face. 'I thought so,' he said. 'OK, here's the play: you've stumbled into something way outside of your job description, Toni, and now it's time for you to back off, do I make myself clear?'

'Perfectly.'

'So, you will recall your man and forget about Cristea Publishing?'

'Of course … I didn't realise they were the sole remit of MI6.'

'Don't get clever with me, Toni. There are forces at work here of which you have no knowledge.'

'Secrets in a secret world, you might say?'

'Exactly.'

'I understand … and I'm sorry if I've stepped on any toes.'

'I'd consider it a personal favour were you to forget about this meeting as well.'

'OK … might I ask a courtesy in return?'

'Ask away.'

'The Finlay PF details the recent attempts on his life and those of his friends. I'm tying up some loose ends. The Anti-Terrorist Squad have Nial Monaghan as being behind it – a vendetta against soldiers his wife supposedly slept with.'

'Embarrassing for Five to have one of their own go off the rails like that.'

Toni drew breath. 'Indeed … Monaghan used contacts and the intel system to work his plan. But I can't access his file or the file of Richard Webb, the Al Q'aeda man he used. Access to both PFs is blocked by Six. I can't even access his DNA profile to confirm it was Monaghan killed in the car bomb.'

'Have you tried a match from his home – a hairbrush, that kind of thing?'

'Not yet, I was going to put a forensic team in but when I went to look over the place I found it had been cleaned. That won't be easy, you wouldn't think anyone had actually lived there. I don't hold with conspiracies, but I would like to know who did the clean-up. It was us, I'm sure, but what department, and who authorised it?'

'Cock-up rather than conspiracy, you think? I'm sure forensics will turn up something you can use.' Howard turned to a small computer terminal on his desk and tapped in the names.

From where Toni sat, she couldn't see the screen but she guessed it was likely to generate information similar to her own. Access denied, with an MI6 reference number.

She was wrong. Howard's higher security clearance did the job.

'Webb was an asset. That much I can tell you,' Howard said, looking at the screen. 'I will speak to his handler to see if we can authorise your access to his PF. Monaghan will be harder. The block on that is at a much higher level.' He turned off the screen and stood up. 'Leave it with me,' Howard continued. 'I'll get back to you in a day or two.'

Meeting over, Howard walked Toni back to the security reception. They shook hands.

'Just out of interest,' he said. 'Have you actually read the *Cyclone* book?'

'Not really, no. I had a scan though a copy and, of course, I read the analyst briefing on it.'

'Well, if I were you, I wouldn't bother. The author has upset some major players by revealing some very embarrassing facts – as per the analyst report – but much of it is fantasy, hardly worth the paper it's written on.'

'Thanks … I'll bear that in mind.'

'One other thing, Toni,' Howard leaned closer to her.

'Something else?'

'Just a reminder. Security on foreign soil is the job of Six, not Five. Leave Cristea to us. We'll find the author and we will find who spilled the beans on the Cyclone operation.'

Before she could respond, Howard had turned away and disappeared back into the building.

Chapter 22

Outside, the rain had eased off but it was still cold.

On the return walk, Toni found herself thinking deeply about what Howard had said and, the more she thought about it, the more she concluded it didn't really matter.

What she had learned was invaluable. MI6 were also interested in Cristea. If Howard saw access to Chas Collins as important enough to warn her off, then, clearly, there was mileage in establishing such a contact. If she could persuade Finlay to take up the offer to travel to Romania, he could provide the very boost her career needed.

It was a competition, and Howard, it seemed, was prepared to play dirty. But she had the edge, she was in front. She had Robert Finlay.

For some time, she had been wondering what to do next. MI5 was a hard act to follow; no office job or commercial career would bring the level of excitement and sense of personal worth Security Service membership provided. But if there was kudos about being an officer in MI5, the mystique surrounding MI6 was all the greater. The fictional life of James Bond may have been just that, but breaking and entering in foreign lands, undermining and spying on both friendly and unfriendly governments, and operating behind enemy lines really were all part of the job. The 1994 Security Services Act had given MI6 immunity from prosecution for illegal acts committed abroad, provided prior authority was given by the Foreign Secretary. So MI6 agents could, and did, break laws and, of course, ran the risks that discovery involved.

Howard Green had hinted he was involved in exactly this type of work – work that appealed to her. If she secured the intelligence MI6 were seeking, she could engineer things to ensure they both shared the limelight; she and Howard. Surely, he would then forgive her for not obeying his orders.

In the coming months, she knew the overwhelming demand upon the Security Services was going to be the threat from Moslem extremists. MI5 would try and deal with the home-grown problems but it would be MI6 that would be facing the greatest challenge. They would need people like her and she was ready to make the move. She could speak Spanish and French, had a working knowledge of Russian and her Arabic was improving by the week.

By the time she turned into Broadway and walked across the front of St James's Park tube station, her mind was made up. As she approached the rotating doors of Scotland Yard and smiled to the two MP5-carrying policemen on duty outside, she was already making plans.

MI6 it was.

Chapter 23

Heathrow Airport, London

'You're brown,' said Jenny.

I grinned, dropped my bag, and threw my arms around her. 'No Becky?' I asked.

'She's at home ... at the house. A new man from Toni's office is looking after her until we get there.'

'No worries.' I placed my hands on Jenny's face, caressed her cheeks and then kissed her gently. 'I've missed you.'

'Likewise. You look really well. And before you say anything, Toni has told me all about your heroism. Saving beautiful Romanian princesses from certain death now, are we?'

I laughed as I leaned down to recover my bag, nearly tripping over it as I did so. 'News travels fast; that's a slight spin on the story, I think.'

Jenny held my arm tight. 'Why didn't you say anything when you telephoned?'

'I didn't want to worry you ... make you think I had been doing something risky. It really wasn't a big deal, I just happened to be there when she got into difficulties.'

Jenny stopped, turned to face me and shook her head, gently. 'That's so typical of you, Robert. A girl owes you her life and you make it sound like what you did was all in a normal day's work.'

I cracked a grin. 'OK ... so maybe I did a good thing. But anyone else would have done the same. Now, where's the car?' For a moment, I thought I detected a mischievous look in my wife's eyes.

'In the short stay, come on ... let's go.'

As we walked to the car park, we chatted and laughed. I felt good, better than I had in weeks. I explained about the extra dive course, the Romanians and who Marica was. Then, as briefly as I could – given Jenny clearly wouldn't rest until she knew everything – I explained what had happened on the day Marica had nearly drowned.

'Well, it sounds to me like you definitely saved her,' she said. 'You must have taken to the diving then?'

'It was amazing. I used to love the helicopter trips in the army but this was way better. It was like being Superman, able to float and fly … to be weightless.'

'Worth the trip, then?'

'More than. And being in the right place for Marica was the icing on the cake.'

'She was grateful?'

'She was *very* grateful.'

'Oh, really?' Jenny answered, coyly. 'How grateful?'

'Enough to invite us both to her wedding in a couple of weeks.'

'She's getting married in Egypt?'

'In Romania, at her home near Bucharest. She gave me an official invitation.'

'What did you say?'

'I said I'd ask you.'

'But you'd like to go.'

'I think so … but I'm not sure if work would permit me the time off. I'm due to start the new job on Monday with a new team. They might not be keen on me taking leave so soon.'

Jenny paid the parking fee with a credit card as we chatted, and then we made the short walk to the first floor and along the lines of cars. Her reaction to the invitation was more positive than I had expected. Somehow she had read about Romanian weddings and was aware they could be great parties with a lot of music and dancing. But the cost, that would be a significant factor. Whether we would be able to afford the trip might decide whether we went or not.

As we drew level with a little yellow car sat at the end of one line, I saw Jenny glance across at it. The familiar shape filled me with sadness. A 2CV. Just like the one that had been blown up on our driveway some weeks previously.

I made to walk on, looking for our Audi, but Jenny turned in front of me, and placed her hand on my chest. Without uttering a word, she held out some keys with a Citroen fob attached. The reason for the mischievous look in the arrivals hall became clear. This was the surprise she had been teasing me about. There were tears in my eyes as I threw my arms around her. Between salt-flavoured kisses and hugs, we eventually put my bag on the back seat and then climbed in.

'You bought it?' I asked.

'It was in the supermarket car park with a 'for sale' sign in the windscreen and a phone number. It was impulsive, I know, but I rang the number straight away. The man who owned it came out of the shop and we agreed a price there and then.'

'Some things are just meant to be, I guess.'

'It was £750. But, I didn't think you'd mind.'

I didn't. Jenny drove us home. I was tired and the surprise of the car had left me feeling a little emotional. For the whole drive home my hand subconsciously stroked Jenny's left knee. I didn't speak, there was no need.

Chapter 24

Reluctant as she was to admit it of someone so new, Toni Fellowes was impressed by Stuart Anderson. A transfer in from the police, he was a quick learner and had a wealth of experience.

He was surveillance trained, an expert interrogator and spoke Arabic thanks to his time in Special Branch. In many ways he was ideal Security Service material. He wasn't a graduate, though, which explained why he hadn't been noticed earlier. It was only recently that the Service had realised the need for Arab linguists. Stuart became one of the fast-tracked entrants. He was yet to complete his initial MI5 course and had been allocated to her department temporarily until he did. As a result, his security clearance was very low, which limited what she could do with him.

Stuart had been a little reluctant about child-minding – that was until he had actually met Becky. Her cheeky laugh and huge smile won him over, as Toni knew they would. Inside of ten minutes, the two of them had been sat side-by-side playing Nintendo on the television.

With Becky now settled on a different game, Toni led the new addition to her team on a tour of the safe house to discuss the layout and security risks. She left doors open so they could be sure their charge was OK.

Stuart's assessment of the house was spot on. With strengthened windows and doors, the building was to some extent a fortress, but one that could only withstand so much. Its real strength lay in its anonymity and secrecy. As they walked around, she brought him up to date on the Finlay family and what she knew about Webb, Monaghan and the hit team that had been employed to kill former soldiers.

Two of the would-be assassins were dead, she explained, and the remaining pair were in the high-security prison at Belmarsh. Of those, one was just a sleeper; he knew nothing. The other, Dominic McGlinty, wasn't talking; as a seasoned IRA man he knew better. Toni had interviewed him briefly, about a week after she had inherited the Finlay case. It had been a wasted exercise.

She also shared her concerns with Stuart about the cleansing of Monaghan's home. Although he was new, Stuart had a policing career behind him, and he agreed with her assessment that the possible removal of any forensic evidence they might have gained was more likely cock-up than conspiracy. Just like the Met, MI5 was a big, unwieldy organisation and was well known for its communication breakdowns, both internally and externally. It was no surprise that a department would be tasked with taking care of a dead operative's house without thinking another department might be investigating his death.

Howard Green, she kept out of the conversation. If he came up trumps then she would learn more about what had driven Monaghan to murder and how Richard Webb had been pulled into the plan. As things stood, Stuart didn't need to know where that information might come from.

They had not long finished the tour of the safe house when the Finlays returned from the airport.

Toni noticed the changed appearance as soon as Finlay walked through the door. A slight suntan made him look much healthier and he was smiling. It was a warm smile, telling her his emotions hadn't been completely killed off by the events of recent weeks. It was a good sign he might just be on the road to recovery, and suggested her decision to send him to Egypt, although convenient, had been the right one.

She introduced Stuart, who offered to make tea and then, as a group, they sat down to talk. Throughout the discussion, she was careful to appear that she was talking from a welfare perspective, but occasionally, carefully, she slipped in a loaded question. Did Robert have any problems saying he was a driving instructor? No. Did the girl he saved have lots of friends with her? Yes; and he provided some useful detail. When he mentioned the incredible coincidence of Marica's family being the publishers of the very book Jenny had given him to read on the holiday, she smiled to herself. It was a pity Chas Collins hadn't been there, but now, with the book so fresh in his mind, Finlay would probably take the opportunity to talk to the author should they meet in Romania. There was one awkward moment – when Finlay asked how she already knew he had saved the girl – but she easily deflected it by reminding him the hotel was approved for use by MI5 officers. The answer seemed to satisfy him. On the subject of whether the couple could afford a trip to Romania, however, she played it safe, suggesting it was unlikely funding would be available for a second trip.

But, all the while she promised herself – hell or high water – Finlay, would be going to the wedding.

Chapter 25

The following day, Toni was working late. It was almost eight o'clock when an email came through from GCHQ. If she had had any doubts about persuading Finlay to take up the wedding invitation, the contents of that email removed them. It concerned Chas Collins' literary agent.

Almost all monitoring of telephones was automated, with certain trigger words being programmed to prompt further attention. If used during the conversations of 'persons of interest', a report would be generated.

The agent was a 'person of interest'.

A short transcript was attached to the email. It read:

Subject: Maggie (Margaret) Price
Occupation: Literary Agent
Date of recording: 10/21/2001
Time of Recording: 1525 hrs
Trigger word combination: Robert Finlay
Type of recording: Cell phone
Transcript part summary:
Incoming caller: *Her bodyguard had to be helped by the tourist.*
Subject: *Really, didn't the bodyguard swim?*
Incoming caller: *I'm not sure. Anyway, I have the man's name. Can you check on him? Marica wants to invite him over here to her wedding.*
Subject: *Give me a minute (pause). OK, what's his name?*
Incoming caller: *Robert Finlay [trigger]*
Subject: *Not heard of him, give me a couple of days. Have you googled the name?*
Incoming caller: *Done what?*
Subject: *Googled. Run the name through a search engine, the internet. That will give you a heads-up on him I should think.*
Full Conversation Time: 3 mins 7 seconds

The email concluded with contact details for requesting a full transcript or recording. A recording would be put on CD and sent via secure mail; it would take up to seven days.

Toni tapped her pen on the edge of her desk. Someone was asking Maggie Price to check on Robert Finlay. She had no doubt in her mind it was a member of the Cristea staff.

She typed 'Maggie Price Literary Agent' into her secure search engine and found the agency's website. She scanned the various pages: how to contact, submission guidelines, fees, clients, etc. Then, on the events page, she found the very information she sought. *Accompanying Chas Collins to the wedding of his publisher's daughter – looking forward to letting my hair down.* Maggie Price was going to Romania ... and so was Chas Collins.

She keyed in the request for the full transcript. It would make for interesting reading.

Chapter 26

Sex Trafficking Unit, New Scotland Yard

The first meeting with my new boss had gone badly. Starting a new job by asking to take a long weekend off was never going to go down well. And Superintendent Max Youldon wasn't known as 'Mad Max' without good reason. The thin walls of his office seemed to shake as he roared his disapproval.

Youldon was an experienced career detective. He had read my police file before my arrival and, as he took pleasure in telling me as I sat down, had immediately gone to see Grahamslaw to register his disapproval.

He pointed out in no uncertain terms that, with the exception of a short stint on a crime squad in Kentish Town, I had no CID experience. I hadn't completed the CID initial course at Hendon Detective

School and I knew little about interrogation, forensics, crime investigation, running informants or any of the other skills he considered essential to detective work, particularly the rank of Detective Inspector. He objected to being, as he put it, 'lumbered' with me.

Grahamslaw, much to my relief, had sent him packing. I was coming to his command, whether he liked it or not.

He stared at me intently for a moment across the top of his glasses, and snarled, 'You, Finlay, are what we call a plastic. You're a cop in name only. You protection people wear the uniform but how many collars have you felt, how many court cases have you put together, how many times have you gripped the rails at the Old Bailey?'

His questions were clearly rhetorical, and I thought it best to keep quiet.

'Right, I'm teaming you up with Matt Miller and Nina Brasov. Matt's also an inspector but he's a proper DI. He's been Flying Squad as well as come through the mill on division. If you drink Penderyn whisky you two might just get on. Nina ... well, you can find out about her yourself, but she won't be with us for long, she's off to the Organised Crime Squad. Now get out of my sight and see if you've got enough detective ability to find them.'

It was as I left the office that I asked about time-off to go to Marica's wedding. I probably could have timed that better.

+

It didn't take me long to find the first of my new workmates. Fortunately for me he was much friendlier than Youldon.

Matt Miller had just transferred in from Kentish Town. We were soon chatting like old mates. It turned out we had attended the same promotion classes when we had been studying for the inspector exam. There were fifty places that year. I had come fourteenth on the list, Matt was sixteenth. The more we talked, the more we realised we had in common. It seemed our paths had nearly crossed many times even though we had never previously spoken.

Nina Brasov still hadn't arrived. 'You'll know her,' was all Matt would say about her.

He was right. At about half past nine, Nina walked in: very tall, probably six foot, with long blonde hair, and, when she removed her long coat and hung it on the back of the door, the most incredible figure. Her tan, knee-length skirt was almost as tight as the black cashmere jumper that accentuated her curves. To say she was built like an Amazon was no understatement.

'You must be Finlay?' Nina shook my hand as I stood to greet her. 'Nina Brasov, DS. I'm your bag carrier, but if you ask me to actually carry your bag then watch out.' She laughed at her own joke, but I understood what she meant. Nina might be my subordinate but this was her world, and I was the new guy. It was clear she was a highly experienced detective and, although I had the strong impression she knew how to use her looks, she didn't take advantage of it.

'I've prepared some files for you to both look at,' Nina continued. 'Then there is a PowerPoint to view and finally some victim statements. Shall we make a start?'

Thus Detective Sergeant Nina Brasov began our education. For the next hour we read and discussed information she had managed to glean from a UN investigator called Irena Senovac. Irena had uncovered sex-slave trafficking across Europe on a previously unimagined scale. She had been sacked from her UN job, according to Nina, due to the corrupt involvement of people she worked with. Irena had taken her employers to an industrial tribunal. She had won her case and been interviewed in both the newspapers and on television.

I had heard of sex trafficking. Like many, I imagined it was a problem that was most prevalent in the Far East. I was only vaguely aware there was some in Eastern Europe. So what I learned from Nina in that hour shocked me.

We were shown personal accounts of women who had been abducted, tricked and manipulated into the trade. Once inside, they found it impossible to escape. We also learned how the trade infiltrated the corridors of power, how influential people became complicit in the business as customers, as organisers or simply by turning a blind eye.

The previous year, the UN General Assembly had debated and approved a resolution that had been called the 'Palermo Protocol', by which the UN Drugs and Crime Office would assist member states to develop anti-trafficking strategies and laws.

For the time being, the Met contribution to the fight was Matt, me and Nina.

One story I found particularly disturbing. A girl called Relia had been tricked into leaving her home in Romania to become a personal assistant in Bucharest. I was drawn to the story, having met so many Romanians in Egypt. Their lifestyle seemed a million miles away from this slave girl.

Relia described how she had been beaten, drugged and raped by more men than she was able to count. Even the women she met on her journey were exploitative and dangerous. She was sold to brothel owners in Bucharest, Milan and then London. Each time her new 'owner' would be provided with details of her family at home so she could be intimidated into work. Every new establishment she entered would warn what would happen to her family if she did not co-operate.

Relia wasn't paid, and she was only given the barest of provisions to ensure she could survive and fulfil her role – to have sex with as many men as the owners decided. With girls like her no longer paid a wage and being required to service many more men, punters who could not have been able to afford the service previously, were now able to. This triggered a new cycle of demand and with it the need to supply more girls. It was a lucrative business for the criminals that ran it and a disaster for its victims.

The girls had a limited shelf life. Relia had been picked up during a police raid on a brothel near Euston Station. Just four hundred yards from where passengers passed by in their tens of thousands, there had been a massage parlour where nearly twenty East European, Thai and Polynesian girls were living in squalor.

Relia had been initiated only two years previously. She was already in her eighth premises and with her fifth different owner. By the time she was freed she weighed just six stone. Records found at the scene suggested attempts had been made to sell her on, but without success. There was a hand-written note against her name on a list that had been found in the owner's filing cabinet. It read 'for disposal'.

That note turned out to be the leverage the Vice Squad had needed to get Relia talking. It was clear to her that her popularity with the punters was low. She had already seen other 'unpopular' girls leave, the owners saying that they had been sold on or had bought their freedom home. Relia suspected otherwise.

Nina knew the truth. Sometimes girls escaped. Sometimes they really did make it home. But many others simply vanished. To Nina, the inference was clear. The girls were surplus to requirement – worn out. 'Disposal' meant one thing. They were murdered. And Relia had been scheduled to join them.

Irena Senovac had told Nina that many UN investigators had seen evidence in Eastern Europe of girls being killed, their bodies disposed of with little care or respect. With ineffective investigation and little prospect of being caught, the traffickers acted with impunity and thought nothing of leaving a corpse at the side of the road.

Here in the UK, it was different. Every single murder the police discovered was thoroughly investigated. Murder squads were well-manned and the very best resources employed. It was no accident that the UK rate for clear-ups in such cases was the highest in the world. If a body was found dumped in London, the Met would not rest until the perpetrator was caught.

But this had Nina perplexed. As she explained to us, there were no reported murders of slave prostitutes, no unidentified bodies found, no sign of girls being smuggled back to the Continent. To all intents and purposes, they simply disappeared.

It was a different type of prostitution from the kind I had been familiar with as a young PC. In the recent past, being 'on the game' had been a euphemism many prostitutes liked to use and we cops had been happy to do likewise.

Even in those simpler days there had still been dangers, of course. Lying in wait for girls coming to London's bright lights to ply the 'game' were the gangsters, the pimps and the drug dealers. As Nina explained, when word spread that the streets of London were not paved with gold, the supply of girls had started to dry up. So the gangsters had adapted their methods. If the girls didn't come willingly they could be forced. The old 'game', in which punters paid individual girls for services, was now a deadly game, one in which life was cheap; the girls expendable.

It was a game our small team was about to join.

Chapter 27

After the presentation, while handing us some further victim statements to read, Nina looked me straight in the eye. 'Standard blade or something special, Finlay?'

The question took me aback. I hadn't heard 'standard blade' used outside the army. Nina was asking whether I was an ordinary Special Forces soldier or had moved on to further things. I decided to play dumb, not quite sure how much my two new friends knew.

'My uncle was a Brigadier. Signals most of his life,' she continued, 'but he did a three-year tour on "A" squadron. My elder brother is Guards Regiment and thinking of doing SAS selection next year. You might say there is a connection.'

'Superintendent Youldon seems to be the only one who doesn't know,' I laughed.

'Oh, he knows, he just doesn't care. He only cares how much detective experience you have, which is none so far as I can see.'

Matt stood, walked over to the office door and closed it before adding, 'We aren't the slightest bit bothered by Youldon's concerns, Finlay. Blokes like you have our respect. You can learn from us ... well from Nina anyway. In return, I'm sure there are a few tricks we can pick up from you.'

'My uncle heard a rumour that Al Q'aeda tried to kill the guys on the Iranian embassy raid and that you stopped them in their tracks,' said Nina. 'Our guess is you are here to maintain a low profile for a while, correct?'

I nodded. 'That's close enough. There are no secrets in this job eh? Does it bother either of you – having me around, I mean?'

Matt replied. 'We all have secrets Finlay. How much you want to tell us about your time in the SAS is up to you.'

Nina extended her hand, warmly. 'So long as you pull your weight, guv. I just hope that you can keep up with us youngsters.'

I returned to the paperwork Nina had given us and was quickly absorbed by the first victim statement I read. It was the story of Relia Stanga, the witness who was now providing first-hand information on the traffickers. Her words made for very uncomfortable reading.

Matt and I finished reading our files at the same time. We both took a deep breath. I could see that Nina was watching us as if she were waiting to see our reactions.

Our silence said everything.

It was time to go to work.

Chapter 28

Toni Fellowes reached Embankment with five minutes to spare. There was no sign of Howard Green. Anticipating a wait, she sat down on a wooden bench and started reading her newspaper.

The minutes rolled by. It looked like he was going to be late. Every so often she would look up from the pages to scan her surroundings. There was no sign of him. She wondered if he was intending to stand her up. It was now ten-thirty and he had said ten o'clock.

It had been a difficult week. Nell's reaction to sending Robert Finlay to Egypt had been positively tranquil compared to how she responded to Toni's plan that both he and Jenny go to the Romanian wedding. Add to that the complete lack of progress on the Monaghan enquiry, and even a meeting with a lecherous MI6 officer seemed attractive. So, when Howard had emailed asking to see her, she had jumped at the chance.

The decision to let the Finlays visit Romania had been a tough one. Despite knowing Collins was going to be there, she was still uncertain about how productive the trip would be. So she had run her idea past Dave Batey, her line manager. They both agreed that it was far too late to persuade Finlay to knowingly work for them, sending a trained agent to act as his spouse; and anyway, the risk that the Cristeas may have seen the photograph of his wife he kept in his wallet scotched that idea. So, as things stood, they had to balance the potential gain of intelligence versus the risk to Finlay and his wife.

In normal circumstances, Batey had explained, the risk would be too great. But these were abnormal times. MI6, the CIA and any number of other Security Services had been publicly caught napping on the day of the 9/11 attacks. Anything could now be justified in the desire to save face, salvage reputations and secure intelligence. The Finlays would be going to Romania.

For the first time in her career, Toni felt guilty about her decision to exploit an opportunity. And she knew why. When she had used people in the past, it had been wholly in the interest of national security. What she was allowing the Finlays to do was more about fulfilling her personal ambitions.

She hadn't mentioned to Batey that Howard Green had warned her off. But that was her risk, not theirs.

She also reassured herself that she had taken every step she could think of to ensure that the couple would be safe. She had fully debriefed Finlay about the Egypt trip, learning as much as she could without alerting him to her reasons for asking. The fake profile Nell had set up had been tight and, from the recorded conversations with Maggie Price, it appeared that her Romanian contact was perfectly happy as to Finlay's authenticity. Collins wouldn't know he was talking to a cop.

There was just one small concern: the bodyguard. Finlay had reported that he had been interested in discussing their shared military backgrounds. If he raised the subject again, her suggestion was Finlay should be economical with the truth. Admit to being a former soldier, she said, just play down what you did. Finlay understood fully.

Once home she would debrief them. Finlay was observant. Without realising it, he would see and hear things that she could use. Jenny was the icing on the cake. She might even spot things he didn't. They were the perfect moles.

A male voice brought her back into the real world.

'Thought you were more of an *Independent* reader, Toni?' It was Howard Green.

She folded the newspaper as Howard sat down next to her. 'I like to keep an open mind. You're late. Do you have anything for me?'

'Yes, and my apologies; a conference call over-ran. So, I have some good news and something to ask of you.'

'Let's start with the good news, shall we?'

Howard handed her a small slip of paper. Written on it were two sets of numbers and letters. 'Your access to Monaghan's and Webb's files has been approved. I've moved heaven and earth to get this for you, Toni. One day I expect the favour returned.'

Her manner softened, the annoyance at having been kept waiting subsiding. 'I won't forget … and thanks. What do you want from me?'

'Dinner. One evening next week, perhaps? On me. A chance to talk about something other than work.'

She hesitated, for a moment uncertain if Howard was up to his old tricks. But it didn't take long to decide; it was clearly in her best interests to keep Howard Green sweet. She said yes.

They shook hands. She was about to stand, but Howard held on to her tight. 'You won't let me down, will you, Toni?' he said, his voice low, and with an intensity that surprised her.

'I said yes. I'll be happy to join you.'

'I think you know what I mean. Don't interfere ... leave Collins to us.'

Toni didn't reply as she pulled her hand away quickly and started the short walk back to New Scotland Yard.

Chapter 29

Did he know?

For the entire walk, Toni asked herself that question. Reaching no satisfactory answer she dismissed her fears. With only Nell and Dave Batey in the loop, there was no possibility. He was bluffing.

In the office, Stuart and Nell were huddled together at a PC. They both had headphones on and seemed oblivious to her presence. It was only when she touched Nell on the shoulder that her researcher jumped and her two assistants stopped what they were doing.

'You need to listen to this,' said Stuart.

'Yes, yes ... listen,' Nell repeated, thrusting her headphones at Toni.

'What is it?'

Stuart handed her a thin bundle of papers in a buff-coloured folder. 'It's the personal file on the literary agent, Maggie Price. The one you requested from GCHQ. The call transcripts are in there too. We're listening to the latest one now.'

'Is there anything new?'

'It's more like before. They think he's a former soldier who now teaches people to drive cars.'

'So, there's definitely no suspicion at their end that Finlay might be a cop?'

'None. They seemed quite laid back about him. The conversation only got really interesting when Mrs Price started to be a bit awkward over one of her authors who is also due at the wedding. They got a bit shirty with her.'

'Anything juicy? That's likely to be Chas Collins they're talking about.'

'That's what's fascinating. Apparently he's been on the television a lot lately. The caller is really adamant Maggie brings him to Romania to see Gheorghe Cristea. But it sounds like Collins doesn't want to go.'

'So is he going or not?' Toni realised her voice was sounding insistent. If, after all her efforts, the author failed to turn up, she would have been risking all for nothing.

'It looks like he is, yes.'

'OK ... great. That's good. Do they say why it's so important to them to get him there?' she asked.

'They don't,' said Stuart. 'And, just out of interest, do we make a habit of tapping the phones of people like Maggie Price?'

Toni laughed. 'The longer you stay in this job Stuart, the less surprised you'll be. Security services have been listening in to authors and their agents for decades.'

Chapter 30

My new Superintendent rarely left his office. I learned that my leave application had been approved via a memo that was left overnight on Matt's desk. In three days' time, Jenny and I would be flying out to Bucharest.

Matt, Nina and I had been collating and researching information on trafficking. So it hadn't escaped me that the luxury trip I was hoping to enjoy was the antithesis of the journeys made by many women who travelled in the opposite direction. Romania was the source of one of Europe's largest number of forced sex workers.

According to Nina, poverty in Eastern European countries had made people desperate. The gangs had seen the opportunity and exploited it. Girls were routinely tricked into travelling abroad on false papers for jobs that didn't exist. Once captured, escape was virtually impossible. Many of the slaves were poorly educated and lacked any knowledge of Western life. They couldn't use public transport, speak the language, use the telephone system or access health services. Most believed foreign police to be as corrupt as in their home towns, so they wouldn't go to the authorities to seek help.

Finding where the slave workers were being kept was now my job; and it was going to be an uphill struggle. But what was causing us the most concern was what happened to the slaves once their working life was finished. Interviews with rescued slaves, carried out by female officers on local domestic violence units, gave us an indication of the numbers of girls being brought into the UK, but not where they ended up.

Matt had uncovered several relevant MISPERs – missing person reports – filed by women's refuges that had taken in young girls from Europe, only to find that they went missing within a few days. Most were put down to the girls simply moving on, but, in several cases, personal effects had been left behind. Those MISPERs remained open and unsolved.

I was at my desk reading one such report when Kevin Jones telephoned. It was good to hear from my old friend.

'You seen the papers, boss?' Kevin asked.

'Not yet. Something interesting?' I asked.

'A major Regiment book has just hit the shops. It's featured in the *Sun*. You'll never guess who the writer is.'

'Try me.'

'Lad calls himself Chas Collins.'

I laughed. 'I read it last week while I was on holiday. It was quite good, all about Operation Cyclone. Toni Fellowes lent it to me and Jenny to read.'

'Bloody hell ... did you recognise him? Collins, I mean,' Kevin asked.

'Can't say as I did. There were some pictures but not of anyone I knew. I half wondered if our job in Peshawar would get a mention, but it didn't. He talked about the kit evaluation a bit and the mule trains bringing bits and pieces from downed Hind helicopters over the border into Pakistan, but he didn't mention us or any of the other lads, not even once.'

'So it didn't ring any alarm bells then?'

'No, not really. It just read like a bloke trying to make a buck out of stuff he found out.'

'Well, that's as maybe. But I can tell you Chas is not his real name,' said Kevin. 'He was on breakfast TV this morning talking live from a secret hideaway somewhere. He's just using the name Chas Collins.'

'Should I know him?'

'You should. He was on the same selection as you. We used to call him "Beaky".'

I had a vague memory of the name. At Hereford, during the early eighties, Kevin and I had worked with a man called Beaky. He had been a selection failure, but he had been a good lad and had come very close to success, so he'd been kept on to have another go. Unfortunately, he'd turned out to have a bit of a drink problem and after several run-ins with the local police he had been sentenced to three months in the Corrective Training Centre at Colchester. After that he was discharged from the army. Last I'd heard, he had moved on to join the 'circuit', the large group of former regular soldiers who moved around the world, doing security work.

'Have you read it yourself?' I asked.

'Not yet,' Kevin replied, 'but it looks like the media are lapping it up.'

I laughed. 'It doesn't say too much, might be embarrassing for a few but most people will think that it's fantasy.'

'He'll be a marked man if you ask me. He must be crazy, or desperate for money. Everybody knew we could never talk about that op.'

'I didn't know he was on it.'

'Nor me; he must have been one of the contractors. Said on the TV that he's living under an assumed name. He'll bloody have to; if the CIA find him, he'll have some serious questions to answer.'

I didn't argue. Since the Iraq War, several former soldiers had tried to cash in on the public thirst for inside stories. Beaky was just another one in a long line, so far as I was concerned.

Kevin promised to get hold of a copy of the book and have a proper read of it. Before we hung up, I told him about the Red Sea rescue, the wedding invitation and the forthcoming trip to Romania. But I decided not to mention the prospect of actually meeting up with Beaky. The timing didn't seem quite right. And Kevin's phone call had also reminded me of a job that I needed to complete.

Using the excuse of grabbing some fresh air, I headed to St James's Park. With people milling about everywhere, the background noise would drown out what we needed to discuss.

Fortunately, Kevin was still at home on sick leave. After a brief discussion, the arrangements were made. I had a safe place for my weapons and kit. We would meet that evening and store them at his allotment.

I enjoyed talking with my old friend. He was doing well. Aside from the bullet wound to his shoulder, the injuries had almost healed.

On a previous call, he had mentioned having taken a real shine to Sandra Beattie, one of the nurses who'd looked after him. Ruefully, he felt there was no chance whilst one of her patients.

Then, after being discharged, Kevin had attended outpatients every day to have the wound redressed. On one of those visits, he told me he had been sitting patiently in the waiting room when Sandi – as she preferred to be called – had walked past. They had chatted briefly and then exchanged phone numbers. They'd now been seeing each other for several weeks.

In some ways, I was envious. Kevin seemed to be putting the events of the preceding weeks behind him. I wasn't finding it so easy, which was something of a turnaround. In the aftermath of the Iranian Embassy operation, my friend had suffered some problems after shooting dead a very young terrorist. He had some counselling and worked his way through it. At the time, it had been my job to support him in any way I could. Now, the situations had reversed. Kevin had noticed I was having problems and, based on what Jenny had been saying in recent weeks, he wasn't the only one.

Chapter 31

Hornchurch, Essex

'It's crap, boss.' Kevin was gripping *Cyclone* in his outstretched fist.

My lips curved into a smile. 'Like I said, it's just an attempt to cash in on 9/11. Did you expect anything else? The publishers were just lucky that such a major attack occurred just as they were ready to launch the book.'

'Not being funny, but you reckon it was just a coincidence?'

I laughed, not just at the idea of Cristea Publishing knowing about the New York attacks but at the way Kevin's Welsh accent became stronger when he was angry. 'I don't think publishers have an inside track on what Al Q'aeda does, if that's what you mean?' I answered. 'Now grab these.' The two black holdalls I was carrying were heavy. I grunted as I heaved them into the hallway of Kevin's house.

'Not sure what I expected, really. I guess I was a bit scared he would name names. Did you read how he always said *with* the SAS rather than *in* the SAS? He's a bloody Walt, if you ask me.' Kevin headed to the kitchen and turned the kettle on, something he always did when under pressure.

'Well, I read it too,' I said. 'And, with the exception of the base Commander, I couldn't work out who he was referring to or even if they were based on real blokes.' I shut the front door and followed Kevin into the kitchen.

'I know what you mean. I reckon I could pick a couple of others out as well. Beaky is a bloody fantasist, though. He talks about his supposed postings with the Regiment as well as his time in Afghan on the Cyclone Op. And did you read about his love life? Better than James Bond's apparently.'

'Lucky him,' I said. 'It's not our problem is it?'

'Not really, no ... but it's annoying. He's either done a lot of talking to guys who should know better, or he was there. My guess – he was one of the contractors who went out there first thing, before the Op really got going.'

'I don't think I met any of them.' I said.

'Me neither. I would have remembered him. Thankfully, he makes no mention of Regiment involvement. There's nothing about the Increment guys either. That's lucky for him, in my opinion. If he'd mentioned their names he would be watching his back for evermore.'

Increment was the code name for the small group of SAS soldiers that went to work for MI6 on a full-time basis. They were given false identities to help with their cover. Increment did the dirty, deniable operations that MI6 required their kind of expertise for. Not surprisingly, they were tough men.

'Recognise anyone in the photos?' I asked.

'Not really ... difficult to tell with the faces blurred out.'

'Nothing to worry about then, Kev. Not like what's in those bags in your hallway.'

Kevin shrugged. 'Cyclone was supposed to have been a black op. How the fuck did a drunk like Beaky get in on the act?'

I decided to take over the tea-making. Kevin was too wound up. For the next twenty minutes I was compelled to listen as he went through page after page of the book, dissecting Beaky's claims and reading out sections that were either inaccurate or could prove embarrassing.

In the end, Kevin reluctantly agreed that *Cyclone* was a mix of fantasy and fact, dressed up to look like the real thing. It exposed the fact that MI6 and the CIA were using the Mujahideen to battle-test weapons against the Russian army but no more. The press would probably lap it up and the public would buy the book. Whatever happened, it wasn't our problem.

☩

As darkness fell, we finished the brew and headed to Kevin's allotment. Beneath the wooden timbers of his tool shed, he had dug a shallow hole into which he had placed a series of small plastic bins. It was secret, perfectly sealed and damp-proof, and it took just a couple of minutes to add my kit to his. There it would remain secure until such time as I would dispose of the weapons properly. I would get them melted down or do something with them that stopped them from falling into the wrong hands.

But not yet. Not until I was sure.

Chapter 32

Bucharest arrivals hall was surprisingly small for such a large city. I scanned the throng of taxi drivers, friends and relatives who almost blocked the route to the exits. There was no one holding a sign bearing our name.

'Finlay,' called a male voice. A muscular arm waved in the crowd. Then there was a beaming face. It was Petre, Marica's bodyguard.

I made to shake hands, but Petre brushed my open palm aside and engulfed me in a bear hug. Then he shook Jenny's hand, gentle and polite, although, from the look on her face, I guessed that she could feel the power of his grip.

With Jenny introduced, and after allowing me a moment to recover my breath, Petre took hold of our bags and led the way across the arrivals concourse to the car park. A blue-uniformed *politia* officer was standing chatting and smoking with the driver of a black Mercedes. When the driver saw Petre, he threw his cigarette into the gutter. This had to be our ride.

Marica had booked us into the Inter-Continental on Nicolae Balcescu Boulevard. It was nice and central, within an easy walk of the Old City and overlooking the National Theatre. Petre did his best to chat during the twenty-minute drive, but the noise of the traffic and the limits of his English vocabulary meant much of what he said was lost in translation.

Arriving at the hotel, Petre suggested we let him take care of the booking-in process, so we handed him our passports and a smart concierge showed us to our room on the third floor.

The room was large and very comfortable. I winked at Jenny as soon as I saw the huge bed. But her response surprised me. The smile that greeted me looked forced. Something had upset her.

'What's up, Jen?' I asked, as the concierge left, having politely refused my tip. 'Don't you like it?' I leapt onto the bed.

'In the car ... did you see what I saw?' she answered.

I shook my head, confused.

'In the pocket behind the driver seat. There was a set of handcuffs.'

I shrugged. 'Maybe the owner is into a bit of bondage?' I said, trying to make light of it. In truth, I was puzzled that I hadn't spotted them. 'Shall I check the bedside drawers,' I suggested. 'See if they've left some for us?'

'Be serious. There was blood on them. At least it looked like it ... dried blood ... and did you see the holes in the back of the seat? They looked like they were stiletto marks.'

I had to confess that I hadn't noticed the cuffs or the puncture marks. I'd been too busy looking at the scenery and passing traffic.

'OK,' I said. 'Let's not go jumping to any conclusions. I'll ask Petre when he brings up the passports.'

Petre arrived about five minutes after the suitcases, while Jenny was taking a shower. In reply to my question about what she had seen, he shrugged, and explained that the car was a spare he had been given to collect us from the airport. Many of the Cristeas' employees used it. He always travelled in the front so he had not seen the damage to the rear of the seats. He promised to ask the driver.

After checking that I had a copy of Marica's itinerary, he said goodnight and left us to it. We would be collected at eleven the next morning.

We ate an early dinner. The waiter seemed to be especially attentive and even knew where we were headed the next day. In good English he told us he knew the Cristeas well: an important family who often used the hotel for their guests, he said.

As we left, he told us that the weather forecast for the next day was good. 'As we locals say, the Cristeas can even arrange the weather,' he said, with a broad grin.

Chapter 33

My first sight of Beaky, or 'Chas' Collins as he was now known, was at breakfast the next morning. It was a buffet and as I helped myself to my favourites, I caught a partially obscured view of a couple sat at the far side of the restaurant. One of them was unmistakably Beaky, my memory of him prompted by my conversation with Kevin. I wondered if he might recognise me; a lot of water had passed under the bridge since the time we'd been on a selection course together, and it looked like we had both put on a few pounds.

Sat next to Collins, with her back to the buffet area, was a woman with bleached blonde hair. My first guess was that she was his wife, although I vaguely recalled Kevin saying that Collins was divorced. Perhaps she was the girlfriend, I thought. On the adjacent table sat two men; they were in their early thirties – tanned and sporting short haircuts, and wearing light bomber jackets over T-shirts and jeans. Just like Petre: personal protection.

One of the bodyguards was watching the room while the other ate. The observer made eye contact with me as I gazed over at Collins, then had a quiet word with his companion. Just as I returned to loading my plate, I saw that both men looked across at me.

Heading back to our table I told Jenny what I had seen.

'Do authors normally employ security, then?' she asked.

'No idea.' I said. 'Maybe it's because he's in Eastern Europe; or maybe he's provoked a reaction with his book.'

'If the Cristea family use the hotel for their guests, I wonder if we'll see anyone famous.'

I sensed that Jenny was starting to feel a tinge of excitement.

As I was finishing my breakfast, Jenny reached across and tapped me on the back of the hand. I looked up and followed her eyes across the room. The Collins party were leaving – one of the guards leading, with the other bringing up the rear. As the group walked past, I was able to get a better look at the woman who had been sitting with her back to the buffet area. Her blonde hair was tied back. She was attractive, but there was a steel in her expression that indicated toughness. I put her in her mid-forties, a bit younger than me. With a confident, determined walk and her black trouser suit, she looked every inch a businesswoman.

✝

Two cars were waiting at the front of the hotel when we came down in our wedding finery. The taste for using black Mercedes seemed to have continued, only this time they were a lot newer than the car used by Petre for the airport journey.

We were being treated like VIPs: a uniformed porter held the rear door of the nearest car open for us; the car smelled new and was in pristine condition. The other Mercedes was in front and appeared to be unoccupied. We waited; there seemed to be some form of delay – the two drivers were very animated, talking heatedly as they prepared for their remaining passengers. I guessed it would be the Collins party and I was right. A few moments later they emerged from the door of the hotel.

It was then that the reason for the argument between the drivers became clear: there wasn't enough seating in the car unless one of the bodyguards sat in the back with Collins and his companion. It looked like they were unhappy with the idea.

The solution was obvious and after a short debate, the driver of our Mercedes opened the door and asked whether we minded if one of the guards rode in the front of our car.

With the passenger logistics sorted, the drive began. The bodyguard mumbled a 'thanks' and shrugged.

'Not a problem,' I said.

'He wasn't happy about one of us riding in the back with him,' he replied, gruffly.

'Likes his privacy, I guess?'

'Something like that. She didn't mind ... *he* didn't like it. I'll be sure not to trouble you.'

The main road away from the hotel was busy but not congested and, save for the occasional delay to overtake horse-drawn carts, we made good progress out of the city.

We headed north. At one point, I noticed Jenny discreetly checking the storage pocket in the rear of the driver's seat. It didn't take much to guess what she was looking for.

For the remainder of the journey, neither the bodyguard nor the driver spoke. After about an hour we turned off the main road into a more rural area – passing through small villages with brightly painted houses and quiet lanes. All the houses had high garden walls along the side that faced onto the road. Privacy seemed to be very important in this country.

In the fields we saw cattle and sheep tended by men with packs of large dogs. There were also people harvesting what looked like maize. They were cutting it by hand, stacking it into huge bundles and then laying it in carts, the horses that drew them waiting patiently. Elsewhere, men were cutting fallen trees with hand-held saws and using huge axes to chop logs.

The two Mercedes saloons seemed incongruous, in this almost medieval landscape.

Chapter 34

Belmarsh Prison, South-East London

Visitors, he thought.

The sound was always the same. All the prison officers carried keys on a belt clip. Not all the keys were the same, but the bunches jingled in a familiar and consistent way as they walked. Hearing the sound stop outside the door to your cell meant one of two things: exercise or a visit; and as Dominic was a nonce, this must be a visit.

He hated the term 'nonce'. A simple prison-service acronym, written on the paperwork of those who were *Not On Normal Courtyard Exercise*, it had grown to become associated with sex offenders who were segregated from the normal prison population for their own safety. Those charged or remanded on terrorism offences faced similar restrictions. On more than one occasion the Irishman had been forced to correct the mistaken assumption of a fellow inmate, normally at the expense of the unfortunate man's face.

Slowly, lethargically, he dragged himself from the lower bunk and stood with his back to the far wall. He knew the form – life was so much easier if you complied with their bullshit rules.

One of the 'screws' turned the small brass lever at the centre of the door that operated an observation flap – the wicket. Designed to allow the passage of goods and supplies to prisoners without opening the heavy door, the wicket could also be used to view the interior of the cell before entry to make sure that the occupant was away from the door before it was opened.

'Stand back McGlinty, your visitors are here.' Senior Prison Officer Parry kept his face a few inches to the side of the open wicket.

Dominic half sneered, half smiled. The prison officer was experienced and knew how easy it was for prisoners to throw the contents of their piss pots into the faces of the screws. Irish lads were well known for the trick. It had become the practice to use the prisoners' first names whenever possible – modern thinking suggesting that it helped to reduce tension and encouraged prisoners to behave. Parry's use of a surname suggested he had people with him that he wanted to impress.

The cell was small, about three metres by four. Painted in a dark-blue gloss, the high walls only served to increase the sense of claustrophobia. Behind Dominic, a reinforced window was protected by four thick iron bars that were caked with dust. Immediately inside the door was a steel washbasin and an open steel toilet, no flush and no lid. All cells now had steel fitments. Previous experience had shown that wood and ceramics could be broken up to make weapons or to be burned. Steel was solid, unyielding and cold. It was also easier to keep clean.

The bunk bed was against the left wall, the lower level used to sleep and the upper for storage. In Dominic's case, the bed held books, lots of them.

Like many prisoners, he spent a lot of time reading, it was the only way to escape to another place – like dreaming with his eyes open.

From along the corridor, two more officers joined a group that waited a discreet distance behind the SPO.

'Turn around McGlinty, you know the drill,' said Parry. A short, wiry man, his voice commanded authority.

Dominic complied without uttering a word. But he moved unhurriedly, a small gesture of resistance. He held his arms out wide to the side, slowly turned his palms to show the hands were empty and then clasped his fingers together against the back of his head. Parry stood to one side as his two officers quickly and professionally searched first the cell, and then his clothing. Only once they were satisfied was he ordered to sit down. He lowered himself onto the small steel chair by the table against the window wall.

'These officers are here to interview you, McGlinty.'

Dominic didn't reply, but he looked, and he liked what he saw. A woman stood behind Parry. He could smell her perfume, it was musky, erotic. Her top was cut low, exposing her cleavage. As he moved his eyes from her body to her face, she smiled. The thought crossed his mind that she was doing it on purpose.

'Fuck a bleedin' duck,' he said, raising his top lip in a sneer.

'Watch the language, McGlinty.'

The female visitor winked as she turned to Parry. 'Could I trouble you for a second chair?'

Dominic noticed that the woman seemed aware of the attention she was being paid. Parry barked an order to the officers outside and within a few moments another steel chair was found. For a moment there was an uncomfortable silence. The woman simply looked at Parry.

The penny seemed to drop. 'I'll be right outside,' he said, 'do you want me to close the cell door?'

'Yes, please.'

With the prison officers waiting behind the closed door, Dominic noticed that the male visitor took up a position near the toilet, where he was both far enough away to watch and close enough to intercede, should there be any unpleasantness.

Although he wasn't planning to make trouble, Dominic decided to start friendly, before he sent these two upstarts packing. In the meantime, he would take his time looking at the woman's body.

'Special Branch? You look like cops,' he said quietly, staring at the man's expressionless face.

'Security Service,' the woman replied. 'We want to show you some pictures and then discuss an offer.'

Dominic repositioned the small steel table between them and beckoned her forward. 'Come a little closer, me darlin',' he smiled. 'One of us may as well enjoy this.'

For the next few minutes he pretended to look at the photographs that were laid, one at a time, on the table between them. He took his time, savouring the opportunity for a little titillation. It wasn't every day he had a visitor. In fact, this was only the second time since he had been remanded. The first had also been a woman from the Security Services. She had kept her distance and was much more businesslike than this one. She had asked him about the bombings, who had recruited him and who he had worked with. Needless to say he hadn't told her a thing. He was no tout.

The new woman asked if he recognised any of the people in the photographs. He denied knowing any of them. Every so often she would tap a particular photo and ask if he remembered a person. There must have been a hundred in total. Some were mug shots but many were taken in the street, in clubs and in pubs.

One photo showed an older IRA member in a clinch with a naked woman that certainly wasn't his wife. McGlinty was careful not to give away the fact that he recognised him but he made a mental note to remember it in case the knowledge should prove useful in the future.

One more seemed familiar, but he wasn't sure. It looked like a picture that Declan had been given. One of the assassination targets. Again, he was careful not to display any sign of interest.

Finally, the woman returned the last photograph to a small briefcase.

'Sorry me darlin', looks like yer wasted yer time,' he smirked.

'The ones I indicated – are you sure you didn't recognise any of them?'

'Ne're the one of 'em.'

'Good. They work for us.'

'To be sure they do; like pigs fly missus.' Dominic gave a forced laugh; his patience was wearing thin.

'I would like you to work for us too, Mr McGlinty.'

Dominic sneered. 'Not a fuckin' chance.'

'I need information, you know the kind of thing.' The smile was warm, intoxicating; her eyes, enchanting.

'Like I said, not a fuckin' chance.'

He knew the score. Talk and your family suffered. Christ he had even done punishment squads himself. But for a squeeze of those tits, he smiled to himself, who knows what I might do? His trousers tightened at the thought.

'Stand up.'

'Sorry?'

'Stand up. I want to show you something.'

Dominic stood – more curious than obedient. As he did so, he noticed the male officer moving to position himself in front of the cell door, blocking the view through the wicket. For a moment it crossed Dominic's mind that things were going to get violent, but the man was relaxed.

He looked down at the woman sitting in front of him. And, for a moment, he was dumbstruck; she had rolled down the front of her top to expose her breasts. There they were, pale and fulsome, just three feet from his groin.

'You've had a hard-on since you saw them, and my guess is they might be the last ones you get to see for a very long time.'

Dominic guessed the trick. Simple sexual blackmail. He could resist threats but how long could he resist the lure of a woman's body?

'Drop your trousers.'

'You serious?' he replied, reaching for the zip to his fly. He looked again at the male officer. The man hadn't moved from the door, he simply winked, as if he knew what was to come.

The woman pushed the small, steel table to one side and slid her chair closer. Dominic rolled his trousers down over his thighs as she moved her head into his groin. She knew what she was doing. Within seconds she had him at her mercy.

'This won't take long,' he gasped, his breathing becoming laboured.

He closed his eyes. And soon, he felt his groin begin to explode. He grunted, moaned out loud. And then, just as he came, the woman moved her face to one side, holding his buttocks tight. He smiled to himself as he felt her squeeze. There was a sharp pain as her ring caught his skin. But he hardly noticed it, such was the pleasure of the moment.

For a moment, he felt giddy. He opened his eyes. The male agent was still standing impassively by the door.

'Yer don't swallow then?' he sneered at the woman.

'Maybe another time, depending on what you do for me, Dominic. Think of that as a little example of what can be done for you.'

'I'll think about it,' he replied, already wondering how many blow jobs he could squeeze out of the bitch without telling her too much.

Allowing Dominic just enough time to fasten his trousers, the male officer knocked on the cell door. It opened immediately.

A few seconds later, the Irishman was alone in his cell, wondering if he had just dreamed what had happened. The mess on the floor told him he hadn't.

+

About an hour later, the late-shift desk officer arrived to finish the cell-visit paperwork. Dominic was on his bed, reading. He had to scan the form and sign it to confirm there had been no incidents during the visit and he had no complaints. He signed without reading it fully. But the names of the officers caught his attention. A cold chill of uncertainty ran down his spine and he missed a breath. The name … Antonia Fellowes. It was the same name as the other MI5 agent – the one that had been in to question him several weeks previously. But today he definitely hadn't seen the same woman.

For a moment he thought to mention it to the screw, but then the door was closed and the opportunity gone. He lay back on his bed. No way could there be two MI5 people with the same name; so one of them had to have been a fake. Or maybe not – maybe they all used the same name when visiting the prison? He rolled over onto his side and as he did so he noticed a small red patch on the threadbare sheet. Blood. From its position on the bed he guessed it was from his buttock, where Fellowes number two had scratched him with her ring.

He touched the spot. It was tender but it made him smile. A worthwhile war wound, he thought, and maybe the first of many.

Chapter 35

InterContinental Hotel, Bucharest

For most of the day following the wedding, I nursed a sore head.

The wedding custom was to serve just one course at a time, followed by an hour of dancing and drinking. That meant the reception stretched well into the early hours. I had intended to last through until the morning, but age and the local liquor caught up with me. By three o'clock, I had been ready for bed and was pleased to discover that Jenny wasn't minded to argue.

During our day at the wedding, there had been a lot of thank-yous.

The first was from the family patriarch, Gheorghe Cristea. Gheorghe had struck me as a generous man, but with a tough streak. He spoke poor English but what he lacked in vocabulary he made up for in enthusiasm. So effusive was his appreciation for my rescuing his daughter that, once again, I felt embarrassed.

And yet, despite his apparent warmth towards me, I sensed Gheorghe was a ruthless and determined businessman, used to getting what he wanted. When, at one point, we had been disturbed by a maid, he had been abrupt in the way he addressed her. I also saw the fear in the woman's eyes – and it was not born of her simple mistake at interrupting our conversation. The poor woman seemed petrified of her employer.

Traditional Romanian weddings are lengthy affairs with festivities beginning on the Friday evening and continuing through until the Sunday. Even before we had arrived, there had been a great deal of celebration: dancing and drinking. Anca – Marica's sister-in-law – had assumed the role of wedding organiser.

As we arrived, a *lăutar* had started to play an accordion and we had been encouraged to try the *horas* and *manea* group dances. There were also traditions to be followed, including the ritual shaving of the groom. All the guests cheered as we adjourned to the courtyard to watch.

After that, Anca warned me to expect a mock kidnapping. She

explained it had been arranged that Marica would be taken at about five in the evening to a neighbour's tennis court, where she would be kept until the ransom was paid. The groom's friends had agreed a payment of six bottles of Scotch whisky. They would carry Marica away, and then one of them would return a few minutes later with one of her shoes – an indication they were willing to do business.

Just before the appointed time, two of the male guests got into a row. Anca stepped in quickly to defuse it, with the result that the men agreed on a short dance competition with their girlfriends performing as good a rendition of the *manele* as their high heels and tight dresses would allow. Both the girls' dresses were bright and colourful, as befitted the warmth of the day. One was blue and green; the other a lovely summer yellow with broad red stripes. The girls were good dancers and gave it their all.

Unable to decide a winner, one of the men had approached Chas Collins for a judgement. There was a tense moment when the security men intervened, but the author had agreed to make a choice.

The winner was given a small bouquet of flowers made up from one of the display stands on the tables. The tension dissipated, the bet was decided and the drinking continued. All was well; that was until the mock kidnapping, when the men arrived to collect Marica.

It all started fairly smoothly, when friends of the groom ran in from the street and started to carry the bride towards the doors. But one of them had come up with what he must have thought was a great way to add a touch of realism. He was carrying a plastic assault rifle; it looked like a Kalashnikov.

The two security men with Collins reacted immediately. It turned out nobody had warned them about the custom; to them, the attack appeared real. In a moment, they had drawn pistols and pushed both Collins and his companion to the ground. One of them turned the table they were sat behind onto its side.

Several women screamed as drinks and food went flying everywhere. Then, two of the Cristea men responded by drawing their own weapons and threatening the bodyguards.

The men were shouting at each other, in both English and Romanian.

It looked like they were all saying to put down their guns, but neither group understood the other.

With nobody able or prepared to break the stalemate, I came to the sudden realisation that I was the only Westerner aware of the misunderstanding.

I quickly nodded to Jenny and then walked into the melée, slowly raising my arms in a calming gesture.

At first, it appeared to be working. But one of the Cristea men wasn't having it. He dashed forward and pushed the muzzle of his Glock into my face. My attempt to resolve the situation had failed.

But the gunman, in his excitement, had put his finger on the trigger guard of the pistol rather than the trigger itself. Noticing it, I realised I had one chance. I lowered my hands as if protesting at what was happening and then, using a move that would have made some of my old instructors proud, I twisted the pistol away from his hand, removed the clip, ejected the round in the chamber and then handed it back to him with a polite smile.

As the other members of the 'kidnap' gang began to laugh, I hastily explained to the security men about the tradition and suggested they relax and put their guns away. They did as they were asked, everybody calmed down and the incident was soon over. The remainder of the evening passed quietly. Petre and Anca came over and thanked me for stepping in. They said I had been brave, I said not. I hadn't had time to think, it had happened so quickly. Brave men are those that face fear and overcome it, I said. Jenny wasn't pleased with me though, and, with the benefit of hindsight, I soon realised the crazy risk I had taken.

✢

Throughout the evening, Collins didn't speak to me. Not a word. In fact, Jenny and I noticed that he didn't speak to anyone other than his female companion throughout the whole day. But it was only when we entered the lift to head back to our room that I discovered the reasons for the author's silence and the presence of the security men.

Jenny had spent a lot of time chatting to Maggie, the companion. It turned out that she was Collins' agent in London. Jenny had warmed to her and found that, after a couple of glasses of wine, Maggie became a bit incautious. It seemed that Collins had attended the wedding under protest; and the scuffle had done nothing to improve his mood. Maggie was cross with him; he seemed determined not to enjoy himself and had made much of the dangers of travelling to unsafe parts of the world. He was also upset because an interview he'd just recorded with the BBC hadn't gone well, just when he had been hoping to negotiate a new deal for future books. Cristea Publishing were also pressurising him to come up with some new ideas. They wanted to cash in on the notoriety that *Cyclone* had generated.

Maggie Price was in the middle. An agent who felt like a referee.

Chapter 36

Thames House, London. Headquarters of MI5

Toni Fellowes sat very, very still. She barely noticed as people filed into the conference room.

Everything she had been working on was now dead in the water. Everything.

It was Saturday, her day off. The Reserve Office had called at six am with a brief message from Director 'T'. *My office, 0900hrs this morning.* It was not a request.

Getting called into work on a weekend wasn't unusual, but a call to a meeting with the Director was only going to mean problems, either professional or personal. And today, it was both.

Her Section Head, Dave Batey, had been waiting for her as she had arrived. Batey was a tough ex-soldier who had transferred from the Intelligence Corps during the Irish troubles and then risen slowly through the ranks. He was now in charge of T2/1 department, which was tasked with both investigating terrorism and liaising with Police Special Branch offices throughout the UK. Batey was also a frustrated field operative who liked to keep his hand in whenever and wherever he could; the kind of man who would never ask one of his team to do something he wasn't prepared to do himself.

Batey took Toni into his office, closed the door, and summarised events for her benefit. Unusually, he suggested she think carefully before commenting.

The purpose of the meeting called by Dirt was to discuss an incident at Belmarsh Prison. Dominic McGlinty had died in the prison hospital. He'd been murdered by a visitor, who had injected him with ricin.

The visitor log at Belmarsh had recorded the name and ID of the visitor; it was Toni Fellowes.

✢

The Director had invited a number of key people to the meeting. Present were the Commander of the Police Special Branch, the Head of the Police Press Bureau and Bill Grahamslaw from the police Anti-Terrorist Squad. The deputy Director 'T' and several Section Heads from other MI5 departments were also in attendance.

Before sitting down, Batey had reassured her that no mention would be made of her name, at this stage. It was a small concession that did little to alleviate the turmoil of her thoughts.

The meeting began. Toni felt all eyes were on her, even though only three of the people present knew how the assassin had gained access to the prison.

Director 'T' started formally, recording the names of those present for the benefit of the minute-taker. He then informed the meeting of McGlinty's death and said, for the time being, the cause of death was being attributed to natural causes. However, he told them it was now certain that McGlinty had been murdered; he had died three days after a visit by two people who had impersonated members of the Security Service.

Suspicions had been raised when McGlinty – in the prison hospital having suffered a rapid onset of diarrhoea, thought to be food poisoning – boasted to another prisoner about a female MI5 officer performing oral sex on him to try and get him to work as a tout. Toni felt bile rise in her throat. Her name was going to be tarred with that brush, whatever the final outcome.

McGlinty's fellow prisoner had repeated the claim to a doctor and the prison staff had, in turn, alerted Special Branch.

The Special Branch Commander asked a question, looking in her direction as he spoke. 'Is that how we get information from terrorists these days, Director?'

The Director ignored the question, moving on to report that, after McGlinty died, a post-mortem had been immediately ordered. The Security Service pathologist had discovered a tiny metal pellet in the victim's buttock. The pellet had been analysed and had been found to contain the poison ricin. The pathologist had confirmed that diarrhoea was a symptom of ricin poisoning. There was no doubt the murder was a very professional hit.

Toni watched the faces around the table; only Grahamslaw's remained straight – the others looked horrified. A couple of questions were asked about whether the use of ricin was likely to become a new weapon of terror. The Director confirmed that several embryonic terror groups were said to be experimenting with the poison, but the reality was, it was a difficult and dangerous substance to manufacture.

It was Dave Batey who suggested the IRA might have been behind the murder. Whilst the use of ricin had not been attributed to them in the past, it is quite possible McGlinty's killing could have been outsourced to another group; one with access to the substance.

Whoever was responsible, the reason for the murder seemed clear: it was to prevent McGlinty from talking.

Toni listened as those present debated various options – from blanket denial through to full public disclosure. Things became heated, with one or two people more interested in finding someone to blame rather than thinking about the consequences should the news become public. She kept quiet, all the while thinking about the repercussions for her career, her ambitions.

Finally, a decision was made. They would recommend the cause of death be attributed to food poisoning. The Director agreed he would take the proposal to the Prime Minister.

As the meeting broke up, Dave Batey walked across to her. 'My office, please Toni.'

She followed him silently along the corridors until his door closed behind them.

'Sit.' It was an order, not an invitation.

'Right,' he continued. 'Continuing where we left off before the meeting, you won't be surprised to learn I've been checking on your movements.'

Gone was the friendly supervisor who had warned her to think before she spoke. She listened attentively as he explained that, at first, he had presumed the visit to McGlinty was genuine. Then he had checked Toni's work diary, only to discover that the prison visit wasn't mentioned. That left him with two possibilities. Either she had forged her diary or the visitor wasn't her. CCTV records from the prison had allayed his suspicions.

She was not the killer.

Batey's orders came fast and furious. She was not to talk to anyone about the murder, not even colleagues. She was to keep him informed of her movements at all times and, inside of three days, she was to compile a thorough list of her movements and meetings over the last six months.

It was a mammoth task but she understood why. Somehow, somewhere, somebody had got hold of both her name and a copy of her identity pass.

Batey also gave her a warning: this breach of security could mean her future as an MI5 officer was compromised. She had already worked that out for herself.

✝

As a dejected Toni Fellowes headed back to the street, she was surprised to find the Director waiting in the foyer. She half smiled a greeting.

'Do you have a minute, Miss Fellowes?' The Director indicated for her to accompany him.

Refusal was out of the question, so, shoulders hunched, Toni followed him along the nearby corridor and up the stairs to his office. He shut the door behind her.

'Please sit down and make yourself comfortable, Fellowes.'

It was only the second time Toni had been in the Director's office. The other occasion had been her first day with the department. The room looked exactly the same – comfortable, but not ostentatious.

'I thought it appropriate that you should attend that meeting, Fellowes. Nasty business about your pass. Do you have any idea how it may have happened?'

Toni was embarrassed. 'I don't ... I'm really very sorry.'

The Director sat down opposite her and smiled. 'Look ... Fellowes. I'll be straight with you here. Right now I'm sure you're thinking this could spell the end of your career.'

Toni lowered her gaze for a moment. As she went to speak, the Director raised his hand to silence her.

'Hear me out, Toni. I want you to know that your work here hasn't gone unnoticed. It's why your name was put forward to do the closing report on the Hastings operation. Once this furore has blown over, I think you would do well to apply for a Section Head position. Your boss, Mr Batey, is due to retire fairly soon. I can see you being an ideal replacement for him.'

Toni was stunned. She had fully expected to be given her marching orders.

'I'm flattered,' she answered.

'Nothing you haven't earned. I'm sure this business with your security pass can be resolved satisfactorily. Just make sure that you give Batey all the information he needs. In the meantime, I want you to do something for me.'

'Anything, sir.'

The Director smiled. 'Nothing too onerous, believe me. Just keep me fully up to date with the progress of the Hastings enquiry, particularly if it takes you anywhere interesting.'

'I will, sir.'

'Very good ... bad business, the way that Monaghan behaved. Could have caused a lot of bad press.'

'The way that Monaghan behaved?'

'Yes. I'm sorry ... I presumed you knew. It will be in his file, no doubt ... something about a personal vendetta. I had a request from MI6 for you to be allowed access and I thought you'd already seen it. I'm sure it will answer any questions you have.'

The Director handed Toni a small business card. She could see there was a handwritten email address on it. 'That's my private, secure email, Toni. Feel free to use it.'

'I will ... and thanks. Thanks a lot.'

Toni was in the process of leaving when a final question occurred to her. 'Do you mind if I ask what you think will happen over the McGlinty death?' she asked.

The Director smiled. 'I shouldn't worry too much about it. I'll be recommending to the Prime Minister that it be kept under wraps. And I don't think McGlinty is going to be missed.'

As Toni headed back to New Scotland Yard, she reflected on the unexpected conversation that had just taken place. She was curious why the Director should be so interested in monitoring her progress, but, such was her relief she still had a job, she wasn't going to question it. The offer was a lifeline, an opportunity to get noticed.

She would make sure he was rewarded for his faith in her.

Chapter 37

Monday morning journeys into London are the worst. I didn't enjoy the tube, even on the rare days that it was quiet. The number of people milling about left me feeling distinctly uneasy. Often I would find my eyes darting from one person to another, trying to make a quick assessment of any threat. It wasn't logical – common sense told me that – but I still found myself doing it.

Emerging from the train at Victoria, I had a choice as to whether to change trains and head for St James's Park station or make the ten-minute walk along Victoria Street to New Scotland Yard. I chose the walk and the fresher air.

I was halfway to my destination when my phone buzzed.

It was Kevin. He got straight to the point. 'Did you see the Sunday papers?'

'No. I haven't so much as turned a television on since we got home from the airport. Why? What's happened?'

'McGlinty's dead.'

It was like a bolt from the blue. I stopped walking, much to the annoyance of the frenzied commuters bustling along the pavement.

I ducked into a doorway as Kevin explained. From what he understood, the papers were saying the Irishman had died in the prison hospital at Belmarsh. The cause of death was yet to be determined, but it was being reported as food poisoning. The conspiracy theorists were having a field day with stories of IRA hit squads sent to silence him and ideas on what kind of poisons could have been put into his food to make him die so suddenly.

To Kevin it was a loose end tied up and I was inclined to agree. If McGlinty had suffered an unexpected end that saved the price of a trial, it was not going to cause us any loss of sleep.

'One other thing,' Kevin continued, 'I've had Gayle Bridges on the phone over the weekend.'

Gayle was Bob Bridges' widow. I hadn't seen her since the funeral, after Bob had been killed in the Marylebone bombing. I had tried to contact her, but she had moved home.

'How did she get your number?'

'She tried you over the weekend but you were away. So she phoned Hereford. They gave her my number. She wants to talk to you.'

I had asked the Police Pensions Branch to forward my number to Gayle. It seemed the message must have got through. 'Did she say what about?' I asked.

'She's just been going through Bob's stuff. She found some papers she thinks we should see. Plus a Browning nine mill, some mags and rounds ... she wants us to get rid of it all for her.'

'How much ammunition?'

'She didn't say. I get the impression that as soon as she found it she froze and decided to contact us.'

I paused for a moment. There was a woman standing just within earshot, lighting a cigarette. I waited until she walked away, before continuing. 'Did you get her address?'

'Yep, want me to text it to you?'

'Do that. And get her contact number as well, could you? I'll call her when I get into the office. Heard any more about Beaky's book?'

'Shit hit the fan,' Kevin laughed. 'The BBC showed an interview they'd recorded with him. They set him up, poor bastard. Anyway, the upshot is people think the whole book is bollocks and that Beaky made it up. The CIA are off the hook for now.'

'I still think the Agency will be looking to have a little word with him.'

'Too bloody right, boss. To be fair to him, it wasn't a bad book, just too many wild stories mixed in with the truth.'

I had to pause again as yet another commuter came close to where I stood in the doorway. With the coast clear, we agreed to head over to see Gayle Bridges in the next couple of days, and that the Browning would best be taken into Hereford so it could be discreetly disposed of.

Returning the phone to my pocket, I headed towards Broadway and the entrance to New Scotland Yard.

Chapter 38

'I don't bloody believe it!' Toni slammed the copy of *Cyclone* back onto her desk. 'Who put this here? Is this your idea of a joke, Nell?'

The target of Toni's anger sat impassively as she answered. 'It wasn't meant as a joke. I thought it was yours.'

Toni hesitated for a moment, realising immediately she had overreacted. Heart racing, fists clenched, she realised she was spoiling for a fight. Nell didn't deserve to be the recipient of her wrath. 'I'm sorry,' she said, finally. 'I'm just having a bit of a bad day.'

Stuart popped his head around the doorpost of the tea room. 'Everything OK?' he asked.

Toni faked a smile. 'Not our finest hour, Stuart.'

'The TV appearance of Chas Collins, you mean?'

'What else?'

'Err ... nothing. But ... well, it was a closely kept secret ... even in the BBC. Nobody knew Collins was going to do a recording with them.'

'That's what you may think, Stuart. Most people in the service will say we're a bloody laughing stock.'

'If it's so important we get to speak to him, why didn't we have him picked up as he came through immigration at the airport?'

'You imagine I didn't think of that? He must have used a ferry or something. God ... if anyone else tells me how to do my job better, I swear...'

Stuart ducked back into the tea room and then re-emerged carrying a mug of tea in each hand. He placed the first in front of Nell before handing the second one to Toni.

'If it's any consolation,' he said. 'I was also under investigation during my last couple of weeks in the Met. Things have a way of working out.'

'Oh, God,' said Toni, realising word had spread. 'Don't tell me you both know about that as well?'

Stuart returned, sheepishly, to his desk, Nell didn't react. For several minutes, they continued to work in complete silence. Finally, Toni stood up and reached for her coat.

'I'm going out for some fresh air,' she announced.

In the downstairs foyer, she walked through a small contingent of press photographers who were waiting for the Met Press Officer and a statement from the Commissioner. The news of McGlinty's death had broken on the TV news channels that morning and the late editions of the national papers would, no doubt, be running the story as well. The journalists were digging. They sensed there was more to the death than had been released through the Downing Street press office. Nobody seemed to be prepared to accept a notorious terrorist could die from food poisoning.

She was feeling frustrated and, generally, hacked off. Her future lay with the investigation Dave Batey had started. If he concluded she was an operational risk then she may well find herself redundant. At the very least, it meant her idea of a move to MI6 would be in jeopardy, however well her unexpected meeting with the Director had gone.

✢

When she returned, Nell and Stuart were busy at their workstations. Thanks to Howard Green providing the necessary clearance, they were both working on the Monaghan enquiry. From their subdued conversation, it sounded like Nell was bringing their new addition up to speed on how far she had progressed.

Stuart looked up and offered to deal with the Monaghan personal effects. An email detailing where and how they could carry out an examination had arrived the previous evening. Things were moving along nicely and getting Stuart to do the leg-work would take the pressure off. She agreed; having him out of the office for the remainder of the day would also give her a chance to talk to Nell.

✢

At Toni's insistence, Nell made some tweaks to the checks they had in place to search media references for Chas Collins. Her researcher had also been embarrassed to discover the author had slipped through the net, but she reacted positively, with a promise it wouldn't happen again. The next time the author appeared in public, Toni would know about it in advance, and the opportunity to ask him some important questions would be secured.

Nell reported that Stuart had been doing some digging of his own. Not only that, he was starting to unearth some strange quirks in the Monaghan enquiry. Having succeeded in persuading the police forensic laboratory to allow him access to Monaghan's briefcase, he had discovered the deceased MI5 officer seemed to have had two other former soldiers in his sights. Two further slim folders contained files on an Iain Blackwood and a Brian McNeil. Both were ex-Special Forces soldiers from the same era as Finlay and Jones. Neither were mentioned in the SO13 Operation Hastings report and, when Stuart had checked with the Met Personnel Office, they were not listed as police officers, either serving or retired.

Aware the Hastings report had concluded Monaghan was behind the attacks on former SAS soldiers, motivated by revenge after he discovered they had been having affairs with his wife, Nell explained that Stuart had checked military records. He discovered there was remarkably little information on either man. She had told him to keep digging. They needed to know why the files on Blackwood and McNeil hadn't been subject to any follow-up enquiry by the Anti-Terrorist Squad.

Nell had also checked on the names. Blackwood was listed as a mercenary, killed recently in a suicide bombing in India. McNeil was reported to be a private security contractor working in Iraq. It was her suggestion that, if Monaghan had also been responsible for Blackwood's death, then McNeil, if he was still alive, could possibly have been another target.

It was when Nell was about to switch off her computer and head home that she stumbled upon a connection between the dead former soldiers that none of them had anticipated.

She had a name for it. Synchronicity.

Chapter 39

Nina was curious to hear about the Romanian wedding.

She wanted to know how I'd coped with all the drinking and dancing that was involved. I laughed her jokes off, most of which were directed at my age. Nina thought such events were better suited to the young, it seemed.

Matt had been doing a little research and had put together some facts and figures on girls reported missing from UK cities. There were very few foreign girls listed as missing persons but, when he had extended his search to include Europe, the list became much larger. Going back several years, the reports ran into thousands. Girls just seemed to disappear from their home villages, never to be seen again.

It was the exact scenario the NATO investigator, Irena Senovac, had alluded to in her reports to the UN. A huge trade in women, most of whom had been forced into the sex trade and some of whom were ending up in London.

Nina was planning to take some photos of missing girls to Relia Stanga, the rescued slave, later that morning to see if she could pick out anyone she knew. She asked me to join her and offered to drive.

Unfortunately for me, I hadn't heard about her reputation or I would have declined the offer. She liked to drive fast, and she was also heavy on the brakes and intolerant of all the 'wankers' that got in her way. Luckily for me, the only car that had been available from the motor pool was a former flying-squad Volvo that had seen better days. It was reliable, but lacked the acceleration Nina craved.

By the time we reached Hampstead, I was feeling queasy. Maybe my system still hadn't recovered from the weekend. For once, I actually felt grateful for a traffic queue. The main road from Belsize Park into Hampstead High Street was bumper to bumper. Nina was quiet as she concentrated on her driving. I wound down the window to the passenger door and gulped in the fresh air.

Nina explained that it was still undecided whether Relia would be provided with safe passage home or if an attempt would be made for her to be granted asylum. The paperwork was complicated but Nina was certain that if Relia went home to what remained of her family, she would be recaptured by the slavers and would either be murdered for talking to the British police or sold back into the sex industry.

The safe house was a flat in a block called Redhill, at the top end of the High Street, close to the tube station. It was privately owned but council funded. There were several in the area that were normally reserved for the victims of domestic violence, but, with good contacts in the Camden Social Services Department, Nina had been able to secure her witness a place.

Relia was at number 43, on the third floor. Nina pressed the buzzer and waited. There was no response.

'I only spoke to her last night,' she said. 'What's the time, Finlay?' She looked a little annoyed as she buzzed the flat twice more.

'Five to twelve. Maybe she's popped out?'

'She doesn't tend to go out in daylight. She's paranoid that someone she knows will recognise her and tell the slavers where she is.'

I could see Nina was starting to get frustrated. A concerned look was registering on her face. 'I'm sure she's fine. Try the concierge buzzer,' I said.

Nina jabbed button 43 twice more before doing as I suggested. A male voice answered and Nina explained who we were and asked to be allowed in. He politely declined but offered to come and help. He would be about five minutes if we didn't mind waiting.

Nina kicked her feet impatiently.

'You OK?' I asked.

'Not really. It's just that I have other things to do today rather than wait for Relia to come home from shopping … and I told her I would be here at midday.'

'Mind if I take a look at the photos?'

Nina handed the document folder over without replying. There were about a dozen sheets, each contained about twenty pictures of varying quality. Most were family pictures of missing girls; some were copies of passport photographs. Each sheet was headed with the Interpol logo. I flicked through them, slowly. They all looked remarkably similar. All women – late teens to early twenties; all white, all looking vaguely Eastern European. All reported as missing.

Nina lit up a cigarette as we waited. The simple action caused me to pause for a moment before continuing to amble through the pictures. It was the first time I had seen Nina smoke. I was surprised. Although she sometimes joined Matt and me at the end of the day to down a small Penderyn, I'd imagined Nina pursuing a healthier lifestyle.

She noticed my reaction. 'Stress, Finlay. I don't smoke many these days, but if I'm stressed I find that a little draw of nicotine gets me through.'

I turned to the final sheet of photographs. It was the saddest of all, showing the bodies and faces of unidentified female murder victims. There were eight, in date order.

'None of my business,' I said. 'Just surprised me a bit…' I stopped mid-sentence. The final pair of pictures caused me to halt the conversation. There was a name at the base of the picture, presumably a village or town, and the country, Romania. The first victim was a poor facial shot of a bruised face with what might at one time have been attractive blonde hair. The second showed the body where it had been found; it looked like a roadside in a wood. The victim's dress was torn and dirty.

'You OK, Finlay?' Nina stubbed the cigarette out on the ground as we saw the caretaker approaching across the small car park. 'You look like you've seen a ghost.'

I stared at the picture. It was the unmistakable dress that the poor girl was wearing that caught my eye.

Yellow with red stripes.

Chapter 40

I paused for a moment before replying to Nina.

'When were these pictures taken?'

'No idea. Recently, though. They only came over the wire this morning. You sure you're OK?'

The dress was very distinctive. Bright yellow, and even with the dirt that soiled it, the stripes were clear.

Just a couple of days previously I had been watching a girl wearing the identical dress lose a dance competition in the courtyard at Gheorghe Cristea's home. I scanned the face in the photograph. It was dirty and dishevelled. I remembered that the girl at the wedding had also been blonde, but the face … it was impossible to be sure.

If it was the girl from the wedding then it might be I needed to do something about it. But it might not be, I thought. For all I knew, that pattern of dress might be common in Romania.

I handed the photographs back and mumbled, 'I'm fine,' just as the caretaker joined us and looked over the warrant card that Nina thrust into his face.

Using a master key to open the street door, our guide led the way up six flights to the third floor. Smartly dressed in matching blue trousers and jacket, the caretaker gave the impression of someone who really loved his job. He was about seventy, but as fit as a flea, and flew up the stairs as quickly as a man many years his junior might manage. Nina tried the intercom at the door leading to the flat corridors. Again, there was no response.

'Do you have a contact number for her?' I asked.

'Yes. Hang on a minute.'

We waited while Nina rooted around in her handbag for her mobile phone. As she tapped in the number, I caught the old caretaker eyeing her up and down. In a black jacket with a white blouse and tight black trousers she could easily have been mistaken for a lawyer rather than a cop.

The caretaker winked and smiled. Lowering his voice, he leaned towards me and whispered. 'Very tall ...'

I nodded without responding. The caretaker was right. Nina was a good two inches taller than me in flat shoes. In heels, she would easily be six feet two.

There was no reply to the phone call. 'Do you have a key to this door as well?' Nina asked the caretaker.

'Yes ... and the flat door if you need to go in.'

Nina turned to me. 'I'd like to, Finlay. OK with you? Just for peace of mind, really.'

I shrugged. It was her call.

The caretaker led the way along the narrow passage. When we reached Flat 43, Nina knocked hard and called out Relia's name. There was no response. She knocked once more, this time harder still.

The corridor lighting was dim but, standing back whilst Nina knocked again and again, I spotted a mark on the door. I held up my hand to indicate that Nina should stop knocking. I looked closer. The mark was familiar. A trace left by the sole of a sports trainer. It was only visible by looking at the door from an acute angle, but it was there. It was the kind of smudge that a burglar leaves when kicking down a door.

'See that?' I pointed to the mark.

'No ... see what?' Nina said.

'Shoe mark. Looks like someone has forced the door.'

'Shit.'

The caretaker interrupted. 'Looks like they didn't get in.'

'Or the door was half open when it was kicked?' Nina commented. 'Can you open it? And try the mortise first, we need to know if the last person to leave locked the door ... and be careful not to touch anything.'

Gently, the caretaker inserted the brass master key into the mortise lock. It was already open; either the last person to leave didn't have the key or hadn't bothered to lock it. The door opened easily as the Yale key turned.

'Better leave this to us, mate,' I said to the caretaker.

With the others stepping back slightly, I eased slowly and gently into the flat. All was quiet.

The door frame was intact with no sign of a forced entry. Behind the front door was a small hallway. Across the tiny space, there were two white doors, both slightly ajar. One appeared to be a bathroom, the other a toilet. To the left it looked like there was a single bedroom. The gentle sound of water running into a sink could be heard coming from my right. I guessed it to be the kitchen and eating area. There was no other sound or indication of life.

'Relia,' I called out.

There was no reply. Edging forward slowly, I headed toward the sound of the water. The door to the kitchen area was only slightly ajar, but even before I opened it fully, I knew what I was going to find.

It was the smell – warm, salty and sickeningly familiar.

The smell of fresh blood.

Chapter 41

Spilled cereal on the kitchen table suggested that Relia had just sat down to breakfast when she was disturbed.

The kitchen chairs were turned over and a drawer pulled open. Several large knives lay on the floor. I wondered if Relia had been reaching for a weapon to defend herself. What was certain was that someone had lost a lot of blood. The kitchen floor was covered in the fresh, congealing evidence of a desperate fight. There were skid marks where feet had struggled to gain grip. Blood was splashed and sprayed up the walls and across the work surfaces, on the unit doors and on the back of the door into the hallway.

A moment later, the caretaker called out. He had found something.

'I thought we said to wait outside in the corridor,' I said.

The caretaker looked ill, as if he were about to throw up. 'Sorry,' he answered. 'I was curious.'

I stepped past him and into the bathroom. Again, the smell of blood hit me. Then I saw the body. A woman. She was in the bath. A bare leg hung over the side.

Nina looked over my shoulder. 'It's her,' she said. She squeezed past me and checked for signs of life. There were none. Relia's injuries were clearly fatal. The killer had left her in a real mess. Blood splashes up the wall and over the shower curtain gave every indication that the attacker had used the bath to start hacking her into pieces. But, for some reason, the attack had stopped and then the assailant had tried to use the shower to clean up, leaving Relia where she was, but using bathroom towels to remove the last of the blood from clothes and shoes, then leaving them in a nasty pink pile on the floor.

As Nina put in a call to the local CID, I stepped out of the bathroom and went to check the front door again. I wondered whether Relia had been expecting someone and had opened it to allow her attacker in. Swinging the door open on the hinges, the hallway light again revealed the mark on the paintwork. I made a mental note to ask the Scenes of Crime examiner to have a look at it.

The local CID were quick to arrive. The caretaker went to open the doors for them and within a few minutes a detective appeared in the corridor with a scene-of-crime kit. A forensic officer was with the caretaker. The Area Major Investigation Team had been informed. It looked like all the bases had been covered.

'It'll be out of our hands now, Finlay,' Nina said, as she joined me in the corridor. 'The Murder Squad will take over. They'll want witness statements and some other stuff but we can take care of that later. I need to get back and brief the boss.'

'What shall I do – wait here?' I said.

'No, you better come back with me. The shit's gonna fly on this, so you can help me dodge it.'

'Why's that exactly?'

'Relia was supposed to be in the witness protection programme. I had a few problems: budgets … that kind of thing. There's going to be people wanting to cover their arses and we need to make sure they don't do so at our expense.'

We headed back to the car. At Nina's suggestion we made a quick call at the caretaker's flat before departing.

When we knocked on the caretaker's door, the forensic Scenes of Crime Officer was in the process of taking a mouth swab from him to collect a DNA sample. He seized the chance to take similar swabs from both Nina and me. The poor caretaker was still shaking at the horror we had witnessed.

I mentioned to the SOCO about the foot mark on the flat door. He promised to make it his next job and we headed back to the Volvo.

Before getting in, I stood for a moment, thinking about what we had just witnessed, the sound of approaching sirens telling me the troops were on their way – uniformed officers who would seal off the entrances to the flats and make sure that the scene would be preserved for the forensic teams.

As Nina opened the car door, I asked, 'Do you think we disturbed them?'

'Possibly. It certainly looked like they left in a hurry. I couldn't work out why the bastards put her in the bath, though. It looked like the fight started in the kitchen, so why not finish it there?'

I looked around the car park. 'Maybe they hadn't finished with her when we turned up … If we did disturb them,' I went on, 'which way would you go if you didn't want to be seen?'

Nina glanced around, shrugged and then indicated the far side of the car park. 'I'd probably have a car waiting over there. Drive away from the main High Street and avoid the crowds.'

'Mind if I have a quick look?'

Nina sighed. 'If you insist. Want me to come with you?'

I did. As we walked together across the tarmac, I scanned the ground. I wasn't looking for anything in particular, just something unusual – a clue that might indicate a route taken by the escaping killers.

I didn't have to wait long. On the other side of the parking area I noticed a well-trodden route across a flower border – a short cut used by residents to enter the streets behind the flats. On a low wall, I saw a dark, damp spot of liquid. Stopping to look more closely, I saw others, smaller and less obvious from a distance.

It was blood. And it was still wet.

'Look at this,' I said to Nina.

She crouched down. 'Looks like she hurt one of them. This hasn't been here long, not even dried at the edges. Wait here ... I'll go and get the SOCO.'

I did as I was told, looking around the trodden-down area as Nina headed off to get help. But within a few seconds, curiosity got the better of me and I started to move towards the street. I was careful where I walked. The last thing I needed was to spoil some forensic evidence that the SOCO might find.

All was quiet. Save for the lines of cars parked along both sides of the road, there was little to see. As the track opened up onto the footway, the direct route across the street was blocked by a shiny new Jaguar.

I pictured men moving at speed and imagined they might bump into the side of the Jag as they ran. I made a mental note to ask the SOCO to check the car paintwork for fingerprints. As I leaned down to check for myself, I saw a faint scuff mark along the sill below the passenger door.

Instinct told me to bend down and look under the car. It was dark. I couldn't see daylight from the other side.

There was someone hiding underneath.

Chapter 42

For a second I stood up and thought. Whoever was hiding under the car almost certainly knew I had spotted them. And I had no radio to call for help.

Just as I was trying to work out how I was going to capture my suspect, Nina appeared behind me with the SOCO.

'Got something, Finlay?' she asked.

I raised a finger to my lips and, with my other hand, pointed to the road beneath the car.

Before we could react further there was a scraping sound from the opposite side of the Jaguar. A small man in dark clothing scrabbled out then sprinted off down the road.

Without a thought, Nina and I both gave chase.

For about twenty-five yards, I kept pace. But Nina did better. The man was fast but Nina had youth on her side and, after fifty yards, she was still with him. I was rapidly starting to lose ground.

I decided that alternative tactics were called for. Nina seemed to be gaining on him. She was tall, athletic and moved freely. And the cigarettes didn't seem to have affected her fitness. But like me, she also had no radio, so if we were going to catch our suspect, we needed a quick plan.

I dived right into a small side street, in the hope that I might head them both off. I soon slowed to a jog, and then a walk as I struggled to regain my breath. I had only gone about two hundred yards when I heard the sound of someone climbing fences in a nearby garden. Whoever it was, they were in a hurry and appeared to be coming my way.

Crouching down behind a low wall, I waited. He was close. A second later and the small man leapt the wall next to me and landed on the pavement.

I made my move.

Only to find myself staring down the barrel of a handgun.

I automatically looked up at the face of my attacker. I'm not sure which of us had the greater shock. In front of me, as large as life, stood the same man that I had disarmed at Marica's wedding.

It was clear he recognised me. His lips opened into a broad smile, exposing broken, yellowed teeth. Just like at the reception, he stood with the pistol pointed at me, the hand steady and near enough for me to grab. I raised my hands to waist height. If I moved swiftly, I just might...

But as I went to grab the pistol my opponent stepped backwards, shaking his head from side to side as he did so. He wasn't going to be caught twice.

The smile faded as his lips curled into a snarl. I saw his hand tighten on the pistol and the index finger slide onto the trigger. He was going to shoot.

I dropped to the floor and dived forward, trying to take out his legs and get hold of the gun. But he moved aside before I reached him. I hit fresh air and landed heavily on the footway.

There was a shout. 'No!' It was Nina. She was behind me.

I looked up. The Romanian levelled the gun at her. Then, he hesitated for a moment, as if unsure whether to fire.

With the gunman distracted, I tried to move closer to him. There was just a chance I could sweep his legs away. Before I had the chance, though, he turned and ran.

Nina bent down to help me. 'You OK?' she asked.

'Yes,' I said. 'Get after him.'

She took off and I dragged myself to my feet and jogged slowly after her. Reaching a junction, I looked left then right. There was no sign of them. I was still breathing heavily. For a minute or so I stood quietly, as I got my breath back and my heart rate slowed. I swore at myself. Once again, I had been very lucky.

Soon, Nina came jogging back to me. She was alone.

'Lost him?' I asked.

'There was a car, a grey one. It must have been looking for him. He jumped into the back seat.'

'Get a number?'

'Too far … sorry … I thought he was going to shoot you back there.'

'Me too. Guess you distracted him.'

'Come on,' said Nina. 'We need to find some uniform lads and get a description circulated.'

Several seconds passed before I summoned the courage to speak. Finally, I blurted the words out.

'I knew him.'

Chapter 43

Nina looked puzzled for a moment.

'The gunman?' she said at last.

'Yes … the fuckin' gunman. Who the hell else did you think I meant?'

'Whoa … steady. I'm not the bad guy here. You mean you recognised him?'

I took a deep breath. 'Yeah … I'm sorry, Nina. I guess I should be thanking you … and yes, I recognised him.'

'It's nothing you wouldn't have done for me. For one moment I thought you were going to try and snatch the gun from him.'

'I thought about it … he didn't fall for it twice.'

'What do you mean, twice?'

'Just a couple of days ago … in Romania. Would you believe I took what might have been the very same gun off that very man?'

'I don't understand? How … how … I thought you meant you recognised him as a known criminal. You mean you've met him before?'

'At the wedding me and Jenny went to. He was one of the men working for the family that invited us … the Cristeas.'

'The Cristea family?'

'Yeah. They're the publishing folks that invited me to their daughter's wedding.'

'Oh my God … oh my fucking God.' Nina started walking in small circles, her head held tightly in her hands. 'You're kidding me … the Cristeas? Seriously, Finlay? This isn't some kind of a wind-up?'

'At a time like this? Are you kidding? Why … do you know them?'

'Do I know them? Finlay … the Cristeas are the reason we have a sex-trafficking problem in London.' She stalked off towards the car park without another word. I followed, my heart beat picking up once again.

When we reached our car, she stopped, opened the driver's door and, jabbing her finger in the direction of the passenger seat, indicated for me to get in. With the doors closed, she paused for a second, appearing to compose herself.

'The Cristeas are one of the reasons this squad has been formed. They're into trafficking in a big way. Relia was going to testify against them.'

'You never mentioned them.' I said.

'Not by name, no. But I would have as you learned more about how things work, what exactly we're investigating and the scale of it. Jesus ... I don't bloody believe it. We are in so much shit. If it gets out that you've been holidaying with them ...'

'But I had no idea.'

'Didn't you think to check them out before you went?'

'Not in detail, no. I think I just assumed, with MI5 knowing about them, they were just a publishing company.'

'Really? Christ's sake. You've been away from real policing for way too long. You should have checked. And I can't believe that Toni Fellowes didn't warn you.'

'You know her?'

'Of course ... our paths have crossed many times.'

'So ... what am I going to do?'

'What are *we* going to do, you mean?' Nina paused, seemingly running things over in her mind. An idea seemed to come to her. 'You definitely haven't done any checks on the Cristeas?' she asked. 'No PNC check, no Interpol, nothing?'

'It never occurred to me,' I replied. 'I just thought they were an ordinary family – pretty well off, but normal. I saw some of them carrying sidearms at the reception, but I thought that might be normal for backwoods Romania. To be honest, I've been a bit distracted since the bombings ... not thinking straight.'

'I'm sure Complaints Branch would be very sympathetic ... just before they sack you. So, there's no trace on any electronic search to say that you could have known that gunman?'

'No ... none.'

'Do you know his name?'

'No ... and one other thing, those pictures from Interpol: there was one with a girl in a very distinctive dress. I couldn't say for definite, but she looks like a girl that lost a dance competition at the wedding.'

'I know the picture you mean, we see a lot like that.'

'A lot of murdered slave girls, you mean?'

'Yes, a lot of them end up dead, dumped at the side of the road.'

'You seem to know so much about trafficking.'

'Let's just say there are family connections. My father was Romanian, worked in the embassy over here, that's how he met my mother. We settled over here but my old man knew a lot of people involved in trafficking.'

'Why is the Romanian connection so relevant?'

'During the war my father's country fought with the Nazis. He told me how the Germans set up what they called "Joy Divisions" in the concentration camps and "*Soldattenbordell*" elsewhere.'

'Brothels for soldiers?' I asked, guessing at the translation.

'Exactly. And they used Romanian soldiers to run them. At the end of the war those men had learned the trade and how lucrative it could be. It didn't take long before they were forcing women into it again.'

'You know a lot about the subject.'

'It's been a particular interest of mine for some while.'

'I'm impressed. But it's not going to help me at the moment.'

'I agree. Didn't you think that maybe you should have said something? I mean, we do have rules about associating with criminals and accepting gratuities.'

I managed a half-smile. 'I'll have to tell the local Murder Squad what I know.'

'They'll hang you out to dry, Finlay. You'll be on a disciplinary hearing faster than you know it. Christ, that bastard Youldon will be rubbing his hands with glee.'

'No choice…'

'Let me think…'

I went to speak but Nina raised her hand to silence me.

After a few moments, she spoke. 'You do have a choice. It's not your fault you're an idiot. To my way of thinking, to err is human. Trouble is … to forgive isn't job policy.'

'Got a suggestion? I have to tell them…'

'No, you don't. You have to give a description and, in case anyone in the street saw the chase, you will have to say what happened. But you don't have to tell them that you'd met the gunman before … you don't have to say that the Cristeas are behind it.'

'Why not, if the Cristeas are the killers, then they'll need to know?'

'You leave that to me, Finlay. Relia was Romanian and came through the slave route … and I'll explain that we were hoping she was going to give us evidence against the Cristeas. I'll tell the Murder Squad that they have to be considered prime suspects.'

'You think that'll work?'

'For your sake … for our sake, I hope so. Now, just do yourself a bloody favour and leave the detective work to those that know what they're doing.'

I didn't answer. Nina was offering to cover for me. She would steer the Murder Squad in the right direction without saying how she knew.

With little option, I had to agree. 'OK,' I said. 'I will. One thing though.'

'What's that?'

'If the gunman dived under the Jaguar straight after leaving the flats, he was hiding there for maybe half an hour. Why not sneak off? Why stay there?'

'Maybe they were still around when we arrived. He saw us and hid in the first available place.'

'But we were a good twenty minutes inside the flats. He could have used that time to make good his escape.'

'Maybe he was waiting to be picked up.'

'Yeah … maybe. Or maybe he was watching us. And only hid when we wandered over to look around the car park.'

'Who knows, Finlay?' said Nina. 'Like I said, we'll leave that to the detectives to work out, shall we?'

Chapter 44

I gave a description of the gunman we had chased to the local CID before we left. They circulated it over the radio and started to organise a search of the local streets. I guessed it would be fruitless. He was long gone.

For most of the return journey to New Scotland Yard, we didn't speak. Nina was clearly brooding, her mood sombre and quiet, her driving more sedate. I didn't push the conversation. I thought hard about the advice she had given me. I had been a fool, there was no doubt of that. Her generosity in covering for me surprised me a little. In truth, she hardly knew me. One day, I promised myself that I would return the favour.

It was pretty clear to me that Relia had been located by the very same people who had brought her into the country. She had known too much and had been willing to name names, identify traffickers and help bring other victims who might also be willing to help. The slavers had found and silenced her.

Breaking the atmosphere, Nina finally spoke – explaining to me what happened when she had tried to get Relia into the embryonic witness protection programme.

'Every resource, every officer was already committed to supergrass enquiries – you know the type of thing: crooks giving evidence in gangster trials. I had to protect an innocent victim on my own. And now, that's cost Relia her life.' Nina sighed deeply.

She was right when she said that the individuals responsible for that lack of support would now be looking to protect themselves from the inevitable criticism.

With Nina's driving now a lot smoother, I took the opportunity to flick through the remainder of the Interpol reports. There were many, almost all involving drug smuggling. We were on the down ramp into the underground car park at New Scotland Yard when Nina suddenly hit the brakes. The files on my lap slipped untidily into the passenger well of the car.

'What's up?' I asked.

'She knew.'

'I'm sorry ... I don't follow. Who knew what?'

'Toni Fellowes ... she knew. She knows about the Cristeas; she has to. I've been thinking about it and it's the only answer I can come up with.'

'I'm not sure I understand.'

'When she arranged that trip to Egypt – did anything happen to throw you and the Cristeas together?'

'I wouldn't exactly say we were thrown together. Marica – the daughter – she wanted to do a course and needed a dive partner. The school suggested that I could do it.'

'And I bet there was an incentive, like it was a freebie?'

'Yes, it was. Are you saying Toni engineered me meeting Marica?'

'It's a theory, but it fits. I bet she couldn't believe her luck when you got invited to that wedding.'

'You're saying Toni wanted me to meet the Cristeas ... that she sent us over there knowing they were criminals?'

'You bumping into one of the Cristea gunmen in the street, having just met him at a wedding is a hell of a coincidence. Isn't it more likely Toni Fellowes had been planning all along for you to have contact with them?'

'But why would she do that? Why put us at risk?'

'She's a spook, Finlay. You of all people should know they only see people like us as assets. She probably figured she could use you to get close to the family. Maybe MI5 has an interest in them too.'

I didn't reply. The trust I had placed in Toni Fellowes had just taken a serious knock.

✠

Matt was waiting for us when we arrived back at the office. News of Relia's murder had filtered through.

'Boss wants to see you both,' he said.

Nina slammed her handbag and the Interpol file onto her desk. 'Does he now?' she replied, angrily.

I made to speak, but the tall DS held up her hand to silence me. 'Leave it to me, Finlay. She was my witness … and it's my head. Besides, I can handle our beloved Superintendent better on my own.'

The phone on my desk started to ring. It was the Hampstead SOCO. He got straight to the point. 'You mentioned a footprint on the entrance door to 43 Redhill.'

'That's right. In the light it looked like the sole of a trainer.'

'Well, I'm sorry … I looked carefully, but there was no mark. No sign of one anywhere.'

I paused for a moment. I was certain I'd seen a mark. 'You're sure?' I asked.

'Definite.'

'Could one of the boys have brushed it off as they walked passed it?'

'Maybe … I guess. But I wouldn't have expected an accidental brush to have removed it completely. Smudged it, yes, but there was no mark at all on the door.'

'Shit.'

I had a shrewd idea what had happened. I'd seen it before. A young DC accidentally damages key evidence and rather than leave it and own up, he removes it completely and denies it was ever there. One of the Hampstead lads had probably brushed against the door, realised their mistake and then wiped the door clean. It was shit practice but it happened.

'One other thing,' the SOCO added.

'Go on.'

'The victim; when we lifted the body from the bath, her left hand was missing … hacked off at the wrist.'

I grimaced. 'Christ. With the cleaver from the kitchen, I guess?'

'Looks like it. Place had been searched as well. No jewellery, no cash to be seen. And our best estimate is there were at least two attackers, maybe three.'

'How can you be sure?'

'Two sets of trainer marks in the kitchen and like I said, somebody searched the bedroom. Whoever did that didn't leave any blood on the floor, so we figure there was probably a third suspect involved.'

'Unless they searched the bedroom before killing her?'

'Could be,' said the SOCO. 'Our boss figures at least two, though.'

'Overwhelmed by numbers. Poor kid never stood a chance. Do you think that the blood trail we found was from her hand?'

'Could well be. It was just a few spots. Not likely to have been from a wounded suspect who was running – that would probably have produced a larger spread pattern. I can't be sure until we compare the DNA to the body, but there was no blood under the Jaguar, suggesting the man you chased was uninjured.'

'No luck with him, I guess?'

'None. Long gone. I'll need you both to come up and look at some pictures of local villains later and I'll need to take shoe imprints from both of you.'

I thanked him for his help and hung up.

Nina was still in with the Superintendent. For a moment it crossed my mind to knock on the door, pull her out and give her the news about Relia's missing hand. The raised voices that reached my ears persuaded me otherwise.

Chapter 45

Later that day, Nina and I drove back up to Hampstead, where we provided the forensic team with samples, footprints and statements. After several failed attempts to contact Toni Fellowes, I left a message with Nell, her assistant. I explained – without mentioning the gunman – that I had learned of the Cristeas involvement in sex trafficking and that I was curious why I had been allowed to travel to Romania. I couched it in no stronger terms than that. Although I was angry, I didn't want to start sounding off; I was hoping there might be a perfectly good explanation. And, I had to remember, Toni had been very supportive and had gone out of her way to help my family. In many ways, we owed her.

That evening, I met up with Kevin to make the one-hour journey from Central London to Gayle Bridges' new home.

Kevin picked me up from Victoria Street at seven o'clock, and almost immediately began to tell me what had happened to Beaky on television. It transpired the BBC had been doing a TV interview when Terry Field, one of the senior NCOs from Hereford, had popped out of the audience with Beaky's personnel file.

The interviewer had then posed Beaky a couple of searching questions about his supposed time in the SAS. It was a set-up. Not surprisingly, Beaky couldn't bullshit his way through the interview with Terry sitting opposite him, the truth in a cardboard folder on his lap. Beaky had lost his temper and stormed out of the studio. Rumour had it he also chinned one of the cameramen. I thought it a sad end to a sorry episode.

It looked like Beaky was going to have the last laugh, though. According to the newspapers, the book had gone to a second print run, such was the demand after the BBC exposure.

I had little interest in Beaky or his book, though. My immediate problem was helping Gayle Bridges dispose of her late husband's trophy pistol. I was also curious as to what might be contained in the paperwork that Bob Bridges had seen fit to keep hidden for so long after his retirement from the army.

✠

As an experienced army wife, Gayle knew how to receive soldiers into her home. The kettle was on and, as she showed us into the front room, there was a plate of Garibaldi biscuits ready on the coffee table. If there was one thing she remembered, it was that soldiers were always thirsty and hungry.

Gayle started out by apologising for not replying to the message I had sent to her through the pension branch. She had decided to cut all ties with her husband's past life. It was only finding the pistol that had changed her mind.

In the car, on the way to the house, Kevin and I had discussed how we would deal with the questions we thought Gayle might ask. It didn't take long before our planning paid off. She soon raised the subject of her husband's murder, the attacks on the other former soldiers and the end result.

Kevin had been uncertain as to how much to say. I had decided. We would tell Gayle about the Irish lads that had been taken out, the Arab who had turned out to be another Irishman, and the fact that the threat was now over. Of Monaghan, the former SAS commander turned MI5 officer, we would make no mention.

Gayle listened quietly while I related the story of how Kevin and I had managed to work out who the terrorists were, how we had then been attacked ourselves and gone on to overcome our would-be killers. I explained that the final terrorist had died of food poisoning in prison, just a couple of days previously.

'Did he die, or was he killed too, Finlay?' she asked me.

'From what I read in the papers, which is really all we know, it seems it was an illness. I suppose we might all hope he suffered a bit, but nobody seems to be claiming it was anything else.'

'I just wondered...' Gale began. And then she stood up and left the room.

I exchanged glances with Kevin. He shrugged. Our shared curiosity was answered when Gayle returned carrying a cardboard document box. She sat down on the settee, placed the box on the coffee table and opened the lid.

On the top of a pile of A4 size papers, about an inch in thickness, lay a Browning 9mm pistol, a spare magazine and three small boxes of 9mm rounds.

'Would you mind taking the gun?' Gayle looked at Kevin as she asked.

Kevin picked the pistol up by the grip, removed the clip and pulled back the slide. A live round flicked out onto the floor.

'Loaded. One up the spout,' he commented, leaning forward to retrieve the bullet.

'Thank you,' Gayle continued. 'It's not so much the gun or the bullets that bothered me. I mean … you've explained what happened to my husband … and who did it. But what I want to know is why? Why after all these years did these men come all the way to London to blow up some old soldiers? And I want to know … I want to know if it has anything to do with this?'

Gayle dropped the pile of loosely bound papers in my lap.

As Kevin unloaded the Browning magazine and placed the rounds carefully with the others in the small cardboard storage boxes, I scanned through the pile of documents. Although there was the odd map and quote in English, they were mostly in Arabic.

I turned to Kevin. 'Did you ever learn to read any of this lingo?'

'Not a word. I picked up a few Farsi sayings on Ops, but reading Arabic script is way beyond me.'

'Me too.' I turned to Gayle. 'What makes you think these are something significant Gayle?'

'I knew he had them,' she answered. 'But he couldn't read Arabic either. Could you get them translated, find out what they mean? Can you do that … and let me know?'

'I suppose we could,' I said. 'The Met has interpreters that do this kind of thing.'

'Just don't say where it came from.' Gayle shook her head and took a deep breath. 'To be honest, I'm surprised you two haven't thought about why someone would single you lads out from all the others.'

'We figured it was due to an op that we were on in Ulster many years ago,' I lied.

'All of you?'

'Possibly; we're not absolutely sure. The people that could tell us aren't really up to speaking about it.'

I continued to flick through the papers. There were drawings, maps of countries, some in the Middle East, others in Europe. A map of the

UK had notes next to it that seemed to be a list of some kind, but it was all in Arabic script.

'Any idea where Bob got all this, Gayle?' I made a deliberate move to steer the conversation away from the events of recent weeks.

'He did some work for the Government after he left the army. Out in the Far East. That man who was made to look an idiot on the BBC ... he just wrote about it.'

'That book, *Cyclone*, you mean?'

'Yes that's the one. Bob was a private military contractor then. He went with a few of the boys out to Afghanistan to help teach the locals how to use guns and things.'

I noticed that Kevin had gone quiet and was staring at me. 'Did he say anything about what these documents are?' he asked.

'Only that one day they would be worth a lot of money. They were his insurance. On his last job out there, the team he was with were ambushed. One of the men with him was killed getting those papers. Bob figured that if they were worth dying for then they had some value.'

'So you think there might be a connection between them and Bob's death?'

'I do. A few years ago, Bob had a telephone call. I don't know who it was but it sounded as if it was one of his old mates. Anyway ... whoever it was told Bob that these pages were dynamite. But he hadn't mentioned them since. It was only when I moved house that I found them ... and the gun, of course.'

Kevin slipped the Browning into his jacket pocket with a promise it would be taken care of. I returned the papers to the document box and tucked it between my feet. The look on Gayle's face told me she was glad to see the back of her husband's mementos.

✠

Teas downed, Kevin led the way back to his car. I asked him to hang on for a minute while I checked it over. His response took me by surprise.

'What are you doing?' he asked.

'Checking the car ... you know, like we should do,' I answered, impatiently.

'For IEDs you mean?'

'That kind of thing, yes.'

'You're serious aren't you? Do you check every time?'

I leaned under the front bumper as I answered. 'Yes ... and so should you.'

Kevin hesitated for a moment before speaking. 'Look, I'm not being funny, boss, but MI5 say it's all over. We can't spend the rest of our lives living like we're under constant threat.'

I smiled as I stood straight. 'I just have to do it, Kev. It helps me sleep easy.'

Kevin shrugged. 'You need to get some help, boss, seriously. Come on ... let's go.'

Chapter 46

As we continued back into London, Kevin strained to look at the papers lying in my lap. In the limited light from the street lamps, I was flicking through the sheets to see if there was anything I might be able to understand.

I had no success, but did have an idea for discreetly obtaining a translation.

I remembered that my Explosives Officer friend, Rupert Reid, spoke Arabic quite well. Rupert was now back at work, I'd heard. The car bomb at my home, which had destroyed my original 2CV, had left him with concussion, cuts and a few bruises. Luckily, the only real damage to the Wookie-sized bomb disposal officer was a perforated eardrum, an injury of the type that he had suffered many times before. It would heal. It wasn't certain that Rupert could read Arabic as well as speak it, but I was confident he would know someone who did.

We were just a few minutes away from my new home when Kevin brought up what Gayle had said about Bob's time in the Far East. 'I never knew Bomber Bridges was on the Increment team, did you?'

'Not until this evening. I remember bumping into him in Cyprus, though. We were just returning from Peshawar, remember?'

'Not sure. We did so many trips they all seem to merge into one.'

'Bomber was heading out to Pakistan on the same aircraft we'd come in on. I remember it well. We shared a quick beer at the airport bar before he caught the plane. I always wondered what he was off to do. Come to think of it, Beaky might have been on that aircraft as well. There were some contractors, as I recall.'

'Well, Beaky had to get his material from somewhere.'

'He might have talked to them on the flight.'

'They wouldn't have told him anything. If they were working for Six, they would have signed the OSA.' Signing the Official Secrets Act was something MI6 insisted on before every covert operation, particularly if it was on foreign soil. It was a little reminder of the consequences of speaking to the press, writing a personal memoir or even talking to your wife. Putting your signature to the OSA form had a way of focussing the mind.

'They came back on a Herc' on one of the other ops as well,' Kevin recalled. 'They travelled back with us, in the rear of the aircraft. They had a coffin with them. Remember that?'

I thought for a moment. I remembered the flights; there were several, always at night. Often there would be passengers in the rear seats of the aircraft who boarded the plane after everyone else and, on arrival in Cyprus, they would exit the rear while all nearer the front had to wait. We always presumed that they were spooks – MI6 or CIA; something of that nature. I couldn't recall having seen Bob Bridges again after that first meeting in the airport lounge.

'No,' I said. 'But from what he wrote in *Cyclone*, I guess Beaky got himself onto one of those teams.'

'Maybe...'

'...Or maybe he got one of the lads drunk, pumped him for stories, and taped it. Add a little imagination ... you got yourself a book.'

Kevin pulled the car to a halt just a few minutes from the safe house.

'When are you planning to take the Browning to Hereford?' I asked.

'First thing, why do you ask?'

'I think I'll come with you. It's been a long time since I saw the place and I've never been in the new camp.'

'I thought Royalty cops like you did bodyguard courses there.'

'We did a week at Pontrilas but never went to Credenhill.'

'Well, if you're sure. I could do with the company, to be honest. It's a long drive on your own.'

'OK, that's settled,' I said. 'You drive around the M25 and pick me up from Cockfosters at eight. I'm on a late tomorrow so an early departure will give me enough time to get back in time for work.' I tucked the document box under my arm, climbed out of the car and headed home.

The walk gave me a few minutes to do some thinking. The Increment lads were specialists. Having left the army, they were between soldiering and civilian life, employed by Security Services to do military-type jobs that the army couldn't or wouldn't do. The Director of Special Forces had heard what was happening in northern Afghanistan during the late 1970s and had been keen for the Regiment to get involved. The Foreign Office decision – the right one – was that it was too dangerous for serving British soldiers to travel into such a war zone. It would be hard to explain the presence of SAS soldiers, should they be captured, or killed and their bodies recovered by the Russians.

We were, however, allowed into neighbouring Pakistan. I remembered the briefings we had been given before several of us had packed our kit and headed off to RAF Northolt. Somehow, a deal had been done between the CIA, MI6 and the Pakistan Inter-Service Intelligence – the ISI – to import weapons into Afghanistan through the Panjshir Valley. The Americans were prepared to fund the supply of weapons to warlords fighting the occupying forces but wanted to avoid overt involvement, for fear of inflaming relations with the Russians.

The Pakistanis didn't have the expertise to train the Mujahedeen, so an incredibly convoluted deal had been done whereby the Americans paid for Russian weapons, purchased from countries such as Israel and

Egypt, and we Brits put men on the ground to supervise their import and teach the locals how to use them.

The Increment lads had travelled into the mountains on foot and on horseback. They set up a training camp in the Panjshir Valley in Afghanistan, using caves for shelter and cover. MI6 officers with them educated local fighters how to get by in English while the ex-soldiers taught them how to use the new weapons.

On the Pakistan side of the border, regular SAS soldiers – including me and Kevin – had a unique opportunity to get hold of examples of the latest Soviet weaponry. The shopping list ranged from small arms, including the new AK74 assault rifle, through to avionics and protection systems for the modern Russian helicopters.

Increment got hold of Russian kit following battles, helicopter crashes and by paying Afghan workers to steal it. The mule trains then brought it across the border into Pakistan. After that, we did some field testing of the interesting bits before boxing up the technical stuff for rendition to the UK.

As a former artillery officer, my specialism had been surface-to-air missiles. That was how Kevin and I had ended up on the operation. Somebody had to teach the fighters on the ground how to use the kit that the Americans had provided.

Cyclone had now exposed the whole complex project.

†

The downstairs lights to the house were still on as I walked up the drive.

Jenny was watching television. As I walked in and leant over to kiss her cheek, the coldness of her reaction surprised me.

Returning to hang up my coat in the hallway, I dropped the document case on the table. When I turned around, I found Jenny standing behind me, leaning against the kitchen doorpost.

The look said it all. I was in the shit.

Chapter 47

I gave Jenny a warm smile – big mistake. It acted like a red rag to a bull.

'You've been out with Kevin Jones, haven't you?' she said.

There was no point in denying it, so I decided to be honest and cough up the reason why we had been to see Gayle Bridges. I explained about the gun, but left out the part about the documents, which at the time were sitting on the hallway table.

Not surprisingly, Jenny was livid. She was no fool. She knew that the Met's willingness to overlook the events of the past few months would only go so far. If we were caught with Bob Bridges' trophy weapon then we would be for the high jump, no question. Then what would I have been left with? she argued. The dole queue? Or driving a taxi, maybe?

My explanations fell on deaf ears. Concepts of loyalty, brotherhood and debt all paled into insignificance when they came between Jenny and her family's future.

What with Nina having lectured me that morning, it was the second time in one day I'd had to swallow being told how stupid I was. I didn't dare mention to Jenny that I had spent part of the morning chasing down a gunman, having him point a pistol at me and then recognising him from the wedding we had just been to. I figured there was only so much openness our marriage could take at any one time.

Luckily, I managed to smuggle Bridges' documents into a briefcase before they were spotted. I had little doubt that the papers were from some kind of terrorist training camp and probably referred to target ideas, guidance to operations, that kind of thing. They would be interesting but were unlikely to be anything that the Security Services hadn't seen before. Even so, I certainly didn't want Jenny seeing them.

After checking in on Becky and kissing her goodnight, I returned to the main bedroom to find Jenny already in our bed. Her orders were clear. Hold her tight and promise to never again do anything that would put us all at risk.

I took a deep breath and made the promise. I just hoped that fate would let me keep it.

Chapter 48

The next morning, Kevin and I were on the road to Credenhill Barracks, Hereford – the new camp of the SAS Regiment. I'd left home early, and with a change to my normal route. This time, I headed north rather than into the city centre. I called the office as soon as I arrived at Cockfosters, and discovered that both Nina and our Superintendent were away doing other things.

Matt Miller suggested I took the day off. I agreed it might be easier. 'People will start talking about you two,' he laughed. 'But make sure you get to Hampstead tomorrow, the Murder Squad want to talk to both of you.'

Kevin had made a break-of-dawn phone call to Tom Cochran, the Armoury Quartermaster Sergeant and explained our need. At first, Cochran had suggested we keep the weapon, but Kevin was persistent and his logic was clear. There was no way he could retain the pistol without knowing its history. If it turned out to be stolen and one of us was caught with it, end of. Nobody would ever believe us.

After a break from the Regiment of many years, it was the third time in as many months that Kevin had passed through the Ministry of Defence Police cordon on the gates of Credenhill. For me, it was all new. As with entry to Scotland Yard, the security checks at the gate were much longer and more involved than I had been used to. We handed over our warrant cards and then waited for a few minutes whilst one of the lads from 'Goon' troop – the men who had just missed out on selection and who were considered good enough to do some continuation training before having another crack – jogged across from the main office to escort us.

As we arrived at the armoury, a familiar voice screamed at the goon for the delay in attending to such important visitors and then dismissed him with a wave of the hand. Tom Cochran was standing behind the armoury counter. A corporal when I had last seen him, he was now the QMS, the Quartermaster Staff Sergeant.

'Sorry 'bout that, gents,' Cochran continued as he pulled three large steel mugs from a cupboard behind where he stood. 'Since those fundamentalist prats decided that New York needed a facelift, we've been weighed down with more checks than you'd believe. CO says all visitors on base have to be escorted, no exception.'

'Not a problem, Tom,' Kevin replied. 'Just glad they didn't check my bag.' He lifted a small backpack onto the counter.

'I told them not to. Last thing we want is some Redcaps getting involved.' Cochran winked at me as he handed Kevin one of the mugs, the tea splashing onto the counter. 'Alright, boss?' he nodded as he took Kevin's bag, removed the Browning, and cleared the chamber with practised ease.

I tipped my head in acknowledgment.

'Magazines?' he asked.

'Two,' said Kevin. 'Both in the bag. Quite a few spare rounds in there as well.'

'Where did you get it? Looks clean; a sleeper. Hardly used, I'd guess.'

A sleeper was a weapon that had seen little use, either for training or in live-fire. Kevin explained that it belonged to an ex-forces lad who now wanted rid of it.

'Want to tell me who?' Cochran asked.

'Can't say. Sorry bud,' said Kevin.

'No worries mate. Heard you two been having some problems and that you got yourself shot, Taff.'

'Word spreads quickly, Tom,' I said.

'Aye, it does that. So … Bob the Builder. To what do we owe this pleasure?'

I smiled at the use of my old nickname. 'Just along for the ride,' I answered. 'And I wanted to have a look at the new camp.'

'Seen one, you seen 'em all, boss. And what about you, Taff? How's the wound healing?'

Kevin swung his arm upwards to show the free movement. 'Not too bad. I was lucky. Bit of nerve damage and stiffness but I'll be OK.'

Cochran slipped on a pair of spectacles and then wrote down the serial number of the Browning on a post-it note. 'Good for you. Nice to see you two took care of business for the murdered lads. Now, give me a few minutes. I can't check the computer to see if the gun is hot in case someone comes along later and notices, but I can have a run through the paper list. Won't take me too long.'

We waited as Cochran walked through into a back room and started flicking through a large file of documents. Sipping the piping hot tea, I peered through the window. In the distance I could see what looked like the new killing house and one of the ranges. There was an exercise in progress. It looked like the DS, the directing staff, were debriefing a team. Four men in black were sat on the deck and from the body language of the DS it looked like they were getting their arses chewed. Nothing changed, I mused.

Cochran emerged with a triumphant look on his face. 'Found it. Lost in 1983 during overseas operations. Reported by Sergeant Robert Bridges. His missus phoned in yesterday, said she needed your number. No prizes for guessing that she found it amongst his kit, eh? No ... don't bother to answer that question; at least we know it's not hot. I'll get it melted down and nobody will be any the wiser.'

Kevin expressed our thanks as Cochran stripped the weapon into its component parts and then threw them into a steel container behind the armoury counter. 'I'll give the rounds to the goons, they can use them up on the range. Fancy a wee dram?'

Cochran reached into the lower drawer of a desk that faced the opposite wall. When his hand emerged it was holding a half bottle of whisky. It was early in the day but, before we could refuse, the top was off and a large slug had been poured into each of our tea mugs.

'You see the BBC interview with Beaky Collins over the weekend?' Kevin asked.

Cochran lifted a levered section of the counter. 'Come in and have a seat ... you could make a squadron out of the number of blokes that wanted to out Beaky over that book. Fuckin' *Cyclone*. I'll give him *Cyclone*. There are some good blokes that have been trying to make a few quid out of their memoirs, real blades, not some fuckin' Walter Mitty like Beaky.' There was venom in his words.

'We heard he laid out a cameraman.' I said.

'We all saw it. The mess was packed. Beaky was sunk. Wanker even tried to pretend that he was just a stand-in for the real author. He always did have a temper did Beaky ... Terry knew it wouldn't be hard to wind him up.'

'I read the book. It wasn't bad, if he'd stuck to the truth he might have done well with it.'

'He might yet,' Cochran laughed. 'Since all the fuss over it, I heard it's been selling like hot cakes.'

'Did Terry find out if any of it was real?' asked Kevin.

I glared across at him, willing him to drop what I thought was a fairly pointless subject. But Kevin was like a terrier with a bone, he wanted more.

'Oh, it was real, alright. It's just that Beaky was nae there. Most of the stories in the book were pure fantasy. Beaky bought a few beers, learned a few tales and then passed them off as his own. But most of the stuff the blokes fed him was complete bollocks.'

'Was he ever out in Afghan at all?'

'Yeah, well OK, he was there a bit, I guess. In the book he talks about getting recruited to do a recce for the spooks. That's all dead gen'. He worked the mule trains in and out of Peshawar Valley. That's where he met some of our blokes who were doing Increment for MI6. I'm surprised you two never saw him at the base in Pakistan. He was there a few times.'

'The lads exposed him ... told Terry, I s'pose?'

Cochran paused. 'No, Terry worked it out himself. We don't have any contact with any of the blokes that went on Increment. There were only about a dozen of them, anyway. Two of them were the Met lads that got killed a few weeks ago.'

'You mean Bridges and Skinner?' The surprise in Kevin's voice echoed my own feelings. Having just learned that Bob Bridges was on the covert operations in Afghan, it was a disturbing coincidence to hear that Skinner was connected with the op too.

A doubt, recently healed, started to reappear. I second-guessed Kevin's follow-up question. 'Do you recall any others that went to Increment?' he asked.

'Like who?'

'Mac Blackwood for one.'

'Yeah, he was there.'

My stomach felt hollow. I'd had no idea there was a connection between the dead lads that we'd never considered.

Cochran continued. 'There were a couple of others from 'A' squadron as well. "Teacup" and "Treacle", we called them. "Teacup" – his name was McNeil, I think. You could ask at the weekend if you're interested. You're coming to the wedding, I presume?'

'What wedding?' I asked.

'Billy, the Fijian. He's marrying a girl from the town. Party Saturday night, church do the next day.' He turned to face Kevin. 'You turning up would be a great surprise for him, Taff.'

'OK,' he replied. 'Count me in. Can you sort me a bed on the base?'

'Nae worries, but sorry Mr Finlay, no Ruperts invited.'

I didn't reply, but I wasn't surprised.

'Why the questions about the Increment lads anyway?' Cochran continued.

'Nothing, really. Just something that Bob Bridges' wife asked us to check out,' said Kevin.

'Something interesting ... or something valuable?' Cochrane looked us both in the eye as he asked.

'I don't follow.'

'You should,' Cochran answered. 'There were stories that those lads brought back something very valuable from Afghan; something they planned to sell when the time was right. It's said that a man with the right contacts could make a lot of money from it.'

'What ... gold or something?' Kevin asked.

'Nobody knows; like I said, there were just stories. Maybe it was treasure or an artefact ... or some kind of weapon. Who knows? But if you're onto something, I know where to find a buyer.'

✠

As we headed home, I had cause to think deeply. Confirmation that Mac Blackwood was in Afghan was enough to drive a cold shaft through my heart. The causal factors we had been searching for before Monaghan was killed had apparently been answered when rumours of the affairs with the CO's wife had surfaced. But that hadn't answered the question over Rod Skinner's murder. Rod had the kind of face that only a mother could love and was the least likely of blokes to have chased married women. I had accepted the affair theory as gospel, particularly when the attacks stopped after Monaghan's death. Now, though, Cochran had cast doubt upon that assumption. And Increment had just thrown another factor into the puzzle.

Chapter 49

MI5 offices, New Scotland Yard

Toni was falling behind and a prolonged telephone conversation with Finlay's wife hadn't helped. Jenny had called for a chat, something she was perfectly entitled to do and which, as her liaison officer, Toni had encouraged. And, in routine circumstances, she would have been happy to oblige, but these weren't normal times.

Toni had listened with limited interest as Jenny reported her husband having had a number of recent conversations with Kevin Jones. She'd confronted him about it the previous evening and Finlay had, apparently, reassured her that nothing out of the ordinary was going on. But Jenny wasn't convinced; she thought the two men were up to something. Toni did her best to sound sympathetic, assuring her that it was most likely nothing to worry about.

There was some good news as well. Robert Finlay's sleep problems seemed to have eased. He had returned from the dive trip happier and more relaxed. However, Jenny was still struggling to come to terms with the fact that her husband had secrets and had expressed her fear she and Robert might drift apart. Toni reminded her that the police counsellor had warned that Robert's behaviour might sometimes appear odd and that she needed to give him time.

'Odd is right,' said Jenny. 'While we were in Romania, I saw some handcuffs and heel marks in one of the Cristea cars. I pointed them out to Robert, but he didn't seemed to have noticed them. He still seems pre-occupied, in a world of his own. Sometimes I speak to him and he doesn't even hear me.'

But then, perhaps in an attempt to demonstrate the conflicting sides to her husband, she described an incident at the wedding in which he had disarmed a gunman, showing, quite clearly, he could think and act clearly in a crisis.

'He seems to have a bit of an Achilles heel when it comes to recognising danger,' Toni had suggested, all the time thinking that her faith in Robert Finlay to handle problems had been endorsed.

With Jenny wanting to continue to chat about her husband, Toni needed to be patient as she tried to move the conversation on to the trip – the Cristeas and what Jenny had seen and heard.

She managed to learn that Jenny *had* met Collins and that he was planning to stay with Cristea Publishing if they could agree a deal. But, otherwise, there was very little about Collins himself. The conversation ended with some news. Jenny had been house hunting ... and she had found somewhere. At least this part of her current workload was going well, Toni thought.

For the remainder of the morning, Toni knuckled down to work, only pausing to refresh her coffee mug. Then, just at the point where it looked like she had caught up with things, Nell remembered she'd promised to deliver a message. Finlay had called. He'd apparently had a run-in with one of the Cristea men near the scene of a murder and had recognised the man from the wedding.

'He was asking why he hadn't been warned about the Cristeas,' Nell said, in a pointed tone. 'He wants to talk to you … and he sounded angry.'

Chapter 50

It was getting late. The list Dave Batey had asked Toni to compile was taking a long time to finish. The daily duty state helped to jog her memory, as did her diary, but there were several gaps. Lapses in memory might be perfectly acceptable in routine circumstances, but in this case, Batey would be expecting a complete record, no exceptions … no gaps.

She had set Nell to work on the Cristeas, wanting to know more about them before she returned Finlay's call. It wasn't long before her researcher had dug up enough to make it perfectly clear that Finlay should never have been allowed to travel to the wedding. The new material also explained what Jenny had said about handcuffs and heel marks in the Cristea car.

That had resulted in an awkward phone call. But the policeman had taken her apology surprisingly well and, in what had turned out to be a much easier conversation than she expected, she ended up increasingly angry at herself. She'd let her enthusiasm cloud her judgement and, in her ambition to secure a departmental coup by locating Chas Collins, she'd made a careless mistake. She thanked God that nothing worse had resulted.

Her offer to have Nell research information on the Cristeas that only the Security Service might have access to was well received; and she accepted that, in the circumstances, it was the least she could do. Finlay even thanked her, and a potential row was averted.

Another idea Nell was working on was one from Stuart – a rather crazy notion that Monaghan might have faked his own death. It seemed a bit far-fetched, but, to keep her assistants quiet, Toni had requested a hurry-up on the DNA tests for the body found in Monaghan's bombed-out car in order to cross-match them with some hair samples Stuart had found in the former officer's flat.

Recalling the Director's wish to be kept informed, she typed a brief synopsis of developments into an email. She decided to include the notion of Monaghan having staged his own death and the steps she was taking to check the idea. It was a fanciful hypothesis, but it was the kind of thing the Director had specifically asked to know about.

Finally, at a little before midnight, she reached the point of a final run-through of her diary report to Dave Batey. She was just about to sign her report when a sudden, horrible thought crossed her mind. There was just one time – one fleeting moment – when her pass had been out of her sight.

It wasn't something that she dare put in writing.

For several moments she sat mulling over the idea that had occurred to her. Right or wrong, the implications were considerable. It might even be better to forget about it. But the more she thought, the more feasible the notion became.

Hands shaking, she flicked through the department directory for Dave Batey's home number. But as she picked up the telephone to dial, her innate caution stopped her. It was quite possible that her department telephone was being monitored. She replaced the receiver and went to find an empty office.

It wasn't difficult. Within a few minutes, she found an unlocked door to a secretary's office, and a safe telephone. Checking the corridor was clear, she dialled Batey's number. For several moments there was no answer. As she waited, her heart began to accelerate.

Where was he, she wondered? Perhaps he wasn't at home?

She was just about to give up when the call connected.

Chapter 51

Murder squad office, Hampstead Police Station

DCI James Bowler was just finishing a summary of the interim forensic report when Nina pushed open the door to the squad office. A projector was displaying an enlarged picture of the bloody scene that we had walked in on at Relia's flat.

The room fell silent. As all eyes turned towards the door, Nina introduced the two of us. One or two nodded their heads in greeting, most simply turned back to face the DCI.

Bowler beckoned Nina to join him in front of the assembled AMIT – the Area Major Investigation Team. 'Perfect timing,' he said. 'You know more about our victim and the trafficking world than any of us.'

For the next ten minutes Nina summarised what she knew of Relia, the circumstances of her being in a police-provided flat and what had happened when we had turned up to show her some mugshots. None of the detectives present had any previous experience of the sex-trafficking trade and even fewer had any grasp as to the scale.

Considering the fact that she was caught on the hop, I thought Nina did a pretty good job. A lot of questions were asked and it was clear that some were critical of the poor level of protection that had been given to Relia. As a victim of trafficking and a key witness to a hugely lucrative criminal activity, most present expressed the opinion that Relia ought to have been looked after – moved further away from the Euston brothel where she was found.

Without being defensive, Nina explained that the witness protection programme had declined to fund a re-location, so the Hampstead flat had been a compromise. She had worked out a schedule of regular visits with Relia and given her specific instructions about leaving the flat, and making contact with friends, either from her home country or in London.

As the organisation charged with protecting Relia, we all felt some guilt. As DCI Bowler continued with his briefing he made it quite clear that he wanted us to find out if Relia had been out and about – where she had gone and at what times.

As the meeting ended, Bowler called me and Nina into his office. The small room smelt of percolated coffee. Documents littered a bulky desk and on the rear wall, there was a large white board with what looked like a flattened spider drawn on it. Bowler noticed me staring at it.

'It's a mind map. It's not much at the moment but, believe me, it will soon be filled as you guys start the information flow.'

As I sat down next to Nina, still puzzling at the spider drawing, Bowler's tone quickly changed. 'Right, first things first: where were you two yesterday?'

Nina answered before I had time to think. 'I was sick, finding Relia like that affected me more than I expected. DI Finlay was with MI5 all day due to his recent problems. I assume you've been apprised of them?'

The DCI snorted. 'Yes … we're well aware. And, as I'm sure you both know, the first twenty-four hours in a murder enquiry can be crucial. So far, we've got nowhere. I've not long come off the phone with your Superintendent. He's OK'd it that, for the next few days, at least, you will be on AMIT with me. Nina, I'm going to ask you to work here with the Office Manager and I will need a statement from you, usual stuff from the scene but also cover everything you know about Relia Stanga – her history, where she hails from, how we came across her … anything really.'

Nina nodded. 'I'll get on it straight away. But I think we should be visiting the brothel where she was picked up.'

'Already on it. And later on I want you to tell me more about this Cristea syndicate,' said Bowler. He turned to me.

'Bob, no disrespect, but in view of your lack of CID experience I've partnered you with DC Bonner on one of the investigation teams. He's a good lad, you'll like him – bright spark with a great sense of humour. I've asked him to wait for you in the canteen. He'll show you the ropes, how to use HOLMES, that kind of thing.'

'HOLMES?' I asked, doing my best not to look too puzzled.

'Our computer system. We've just switched to the new version – HOLMES TWO. It makes sure that people like me can process the tons of information that people like you will be bringing in so that we don't overlook any clues.'

Nina and I left our new boss making telephone calls. The main enquiry room was already buzzing with activity. In some ways it resembled a small call centre, with operators busy on telephones in front of computer screens. All those present, however, were focussed on one task: finding Relia's killers.

'Thanks for covering for me,' I said to Nina quietly as we entered the main enquiry office.

'No problem. Do the same for me one day.'

Before heading off to the canteen, Nina introduced me to another Detective Sergeant, Naomi Young, who had been appointed as the Office Manager. Determined to strike while the iron was hot, the two of them patiently attempted to explain to me how HOLMES worked. But, almost instantly, my eyes began to glaze over and the detective saw it.

'Bit technical?'

'Yes ... computers really aren't my thing. I've only just discovered the internet.'

'OK ... sorry. I'll keep it simple.' Naomi turned to her desk, tapped a few keys on the keyboard and indicated a complex looking screen that appeared on the visual display unit.

'This is HOLMES TWO. Stands for Home Office Large and Major Enquiry System. HOLMES ONE was OK but it couldn't link between different police forces or even between different enquiries. The updated version can, so if, for example, we have a serial killer operating in Yorkshire, Devon and the Met, we ought to be able to see the common factors.'

'Sounds good,' I replied.

'Oh, it is good. But it's only as good as you guys on the ground. The better the information you give us to put into it, the more valuable the data it can produce. Conversely, shit data produces shit intelligence, so to speak.'

'I think I get the idea.'

'My best advice to you is not to think like a layman. For example, something that may seem to be a simple coincidence could actually be a thread of information. Weave a few threads together and they start to form a picture. Our job, as detectives, is to recognise those threads and to create that picture. HOLMES helps us do that.'

'Does it actually solve cases?' I asked.

Naomi chuckled. 'Not exactly. Think of a crime as being like a mirror that's been smashed into fragments and all those parts have been spread to the four winds. HOLMES helps us piece things together so the image is revealed. It might not tell us the whole story but it can fill in detail – timings, where people say they were, comparing one person's statement against another, that kind of thing.'

'But more complicated?'

'Of course. And often we don't need the whole mirror image to be able to solve the crime. Most of all, HOLMES helps if we're struggling with the biggie, what is arguably the single most important clue in any investigation.'

'Which is?'

'The motive.' She patted the top of her screen as if it were a favourite pet. 'Find *why* someone was murdered and you're halfway to finding *who*. But remember, although it's a good system, it will never replace a copper's gut instinct. So ... if you simply follow what the computer says, you might catch villains, but you'll do nothing that coppers haven't been doing for years using their brains.'

I smiled. Despite being a techie, our Office Manager was still a detective.

My introduction to the electronic side to a major investigation over, Nina led the way to the station canteen. As soon as we were alone in the corridor, I asked her a question that had been nagging at me all morning. Did she think her plan had worked?

'I think so,' she replied, somewhat nonchalantly.

'You *think* so?'

'OK ... I'm pretty sure. The DCI has the Cristeas on his radar. It was my idea that he employ you on the enquiry team and put you on door-to-door.'

'Teaching me the ropes?'

'Something like that. Just remember: you're an eye witness to a suspect. You remember what Naomi said?'

'Which bit?' I asked.

'About coincidence being a clue. You chasing down that gunman and finding he was the same bloke you met in Romania was what Naomi referred to as a layman's coincidence. To a detective, it's a line of enquiry ... and it will help with building up a picture of what exactly happened to Relia and why. It was chance that you clocked him, pure luck, maybe ... but you *made* that luck by being determined to check for the killer's escape route.'

'So why put me out knocking on doors?'

'Because you know exactly who we're looking for, Finlay. If you see him or his friends, or any clue as to their whereabouts, then you are going to recognise it when others might miss it. They were here, in this very area, on these very streets and people saw them. Those are the same people that you are going to be talking to ... and one of them might hold the clue we need to put a name to the face you recognised.'

'Sounds good. So ... what am I going to do about my other problem?'

'Toni Fellowes, you mean?'

'Yes. I called her and she apologised. But I'm not entirely sure she took it on board.'

Nina leaned toward me, her left hand moving to gently adjust the lapel of my jacket. 'You leave her to me.'

✝

A few moments later, we located Josh Bonner, my working partner for the day. He was in the canteen, sat with his back to the door, talking to two of the other members of the team. The group were just finishing chatting as I walked up. Nina left us to get acquainted.

Josh stood up, his chair dragging noisily on the linoleum floor. As

I reached out a hand in greeting, the two other detectives stood. For a moment, it seemed they were also about to extend a welcome. Then, without uttering a word, they both turned and strode quickly to the door.

'Something I said?' I asked my new companion, as soon as we were alone.

'Bit awkward guv,' Josh replied, as we sat down. He took a deep breath.

I sensed what was coming.

'You see ... we know about you. It's gone round the job like wildfire. It's not every day the IRA start targeting coppers, and everyone knows they earmarked you for some special attention.'

I thought carefully before replying, recalling how the assembled detectives had fallen silent as Nina and I entered the briefing room. I had considered it a fairly normal response to the arrival of strangers. Now, what Josh was saying cast the reaction in a new light. 'So, are they OK with me being around?' I asked.

'Most of them don't give a toss, but a few – like those two – think you might ... well ... be a bit of a bullet magnet.'

I sighed. It seemed that, for a while, this was a situation that was going to follow me wherever I went in the police. Until people started to forget about what had happened, I would have the shadow of it hanging over me.

'Listen Josh,' I scowled. 'It wasn't the IRA; just some idiots with a grievance. The combined efforts of SO19 and the Anti-Terrorist Squad managed to take care of them. I'm just trying to get on with my life.'

'Sounds like a helluva story. Any truth in the rumour that you were SAS?'

I took a deep breath. 'Yes ... a very long time ago. You were probably still wearing shorts.'

'Guess so ... sorry. Just that you guys are heroes of mine. That's why I agreed to be posted with you when we were all asked.'

'You were all asked?'

'Yeah, everyone knows, DCI included. You can't keep things secret for long in this job. We were all given a choice about working with you.'

'OK, Josh.' I stood up, realising that I needed to get out in the fresh air before I lost my temper. 'It's time you started teaching me how to be a detective.'

Chapter 52

Wearing out shoe leather is a basic necessity of being a detective.

Josh Bonner and I we were tasked with visiting shops on the east side of the main Hampstead High Street and showing Relia's photo to anyone we met. There were dozens of potential sources of information: boutiques, mini-markets and several estate agents stood side by side with solicitors, banks and even an internet café. They all had to be visited, and all the occupants interviewed.

We were expected. Word had spread of the murder and I was relieved to discover that, in the main, people were more than helpful. It differed from times when, as a PC, I had been drafted onto similar squads to do the legwork. There were all too many areas in London where cooperation was not at all guaranteed. Hampstead was an exception, rather than the rule.

Many people were curious. They wanted to know who Relia was, where the murder had occurred and what had happened. Josh did most of the talking but kept it brief. The DCI had given instructions that any shops with Eastern European employees were to be noted, especially if they shared the language of Relia's home country, Romania. He was of the opinion that Relia may well have given away her location to the traffickers by talking in her native tongue to somebody local. It was a reasonable starting point in our effort to establish a trail to the killers.

Every location we visited was logged, each person present was spoken to and their details recorded. Everyone absent was listed for a follow-up visit. The HOLMES demand for data input was thorough and colossal.

Before long, we were becoming hungry, so Josh suggested a diversion to the nearest petrol station. It had a small sandwich shop and was on the list for us to check, so we were killing two birds with one stone.

The pay desk at the petrol station was manned by a single, not very helpful, Asian lad. Fortunately, his mother was sitting in the office at the rear and she proved to be the antithesis of her son. Neither of them recognised Relia from the rather worn photograph. But they did have a CCTV system and they were willing to allow us to sit and watch it from the comfort of the back office.

The CCTV was modern, using a digital recording system that stored several weeks' worth of images. The owners of the petrol station used it to deter shoplifting and to record the registration numbers of the cars when the drivers made off without paying. As we sat watching the screen, paper cups of tea and packs of sandwiches to hand, I asked about Eastern European customers, on the off chance they might remember something.

As Josh had told me, 'The more questions you ask, the luckier you get.' And we were in luck: what the lady owner remembered was vital.

She recalled two foreign men, the previous Sunday evening, asking for directions to Redhill Flats after buying petrol. It had stuck in her memory because her sister also lived in the block. The men had paid cash, using a crisp, new fifty-pound note. It was still in the safe. The owner knew it was the same one as they rarely saw them. Most people paid by card and traders generally avoided large notes, for fear they could be counterfeit.

Josh immediately asked to review the CCTV for the Sunday evening. With the review set to double speed, we focussed on the counter camera, looking for the moment that the two foreigners would appear.

As the clock reached 8.22 pm on the CCTV recording, I leapt up and stopped the player. If I hadn't seen it with my own eyes I would not have believed it.

There, on the small screen before me, was the gunman from the Cristea wedding. The same man who escaped from me and Nina two days previously. Also on the monitor, just behind the gunman, stood a well-built and very familiar figure.

It was Petre, Marica's bodyguard.

Chapter 53

As Toni entered through the security door, it was immediately clear Nell was finding it hard to contain herself. The speed at which her researcher typed seemed to reflect her mood. Angry or excited, her fingers were a blur of activity.

Nell pointed at the PC screen. 'Read,' she said.

'What's so urgent, Nell?' Toni replied as she dropped her handbag and pre-packed sandwich on the desk and pulled up a chair.

'I did what you asked. You'll need to follow my report to understand it fully, but I established an unlikely connection between the author you were looking for and the Operation Hastings murders.'

'Seriously? What kind of connection?'

'Just read.'

On the face of it, Toni had given her assistant two completely unconnected lines of enquiry: Operation Hastings and Cristea Publishing. Hastings to tie up loose-ends, and Cristea to try and help Finlay. As Nell had continued to dig, the more she had looked, the more she had found. As they sat together reading through Nell's report, Toni learned why her researcher was so excited.

MI6 files from the 70s and 80s had only recently been transferred into digital form but Nell reported the job had been completed conscientiously. Toni had no doubt that some poorly paid clerk had been given the rather tedious scanning task, spending many hours going through hundreds of handwritten and typed reports, in case, one day, someone should need to see the information they contained. On this particular day, Toni was that someone.

Nell's report was detailed and comprehensive. It began by describing how the Cristeas were originally a farming family who had grown in stature since the mid-80s, when the senior member of the family, Gheorghe Cristea, had expanded his honey production business. Using established trade routes through Afghanistan and Pakistan, Gheorghe had started importing opium. He had first come to the notice of MI6 in 1983, when information had reached the ears of the FIA, the Federal Investigation Agency at Islamabad in Pakistan. The Cristeas then used those same routes to transport arms to Ahmad Shah Massoud, a military leader from the Panjshir valley in northern Afghanistan. An MI6 PF had been created for Gheorghe Cristea.

'Cristea has a personal file?' she enquired.

'You'd better believe it,' said Nell.

Toni read on. The family had continued to expand their interests. Honey routes became regular opium trails, which also started to see the movement of precious stones, such as emeralds and lapis lazuli, which were mined and exported through northern Afghanistan. These were then exchanged for what were becoming the most valuable and sought after commodities in the area: weapons and armaments.

With burgeoning income streams, the Cristea empire grew. However, when the demand for weapons diminished, a switch had been made to what was fast becoming a highly lucrative trade. The trafficking of sex workers. The Cristeas had even been mentioned in a United Nations report on links between UN-appointed contractors and the organised slave trade. In 1996, Anton Cristea, the eldest son of Gheorghe, had been killed in a shoot-out with local police in Georgia. Anton had been transporting women who had been abducted and were destined for the sex-slave trade.

Toni stopped reading. 'Sex trafficking? You're telling me Cristea Publishing is a front for drugs and people trafficking?'

'Hard to believe, isn't it?'

'This is really interesting, Nell. But what does it have to do with Chas Collins or Finlay and the Hastings report?'

'There's more, trust me. It's what was *missing* from the FIA reports that gives it away.'

As Toni read on, she began to get the picture. Nell's eye for detail was incredible, particularly when it came to documents and reports. She assimilated information at a phenomenal rate and her memory never failed to amaze. These skills meant Nell had noticed one report was absent from the 1983 weekly FIA reports from Pakistan.

'There's a lot to read, Nell. Couldn't you just summarise it for me?'

Nell sat back in her chair. 'OK, but it's all in there.'

'Pretty please?' said Toni.

'Alright, it's like this. Did you see I mentioned a man called Ahmad Shah Massoud?'

'Yes … the Mujahideen leader?'

'Exactly. Until his death, Massoud was the Cristea contact in Afghan. He ran the heroin trails … and he also ran weapons. The FIA reports on Massoud being supplied with American-manufactured weapons to use in the fight against the Russians would normally have been a distraction and outside my research brief. What spurred my curiosity was the coincidence that Massoud had been assassinated just before the 9/11 attacks.'

'You think it was connected?'

'Maybe, maybe not. Anyway, that led me down a route that I thought was a blind alley, but I did notice that it happened on the same day as the Chas Collins' book came out and, well, you always say not to believe in coincidence.'

'You're learning. Go on.'

'OK, so the Cristea link led me to the FIA reports. The FIA gave a name to the CIA operation in Afghanistan. It was called 'Operation Cyclone'. You know? The same name as the book?'

'I thought you knew that's where he got the name from, Nell?'

Nell stopped for a moment, a puzzled look on her face. 'If I'd known, I would have said so.'

'OK, no matter. So what's the relevance?'

'Cyclone was mentioned in one of the career histories of the SAS soldiers that you asked me to look at: the one called Bridges. Cyclone is the connection.'

'I don't get you. Why ... I mean *how* does the name of one operation that Bridges was on establish a serious connection?'

'Through Massoud!'

'Who is the man that was assassinated the day before 9/11, I know. On the same day the Cyclone book came out?'

'That's it. That's the connection.'

'I still don't understand. How does that link the Cristeas to the Hastings enquiry? What else do you have on Massoud? I need a bit more than a reference to Cyclone on the Bridges file to have us start a whole new line of enquiry into his past.'

Nell sighed. Ahmad Shah Massoud, she said, was a fascinating character. He was a Sunni Muslim, also from the Panjshir valley in northern Afghanistan, where the Cristeas had established their connections. The son of an Afghan army officer, he had studied engineering and obtained a degree at Kabul University. When the Russians invaded to support the weak communist government, Massoud joined the resistance in the mountains.

It was easy to see how Massoud had hooked up with the Cristeas. They had an established import/export route through the mountains of Pakistan and Iran into Eastern Europe. Massoud needed weapons and had access to opium and precious stones. The Cristeas provided the connections.

Having satisfied her interest in Massoud, Nell explained, she had been about to switch back to the Operation Hastings enquiry when, out of idle curiosity she had typed Massoud's name into the video website YouTube. Several links came up. Most were entirely in Arabic but in one – an interview with an Irish journalist – he spoke in English.

Nell had watched it. During the ten-minute clip, Massoud was asked his opinion on several subjects, including his frustration at not receiving help from the CIA during the fight against the Soviets. Massoud was effusive in his condemnation of the CIA operation and how it had favoured what he referred to as 'bad people' who would one day use the American weapons against the very people who had supplied them. He talked about Al Q'aeda and the rumours of Afghan-based training camps.

'Should we watch this video you mention?' Toni asked.

'Already lined up. It's an oldie, but I think you'll find it interesting.' Nell rotated the nearest computer screen and pressed a key.'

It was as Nell had described. Toni was surprised at the standard of Massoud's English. His accent was strong, but he was easy to understand. She picked up on one expression that she hadn't heard before. Massoud used it several times. He referred to something called 'Al Anfal'. She made a note to google it.

It was, however, a single word that he used towards the end of the interview that caused Toni to sit upright. He referred to the CIA operation, and he called it 'Cyclone'. He knew the name, even back then.

She checked the video listing. It had been uploaded before Massoud's death but looked to have been recorded many years previously. Just as the recording was drawing to a close, Nell leaned across the desk and tapped the pause key.

'Look at the men in the background.'

Toni did as asked and, within a few seconds, spotted the very thing that had caused Nell to become so animated.

In the background, clear as day, was former SAS Sergeant, Bob Bridges.

'That's amazing,' said Toni.

'And it's not the best bit.' Nell held her hand over the open page of her report, her index finger indicating a particular section of text.

Toni pulled the file closer to get a better look and, as she did so, the true cause of her researcher's excitement became very, very clear. The Personal File in the name of the Cristeas had been created by none other than Howard Green.

Chapter 54

Hampstead, North London

Rewinding the CCTV recording provided absolute confirmation that I was right.

On the station forecourt stood a black Mercedes, of the type that appeared so popular with the Cristeas. The registration mark was easily readable. As I read the number out loud, it dawned on me that I was off the hook. The car was the key to identifying Relia's killers.

Josh telephoned the office to report what we had learned.

After updating Naomi, things moved very quickly. Back at the enquiry room, the office team made calls. The Mercedes was a hire car. Within just half an hour of me telling the DCI that I had recognised the escaped gunman on the CCTV, detectives from Heathrow were seizing paperwork from the hire car company.

Before the hour had elapsed, Immigration Control at Heathrow Airport had come up with a list of four male East Europeans who had arrived as a group on the Sunday morning. They were Constantin Macovei, Iulian Roman and Marius Gabor from Romania and a Serbian, Petre Gavrić.

Iulian Roman and Marius Gabor had provided the Border Agency with an address in Ealing. It matched the one given to the hire car company. Plus, the desk clerk had taken copies of the men's passports.

At seven that evening, I was able to confirm, from a photograph, that the escaped gunman was Marius Gabor. The DCI even congratulated us. I began to feel like a proper detective and, best of all, Gabor was identified without my having to say how I knew him.

By seven-thirty, the address provided by Roman and Gabor was under surveillance by local CID. They were relieved by the Met Specialist Surveillance Team, SO11, at eight-thirty.

SO11 confirmed that the house was occupied.

SO19, firearms branch, sent their initial assessor onto the plot at ten.

By eleven o'clock, Josh and I were with DCI Bowler and six of the AMIT team, sitting in the rear of a dark-grey Luton van parked around the corner from the house.

By eleven-thirty, the SO19 arrest team were ready to go.

Chapter 55

In the rear of the SO19 Rapid Deployment Vehicle sat eight black-clad figures. One of them, much smaller than the others, was the first to emerge from the rear door of the vehicle.

Lynn Wainwright was a rarity in a male dominated world. One of only two female specialist firearms officers in the department, her job on this operation was to use a Remington semi-automatic shotgun loaded with Hatton rounds – made to destroy locks and hinges, but not harm anyone behind the door – thereby getting her team through any locked doors quickly.

A twelve-man SO19 team was to be used to secure the house quickly and ensure minimum risk to life. At the pre-deployment briefing, she and the others had learned that one of the AMIT detectives had previously seen a suspect with a semi-automatic pistol. As a result of that warning, it had been decided that SO19 would make the initial entry, secure the premises, and then hand over to the CID officers.

Surveillance officers had reported movement at the house. Lights had been turned on and off, and shadows had been seen in both upstairs and downstairs rooms. Initial estimate was that there were at least three occupants.

Two hours after arriving on the plot, the CID officer in charge had called a meeting. The firearms tactical advisor, an SO19 inspector, returned after about half an hour with the surveillance team report. They moved into attack positions fifteen minutes later.

The house was reported to now be in darkness. It was a standard

1930s three bedroom semi-detached. There was rear access via a car-width alleyway to a separate garage at the end of the garden. A gate on the left-hand side of the front door provided access to the rear. The back garden contained a skip that was full of earth and rubble. It would provide good cover for the team at the rear.

The briefing from the inspector had detailed expected room layouts with three downstairs, including the kitchen, and four upstairs including a bathroom.

Lynn was assigned to the initial entry team. She would work closely with Brad, the shield man, and Tony, who would open the front door with the 'big key'. Tony was a sixteen-stone weightlifting enthusiast who handled the 'Enforcer' battering-ram door-opener as if it were made of balsa wood.

As number three behind Brad and Tony, Lynn's Remington would open anything the Enforcer didn't. Her prowess with the weapon had resulted in her affectionately being known as 'Avon calling'. The nickname was the only hint of a joke that Lynn was ever subject to; she knew she had the respect of her colleagues.

At 01:15 hrs, under cover of darkness, they took up positions as briefed.

At 01:30 hrs, the inspector radioed that all officers were in place.

At 01:32 hrs, the 'GO' command came over the radio network.

Chapter 56

Tony had the front door down in an instant. It was UPVC and, despite having security bolts, offered little resistance to the Enforcer.

With the Remington surplus to requirements, Lynn tucked in behind Tony's ballistic shield as the remaining team members entered the hallway and dispersed to clear the rooms. The first four black-clad officers dived past her and Tony, moving towards the ground floor rooms. Five more then followed the two of them up the stairs to the bedrooms.

The house was secure within twenty-five seconds of the front door going in. It was also empty.

Immediately, the Inspector gave the command to check the garage and the understairs cupboard. Within a couple of minutes, Lynn heard the transmission that they had been cleared.

That left the attic.

Lynn knew the team Sergeant wouldn't relish that prospect. Attic entry had its own particular problems. Not only would any suspect have the high ground, they would also have the opportunity to place themselves anywhere within a three hundred and sixty-degree arc of fire. The officer entering might be backlit and the suspect hidden in the darkness.

The surveillance team had confirmed multiple occupants, so unless they had made some kind of unholy foul-up, there were several people up there.

Tony was called up to remove the ceiling hatch. Manoeuvring the ram above head height wasn't easy, but Tony was strong. One hard swing and the flimsy wooden door burst open and flew away into the dark loft space. Ron, the Sergeant, called upwards for those inside to come down. There was no response.

From her position in the hall, Lynn was vaguely aware of whispered voices at the top of the stairs. A few moments later, the Sergeant came down to speak to her.

'Hatch is too small for us lads. With kit on, we can't get into it quick enough. Sorry Avon, but I'm gonna have to ask you to do the entry.'

Lynn was horrified. For some, fear of the dark is culturally indoctrinated, for others, her included, it was instinctive. Darkness spelled danger.

Any lone cop, faced with unknown horrors in the dark, knows that he doesn't have the luxury of a computer-generated restart or an extra life. So Lynn was already starting to sweat as she trudged up the stairs to the landing. She wondered how the average member of the public would feel about poking their head into a dark and dusty attic expecting to be confronted by an armed and cornered criminal. Peering into the darkness to find herself lit up by a bright-orange flash was not what she signed up for.

But, as the smallest member of the team, there was no way she could turn down the request.

Ron handed Lynn an MP5 then outlined his plan. They would balance her on the ballistic shield, just below the hatch. Brad and Tony would stand by with a small aluminium ladder. All lights would be killed and then they would wait for a minute and listen. Ron would then throw two flash-bangs into the attic and exactly three seconds after the second grenade exploded, the two lads holding the shield would launch Lynn into the loft like a jack-in-a-box. Once inside, she should step to one side and use the Maglite on the MP5 she was now carrying to light up the east and south faces of the house.

Brad would be behind her in the loft space. Ron figured Brad would be slim enough to squeeze his upper body through the space so that he could cover the north and west aspects. It sounded a reasonable plan, if it wasn't for the darkness.

Two minutes later, Lynn was balanced and standing on the shield, her head just below the roof-space entrance. She closed her eyes to buy a little time and allow them to get used to the darkness. A moment later, all lights were killed and they waited.

Silence. Nothing stirred.

The grenades went in. Lynn closed her eyes and pressed her hands hard against the gas mask to shield her ears and minimise the percussion effect.

In an enclosed area like a roof space, stun grenades were at their most effective. Both exploded, almost simultaneously. Lynn waited, counting the seconds.

The flash-bangs were designed to emit a blinding light and a noise so loud that it caused temporary loss of hearing. They would give the incoming firearms team a momentary advantage over any waiting suspect.

Lynn was all too aware that the grenades also came at a cost, though. The element of surprise was lost as the defenders knew you were coming and the dust cloud that was thrown up in the attic obscured any view. She braced herself for launch.

A hand tapped her left shoulder and in an instant the shield lifted and she was thrown through the hatch into the darkness.

Lynn dived right, away from the opening. Switching the Maglite torch on, she scanned her designated sides of the roof space while moving down and to the left to get clear of the opening. The dust cloud was thick and almost impenetrable. The light picked up dirt particles, swirling and choking the air. To her right, someone coughed. She swung the MP5 towards the sound.

Ron's plan hadn't allowed for the dust disturbance, she realised. If someone fired at the source of the beam, she would be toast. There was more coughing, then a voice, female. The accent, foreign.

'Please … don't shoot. Don't shoot.'

She called out. 'Armed police. Step forward.'

There was a movement, just discernible through the dust cloud. To her left, there was scuffling. Brad was squeezing through the loft hatch.

There were no orange flashes from the darkness, no shots, no sudden pain or explosion of movement of the kind that she had prepared herself to face. Just a woman, in underwear, coughing and choking on the dust as she struggled across the joists that made up the attic floor.

'Hands out. Stand still,' she shouted, her voice muffled by the mask. The half-naked woman stood.

'Lie down, keep your hands in front of you where I can see you.' The woman hesitated.

'Lie down … *now!*'

Lynn kept the woman covered with the MP5 and Maglite beam as Brad squeezed through the hatch and then stepped forward to plasticuff her wrists behind her back. The dust was clearing. A third black-clad figure appeared from below. A voice crackled though her earpiece.

'Trojan five. Multiple movements from adjacent house.' The neighbours were awake.

Brad lowered the woman through the loft hatch. She was skinny and fitted through easily. There was a muffled voice from ahead of her.

The third firearms officer had found something.

Chapter 57

With the house secured, the DCI called us in to have a look around.

I was one of the last to enter. Josh volunteered to check though the downstairs rooms. The DCI winked at him as I was despatched up the stairs to take a look at what had happened in the loft area.

I was slightly surprised that the SFO team had chosen to use flash-bangs. At the Iranian Embassy siege, the heat generated by the grenades had been responsible for starting the fires that gutted the building. In the cramped space of the attic, any inflammable materials might have caused severe problems. That said, any operation that ends in success without loss of life is a good one. The debrief would be the time for questions.

An eagle-eyed member of the firearms team had spotted the reason for the apparent lack of people in the house. In the attic space, behind a cardboard box that had been pulled against the wall adjoining the next-door property, he had spotted a hole cut into the brickwork. Enough bricks had been removed to allow the occupants of the target house to escape and then pull the box behind them to conceal their route. The first woman found hadn't quite made it in time.

The firearms team had moved quickly to seal off both houses. With no further escape possible, they had entered the second house. In the upstairs rear bedroom they found the remaining occupants. Cowering in the dark, their faces pale and petrified, were seven more women. All were dressed as the first, in just underwear. There was no light bulb in the room and no heating in the house.

And there was no sign of the Romanian men we were looking for.

One of the women spoke enough English to explain that the room in which they were found was their living quarters. They had four single mattresses between them and no bed linen. The mattresses were old, stained and smelled of urine. They shared one toilet and a bath with a single tap that only produced cold water. All the other rooms were for entertaining clients.

According to the woman, the men who ran the brothel had fled about an hour before the raid. They had ordered the women to hide in the second house and keep quiet. If it hadn't been for one of the women being unable to get through the hole in the brick wall due to a back injury, they might not have been discovered.

The DCI made arrangements for the women to be looked after by local uniformed officers and two detectives from the divisional domestic violence unit were called in from home. They would arrange physical examinations, taking of statements and temporary accommodation. It was going to be a long night.

A large number of passports were found in an understairs cupboard. Some of them belonged to the girls who had been living at the house, but many more bore details of other women – as likely as not those working as sex slaves in similar houses elsewhere in the capital. The girls had one thing in common that we quickly picked up on: they were all from Eastern Europe.

It looked like the houses had, at one time, been converted for student accommodation. All the 'entertainment' rooms had a double bed, a sink and heavy curtains. There were no carpets. The lower rooms had large rugs in front of the fireplaces, which partly covered the floorboards and offered a small amount of comfort to the occupant. In some rooms there was a single, central ceiling light, but in most the power was turned off at the mains circuit board. The men in charge of the houses even controlled the electricity supply.

One room did have working power points; it was set up with a camera tripod and lights and was cleaner than the others. Beneath the bed and in cupboards the detective allocated to search the room found sex toys, condoms, outfits and sado-masochistic equipment. It didn't take a lot to work out what was filmed in this improvised studio.

I sent Nina a text; I knew she would want to be involved in interviewing the women. She was starting to build up a decent network of contacts and knowledgeable interpreters. It might well be that the women would know things that might help in identifying Relia's killers. Whether they would be willing to talk was another question. As Nina had explained when I first met her, in their home countries these women were used to a police force that either turned a blind eye to the slave trade or was actively involved in it. Persuading them to trust anyone in authority was nigh-on impossible.

For me and the other members of the AMIT team, our role at the houses ended at gone four in the morning when the forensic team arrived to undertake a more thorough search.

✢

It was six o'clock when I finally made it home.

The house was quiet.

I crept upstairs, sneaked a peek at Becky and then undressed in the spare room. As I crawled into our bed, Jenny was breathing gently. Beneath the duvet, the bed felt warm and welcoming.

She stirred, her arms reached out for me. As we pressed together she shivered briefly. I kissed her cheek.

'You're cold,' she said.

'And knackered,' I whispered.

'I missed you this morning. I had something to show you.'

'Something nice?'

'I think so. It's some estate agent blurb. There's a couple of nice ones.'

'Can I look at it in the morning?'

'It's already morning. I'm up soon to go and see mum, remember?'

I was vaguely aware of Jenny saying something more but it didn't sink in. Exhaustion got the better of me. I was quickly asleep.

Chapter 58

MI5 office, New Scotland Yard

Nell was in danger of turning their research into a race. Toni smiled as she saw the focussed way her researcher applied herself to her work. They both knew there was more to find, especially now that they suspected Howard Green to be a common factor.

The coincidence had set Toni thinking. On the train journey home the previous night, and even as she had settled down to sleep, it had dominated her thoughts. The meetings, the warning not to get involved, his interest in Robert Finlay; it all added up to something. It was just a question of what.

There was one other thing that kept her awake, one factor that she hadn't dared share with Nell. Her concern regarding the security pass and the one occasion it had been out of her control. Dave Batey had scoffed at the notion someone in MI6 may have been responsible. But now, if they found anything else to implicate Howard Green, the coincidences would be mounting up, even to the point of conspiracy.

On a flip chart, Nell was drawing up a list of facts. Nell didn't really like theories, they relied too much on imagination. She was happy to leave the creative thinking to Toni.

And the facts had started to stack up. Nell had already recorded that Robert Finlay and Kevin Jones had similar gaps in their army service records from late in 1980 through to 1984. Toni had looked through them in some detail. There were training reports, expense claims, a disciplinary matter and other small clues that put them both in the UK for a part of the time. But there was no information on overseas deployments. Either someone had removed it or it had never been recorded.

The Falklands conflict had taken place in early 1982. With so many Special Forces soldiers having been involved and quite a few being killed, Nell had queried why there was no mention of either Finlay or

Jones on any paperwork relating to SAS operations at the time. Where had they been, she asked?

Toni checked on the two policemen who had been killed in the recent London attacks: Bridges – who they now knew had been in Afghanistan; and Skinner. Both had left the Army in late 1980. Both had joined the police force several years later: 1984 in the case of Bridges, '85 for Skinner. No records for the interim period.

When Nell discovered files in the name of Iain Blackwood, a picture started to form. Blackwood had also left the army towards the end of 1980.

And there were two other soldiers who had left with Skinner and Bridges: Brian McNeil and Chris Grady. McNeil had been mentioned in reports as working as a security operator and was last heard of in Iraq. Grady had dropped off the radar.

So, Toni asked, as they broke off for a coffee and to review their progress, what had happened in the early 1980s to prompt five Special Forces soldiers to leave the army and then for all their records to show similar gaps? And why were there similar breaks in the service records for Finlay and Jones?

Nell mentioned the missing Federal Intelligence report from Pakistan, which had led her down a blind alley. It dealt with the rendition of a terrorist suspect from Pakistan by the CIA. There were no names on the report but the details of the flight, the departure point and the destination told Nell what it was.

Toni suggested they switch focus to men who had left the SAS at about the same time as the others – in the early 1980s. They found there were twelve of them. Hunched over the computer, Nell searched military records, salary payments, newspaper articles and all manner of sources in an attempt to trace any common link.

It was when Nell decided to check pension and life insurance records that her efforts bore fruit. In ten cases, the immediate dependants of the men who had left both the SAS and the army between April 1980 and February 1981 had claimed on life-insurance policies. All had paid out.

So, ten out of the twelve who left the SAS between 1980 and 1981 were dead. The only ones alive were Grady and McNeil. Nell wrote in red ink on the flip chart, underlining her words.

Toni started searching names but produced nothing of note. It was as if the men had disappeared off the face of the earth between 1981 and 1984. There weren't even any social security claims. Nell in the meantime beavered away at Government databases. She, of course, came up trumps. She had switched tack to regular outgoings – the kind of thing that everyone pays: car insurance, national insurance, even income tax.

By tracking the sources of the national insurance payments, Nell was able to identify bank accounts. Most were now closed, but two were still open. They were joint accounts shared with surviving partners. Within a few minutes she had details on her screen of two accounts that bore the names of deceased soldiers. Both had received salary payments. Both from a company called Black Suit Travel, listed as BST on the bank statements. Nell checked Companies House. There was no such organisation listed.

Dead end.

She started on Bridges, Skinner and Blackwood again. All had changed accounts, but the banks were thorough and kept detailed records going back for decades. It wasn't long before Nell found what she was looking for. BST had been paymaster to all three throughout the important years.

It was the same for McNeil and the others.

Bingo.

With the exception of Chris Grady. For him there were no NI payments, no benefits claims, no bank account, no records. Chris Grady had disappeared from the electronic world.

Then, as Nell added to her fact list, a thought occurred to Toni. Something Finlay had said about the *Cyclone* book, which, she remembered, was also set in the early 1980s. She saw that Stuart had left the office copy on his desk. She picked it up and, returning to the comfort of her chair, opened the front cover.

Chapter 59

I woke up late.

At least, it might have been called late on a normal day. As the alarm wrenched me from a deep slumber, I had been in bed for just three hours.

Staggering towards the shower, I noticed a note on the chest of drawers next to the bedroom door. It was from Jenny. I was not to be too late home from work. I smiled. Chance would be a fine thing.

The DCI had suggested we get into the office by noon. Josh proposed we meet in the canteen for a brew before starting work. We would both need the caffeine to kick-start our brains.

I could have easily succumbed to temptation and spent another couple of hours under the duvet, but I had an appointment to keep.

Rupert Reid was now back at work and fully recovered. I had sent him a text while we had been waiting for SO19 to turn over the Romanian house, asking him if he could look at something for me.

Despite the unusual hour, Rupert had replied almost immediately. My instructions were to attend his office on the sixteenth floor, Scotland Yard, Room 1604 at 10.30. It would be great to see the old guy again. The last time that we had spoken was just before he had warned me not to trust either MI5 or Nial Monaghan. How right he had been. The bomb that went off beneath my car had been just far enough away from him to spare his life.

✢

I arrived at Rupert's office just as his clock showed ten-thirty.

There were two mugs of coffee waiting ready near the kettle. A huge bear hug and much hand-shaking later, I showed Rupert why I needed his help.

As I laid out the contents of the yellow folder on an empty desk, I could see from Rupert's facial expression that there was going to be a problem.

'It's Arabic, Bob,' he commented, as he donned tortoiseshell-framed reading glasses and leaned heavily over the desk for a closer look.

'Which is why I came to you, Rupert,' I replied.

He took a deep breath, exhaling slowly as he flicked over the sheets of paper. 'I don't read Arabic as well as I speak it, but I can tell you what it's from.'

'That's a start. Can you work out what it says?'

'Well...' he paused. 'It looks like it might be something from a collection of Islamic works called *Mawsu'at al-Jihad*, the 'Encyclopaedia of Jihad' ... but it's not a section I have ever seen before.'

'I've never heard of it.'

'After your time, Finlay. We first came across sections of the *Mawsu'at* in the late 1980s. It was written by people working for a man called Abdullah Azzam. Your extract seems to be slightly different; it's called "Encyclopaedia of Political Jihad" – maybe a localised version?'

'Political Holy War?' I asked.

'Not Holy War. It's a misconception that "jihad" means "holy war". It actually translates as "struggle or effort in the name of Islam", so what we have here is something about political struggle.'

I sat down. My lack of sleep was already starting to catch up with me. Rupert stopped talking for a moment, walked across the office and returned with one of the mugs of black coffee. 'Here, get this down you,' he said. 'This could take a while.'

I sat and listened as Rupert continued to browse the documents. Here and there he could pick out words he knew – signs and names that were familiar. Azzam, he explained had been a co-founder of the Palestinian Hamas organisation. He had commissioned the 'Encyclopaedia' as a means to teach Mujahideen how to resist the Soviet invaders.

'Sounds like a nice bloke,' I commented.

'Not really. He's widely reported as having been responsible for persuading Bin Laden to travel to Afghanistan and get involved in what he called the "global jihad". Azzam met Osama Bin Laden in Saudi when he taught him at the university. Bin Laden fell under his spell.'

'The same Bin Laden that they say is behind 9/11?'

'The very same. Azzam recruited him.'

'He'll be high on a CIA hit list then?'

'Not anymore, Finlay. Late 1989, Azzam was driving his father and brother to prayers when they were taken out by a roadside bomb.'

'CIA got him?'

'One of many suspects. Serious money is on Bin Laden taking out his old mentor when they started to head in different directions. Sure as eggs are eggs, if Azzam was alive today then it would be him in charge of Al Q'aeda, or whatever it might have become.'

'The King is dead, long live the King. Bin Laden takes out his biggest rival leaving the path clear?'

'Got it in one, Finlay. Makes you wonder who taught those guys how to make bombs like that.' His eyebrows raised, Rupert looked hard at me over the top of his reading glasses. He knew what I would be thinking. I paused for a moment before answering him.

'I know what you're saying. We did, mostly ... me and a few others. We had quite a few of them over here in the eighties. Mostly up in Scotland. We taught them a lot of ways to kill Russians.'

'It's a murky world. I saw that Collins lad on TV last weekend. He's stirred up a real hornets' nest. I had a feeling when I looked through the book that some of your lads might have been involved ... but I didn't think you were a munitions specialist?'

'I'm not, I was sent up there to train them on missiles. First it was the Milan, but they couldn't get the hang of the wire guidance system. A year or so later the Americans managed to sort out some Stingers. The Afghans were much better with that. Fire it, forget it.'

'And once they got the Stinger, Russian air immunity was defunct.'

'Exactly. And, like Beaky wrote in his book, war games for the Americans.'

'Beaky?'

'Chas Collins, the author you're referring to. Me and Kevin knew him. He was on Goon troop for a while before he quit to work the circuit.'

'So, he was SAS then? That TV programme at the weekend made out he was fake ...'

'No, Rupert. He told some porkies and paid the price. Beaky wasn't badged; he never passed selection.'

'Hardest course in the army.'

I laughed. 'No, that's the one run by the Catering Corps. Nobody's ever passed it.'

We laughed together. It was an old joke.

Rupert continued to mull over the papers, making notes on a jotting pad as he slowly worked his way through them. After about twenty minutes, he admitted defeat. Slamming his pencil onto the notepad he swore under his breath.

'It's got me, Finlay,' he said. 'The text is confusing. Some parts I can work out, then, in the middle of a sentence the language seems to change. It's really odd. Like it's been put together by several different people.'

'That might be the case if it is what you think. I doubt if Azzam wrote it all himself.'

'Can you wait a minute while I "phone a friend", so to speak?'

I readily agreed. While Rupert headed off to his desk in the corner of the room, I stared out of the window.

It was a grey October day. In the street below, hundreds of people were going about their working lives. Not far away, the River Thames was visible as it cut through the heart of the city on its way to the sea. A small boat was struggling eastwards against the flow of water. Somewhere out there, I thought, Jenny was shopping for our new home.

I had an idea what she would be looking for. I had seen the latest estate agent blurb on the kitchen table before I'd left that morning. Over the preceding weeks, there had been piles of property listings arriving in the post. I had scanned through them but none seemed to excite me. The listing that had been sitting on the kitchen table for the last few days was different, though. Quiet, rural and with roses around the door, the house was described as having nice views and no neighbours. Jenny didn't like having neighbours; it was a trait that we shared.

A few moments later, Rupert returned.

'Good news. A mate of mine who works over at the Ministry of

Defence will have a look at it for you. He's a top-drawer translator; bit of an oddball, but great with languages. One of the few blokes in the UK who can debate the Quran with a Muslim cleric without getting into a heated argument.'

I hesitated for a moment. The idea of allowing an MOD employee to have the file troubled me. I had promised Gayle Bridges some answers and I didn't plan to get us all in the mire by having it handed over to the Ministry of Defence.

'Can he be trusted … I mean, can he work without the MOD knowing what's in the file?' I asked.

'If that's what you want. He might work for the Government, but he's discreet. If you want a private job done then I can vouch for him.'

'OK, what's his name?'

'Dr Julian Armstrong. He's a Taff, like your mate Kevin Jones. Lives in the Black Mountains, gets up at some God-earthly hour to get to work in London. Just don't get talking politics or religion with him is all I'll say.'

'Why's that?'

'He hates politicians and, when it comes to religion, he follows a Buddhist order that dates back to the eighteenth century. He might try and convert you.'

'You want me to take the folder over to him?'

'No, leave it with me. I'll pop it over to him in my lunch hour. Give us a chance for a natter.'

I agreed. I was left with an hour to get to Hampstead.

Chapter 60

It was back to square one for the murder enquiry team.

By the time I reached Hampstead, the DCI had sent several detectives to Ealing to sit in on the interviews with the slave girls. It was unlikely they would know where the Romanians were heading when they fled the house, but we had to try.

I was sent with Josh Bonner to wear out some more shoe leather, knocking on doors in the High Street. It was tedious work, especially after the excitement following the lead we had gained from the CCTV at the garage.

Several hours' slog produced no rewards, save for the knowledge that Relia hadn't been frequenting the local shops. That made how her killers found the safe house even more of a puzzle.

Rupert rang me at about three o'clock. Julian Armstrong had given the document a quick once over during their lunch together. The reason Rupert had been unable to translate it was due to the fact that it was written in a number of versions of Arabic, as if it had been written by a Palestinian, edited by an Egyptian and then proofread by someone from Saudi. As Armstrong had been able to recognise all of the language variations, he had found reading the text less of a challenge.

Rupert warned me to be patient for a result on the translation. Armstrong had proposed doing a superficial analysis, with notes, to see if the document was of any interest or significance. He would be in contact in a few days if he had anything to report.

I got the distinct impression, though, that Armstrong didn't consider the extra work to be a high priority. Although Kevin seemed to be anxious to know if the document had a monetary value – maybe even the kind of figure that could buy an early retirement – he was going to have to learn to be patient.

Rupert wanted to know if I had ever heard of something called 'Al Anfal'. I hadn't. Apparently, the name was mentioned in the Chas Collins book and in several of the document pages that Armstrong had scanned over lunch. It seemed to be the name for another group, similar to Al Q'aeda. I had to confess to having skimmed some of the Collins book, so I wasn't too surprised that I didn't recall reading the name.

We ended the call and I returned to Josh and the job at hand.

Chapter 61

Ealing, West London

Lynn Wainwright turned the Rover into the side street. In the daylight, it looked very different. The local station had mentioned there would be a PC standing outside and there he was, halfway along, looking chilly and bored.

He watched her as she parked the car. Waiting for her to mess up a parallel park, she mused. If so, she disappointed him. One swift movement – a perfect manoeuvre.

She climbed out of the car and greeted him. 'Hello, mate. I'm Lynn Wainwright from SO19. Just popped back to pick up my torch. I left it here during the entry.'

'Lucky you, I've drawn the short straw. No warm cars for me ... Nice bit of parking, by the way.'

Lynn smiled in appreciation. 'You're on stag, I guess?'

'I've been standing outside these empty houses for the last two hours. Best entertainment I've had has been staring at the windows of the places opposite. Highlight was at about seven, when the lights started to turn on. Would you believe, the routine is almost the same in every house? First the bedroom light, then the bathroom. A few minutes later the hallway and then the kitchen.'

'Alarm, toilet, cup of tea, shower,' said Lynn.

'Exactly. It's the same in my house too, probably the same for you.'

'Just starts a lot earlier.'

'They tell me this was a brothel, which made me wonder why SO19 had done the raid. Prostitution wasn't normally your thing, I'd have thought. But I guessed maybe the pimps have started carrying guns.'

'Something like that.' Lynn looked along the front paths to the houses. It looked like the Murder Squad forensic team had been on scene as well. Both were now closed up, the windows sealed with masking tape. All views from outside were blocked by sheets hung across the window frames. 'Police Line – Do Not Cross' tape was tied against the doors of both houses. 'Do you have a key?' she asked.

'It's all locked up, I'm afraid,' the PC replied, somewhat meekly. 'Shall I radio the nick to see if we have one?'

Lynn noticed him glance at her left hand. He was looking for a ring. 'It's OK. I have a set in my pocket. But I'll need you to come with me.'

'Why's that?'

'So I don't get accused of interfering with evidence or anything like that. I just need you to verify that I went straight up to the loft and came straight out again.'

The PC shrugged. 'Seems fine to me. Are you one of the SFOs, then?'

'That's right ... you're detective material I see.' She smiled warmly, keen that he should see her comment as a joke rather than an insult.

He laughed. 'Yeah ... sorry. Just didn't realise there were any women in specialist firearms.'

'There are two of us. Now ... shall we get my torch?'

Reaching into her trouser pocket, Lynn produced a small bunch of keys. 'Fancy a look inside?' she said, coyly. 'What's your name?'

'Alastair McCulloch. But call me Al, everyone does.'

There were several keys on the bunch. Lynn struggled to find one to fit the newly repaired front door of the left-side house. Al offered to help.

'Go on,' she said. 'If you can do it, I'll stand you a tea at refs break.'

Al took the keys and, in turn, tried the three keys in the lock. In the event, only one would actually go into the lock. He twisted the key gently so as not to break it. The lock was stiff, but it moved. A moment later the door popped open. They were in.

As he turned back towards Lynn, she noticed a look of disappointment on his face. The reason was approaching from behind her. Two men had walked in from the pavement and started up the garden path. They looked like CID – both in suits, one much younger than the other. The older one was purposeful, in a hurry, but it was the younger one who spoke.

'Hello you two. DC Bonner from AMIT. Mind if I ask what you're doing?'

Al turned sheepishly to face the new arrivals. As he stumbled for an explanation, Lynn came to his rescue.

'Sorry gents,' she explained. 'Spoke to DCI Bowler first thing. He OK'd it for me to come and collect my torch.'

She could see the two detectives start to relax. Perhaps they weren't in the shit after all.

The DC introduced the older detective. He was a Detective Inspector. She didn't quite catch the name. It seemed they had called to check out a theory the DI had been working on. As the forensics team had now finished with the house, they had been cleared to have a poke around.

Lynn pushed open the front door. The hallway was bare floorboards. She remembered the smell from the night before; a mixture of stale sweat and spray deodorant. A bit like an empty locker room following a tough game, the team having just headed off to the pub.

The two detectives walked through and turned into the front room, the older one leading the way. She trotted up the stairs. Her new friend chose to stay with the detectives.

On reaching the landing, Lynn realised she was going to need a hand to get into the loft area. She'd forgotten just how high the ceiling was. Returning to the ground floor, she found the others in the front room. The two detectives were in the process of tipping a double bed onto its side and pushing it against the wall. As she continued to watch, the younger detective, Bonner, pulled back the rug in front of the open fireplace. There was no carpet. The DI finished rolling up the rug and leant it against the bed. He scanned the floor.

'Check the floorboards, Josh,' the older detective said. 'Look for cuts, missing nails. Anything that might look like a hide or a trapdoor.'

She was curious now, figuring the Murder Squad must have had a tip that something was hidden beneath the floor. For several minutes the two detectives tapped timbers and prised at the gaps to see if anything was loose.

'Nothing?' said the older man.

'Let's try the back room,' said Bonner.

It was Lynn's chance. 'Al … come and give me a hand will you? I can't get up to the loft.'

'Teas are *definitely* on you then,' he quipped as they ran up the stairs.

He cupped his hands to lift her up. For the second time, she entered the dark void. Fortunately, the torch lay just inside the opening. She dropped it into a retaining loop on her belt and climbed back into the hatch.

And that was as far as she got. As her equipment belt jammed against the wooden frame and then dug her holstered Glock pistol into her side, Lynn realised she was stuck, unable to drop or to climb back up.

Al sniggered.

Lynn was not amused. 'Just give me a hand.' She twisted and groaned, unable to move or even breathe properly.

'How about we make that tea you promised me into dinner one evening?'

'You cheeky fucker,' Lynn replied. 'When I get down from here I'll be shoving this torch somewhere the sun don't shine. Now get under me and help me push upwards.'

Al waited. 'Dinner would be nice, Alastair. Thank you,' he said.

Trapped and unable to move, Lynn took a deep breath. 'OK, dinner it is … and if you tell a bloody soul how you got me to agree I'll—'

'OK, OK … I get the drift.' Al cupped his hands once again and placed them under her black, hi-tech boot.

There was a voice from downstairs. It was the DI. 'We're nipping next door to check the downstairs rooms there. When you two have sorted out your social arrangements, make sure you shut the door behind you.'

Lynn smiled as she dropped down beside Al. The DI must have heard. Luckily, he also had a sense of humour.

'You cheeky bugger,' she said, cracking the torch onto the badge at the front of his helmet. 'No way are you getting me to buy you dinner. You'll get a brew and be grateful.'

Al shrugged. 'It was worth a try.'

Lynn started down the stairs. 'What were those two looking for?' she asked.

'A hidden room. They seemed to think there might be something under the floors downstairs. They've gone to check next door now.'

As Lynn walked into the front room, Al followed. 'I've got a hoolie bar in the car,' she said. 'That'll lift the floorboards. I'll go ask them if they want to try it.'

Al agreed to wait in the first house until Lynn could return. The hoolie bar, or hooligan bar, was an adapted crowbar that would give the necessary leverage to prise up any floorboards. She headed back to the ARV car, opened the boot, pulled out the heavy metal tool and then walked up the adjacent path to the next door house.

Chapter 62

As the WPC started to prise open the first of the floorboards, there was no clue as to what lay below. Then, as what appeared to be a hollowed-out cellar beneath the floor was revealed, there was a yell from the front room next door, followed by the sound of a shot.

I was first to react. 'Josh ... stay here,' I said firmly. 'Lynn ... with me.'

Lynn dropped the bar and drew her Glock from its belt holster. She was right behind me as we ran out into the front garden. We were just in time to see two men – one in the street and another in the process of exiting the adjacent front garden.

The suspect closest to us was barefoot, explaining why he wasn't moving as fast as his friend. He stopped, raised a pistol toward us and fired.

As a round zipped over our heads, I dived for cover behind a low wall; Lynn tumbled forward and low onto the grass. Rolling over, she regained a crouch position with her Glock ready. She was fast, very fast. I was impressed. At a distance of about fifteen metres she put two rounds into the torso of her target. Both hit the chest area. It was instinctive, point and shoot, and as good as I had ever seen.

'Armed police', she screamed.

Too late, I thought, until I realised that her warning was directed at the second suspect, running up the street.

Save for the rapid beating of my heart and the sound of Lynn's heavy breathing, the street was now silent.

I stood up slowly. There was no sign of the second suspect. In the adjacent garden, Lynn's target lay still and on his back. A large red stain was spreading through his white shirt.

'You check him,' I yelled. 'I'll look for the other one.'

I moved out into the street, ducking behind anything I could use as cover. There was no sign of the second man. Returning to the front garden, I found Lynn checking for a neck pulse with her left hand, her right still holding the Glock. She was shaking, her face pale.

Her voice trembled as she spoke. 'He's dead.'

'Probably before he hit the ground,' I replied. 'That was an incredible piece of shooting, miss.'

I realised then that the PC from the first house hadn't appeared. I was just about to storm in through the front door when Lynn held me back.

'Wait … there may be others. We should call in help.'

'No time.' I called into the house for any signs of life. No response.

Lynn led the way inside, Glock at the ready.

We found the young PC in the front room. He was still alive, but weak from blood loss. Slimy red foam was bubbling from his mouth and nose.

'Al … Al,' Lynn yelled at him as she knelt down. 'Stay awake mate, stay awake.' She pressed the transmit button on her personal radio. *'Trojan this is Trojan five three … Officer down … Ambulance…'*

'Can't … breathe,' the PC hissed.

For a moment, I was back in another world, one I hadn't experienced for a very long time. A man lying before me, bullet wound to the chest, familiar symptoms. So long ago, it felt like someone else's life.

'Tension haemothorax,' I muttered to myself, under my breath.

Lynn turned back to me. 'What did you say?'

'Tip him up,' I said, trying my best to sound calm.

'We should keep him still,' Lynn argued.

There was no time for debate. If I was right, the PC was close to death. I pushed past Lynn and ripped open his tunic. One wound; lower left chest, into the lung area.

'We need to look for an exit wound,' I said, my tone urgent.

Lynn did as I asked without further question. Dark-red blood oozed slowly from the entry wound. There was no corresponding wound to his back.

'Looks like a nine mil' entry wound, round still inside.' I was talking as I thought, deciding my options, reliving times past to work out what to do next. 'Get me your trauma kit from the car,' I ordered.

Lynn hesitated for a moment, as if unsure whether to leave the injured PC.

'Go,' I yelled.

As she headed back to the street, I kept talking to the PC. It was important to keep him awake, stop him falling into unconsciousness. I was right, I had seen these exact symptoms before.

'Al ... Alastair,' I said. 'Come on you bastard ... stay with us. Think of the dinner Lynn's gonna buy you ...'

Badly injured and bleeding, the PC grimaced through his pain. He was now grey, his skin turning cold and clammy. I gripped his hand. It was wet ... sweaty. I pressed my fingers into his neck, found the pulse. Fast ... very fast. A heart powered by adrenalin, trying to maintain blood pressure.

Lynn returned with the first-aid kit and Josh Bonner. 'I've called an ambulance,' he said.

'Do you have any duct tape?' I demanded.

'Duct tape?' Lynn replied. ''What for? There's micropore tape in the trauma pack, will that do?'

'It won't stick. I need duct tape ... sticks better when there's blood.'

'There's some in the boot of our car, guv,' said Josh.

'Get it. Be quick.'

Hoping all the while a paramedic would appear in the doorway, I mentally rehearsed what I needed to do. Improvised occlusive dressing. Seal wound. Tape three sides to create one-way valve.

I ripped open the first-aid kit and started to clean the blood away from the PC's chest. Bandages, a scalpel, scissors, forceps and a plastic sheet fell beside me.

'He's slipping away.' Lynn said, in a low voice.

I tapped Al's chest, around the wound and across to his sternum, doing my best to look calm. The last thing I needed was for Lynn to continue to argue with me.

'What are you doing?' she asked.

'Listen,' I said. 'His chest cavity is full of blood. It should sound hollow. It's why he can't breathe.' I was remembering lessons on battlefield treatment of casualties that I had attended over two decades previously. 'We need to help him,' I continued. 'Rip open a scalpel pack and cut a piece of that plastic sheet to the size of a credit card.

Josh returned and went to hand me the duct tape.

'Tear me three strips about six inches long,' I said.

Josh and Lynn performed their tasks without objection.

'Now keep him still,' I urged as I used the tape to stick the plastic over the bullet wound to create a seal. If I was right, it would allow him to breathe. As the final strip stuck fast to the surrounding skin, Al's breathing took a serious turn for the worse. It wasn't working. The dressing had failed.

Al was now beginning to panic, his legs and arms starting to shake uncontrollably.

I took a deep breath, trying to buy myself some thinking time. 'Any sign of the ambulance?'

There wasn't. We were on our own, and we knew it. And I knew what I was facing.

'Right,' I said. 'I need some pipe … something like a hosepipe, about ten inches of it, maybe. And something like a balloon that we can tape onto the end.'

'What for?' Lynn asked.

'We need to drain the blood from his pleural cavity.'

'What ... like make a hole in his chest, you mean?'

'That's about the sum of it.'

'How about a biro? I've got one in the car. And I think there's a hosepipe in the back garden.'

'Biro's too narrow ... garden hose too big ... something inbetween. Do you have a stethoscope in the car?'

'Petrol siphon pipe do you?' said Josh.

'Perfect. Lynn ... this was a brothel. Have a look around the other rooms ... I remember seeing some condoms somewhere, and be quick ... both of you.'

As I waited, I taped down the fourth side of the plastic square now covering the entry bullet wound to Al's chest. His chest movements had become very fast and shallow. I knew what was happening. His pleural cavity, ruptured by the bullet, had now filled with blood and air, so his diaphragm was losing the means to operate. We needed to get the blood out from that cavity, and we needed to do it fast.

I pulled Al's shirt back so as to expose the sides of his ribcage and moved his left arm up and away from his chest. I'd seen this demonstrated several times in theory but only the once in practice, and I'd never done it myself. Placing my hand into his armpit, I used its width to estimate where I was going to have to cut. 'Between the seventh and eighth ribs,' I said, talking myself through what I was about to attempt.

Josh appeared behind me with a small length of clear hosepipe.

'Clean it, best you can. Use one of the alcohol wipes.'

Lynn came barging into the room. 'Got one,' she yelled, as she thrust the sealed foil packet into my hand.'

'Open it up and tape it over one end of the tube, quickly.'

As Lynn did her job, I reached for the scalpel and then felt for the softer area between Al's ribs. My hand shaking and slippery with blood, I struggled to grip the slim metal handle. As the point of the blade touched Al's skin, I uttered a silent prayer. Then, it was too late. I was in.

'One inch cut, just the skin, no deeper.' The words of our medic instructor – drilled into me nearly twenty years before.

Although he was now semiconscious, I felt Al wince in pain.

Next came the separation of the muscle fibres to allow access to the pleural membrane. I tried to picture it in my mind as I placed the scalpel to one side and switched to using the forceps. Gently, tentatively, I worked my way in, levering the muscle tissue aside until I felt a solid resistance. Pushing harder, I prayed again. Then … the sound I wanted to hear as the membrane succumbed to my efforts. It popped, just loud enough for me to hear it. I was there.

Quickly, I reached for the petrol hosepipe and squeezed it into the hole I had created. For a second, nothing happened. Then a small ball of dark red blood appeared just near my trembling fingers. I resisted the temptation to push the tube further in. If the lessons I remembered were right, the blood should exit along the pipe, fill the condom and then, as the pressure in the cavity reduced, Al would be able to breathe. With the tube sealed to the outside air, and as his diaphragm started to work, air would be prevented from being drawn in to fill the void.

Blood began to flow, slowly at first, and then in greater volume. It was working. I held the tube tightly in place and watched to see if Al reacted.

He did. No more than thirty seconds from the moment I pushed the pipe between his ribs, his chest started to expand. At first the movement was barely noticeable, but with every subsequent breath he became stronger and the breaths deeper. After a minute or so, his face started to gain colour.

I closed my eyes to say a silent thank-you and, as I did so, became aware of movement behind me. Two paramedics.

The cavalry had arrived.

✠

The paramedics worked speedily and efficiently, replacing my home-made chest drain with a non-return device designed specifically for the job. I sat back against the upturned bed and watched as they worked. I was totally exhausted.

A few minutes later they lifted Al onto a stretcher and carried him out to the waiting ambulance. Lynn decided to go with them.

With Josh's help, I got to my feet and, returning to the front garden, we found a colleague of Lynn's in the process of pulling a sheet over the body of the gunman.

'Hold up,' I said. 'I just need a quick look at him.'

As I suspected, it was another of the men who had arrived in the UK with Petre. I guessed the one who had escaped was Marius. That was the second time he had gotten away from me.

As we stepped back, Josh took hold of my arm. 'What you did in there was pretty awesome, guv,' he said.

I didn't answer, my thoughts, elsewhere, promising myself there wouldn't be a third time for Marius.

'Something tells me you've done that before.'

I smiled. 'Grew up on a rough estate, Josh.'

He laughed.

☩

Within half an hour of Lynn downing the gunman, the street was sealed off and the area was alive with searching police officers. An SFO team arrived about twenty minutes later. Josh and I left it to them to clear the two houses and do the initial search of the priest hole. It only took them a few minutes. They used a K9 – a police dog trained to work with the firearms teams. The dog went first to check the house before the SFO team swept through.

Half an hour after the dog went through the door, I followed Josh through the gaping hole in the floor to explore the hide.

As we finished, I pulled myself from the concealed chamber and brushed the dust from my trousers.

The dug-out was devilishly simple in its construction, yet almost impossible to detect. In both of the semi-detached houses, the ground-floor, front-room floorboards had been removed to allow a six-foot-deep void to be created under each room. A four-foot-high tunnel linked the two. Each contained a small cot, a cupboard and enough tinned food to last a man for several weeks. There was bottled water, a small sealed chemical toilet and several books.

The builder of the modern-day priest holes had even provided an electricity supply by splicing into the mains feed before it reached the meter. From above, there was no clue that there was anything beneath the floor. If it hadn't been for Lynn Wainwright offering us the use of a huge crow bar to try and loosen the floorboards, the two men hidden within might well have remained undiscovered.

The idea of there being a hide beneath the floor had occurred to me after reading the estate-agent listings Jenny had left for me. One had described an old rectory with a priest hole as one of its 'original features'. The skip in the back garden of the brothel house had been a clue, and, combined with my thoughts of hiding places in walls and under floors, my suspicions had been triggered. The earth the skip contained had to have come from somewhere. It reminded me that the hide beneath Kevin's shed must have produced quite an amount of spoil as well. With no obvious landscaping in evidence, a hidden cache under either the garage or the ground floor seemed to be a possible answer.

I had wondered if we might make a gruesome find. The question was still unanswered as to where the retired and exhausted slave girls went once they had served their useful purpose. What I hadn't anticipated was that the chamber might conceal living people, or that they might be armed.

That was my mistake.

Chapter 63

Waiting around in police stations was starting to become part of my daily life. With a gunman killed, a PC badly wounded and a murder suspect on the run, I wasn't going anywhere soon.

After cleaning off the worst of the dirt from the modern-day priest hole and doing my best to sponge Al McCulloch's blood from my trousers, the first thing we were told to complete was a duty statement. While events were still uppermost in our minds, Josh and I were ordered to sit at opposite ends of the local CID office at Ealing and describe everything that had happened both inside and outside the traffickers' hideout. I was just at the point of describing when Lynn shot the gunman, when my telephone started buzzing in my pocket.

It took me several moments before I was able to understand the hysterical scream, and a number of angry sentences before I actually recognised the voice. It was Gayle Bridges. She was in a rage. Amongst the insults and threats, the words 'betrayal', 'bastards' and 'search' seemed to figure. Getting a word in to respond proved impossible. Before I could speak, the phone went dead. She had hung up.

I sat for a moment, wondering if I should leave it or call back straightaway. At the opposite end of the office, two older detectives in dark suits had walked in and were chatting to Josh. From the matching ties, I guessed they might be from the Complaints Branch, CIB.

Gayle's anger seemed aimed at me. For several seconds, I stared at the phone before scrolling the menu to 'Return Call'. I took a deep breath before tapping the button.

Engaged. I waited and then tried again. Same result.

I wondered why she was so angry. With her husband's pistol safely returned to Hereford, it had to be about the document she had given us. For a moment I felt guilty. She had said it had value, but as yet we didn't know why.

I took another deep breath, blew out my cheeks and exhaled slowly. The suits were now sitting down with Josh. I had time to find out what Gayle wanted. On the third attempt, the call connected.

She answered almost immediately. 'What?' The anger was still plain in her voice.

'It's Bob Finlay, Gayle. You just rang me.'

'I know that. I'm not an idiot.'

'Err ... it's just that I didn't quite catch what you said. Well, it sounded like you're cross about something?'

Gayle sighed expressively. There was a pause. I imagined her pacing up and down the hallway of her house, frustrated by the prospect of having to repeat herself.

'I've called Kevin Jones as well. Gave him what for.'

'Is that why your phone was engaged when I called you back?'

'Yes. He says you knew nothing ... says he's going to look into it.'

'Into what, Gayle? What's happened?'

'It's your lot. Coppers ... filthy boots, all over my carpets ... pawing through my underwear ... they even looked through my rubbish bins.'

'I don't understand.'

'They turned up at my house. My mother was here. Christ, it was so embarrassing. They had a warrant to search they said. Claimed they had information I had a gun in the house ... they searched everything. They even went in the attic.'

It took several minutes to tease the whole story from Gayle. It wasn't so much hysteria and anger, more that she felt powerless and humiliated. Her only previous experience of police officers had been the friends of her husband that she had met socially.

Somehow, word must have reached the local station that Bob Bridges had a trophy weapon at home. A few days earlier and a search of the loft would have revealed where Bob had concealed it – in the box with the Arabic documents. No doubt, if they had found the gun, the papers would have been seized as well.

From Gayle's description, they had all been CID and had turned up earlier that morning. Gayle and her mum had been taken completely by surprise. Seemingly unconcerned by Gayle's protests, they had probed, sifted and scoured through every drawer, cupboard, box and container in the house. They had removed books from shelves to look for hollowed-out hiding places, flicked through the pages of magazines and even removed doors from hinges to look for secret compartments. It had been a thorough job – unusually so.

Something rankled with me, though. Gayle mentioned the questions the lead officer had asked: Had any of her husband's former army colleagues been in touch? Had anything else been removed from the house? These questions, and the professionalism of the search seemed more in keeping with the activities of the Anti-Terrorist Squad … or Special Branch, not a small team of local CID officers.

Gayle had jumped to the conclusion that Kevin and I had been responsible for the invasion, which was why we were the targets of her wrath. Kevin had managed to convince her otherwise and, by the time my call with her ended, she was calming down.

I was left with an uneasy feeling. Things didn't seem to add up.

Chapter 64

Complaints Branch kept us hanging about for three hours.

Everyone had to write statements, complete suspect descriptions and sketch a drawing of the shooting scene before the Complaints Investigation people would allow us to depart.

Word had reached the media world quickly. Within an hour, PCs posted to perimeter control were being approached by local hacks keen for an exclusive. Not long after, the press was turning out in force. Extra officers were called in to deal with the growing throng as they jostled and manoeuvred for the best position to secure a photograph. A large white van with an aerial projecting from the roof signalled the arrival of the first television crew.

From the hospital came good news. Al, the injured PC, was expected to pull through. The police station itself was a hive of activity, its yard crammed – the shooting having resulted in a lot of people being called into work.

I was watching Josh Bonner trying to get into our car in the Ealing police station yard so we could head back to Hampstead when Kevin called me.

It sounded like Gayle had also given him a real ear-bending. I told him I would need to check, but it was my guess that the search team was either from the National Crime Squad or the Met Complaints Unit. Someone may have given them a tip-off. I wondered if anyone else had known about the pistol that Gayle had asked us to lose for her. It would be easy enough to find out. All searches were recorded on the Met SO11 database for intelligence use.

It was nearly three o'clock before we made it back to New Scotland Yard. The office was empty apart from Matt Miller, who was on the phone, trying to persuade someone to let our squad have some extra staff. Nina was on the phone trying to get hold of Lynn Wainwright.

Once the Complaints Department scene investigation was complete, the Major Crime Team would need a statement from Lynn, as she had been the only person at the scene to get a decent look at the fleeing gunman. Apparently, Lynn wasn't answering her mobile phone, so Nina had contacted her office in the SO19 North London base at Old Street Police Station. They confirmed that Lynn was on duty the following morning and would be available for interview after her post-incident debrief. Nina made an appointment. She also wanted Lynn to look at some photographs of known Romanian criminals and at a few Immigration Control stills to see if she could pick out the escaped gunman. The squad were hopeful that the suspect was one of the men recently seen entering the country through Heathrow.

I offered to go with Nina. At first she seemed reluctant – irritated even, by the suggestion. But Matt overheard her talking to me and pointed out that, as I had been with Lynn at the time of the shooting incident, it made sense that I should also go. Just before Nina headed home, we arranged to meet at King's Cross the following morning. I would take the tube in to work and Nina would pick me up at nine.

With Matt busy on the telephone, I made some calls to see if I could find out anything else about the search at Gayle's house. I drew a blank – no record of either a planned or a recorded search. I hung up the phone and sat back. I must have looked frustrated. With my chin sat firmly on my chest, I had my hands across my stomach, fingers entwined.

'You OK, Bob?' Matt asked.

'It's probably nothing,' I said. 'You remember the Marylebone Inspector who was killed in the Selfridges bomb in September?'

'Sure. Friend of yours, Nina said.'

'That's right. Well, his widow was turned over by some of our guys this morning. Full search, gave her a real fright. Said they were looking in case he had left a trophy weapon behind in the house.'

'They find anything?'

'No ... and I can't establish who they were. I wanted to find out who was the lead on it; they really put the frighteners on her. A few words of apology might help avoid an official complaint.'

'Nothing on registry?' Matt asked.

'Nobody has even flagged the address as being of interest and definitely no mention of a search.'

Matt thought for a moment. 'Get a copy of the warrant. Even the Complaints Unit or the army SIB have to have one. That will tell you who did the spin.'

'Great idea.' I picked up the phone to call Gayle. The army Special Investigation Branch hadn't occurred to me. It would explain why there was no register of the search.

The call to Gayle Bridges, however, produced further frustration. The detective in charge hadn't left a copy of the warrant. Matt Miller's conclusion didn't make for comfortable hearing. No register record and no warrant might mean it was the Security Services.

Then, to completely spoil the day, Kevin Jones called again. He was with Rod Skinner's wife. Rod had been shot dead on his driveway not long after Bob Bridges was killed. The Skinner home had also been searched. It sounded like the same team. Again, no copy of the warrant had been left and no weapon had been found. But, from what Rod's widow was claiming, it wasn't just weapons that they were looking for.

In a box of her late husband's personal effects, the search team had found some documents. As soon as they had been shown to the lead detective, the search of further parts of the house had been abandoned. It looked like they had found what they were looking for.

Although June Skinner had never seen the documents before, she had glimpsed them when the detective had pulled them from their box. She described one as about two inches thick ... with a front cover written in Arabic.

Chapter 65

At a quarter to nine the next morning, I was waiting next to the taxi rank at King's Cross rail station.

I felt tired. After many days without intrusion, the previous night had seen vivid nightmares return to disturb my sleep. Although the news on Al McCulloch was good, the experience of treating him had, once again, triggered a series of distant memories. I found myself reliving the incident, getting things terribly wrong and then having to face the wrath of those around me.

Jenny had been great. She'd noticed me 'chasing rabbits' and, as I woke, she grabbed a towel from the bathroom, dried off the sweat and then cuddled up to me until I relaxed. I drifted in and out of sleep for the next couple of hours, but when the alarm finally went off, it felt like I had only just closed my eyes. My body now ached and I'd fallen asleep twice on the short train journey to King's Cross. It was going to be a long day.

The sound of a horn close by caught my attention. Glancing across the line of waiting black taxis, I could see a small silver sports car. It was Nina. She waved to me frantically from where she was blocking the entrance to the taxi rank.

I jogged over to the passenger door, ignored the disapproving glares of the taxi drivers, and dropped heavily into the seat next to Nina. Allowing no time for me to slip on the seat belt or even mutter a 'good morning', she slammed the little car into gear and darted into a line of traffic, narrowly avoiding a fast-moving cyclist who was speeding up the inside of the queue.

The lights on Euston Road were at red and, with the junction blocked by a bus, it looked like it might be some time before the traffic got moving.

'We'll go the back way, hold on,' Nina said, as she forced a path between the second line of cars and made a right turn away from the lights.

Moments later, the congestion of King's Cross was fast disappearing in the rearview mirror as we headed north towards Islington.

Our appointment was at the ARV Headquarters at Old Street Police Station. Nina had telephoned ahead to arrange to see Lynn Wainwright in the canteen at ten. We found her fairly easily. Nina bought teas and I ordered a breakfast. By the time I returned to our table, they had already started work.

From her briefcase, Nina had produced several photos that she was in the process of spreading out on the canteen table. Lynn was studying the collection of pictures. Three were from police records – photographs taken as part of the fingerprint identification process in a custody suite. The remainder were from passport control, with one or two being stills from CCTV cameras.

The quality of these latter images wasn't great and, as I glanced over Lynn's shoulder, I wondered how anyone could be expected to pick someone out. The rest of the photos were surveillance close-ups taken by someone who clearly knew what they were doing.

One of the poor-quality pictures was of Marcus, the Romanian from the petrol station. I knew that both Nina and I were wondering whether Lynn would pick him out. Lynn turned towards me as I sat at the adjacent table, a welcoming smile on her face.

'I hadn't realised you were going to be here,' she said, warmly.

'Not a problem, is it?'

'No … not at all. In fact, I'm pleased you came. I just wanted to say how incredible you were at the house yesterday. The paramedics said you most likely saved Al's life.'

'To be honest, I've never done anything like it before, but I knew we had to do something.'

'That training as a medic came in handy, I guess?' Nina interrupted, winking at me while Lynn was distracted. She was diverting the conversation, avoiding any chance of my becoming embarrassed.

'Yes … I guess the teaching was better than I realised,' I said.

'Lynn was just telling me that she's in the sin bin for the next month or so.'

Topic changed. Nice one, Nina, I thought. 'The sin bin?' I asked.

'My firearms authorisation is suspended until the IPCC finish their initial investigation,' Lynn explained. 'That's supposed to take twenty-eight days but the Federation rep says not to hold my breath. He's known it take longer, particularly when it's a fatal shooting.'

'Were the Federation ok with you talking to us?' asked Nina.

'Just so long as we don't discuss what happened. A Federation lawyer is meeting with the post-incident manager as we speak. After that I'll follow a PIP that they've prepared for me.'

'A PIP?' I asked.

'Post-Incident Plan. For example, I can do you a quick statement if I happen to recognise the man that escaped, but I have to sign it Charlie Four.'

'A cipher?'

'Exactly. There will be an inquest and an enquiry, so my identity needs to be masked straightaway.'

'Who's the post-incident manager?' Nina enquired. 'We may need to speak to him later.'

'Our Ops Superintendent, Ron Glover.'

'I know him, thanks.'

Lynn had been flicking through the pictures as we spoke. She didn't recognise anyone and, after several minutes, she admitted defeat. It was completely understandable; her view of the fleeing gunman had only been peripheral as she had concentrated on bringing down the most immediate threat to life. By the time her focus had shifted, the man had been on his toes and away down the road. The merest glance of a face from the corner of her eye wasn't enough to identify him.

As Nina was putting the photographs back in her briefcase, she stopped and lowered her voice. 'Woman to woman, would it help if I ran through a few things for you?'

Lynn glanced at me before replying. 'How do you mean ... ?'

'I've been an investigator for a lot of years, Lynn. You're going to be interviewed as a suspect. It might help, off the record, to just hear what the Independent Complaint Commission investigator will want to cover.'

'Won't the Federation do that? It's what we pay our subscription for, isn't it?'

'They might. But we have a few minutes here and now; I think it could help.'

Lynn looked to me again, as if seeking a second opinion. I simply grunted my approval of the offer.

'OK … I guess I have nothing to lose.'

Lynn nodded attentively as Nina spoke. To me, it was clear that slave trafficking wasn't my colleague's sole field of expertise. Soon, Lynn began to open up. I listened as detective and firearms officer talked through the decision to open fire, what threat Lynn had perceived and her justification for using lethal force. Nina even asked how Lynn had been affected by the incident, whether her sleep patterns had changed; had she experienced dreams or flashbacks. Everything was covered, even the time Lynn had dragged herself out of bed, what she had to eat that day, what time she had paraded for work, where she had loaded the Glock pistol and how many rounds she had placed in the magazine.

I finished my breakfast just as Nina was bringing the chat to a close. Lynn opted to escort us down the stairs, through the radio room and out into the yard.

As we left the station yard, Nina spoke.

'I hope you didn't mind me saying you were a medic?'

'Not at all. I'm pretty sure I understood the reasons.'

'I guessed you might. What you don't know is there is a fair bit of resentment in SO19 about what happened during Operation Hastings.'

'Any bit in particular?'

'Mostly centred around the fact that someone dressed up like an SAS soldier opened fire on their blokes a few weeks ago and they've been told not to discuss it.'

'I hadn't heard.'

'About the shooting incident or that they've been told not to discuss it?'

'Both.'

'... If you say so, Finlay. Anyway ... with regards to the warning, it's in-house only. You remember I mentioned I know Ron Glover?'

'Their Ops Superintendent?'

'Yes. Ron was told in no uncertain terms there would be no investigation to find who the SAS lads were and that any member of SO19 who was caught talking about it would find themselves in front of a disciplinary board.'

'Did he say who told him that?'

'No ... but he hinted that it came from the very top – maybe even the Home Secretary.'

'So, Lynn Wainwright learning that I'm ex-22 might make things a bit awkward?'

'We'll make a detective out of you yet, Finlay.'

For the remainder of the drive back to New Scotland Yard we hardly spoke. I had a feeling that Bill Grahamslaw probably knew about the warning that had been issued to everyone in SO19, if he wasn't behind it himself. I couldn't see any point in asking him and, as I thought about it, I was quite pleased to hear that it had happened. Given time, the frustration the SO19 lads felt would fade and what had happened would become a story for them to tell their grandchildren. And Nina was right; it was for the best that Lynn hadn't made the connection.

✠

As we pulled into the car park approach at New Scotland Yard, Nina asked me if I was going to the big Regiment wedding at the weekend. She'd heard about it from her uncle. I wasn't. 'No Ruperts,' I said, and she grinned.

When we reached the sanctuary of the SO13 offices, I rang Kevin and asked him if he was still intending to go. He was. I couldn't help thinking the trip might create an opportunity. Tom Cochrane had suggested Kevin talk to some of the older hands who may have known Skinner, Bridges and some of the others who had left the Regiment to work abroad. Kevin agreed, and promised to try and find out what Bob

Bridges had been doing when I saw him in Cyprus, apparently on his way home from the Far East. It might give us an indication whether the Arabic documents were of any significance. He would also try and find out if there had been any other house searches.

Kevin also suggested, rightly, that we needed to find out what Armstrong, the translator, had to say. That could tell us why somebody else might be looking for the document.

It occurred to me to ask Toni Fellowes about the searches. She was in charge of the enquiry into the attacks on the ex-Regiment lads, after all. But I ditched the idea when Kevin pointed out it might actually be Toni who was behind them.

As I hung up the phone, a familiar shiver ran up my spine. It was a sense of foreboding I'd paid insufficient heed to in the recent past. Abstract and lacking substance, it troubled me ... but I now knew not to ignore it.

Chapter 66

The next morning, Toni arrived for work early.

A day at home, away from the workplace, had recharged her batteries. It had been a last-minute decision. She needed time alone, time to think, and to read.

After getting up late and spending the day lazing around her flat, the weakening winter-afternoon light saw her reaching for the light switch in order to explore the real reason for her absence from the office: to take a proper look at *Cyclone*.

Howard Green had described Collins' book as both revealing and fantasy. Not many books were the subject of Security Service analyst reports, and not many authors found themselves targeted for interview in order to identify their sources. But there was something about the not-too-friendly warning from Howard to leave Collins to MI6, and, preceding that, his opinion that the book wasn't really worth reading that had triggered her instincts; there might be more to the book than was apparent in the analyst's report. She had a feeling that somewhere in the content would be the clue to locating the author.

She had therefore pulled *Cyclone* from her briefcase, initially with the intention of scanning it for an hour or so over a cup of tea.

> ***Chapter 1, 'The Great Game' – The continuing rivalry and conflict between the British and Russian Governments for control of Central Asia.***
> *For decades the British have perceived that India, their jewel in the Crown, has been under threat from Russian invasion through Afghanistan…*

As Toni read, she learned, and the maximum one-hour she'd promise herself was soon exceeded. From before the time of the British Raj in India, the strategic importance of Afghanistan was recognised by both the British and the Russians. 'The Great Game' was coined in the nineteenth century to describe the manoeuvrings – political and military – played out by the competing states as they sought to establish advantage and influence, with India the prize.

The British, it seemed, had seen Afghanistan as a buffer state, one which, so long as it remained independent of Russia, would deter any invasion of India. As the twentieth century moved on, instead of competing for control over geographical areas and trade, pipelines, tanker routes, petroleum consortia and contracts became the new prizes in 'The Great Game'. The ruthless pursuit of influence remained.

All this was interesting, but as the book moved to modern times it mentioned dates that really grabbed Toni's attention. She noted with increasing interest how events the author described corresponded with gaps in the records of the soldiers listed in the Hastings file. The covert activities of the CIA in Afghanistan caused her to check, and then recheck her notes from Nell. And then, in Chapter 6, she learned about Increment, and the hairs on her neck stood up.

The author described them as *'A force of semi-retired SAS soldiers recruited by MI6 to help the CIA move weapons into the area so that the Mujahideen could fight the Russians. The Americans supplied the weapons, the Brits taught the locals how to use them.'*

The soldiers had been given false identities in case they should be killed or captured in enemy territory.

In Chapter 8, Collins described a falling-out amongst the soldiers that had resulted in one of them being killed. The argument had, apparently, been over something valuable. He called the precious thing 'Al Anfal', the same name that Massoud had used in the YouTube video. The reference was vague – an artefact of some kind, possibly some form of treasure. Whatever it was, it seemed to have been important enough to result in a death.

Collins claimed to have joined Increment after the death of that soldier. He described his trip to London to be interviewed for the job. The name of the company doing the evaluation was Black Suit Travel. An MI6 officer had been his recruiter, a man called Howard Graham. Toni wondered at the name. Could this be Green? Was this the real reason he was looking for Collins?

✠

Toni dropped her handbag to the side of her desk. Nell had left a post-it note stuck to the PC screen telling Toni to check her email. She switched on the computer and then went to make tea. The quiet hour before the others arrived would allow time to catch up on developments, make a couple of calls and bring herself up to speed with Nell's research.

The report from Nell was long. Never one to pad her prose, Nell had nevertheless written fourteen pages, crammed with the detail of her and Stuart's enquiries and with links to internet sites, plus pictures and document scans, and references to outside data sources.

Toni decided to postpone reading it to allow time to do some research prompted by *Cyclone*. First, she searched on the Security

Service database for Howard Graham. There was no reference; it was a false name, no doubt. But the notion that MI6 could have been responsible for putting men on the ground fitted with Collins' claims.

In fact, if Finlay and Jones were taken out of the equation, it all fitted. The dead soldiers were all absent from the UK at the key time. And they had all worked for Black Suit Travel.

She wondered what the statistical probability was that all the men listed would have died, either through natural causes or even as a result of their paramilitary work. Unlikely, she figured. What seemed more likely was that they had all been in Afghanistan. And it looked likely that Black Suit Travel was an MI6 front company to recruit soldiers into the Increment team.

She moved on. Bridges and Skinner had been killed in London. Iain Blackwood had been taken out by a random suicide bomber. She wondered whether Blackwood had been targeted as well. Brian McNeil was still working in Iraq. Quickly, she word-searched Nell's report. Of Chris Grady there was still no trace, still no record.

Nell had created an annex on the life-insurance claims for the soldiers recruited by Black Suit Travel. Two were killed in car accidents, one in a fall whilst climbing. The remainder had been killed undertaking contractor protection work in various countries in the Middle East. None had died of natural causes.

To the notes she was making, Toni jotted down a simple, yet alarming fact that she had discussed with Nell. Including the first man mentioned in the book, ten former soldiers were prematurely deceased. Were they looking at evidence of a falling-out amongst thieves? Had a dispute over the 'Al Anfal' treasure resulted in so many deaths? Was Collins right?

Finally, it was time to go through Nell's report. Toni made herself another large mug of tea, stirred in a spoon of sugar and settled down, ready for a long read. An hour later, the office door opened. A very wet Stuart Anderson dropped his umbrella on the floor and then swore under his breath.

'Morning,' he said, as he removed his jacket to shake the rain off.

Toni held up her hand, her gaze remaining on the screen. It was not so much a hint as an order: no conversation. She was busy.

Nell arrived a few minutes later to a similar response. Toni cast a quick glance over her shoulder, gave her a nod, and saw a huge smile crossing Nell's lips.

The word coincidence didn't seem at all sufficient to describe the common factors Nell had found, linking the dead soldiers, Increment and Operation Cyclone.

Testing her researcher's theories, Toni again tapped the names of Chris Grady and Brian McNeil into the Security Service internal search engine as well as into Google. She also tried the term 'Al Anfal'. With her higher security clearance, she hoped it might produce something Nell had been unable to access. The result was the same as she had experienced earlier. There was one other possibility – personnel records.

A telephone call to MI5 HQ at Thames House produced an answer. Rod Skinner, Bob Bridges, Mac Blackwood, Brian McNeil and Chris Grady were *all* on a twelve-strong team that had been deployed on overseas operations during the early 1980s. Ten of that team were now dead: Skinner, Bridges and Blackwood amongst them. McNeil was understood to be working in Iraq as a bodyguard to visiting journalists. Again, there was no record of anyone called Chris Grady.

Toni leaned back in her chair and stretched. Sitting for so long in the same position was starting to take its toll. Nell was watching her.

'Good report,' said Toni.

'Did you get to the best bit?'

'I'm not sure. It's all good ... very good.'

'I mean the video. Did you look at it, like I suggested?'

'Not yet, no.'

'I didn't think you had. I've lined it up on my screen. Trust me; you won't want to miss it.'

Curiosity aroused, Toni eased herself out of her chair and crossed the office to stand behind Nell. On the screen, her researcher had freeze-framed a section of the same video of Massoud in which they had spotted Bob Bridges.

'It's the same one we watched before, Nell.'

'I know … we missed something. Focus on the man to the left of the picture who turns away from the camera. He clearly doesn't want to be filmed, but you just get a glimpse of his face.'

Toni watched. Just as Nell had described, one man kept his face turned away from the camera. As Massoud finished speaking he turned back momentarily, possibly believing the recording to have concluded. He soon realised his mistake, and twisted away again. 'It was too quick,' she said. 'Can you slow it down?'

'Give me a second.' Nell made some adjustments to the playback settings, rewound and then played the scene in slow motion. As the all-important frame appeared she pressed 'pause' and then magnified the image.

'My God,' said Toni. 'Synchronicity, Nell,' she said, softly.

It was Howard Green.

Howard was the connection they were looking for. Collins had indeed named him as Howard Graham. It all added up: Green's interest in the case, and his warning not to try and locate Collins. For Howard Graham, read Howard Green.

As Toni turned away from the screen, Stuart appeared behind her. It looked like he wanted to chat.

'Not now please,' she said, holding up her hand to him. 'We'll have time to talk later. Nip down to the underground car park, get the car and meet me out the front in five minutes. We're off to Hornchurch. After that, I've got a little job for you.'

Chapter 67

But, despite Jones's line management assuring her he was at home still recovering from injuries, it had been a wasted journey. The door had been answered by an attractive blonde woman who had introduced herself as his girlfriend. Apparently Kevin had gone to Hereford for several days. He was a guest at a Regiment wedding.

It was time to amend the plan. With time limited, next stop would have to be Finlay, although it would be harder to get him to talk. At the moment, she wasn't exactly in his good books. If there was something in his past he wanted to hide, he wouldn't be about to disclose it in answer to a straight question.

She would need a strategy. It didn't sit comfortably as she had grown to like the family, but Toni wanted answers now, and she had a feeling the key lay with how important Finlay's family was to him. If he thought they were under threat once again, he would talk to keep them safe. She just had to get under his skin, persuade him it was in his best interests ... and then see what he revealed.

Just as Toni closed the car door, her phone rang. It was Nell. The results had come through on the body in the car. They confirmed a match between the Home Office records for Nial Monaghan and the hair samples Stuart had managed to find in Monaghan's flat. And Nell had a further message. Dave Batey wanted to see Toni, urgently.

The moment the call ended, Stuart began questioning her about Nell's research. He seemed determined to understand the significance of looking into the Cristea family. Toni's mind was on what her department head wanted. It had to be about the copied security pass.

'Surely it's police work?' Stuart asked.

'What is? Oh ... maybe,' Toni mumbled, distracted by thoughts about Batey. 'But a lot of what the police do overlaps with us, and vice versa. That was Nell. Body in the car confirmed as Monaghan.' She hoped that the change in tack would steer Stuart away from the Cristeas.

'Well, at least we know, then. So, why ask Nell to dig around in this case? Do you think the Cristeas are connected to the attacks on Finlay and his mates?'

Toni sighed. 'No, nothing like that. We're just being thorough ... which we weren't last week. Finlay met them on holiday, saved the daughter from drowning and then got invited to attend her wedding in Romania. In normal circumstances that would have been fine, but it turns out that, far from being simple publishers, the Cristeas are, essentially, a Mafia-type family.'

'Ah ... I see. So we exposed him to a risk?'

'It's very kind of you to say *we*, Stuart. Actually it was me. So now you know why I'm on restricted duties,' she lied.

'Because you should have checked on them first?'

'The family are my responsibility. Fact is, we may not have learned about it except for the fact that a couple of days ago Finlay saw one of the Cristea people fleeing the scene of a murder.'

'He made the connection himself?'

'Yes, and he wasn't happy. So, I promised to make it up to him by digging up as much as I could on them.'

'To help identify the gunman?'

'Amongst other things, yes. It's the least I can do in the circumstances.'

'Did you see the report Nell did on Cristea Publishing's distribution centre in the Forest of Dean?' Stuart asked.

'Yes. They seem to be putting the proceeds of their criminal enterprises to good use.'

'Why would a publisher distribution factory want an incinerator?'

'You're referring to the planning application?'

'Yes.'

'You want a steady-Eddie answer or something more imaginative?' Toni fixed her companion with a firm stare.

'Try me with both?'

'An acceptable reason would be to destroy unsold stock, spoiled books, that kind of thing.'

'And the imaginative?'

'You don't want to think about it.'

Stuart paused for a moment as he slowed down to stop at a red light. 'Try me.'

'We know the Cristeas are into slave trafficking. Ever thought what happens to the women once they are no longer useful?'

Stuart stared at Toni, a look of horror on his face. He missed the light turning green and jerked into action as someone behind sounded their horn. 'Body disposal, you mean?' he said, once he'd recovered his voice.

Toni looked straight ahead. 'Like I said, it's only an idea.'

The remainder of the journey took place in virtual silence. Toni was too preoccupied to talk. By the end of the day, she might well be out of a job. Or, if she was lucky, Dave Batey might go along with an idea she was formulating.

And that would be where her new friend Stuart Anderson would come in.

Chapter 68

SO19 Firearms Branch, Old Street

For Lynn Wainwright, the late-turn reserve shift was dragging on.

With her firearms authority suspended for the period of the investigation, she felt like a spare part. The lawyer appointed by the Police Federation was optimistic, though. It was clear that the dead suspect had opened fire, and she had responded appropriately. Her version of events had been corroborated by the only witness, Detective Inspector Finlay, who also spoke highly of Lynn's skill and her reactions to a life-threatening situation. The lawyer felt she would be returned to full duties in a month or so.

Outside of the SO19 base, London was its usual cocktail of night life – with fun-seekers mixing with troublemakers. Almost every call for police help would, in some way, be related to either drug or alcohol use. The police officers on the streets reacted to each and every 'shout' with varying degrees of urgency, and in the background, the Trojan cars – the Armed Response Vehicles – cruised, ever patient, and always ready to be deployed.

With only one late-turn crew due in, Rod, the shift sergeant had suggested Lynn slide off early. He could see she was bored and her presence in the office was superfluous. Lynn already liked the sergeant and the offer of an early finish raised him even higher in her estimation.

She varied her route home, not due to any perceived threat of a security risk, but simply to try and avoid the worst of the traffic. At ten-thirty there would also be a higher number of drink drivers out on the street. There was no easy route at this time, but the City seemed to present the easiest option.

She was about halfway into the journey, stopped at some lights, when she felt the thud as a car travelling behind her made contact with her rear bumper. She swore, then raised her eyes to the heavens. This was all she needed.

With my luck it will be a drunk driver, she thought. She was in half-blues with a small, dark jacket pulled over her uniform shirt to provide extra warmth. Normally she would have changed into civilian clothes but tonight she was tired and had just wanted to get home to a hot bath.

There was no choice, she would have to get out and take a chance. If the people in the car behind recognised the uniform beneath her jacket, things would either go more smoothly or turn really awkward. It would probably depend on whether they were the worse for drink. Swinging the door of the VW open, she stepped out into the street and walked around to the back to see if any damage had been caused.

Apart from her car and the old, black Mercedes that sat behind it, the street was deserted. Lynn waved to the man in the driving seat, beckoning him to get out and to join her in checking for damage. The man looked foreign, maybe Greek. After a moment he seemed to understand her sign language and opened his door.

He *was* foreign. Perhaps she was in luck, after all. The damage to the Golf was minimal, just a scratch, and the Mercedes seemed untouched. There was a chance she might be able to ignore it and be on her way.

By waving and pointing, Lynn managed to get the Mercedes driver to look at the two car bumpers. They both leaned down to have a closer look. She could smell cigarette smoke as he breathed, but no sign of drink. Another blessing.

As she straightened up again, Lynn became aware of another figure behind her. She guessed it was the passenger from the Mercedes.

She turned to check, and a strong hand was immediately reaching around her face and squeezing some kind of gauze pad over her mouth and nose.

Her reaction was instant. She twisted, ducked down, and swung an elbow towards her assailant. At that same moment, something heavy connected with the side of her head. It knocked her to the ground.

She was stunned, struggling to comprehend what had happened. Then, it seemed that one of the men lay on top of her, pinning her to the road surface.

The gauze pad was, once again, forced over her face. Now, she could smell chemicals. She struggled in vain to twist, to kick out, and to breathe.

✠

Semiconscious, Lynn only barely registered her ankles and wrists being bound together and what felt like duct tape being stuck over her mouth, leaving just her nose to allow for breathing.

Next she felt what must have been a hood being pulled over her head and fastened around her neck with a cable tie.

One of the men lifted her with apparent ease, then dropped her again, into what, in her haze, she guessed was the boot of the Mercedes. The boot lid slamming shut brought her to her senses for a moment.

She listened, straining to hear a clue; anything that might tell her what the hell was going on. There was nothing.

Chapter 69

Jenny wasn't happy that I was working on a Saturday.

She repeated several times, before I left home, that the whole reason I had quit Royalty Protection – where seven-day working was the norm – was to be able to spend more time with my family. There wasn't much I could say to defend myself. It wasn't that I was married to the job, far from it. But the murder of Relia had got under my skin. Add to that the fact I had been so close to catching the gunmen who were hidden beneath the Ealing house and I knew I wouldn't be able to rest until her killers were caught.

Jenny said I was becoming obsessed. I ended up leaving the house without kissing her goodbye. It was the first time that had happened.

And I told myself it would be the last. The drive into work gave me time to reflect. Jenny was right. I still wasn't myself. I knew I should be talking to her more, reassuring her that the threat to our family was over, but I found it impossibly difficult to talk about. Finding Relia's killer stopped me from thinking about other things. Concentrating on work helped keep me sane. But I knew I couldn't keep avoiding the discussion that Jenny seemed so keen for us to have. She wanted to talk about our relationship. But I was beginning to fear what she wanted to say, that she would come out with something from which there would be no turning back.

We just needed time, time to settle. A new home, a period of peace and we would be fine. I knew it. And I would make sure never to leave the house again without kissing her.

✢

I arrived at the Murder Squad office just after eight. Although it was early, I was surprised to find that, apart from the Officer Manager, Naomi Young, and the DCI, the Incident Room was deserted.

I chanced a look through the large window into the DCI's office.

The mind map on the wall was starting to fill up with photographs and notes. Different coloured lines drawn with marker pens joined sticky notes to other seemingly connected lines of information and enquiry. Naomi was making coffee.

'Got a spare one?' I asked.

'You're an early bird today,' she replied as she poured a second cup and pulled a third mug from the cupboard.

'Things to do, people to see. You know how it is.'

'Well, you can start by taking this coffee in to the governor. He asked me if you were in today, there's been a DNA match from that cellar you found under the floorboards at the house in Ealing ... and there's more good news from the hospital. PC McCulloch is on the mend.'

I felt a wave of relief, picked up the drinks and tapped on DCI Bowler's door. He called me in immediately.

Naomi was right. I was told to sit down on the opposite side of the desk and then informed that we were going to brainstorm. There was to be no 'how-are-you, how's-the-family' type chat. It was straight to business.

'You've got a good brain, Finlay,' Bowler said. 'Nobody else even thought about the possibility of a hidden chamber under the house. Now bear with me while I go through what we've got so far, I want to make sure I'm not missing anything.'

The DCI confirmed that a DNA sample found in the cellar had been matched to the scene of Relia's murder. He also revealed that fingerprints found in the Ealing house belonged to one of a group of Romanian men who had arrived at Heathrow airport just a couple of days before the killing.

'It looks like they were a team brought in especially to carry out the job,' he said.

My guess was he was right and, chances were, they had already been spirited away to safety.

Moving onto the interviews with the sex-slave girls rescued from the house, Bowler told me these had produced very little. They were a wide range of nationalities – from Algerian to Moldovan, French to Italian. The one common factor was they were all from very poor families.

None of them had expressed a wish to return to their homes. All feared being re-abducted and, without exception, they viewed the possibility of life in the UK as a far better alternative to repatriation. The women had also been able to confirm that the gang running the trafficking route was Romanian.

My phone had beeped while we were chatting to alert me to a text message so when we broke off for a few minutes for the DCI to answer a call, I took a look.

The text was from Jenny. '*Ring me. Urgent.*'

I felt my stomach turn over. My hand trembled as I pressed our home number.

I forced myself to think sensibly. Hopefully it was news resulting from the estate-agent particulars we had been looking at. But the reason for the text had nothing to do with houses. There had been an email from Marica in Romania. Jenny read it to me, her voice trembling.

> *Robert, this is very hard for me to believe. Today, I find that you are a spy. I hear that you made it look like you save me from drowning when it was excuse to get inside my family. My father is very, very angry with you. He tells me you are a police spy and that if he ever sees you again he will kill you. Robert, I know what happened in the sea so I know I do owe you my life so this is why I make you this warning. Please do not come near me or my family again. Please be careful. Marica.*

For a moment, I was stunned into silence. Jenny and I shared an email address. It was the kind of message I would have preferred her not to see, but now the damage was done.

'What does it mean?' Jenny asked. I could hear her voice starting to break. She was near to tears.

I tried to be strong. 'It means what it says,' I said. 'You remember we talked in Bucharest about the Cristeas – what they did? Remember that car, the damage to the rear seats?'

'Yes. You said you were going to ask Petre about that.'

'Well, after we got back, I did some digging. I had a feeling the family were hooky and what I found confirmed it. To put it simply, the Cristeas are criminals.'

'What the hell's going on, Robert? You're leading us from one disaster to another.'

'Whoa Jen,' I pleaded. 'I had no idea before we went what they were like.'

'So, who are these bloody Cristea people? Is Marica serious? I mean ... for God's sake Bob, we only just got through some people trying to kill us and now we're gonna go through it again. I can't handle this ... I really can't.'

'They're crooks Jen ... but just in Romania. They can't touch us here.'

'You promise?' Jenny was crying now. Between the sobs, she continued. 'So why didn't the police stop you from going there, to Romania? They must have known it was risky.'

'They didn't know. I didn't know. Nobody knew before I checked what these people were like. I had no idea ...'

'What do they do ... I mean what kind of people are they?'

'Drug dealers.'

'... And you promise they can't touch us in England?'

'I promise. They're small-scale, local. They don't operate over here.'

Jenny stopped crying. The line went quiet for a few seconds.

'Robert,' she said, breaking the silence. 'We need to talk.'

'I know. Tonight ... I promise.'

'OK ... bring some wine home?'

The hole in my stomach reappeared as we ended the call. I hated lying about the Cristeas, but, caught on the hop, it seemed the best thing to do. I hoped, prayed, that I was right.

Marius Gabor had recognised me. Word had reached the Cristeas and now Marica knew. I shrugged it off. It didn't matter. I doubted if our paths would cross again. And if they did, it wouldn't be on their turf, it would be on mine.

I'd been lucky; in fact Jenny and I had both been lucky. The prospect of having been exposed while in Bucharest was too unpleasant to think about.

✝

Naomi joined me as I was returning to the DCI's office.

'You OK, Finlay?' she asked.

I nodded.

She frowned. 'You look like you've seen a ghost.'

'I'm fine, really,' I said. 'Your coffee is actually quite nice.'

Naomi laughed, her curiosity seemingly diverted.

As we sat down, the DCI explained the office-based detectives had put a lot of hours into identifying the connection between the murder victim, the dead gunman and the suspects from the petrol station. The telephone call that had interrupted us earlier was news that the dead gunmen's phone had been used in a number of areas around London and, on two occasions, in the west of England.

I reiterated what I had learned about the Cristeas from Interpol. Naomi left us for a few minutes to run some checks through the Police National Computer.

When she returned, she was smiling. 'Found them,' she said.

'Names and addresses for our suspects, you mean?' said Bowler.

'No, but a list of known associates; houses they use, phone numbers, et cetera. Just a question of time, now. I can start drawing up a list of places to turn over. If we can relate the forensics we have from the murder scene to similar samples from new scenes, we can start to narrow down the identity of the killers. If we strike lucky we might even find the actual people during the searches.'

Bowler slammed his pen on the desk. 'Brilliant; get on it Naomi.'

I was just about to leave when a thought occurred to me. 'I know it's a Saturday,' I said, 'but I thought there would be more than just us in today?'

'There are. The other two have gone over to Old Street. The WPC who saved your bacon didn't turn up for work this morning. They've gone with her sergeant to check her home and make sure she's OK.'

Chapter 70

The cell was dark.

Occasional light came from torches that the guards carried. From these glimpses Lynn had discovered that immediate escape from her prison was unlikely. The only way in or out was the solid wooden door. It opened into a space that seemed to have been hewn from rock. The rear wall of the cell was concrete blockwork – a possible weakness, she'd hoped. But after a few minutes exploration she found that it, too, was solid and, without tools, impregnable.

On first waking, Lynn had been utterly confused as to where she was. At first, she had expected it to be her own bed, but the cold, rough feeling of the damp blanket covering her brought with it the memory of the kidnapping.

Whatever drug they had used to knock her out had left an acrid taste in her mouth, and a God-awful headache. It was like a bad hangover. Cold, headache and a severe thirst.

There was no telling how long she had been unconscious. In the dark, she now checked her limbs. No pains, no injuries. Clothing seemed intact. That was good. Sniffing her armpit produced little by way of an odour, which suggested she had only been out for a few hours at the most. The final check was the toughest.

Unbuttoning her trousers, she slid her hand slowly into the top of her knickers. Carefully, she checked for any sign of injury or sexual assault. There was none. As she re-buttoned her waistband, she let out an audible sigh of relief.

With no idea where she was or what her captors were planning, Lynn mulled over her options. There were several, but all depended on knowledge. For the time being, there was little she could do other than wait. She had no idea if she was even in the UK. Extreme possibilities plagued her. If the kidnappers were terrorists, then her fate didn't bear thinking about. It was possible, though, her captors just planned to use her for sex. If that were the case they had better watch out, she thought.

One chance would be all that she would need to turn the tables on them.

Lynn forced herself to think sensibly. She wasn't an obvious target to secure a ransom pay-out. Her parents were ordinary, not wealthy, and the idea that someone would kidnap a cop for ransom seemed absurd. Chances were the men didn't even know she was a cop, so wouldn't realise that, before very long, her colleagues would be looking for her. She knew the lads would stop at nothing to find her.

Thoughts of the kidnappers being terrorists were daft, she told herself. It was just a case of a group of men who had stumbled across a lone female motorist at night and had taken the chance to grab her. The drug and face mask suggested they were prepared, though. Perhaps she could tell them she was a cop? That might persuade them to dump her, let her go. But the more she thought about that idea, the more she dismissed it. Knowing they'd kidnapped a police officer might make them panic. Their solution might be to kill her and hide her body.

No, best wait, she decided. Wait until I find out what is going on and then think about how the hell I'm going to get out of this.

✠

An abrupt burst of bright, wavering light from outside the door was her first indication she had a visitor.

The door burst open. Two torch beams pierced the gloom, pointing into her eyes, making her squint.

'Step forward.' The man giving the orders barked the instruction. His voice was deep, strong.

Lynn pictured a powerful man behind it. This was not the time to try and escape.

As she stood to obey, Lynn felt two sets of hands grab her arms from the side and force her hands behind her back. Next moment, a set of rigid handcuffs were clicked into place over her wrists.

She kept silent, but her mind was racing. The men had found *her* handcuffs. They had been in a bag on the back seat of her car. If the kidnappers had found them, they probably had her warrant card, too, and that meant they knew she was a cop.

Silently, the men guided her along a small corridor and out into a larger, cooler area. It remained dark, but there were more torch lights, perhaps six or seven. More men then grabbed her, stopping her from walking any further.

Her arms held tight, Lynn glanced around her, trying to gain a perspective on where she was and how many people were holding her. Her guess was that these were minions who had brought her out to meet the boss. Perhaps now she might learn what was going on.

'Close your eyes, Miss Wainwright.'

They knew her name. Why did he want her to close her eyes when there was so little light? It was the same powerful, accented voice she had heard in the cell. He was maybe fifteen or twenty feet in front of her, hidden in the darkness.

'You know my name,' Lynn said. 'What is this, some kind of hostage thing?'

The hard slap to the back of her head caught Lynn completely by surprise. If it hadn't been for the support of the men holding her arms it would have been enough to floor her. Stunned for a moment, she only just caught the repetition of the instruction.

'Close your eyes.'

Once again, a torch beam lit up her face. Lynn did as she was told.

From behind, someone slipped a small hood over her head. From some distance away there was the sound of an engine starting up. A generator. Lights came on.

Lynn took the chance, and opened her eyes, looking down past the edge of the ill-fitting hood. To each side she could see boot-clad feet; black, military type. The kind that police wear. The kind that she wore. For a moment a forlorn hope entered her mind. Was this a practical joke? Some kind of test? Why had they needed to hit her so hard, then? Met coppers were renowned for their creativity in putting together tricks to play on their fellow officers, but this was too much.

To her right she heard shuffling. People walking quietly. Lots of people. What was this, some kind of audience? For a moment, she felt sick. Then, bar the distant drone of the generator, all was silent.

A hand snatched at the hood and pulled it back, away from her head. For a moment, the lights blinded her. Then her eyes adjusted to the brightness, and she was able to focus on her surroundings. They were in a cave of some kind. The walls and roof were a dark grey.

A man in grey military-type fatigues was standing looking at her. Next to him was a woman, her head bowed, looking at the floor. Like Lynn, she too seemed to have her hands tied behind her back.

This wasn't a joke.

Glancing across to her right, Lynn saw the cause of the shuffling noise. There were about thirty or forty women, most with their hair tied up, all facing the man that stood in front of them. They stood in complete silence. Behind the women, to their side and near to her, she quickly counted eight guards. No chance of escape.

There seemed to be no reason for the hood. Placing it over her head had to have been a mind game, a ploy to create fear. It had worked.

'We have new girl,' the man in front said. He seemed to be addressing his words to the women.

Lynn looked at them. Their shoulders were hunched; faces drawn and pale. They looked like junkies – a line-up of forty or so drug addicts. Lynn felt a shiver run down her spine.

'... And we have problem. *Big* problem.' The man shouted the word as he turned towards the figure at his side.

The woman cowered away from the gaze of the silent audience. Only Lynn could see her face. The eyes were swollen and red. The poor wretch kept her vision fixed to the floor, only raising her look for one fleeting moment before the speaker continued.

In that instant, Lynn saw fear and desperation. A plea for help.

'This ... piece of filth went to police. This piece of shit tried to escape.'

Lynn wondered what the hell was going on. The man's voice was like the others – East European. But he spoke in English. Were all the women English? Was she still in England?

'Today, we are joined by new girl. Like we have warned you and we now warn this new girl. If you run, we will find you. If you go to authorities, they will bring you back to us. When we catch you, we will punish you. If we do not catch you, we will punish your families.'

Lynn quickly ran her eyes over the men. No weapons that she could see. How were they keeping the women under control? It must be fear, but fear of what? Her question was answered almost immediately.

The man at the front pulled a pistol from where it must have been tucked into his trouser belt. With practised skill, he cocked the gun and then pointed at the head of the woman next to him.

There was no hesitation, no opportunity for a last word, no respect for the taking of a life. As the pistol roared, blood, hair and skull fragments splattered across the floor. The woman's lifeless form collapsed in a heap at the man's feet.

Lynn felt her hands begin to tremble. From the watching women, there was no word, no reaction. Just the same thousand-yard stares.

The man walked towards her. He raised the pistol. Lynn could see it was a Glock. The barrel pointed at her eye.

My God, she thought. He's going to shoot me.

But he didn't. He just smiled.

'WPC Lynn Wainwright. So very nice to meet you. You killed one of my men; now you will work to pay debt you owe us.'

Lynn didn't reply. The obvious truth she'd avoided for the past few minutes was confirmed. These were the slave traffickers. They had come back for her. These men must be from the gang they had been looking for at the house in Ealing.

Her mind raced. At least she now knew why she was here, wherever 'here' was. What the speaker meant by working off her debt she would no doubt learn. They didn't plan to kill her, it seemed ... at least not immediately. Shooting the poor woman was clearly a lesson – to her and to the others.

'Take her away,' the man barked to the two men who held Lynn's arms.

As they spun her around, Lynn caught a glimpse of a tattoo on the forearm of the man who she had thought was about to execute her. She recognised it.

'*Legio Patria Nostra*'.

Chapter 71

The news about Lynn Wainwright didn't take long to reach me.

It was midday and I had just arrived outside Scotland Yard. I was parking the Citroen when my pocket started buzzing. It was Josh ... he sounded concerned. Together with the SO19 duty sergeant, he had been to Lynn's house to verify the local inspector's report that nobody was at home. The bed didn't look like it had been slept in and the neighbours had noticed that her car hadn't been in its usual spot. Lynn hadn't gone home the previous evening.

As Nina and I had been amongst the last people to see Lynn, Josh had been tasked to call us. I wasn't much help. Nina had spent more time with Lynn, so I suggested she might be a better person to speak to.

Josh told me discreet checks had been made at hospitals covering the route Lynn would take to work and with the Police Information Room to see if there had been any road accidents involving her car. With no reports of sightings and no clue to her whereabouts, ninety minutes after having noticed her absence, the SO19 duty inspector put in a call to his Chief Superintendent, Peter Ackerman.

Phone calls were made to Lynn's friends and colleagues. Did she have a boyfriend she might have stayed overnight with? Had she gone somewhere that might have delayed her getting to work? Was she depressed or particularly upset at being suspended? All responses came back negative.

Lynn Wainwright had disappeared.

And there was an even more worrying development. Josh was calling from Lambeth car pound. Lynn's car had been found on a removal lorry on its way to their lock-up facility.

It had been found abandoned in the middle of the street.

I had just finished the call with Josh, slipped off my seat belt and reached for the car door, when the phone rang again. It was Toni Fellowes. She wanted a chat.

'On a Saturday?' I asked.

'Yes,' came the brittle response. 'On a Saturday. Are you in your office?'

'I'm outside. Just parked the car. I'll be there in a few minutes.'

'I'll be waiting.'

☩

As I walked into our squad office, Toni was standing, looking distracted, as if something was playing on her mind. She wasn't the only one. After the earlier call from Jenny, I wasn't minded to give our liaison officer an easy ride. I wanted answers.

'How are you?' she asked, as she pulled up a chair and sat down. She indicated that I should do likewise – and in my own office, I thought.

'I've been better. Have you spoken to Jenny today?' I asked, bluntly.

'I haven't. Should I have?'

'Perhaps, yes. I imagined after exposing your charges to a risk like the Cristeas, you might be being extra careful.'

She held her hands up in apology. 'Look … I know. Believe me, if I could turn the clock back I would. Like I said on the phone, it was an oversight. I thought someone else was doing the checks; they thought I was. Left hand, right hand.'

'A little bird told me you knew about the Cristeas.'

'Nina Brasov, I'd bet.'

Not being the best at masking surprise, my reaction gave me away.

'I thought so,' Toni continued. 'She called me. She seems very protective of you.'

'We get on pretty well … she's a good detective.'

'Well, she was an angry detective when she called me. I tried to reassure her that I hadn't known the extent of the Cristea criminal connections, but she was having none of it.'

'Is she right?' I demanded. 'When I first asked you about it, I thought it was a case of you being careless. Now, it strikes me as a bit of a coincidence you gave me and Jenny a copy of a book that Cristea Publishing put out, just when I'm about to take a trip to the same resort they're staying at.'

'She's not … I promise you. Slave trafficking is not on the MI5 radar, especially not at the moment.'

'But what about the more obvious reason – that you were setting me up to try and locate Chas Collins? It's been in all the papers that the CIA and people like you are looking to have talks with him … and we all know what that means, don't we?'

'Believe me, this was a simple cock-up, not a conspiracy.'

I gave her a wry smile. I didn't believe her, and I made sure she knew it. Truth is, I'd never yet met a spook who was completely trustworthy. The fact that Toni had been pursuing an agenda shouldn't really have been a revelation to me.

'OK … let's leave it,' I said. 'I asked you if you've spoken to Jenny because the Cristeas have been in touch.'

'Contacted you, you mean?'

'It looks like the family sent a team over here to kill off a witness who was going to give evidence against them.'

'And they contacted you about that?'

'Not exactly. We had an email from the daughter, Marica. Like I told Nell, I saw one of their men near the scene of the murder this week and I was sure he clocked me. Well, it looks like I was right. He did recognise me and reported it home. The email was a warning to keep out of her father's way.'

'She threatened you?'

'It was a warning to a friend she considers she owes her life to. Unfortunately, Jenny opened it.'

'Christ … I'm sorry. Is Jenny upset?'

I stood, walked to the office door, and closed it gently before answering. 'You could say that, Toni. Or you might even start to think she is running out of patience. I'm heading home soon and she wants to talk. I put her through enough with what Monaghan tried to do to us. I hadn't wanted her to know anything about the Cristea family or the risk you exposed us to in Romania.'

'She would have found out eventually.'

'Would she?' I demanded, my voice revealing the anger I felt building. 'Sometimes ignorance is bliss, wouldn't you say?'

'And look where that got you before, Finlay. You kept your past secret for too long, and from the one person best placed to help you.'

'That's completely different,' I snapped.

Toni raised her hands again. 'OK ... OK, let's not argue. It's not going to get either of us anywhere. What's this I hear on the news about a missing WPC?'

She was changing the subject, but she was right: arguing got us nowhere. 'Bad luck seems to be my shadow at the moment,' I answered. 'We were involved in a shooting in West London. She shot one of the Cristea goons.'

'Dead?'

'Yes. And one escaped; I think it's the one who recognised me in Hampstead.'

'If there's anything I can do?'

'To make things up to me, you mean? Well, hold on to that thought, Toni, because you never know.'

'Is the WPC suspended?'

'Just from carrying a weapon, not from duty.'

'She's probably fine. Things like that can affect people. Maybe she's lying low for a while.'

I looked at Toni, aware she was tempering the conversation, trying to calm me down. 'Who knows? But, from what I'm being told, her disappearing like this is completely out of character. Anyway ... if you didn't ask me up here to talk about the Cristea email, what do you want?'

'I need to ask you some questions, some of which may seem a bit random. But I need you to be honest.'

'Sounds ominous. But fire away.'

I sat down and, for the next few minutes listened in silence while Toni spelled out the progress she had been making on the enquiry into Monaghan and Richard Webb. It wasn't good news. Her researcher,

Nell had uncovered even more links between the dead men than Tom Cochran had suggested when Kevin and I visited Credenhill.

The longer Toni spoke, the greater became my sense of impending doom. She asked a lot of questions, some of which I would have preferred she hadn't. I explained that I hadn't heard of Black Suit Travel but I knew there were people who did that type of work for MI6 and, yes, I was aware they were called Increment. I also confirmed I was aware Bob Bridges had been in the Middle East on operations with Increment after he left the Regiment.

Toni wanted to run some names and facts past me. First was Brian McNeil. The name was only vaguely familiar and no, he wasn't on the Iranian Embassy operation. Apparently, McNeil was another name from the same Black Suit Travel organisation. It employed another man she wanted to know about: Chris Grady. Grady I did remember – a Sergeant from 'D' squadron during the early 1980s. Grady hadn't been at the Embassy either.

'Are you in touch with any of the other men on the Increment team?' she asked.

'No … I lost contact with everyone from those days, apart from Kevin … although I bumped into Bob Bridges a couple of times after we both joined the Met, but we didn't keep in touch.'

'Have you ever met a man called Howard Green?'

My hesitation and the resulting look on Toni's face gave things away. The answer was yes. I did know a man called Howard Green.

'How do you know him, Finlay?' she asked.

I stalled. 'I'm not sure how to explain. About the same height as me, skinny?'

'Sounds like him. Let's continue with the honesty, shall we? I'll be open with you and, in turn, you tell me the truth.'

'Sounds good to me. Why are you asking about Howard?'

'I know there is a connection between you, him, the dead cops and Afghanistan.'

'Is there really?' I asked. 'And how might that be?'

'The book … *Cyclone*. The author changes names but it's pretty clear to me that it was Howard Green pulling the strings of the Increment team that were sent in to deliver the CIA weapons.'

'Green was with Six in those days,' I said. 'For all I know, he still is. Do you know him as well?'

'Yes, I do, and he's still with MI6. I think he holds the key to what was really behind the killings.'

'What do you mean, "really behind the killings"? Are you telling me it wasn't a case of Webb and Monaghan settling old scores?'

Toni hesitated. 'I can't be sure … look, I don't want to alarm you, but it's beginning to look that way. Yours and Kevin's army records have the same gap at the same time as the men who were killed. What were you two doing during that time?'

'Are you saying that me and Kevin are still targets?' I demanded. Even as I uttered the words, I felt myself getting hot, and my chest tightened. I could hardly believe what I was asking. I thought once more about what Jenny had said and what she wanted to talk about that evening. With the promises I had only recently made, I wouldn't want to tell her that the threat was back unless I was sure.

'I'm not saying that, no. I'm just saying that I can't solve the riddle until I have the whole picture.'

'For Christ's sake, Toni. That's not good enough.' I didn't care that I sounded angry now.

'OK … Ok. I'm sorry. Look, if I thought there was an immediate risk to your family I would have you out of that house straightaway. I don't … I'm just trying to piece together Monaghan's motives.'

I breathed more easily, but only slightly. 'OK …' I said, unsure if my honesty was being reciprocated.

'So … how do you know Howard Green?' Toni asked calmly. From her jacket pocket, she produced a small writing pad.

As I talked, she jotted down notes. I explained that, in the early 1980s, MI6 had brought Mujahideen fighters over to the UK to undertake weapons training and battle tactics – skills it was intended they took back to their home country to use against the occupying Russian forces. Kevin and I had been given the job of teaching them. Most of the theory work had taken place at a camp in Hampshire and then we had bussed them up to Scotland to do some live training in the Cairngorms.

One of the weapons we had taught the Afghans to use was Blowpipe, our UK surface-to-air missile. The Afghans were good students and quick to learn. They were also extremely brave fighters. Using the Blowpipe, they needed to be. Unlike the fire-and-forget missiles that superseded it, the Blowpipe was user-guided onto its target. That gave it the advantage of being able to hit both side-on and oncoming targets, but also meant that the firer had to break cover to be able to see what he was aiming at. The Mujahideen soon found out what we already knew: if you missed, or if there were other enemies in the vicinity, all hell would bear down on your position.

In the end, the fighters grew to hate the weapon and in fact had very little success with it. The CIA became involved and, not long afterwards, someone got hold of a load of American Stinger missiles. And that was when we met Howard Green.

Toni listened intently as I related how Howard had briefed Kevin and me and then travelled with us to the Peshawar Valley on the Pakistan border. There, we taught local fighters how to use the Stinger. The version they were supplied with was an old one, I explained, but very effective. Soviet air impunity was compromised, and the tide was turned in the war against the Afghan occupation.

I stopped talking, and Toni remained silent. She had stopped making notes. I wondered if I had revealed too much, even to an MI5 officer.

I waited. Finally, she spoke. 'I had no idea,' she said, her voice low, as if she feared we might be overheard.

'About the kind of operations our Government sends us on, you mean?'

'Yes … and the type of things you've personally been involved in. I think I now understand why you've never confided this in anyone.'

'It was a black op – a secret. Collins shouldn't have been allowed to get it published.'

'If it had been a UK publisher, he wouldn't. But that's not what I mean. I mean that, if what you're saying is true – and I'm certainly not implying it isn't – we were responsible for training the very people that our troops could be fighting in Iraq. And, if we go into Afghanistan, as the Americans are suggesting we will, our boys could be up against weapons we supplied used by people we trained.'

'*If* we go into Afghan. There's no certainty we will.'

'It's no wonder there's a gap in both yours and Kevin's military files.'

'Sometimes what's missing can tell you more than what is there,' I said.

'Someone else said that to me just recently.'

And then, Toni asked her final question. It rocked me to my core. 'Have you ever heard of something called "Al Anfal"?' she asked.

My expression gave me away once again.

'You have, then?'

'I have. But only recently,' I answered. 'I hope I can trust you, Toni.'

'What do you mean?'

'People have been searching homes of old mates. People who I think might be from the Security Service.'

'Me ... you mean?'

'Maybe. Was it you?'

'No, I promise you. I have no knowledge of any searches.'

Once again, I decided to trust her. 'OK ... I'll tell you. Bob Bridges left a document. His wife found it amongst his stuff after he died. It mentions the name "Al Anfal".'

'Christ. Does she still have it? Where is it now? Can I see it?'

'It's with a mate who speaks Arabic. He's trying to translate it for us. He also asked us if we knew the term.'

'Us ... who's us?'

'Me and Kevin. He was with me when we picked it up from Bob's house. Why do you want to know about it ... and what is Al Anfal anyway?' I demanded.

'Something or nothing. I'm not sure. Were you aware it was mentioned in the Chas Collins book? Something about a falling-out between the soldiers that resulted in one of them getting killed?'

'I wasn't. I've read the book and I remember reading about that fight, but I think I scanned through the bit that mentioned "Al Anfal". It mustn't have struck me as important at the time.'

'Well, trust me, it is important. I'd very much like to see that document as soon as possible.'

'I could do that I expect.' I thought as I spoke. Armstrong, the translator, was just across the border in Wales. It wouldn't be that easy to get the document back quickly, and I was also keen to know what it contained before I let Toni see it.

'Yes, do,' she said. 'I'll get back to you. In the meantime, try not to let my ideas get to you. It's probably nothing, I just have to make sure we have everything tied up before my final report goes in.'

'OK, I understand … and Toni?'

'Yes?'

'Make sure you're right. I made a mistake when I first learned of a threat to my family. I reacted too slowly … didn't take it seriously enough. It nearly cost me everything. So don't go giving me notions and theories and then wait until you're a hundred percent sure. If you think we're at risk, I need to know.'

Chapter 72

A few minutes after Toni headed back to her own office, I made my way to the basement.

Other than to access the underground car park, I hadn't visited the lower levels of New Scotland Yard in several years. As a result, it took me several attempts before I located the correct set of stairs. I was looking for the boiler room. As the dryness of the air increased, I knew I was getting closer. Finally, after the frustration of finding a couple of access points locked I located the one I was looking for. The wooden door felt warm to the touch and, as I pushed, a waft of hot air hit my face. This was it.

I closed the door, slid across the bolt to lock it and removed my jacket. I was alone now. The boiler room at New Scotland Yard was one of several places I came to when I needed solitude, somewhere to get my thoughts back in some sort of order.

The tension that had gripped me in the immediate aftermath of my conversation with Toni Fellowes began to fade as my heart rate slowed and the warmth relaxed me.

Now … I could focus.

I remembered Howard Green well. Kevin and I had shared many an hour with him in a Pakistan hotel and on the ground in Peshawar. He knew how to look after himself and he looked after us. He was a pro – well prepared and competent. Someone I had come to respect.

If Toni had another theory for the murders, I wasn't ready to buy into it. I had been with Jenny and Becky in a safe house, but Kevin, he had stayed in his own home and had been in hospital after being shot. He would have been an easy target if someone had wanted to get at him. No, I thought, Toni's idea didn't make sense.

But something did. Something Nina had said about Toni having a reason for wanting me to meet the Cristeas. We'd been on the wrong track in assuming the family were her interest. It was Collins, the author. That was the reason for the MI5 interest. It was Collins that Toni had been trying to get me close to, and she'd carelessly let me know it.

✢

By the time I emerged from the basement, the evening was drawing in but I was feeling better. And I'd made a decision. If Toni Fellowes had been trying to get me close to Chas Collins then it hadn't worked. Jenny and I had got home safe and the Cristeas were a problem that really was unlikely to affect us. I was going to forget about what Toni had done; Jenny and I were going to move out of the safe house, and we were going to get our lives back on track.

As I crossed the street near to St James's Park, I was whistling a tune that reflected my improved mood. Outside the tube station, the phone in my jacket pocket began ringing again. Josh, I thought. Hopefully with good news about Lynn Wainwright. But the number showing on the screen wasn't one the device recognised. I pressed the 'answer' button, feeling a sense of apprehension as I did so.

It was Julian Armstrong, Rupert's friend who was doing the document translation. I hadn't been expecting to hear from him for some time. He had been working on the document and it sounded like he was in a bit of a rush. He wanted to meet and also wanted to know where I was.

Perhaps Toni was going to get to see the document earlier than expected. I smiled to myself. I knew I was going to be busy, so I suggested getting together in the middle of the week.

Armstrong was having none of it. 'I really can't stress the urgency of this enough and, to be honest I don't think we should speak on the telephone. There are some things I need to show you. This really is very, very interesting.'

'OK,' I replied, stalling as I thought. The following day was a Sunday, so it was just possible I could drive down to Armstrong's place. It would also give me a chance to bring the document back to London so Toni could have a look at it.

The biggest problem would be squaring it with Jenny. I was already on a verbal warning; our last conversation having left me in no doubt that she was worried about our future. If I could leave early the next morning, I might get home by lunchtime. Traffic would be light so it wouldn't be too much of a chore to make the drive and if the document contained a key to what Bridges and the others might have been up to, I needed to know.

Armstrong wouldn't be drawn on what he meant by 'very interesting', just that I would understand once I had seen the translation work he had managed to complete so far. I jotted down the address, some rough directions and promised to try and get to him by about ten.

I decided to update Kevin. The connection cut through to his answerphone. I checked my watch, and realised he would be at Billy Lacanivalu's pre-wedding drink.

Chapter 73

MI5 HQ, London

The phone rang twice before Howard answered.

He seemed pleased, if a little taken aback, to hear from Toni. But the moment she mentioned getting together for dinner, he agreed.

And when she suggested making it that very evening, his enthusiasm was almost palpable. She explained that, as her home central heating had broken down, her plan was to work late and then find a room through one of the late-booking websites. It would be a great chance to have supper and catch up.

Not surprisingly, Howard had a better idea. He suggested they meet at One Aldwych, a hotel at the western end of Strand. It was a comfortable and convenient place for an officer to stay if they found themselves stranded in London without transport. The rates exceeded normal Security Service limits, but Howard explained he had a good contact and could book Toni a room without any great difficulty.

It was arranged. They would meet at eight.

One Aldwych: very nice, she thought. Howard was nothing if not predictable. And the bait was taken.

An hour later, Toni finished the fastest shopping trip she had ever managed. Surprisingly, it had been Stuart who first proposed the idea. 'Let him think he's on a promise,' he said. 'A honey trap.' First on the list was a new dress. She had chosen carefully and had settled on a black one, knee length, tight and with just a little cleavage on show. Nothing too obvious, just enough to keep Howard interested.

The shoes were also black, shiny and with three-inch heels. They would show off her legs nicely. As she checked herself over in the mirror, she noticed the approving looks from both Nell and Stuart.

'Not too tarty?' she asked.

'Perfect,' they both said simultaneously, almost as if they had rehearsed.

✝

Howard was true to his word. When Toni arrived at the hotel reception, an attentive maître d' saw her to a table tucked away in the corner of the restaurant, a discreet distance from other diners. Her date was waiting.

He was the perfect host. Helpful, but not patronising, he chose a good wine and then guided her through a menu he clearly knew well. As they chatted freely, she was careful to respond warmly to his overtures, smiling coyly and holding his gaze just a little longer than usual. As opportunity arose, she dropped the smallest of hints they might become more than just professional colleagues.

The evening was going well.

If there was one thing Howard wasn't, though, it was a fool. Years of work in the industry had clearly left him with a leaning towards cynicism. They were waiting for coffee to be served when he turned the subject of their conversation to work.

Then he looked her straight in the eye and asked about the real reason for their date.

She answered him without hesitating, having anticipated the question and conceded there would have been no point in denying an ulterior motive. She just had to hope he wanted her so much that he would be willing to barter information in exchange for her favours. First, she asked what he knew about the searches of the deceased soldiers' homes.

His reply was non-committal and disappointing. Howard Green wasn't that easily bought. But he did hint. He suggested he was in possession of the kind of knowledge she sought, and that, depending on how the evening progressed, he might be persuaded to be forthcoming. The ball was in her court.

Then Howard changed the subject. 'Have you had a chance to see your room yet?' he asked.

Toni admitted that she hadn't yet checked in. She also explained that she would be heading back to Scotland Yard in the morning in the same dress she was wearing for dinner.

He smiled broadly. 'No matter, I've managed to get you an upgrade. It's a suite; would you like me to show it to you? It overlooks the main road but it's very quiet. I took the liberty of asking them to put some champagne on ice, in case you would like a glass before turning in for the night.'

Toni returned the smile as she stood. 'Yes, that would be nice, on both counts, thanks.'

Inside, she was cringing. Aware that she was leading this man on in the hope that he might be persuaded to talk. This was going to be such a gamble; she just hoped her suspicions of him were correct.

Howard behaved himself both in the lift and along the corridor, but it was clear that he was reacting as Stuart had predicted. Now ... it was his turn to be disappointed.

As he opened the door to the suite, just as she'd planned, Toni's mobile rang in her handbag. With profuse and rehearsed apologies, she answered the call, listened to the prearranged report and then hung up. She trusted her acting skills were convincing.

She sighed and then shoved the phone into her bag, as if angry. 'I'm really sorry Howard, but we're going to have to take a rain check. This can't wait; I'm going to have to go.'

For all the disappointment her companion must have been feeling, he remained calm. 'Can't it wait, just for an hour, perhaps?' he asked in an uncharacteristically boyish voice.

She almost felt sorry for him. 'It can't,' she replied. 'I'm so sorry, Howard.' She placed her hand gently on his arm and kissed his cheek.

Then, as the door closed behind her, she let out a gentle sigh of relief. Howard Green had been expecting to get laid. What he did next would dictate the success or failure of their plan.

Chapter 74

Two floors below, Toni tapped gently on the door of room 104. The familiar features of David Batey appeared as he let her inside. Ditching her coat and handbag on a settee, she joined Nell and Stuart hard at work at a desk, open laptops before them, their focus on what they were listening to through the headphones they wore.

'What's he doing?' she asked.

Nell pressed a finger to her lips, and then tapped a key on her laptop. A voice started up from the speaker attached to the device. It was Howard Green.

'It's me,' Howard began. 'I have a nice hotel room and two hours to fill. Tell me where you are and I'll send a taxi.'

Toni grimaced. This wasn't part of the plan. There was a short pause as the recipient of the call appeared to be speaking. She glanced at Stuart and he did a thumbs-up. He was listening to the woman Howard was calling.

'What do you mean you can't?' Howard continued.

To her side, Toni heard Dave Batey mutter a stifled sigh of relief.

'What?' Howard said. He was sounding angry, an encouraging reaction. 'Not even for an hour or so? I'll double your rate.'

Don't go for it, Toni thought.

'OK,' said Howard. 'Give me half an hour.'

The speaker went quiet.

'He's ended the call,' said Stuart.

'What happened there?' Toni demanded. 'I thought he always went to see his little prostitute on this particular evening?'

'He does,' said Batey.

Stuart interrupted. 'He must have fancied the chance to use the hotel room. Luckily for us, she wasn't up for it and she suggested the usual place. We'd better get moving if we're going to be ready for them.'

'Well, it's just as well she did,' said Toni. 'For one minute there I thought we'd blown it.'

As Nell and Stuart gathered their kit, Toni headed into the alleyway behind the hotel and climbed into the waiting taxi cab. If their predictions were right, inside of half an hour Howard Green would be walking along St Pancras Way, having made the short tube ride to King's Cross. It was a journey he did every night, and from the mainline station he would catch a train to his home in the countryside.

It had taken some considerable effort on her part to persuade Dave Batey to authorise surveillance on a fellow Secret Service officer. At first, he had dismissed as complete nonsense her suggestion Howard Green was behind the use of her security pass. But, the more they had discussed it, the more it had made sense. Batey had eventually conceded that, when Toni had disobeyed Green's warning to keep away from Chas Collins, he'd followed up with an effort to discredit her. And that meant Howard Green was behind the killing of Dominic McGlinty. Faced with a good reason for the assassination, Batey had come round to Toni's way of thinking.

Soon after, he'd had Howard watched as he headed home from his office. It was impossible to listen to his workplace calls inside MI6 headquarters, but both his mobile telephone and his home line were now the subject of twenty-four-seven monitoring. It hadn't taken long for the surveillance to produce something Batey knew they could use.

Amongst the commuters, Howard was anonymous. He was one man – dark suit and overcoat, umbrella and briefcase; just another city-type journeying home. Nobody paid him any attention. Everyone on the evening trains kept themselves to themselves, heads down, collars up, unaware of the melee that surrounded them. But every so often, Howard slipped away from his fellow travellers and varied his journey. By checking CCTV from the station, the surveillance team spotted a regular break in his routine. And they soon found out what it was he was doing. He had a rendezvous to keep.

Howard would walk to a small block of flats about four hundred yards from Euston Road, nestled between King's Cross and St Pancras Stations. The surveillance team had reported, as he entered the backyard of the flats, it was clear he was familiar with the route. They saw how, with only limited light from a nearby lamppost, Howard easily found the fire escape stairs leading to the flat roof which, they noted was high enough to be above the reach of the street lights. In shadow, it was a perfect meeting place.

In the darkness, Howard's appointment would be waiting. He would hand her some folded-up cash and then, without a word, she would turn and place her hands on the parapet wall that overlooked the street.

Howard's response was the same each time. He would lift the woman's short skirt, stroke the skin of her buttocks for a few seconds and then start to spank her. He always used his bare hand and always struck her six times. It was his routine. Then he would unzip his trousers and take the object of his lust from behind.

Toni had been shocked as Dave Batey presented her with the photographs. His reaction had been more cynical. He'd heard rumours – nothing concrete, but enough to suggest what his team might uncover.

It was the supposed normality of it that Toni found hardest to comprehend. Within a few minutes of experiencing open-air sex with a prostitute in the middle of London, Howard would return to the station concourse as if nothing had happened, as if it were all part of his normal working day. And to any casual observer, he was perfectly normal. By then, he was just another man heading home to a warm house, a hot dinner and a dutiful wife. Just another man in a suit carrying an umbrella and a briefcase.

Just another man with a secret.

Chapter 75

Howard leaned over the parapet, apparently checking that the taxi had departed. The woman was waiting for him, as promised. She turned, faced the wall and hoisted up her skirt.

Toni checked the clock on the screen of her laptop. She was timing him, hoping against hope he took long enough for Stuart to get in position.

Seven minutes later, Howard tucked his shirt into his trousers, zipped his fly and straightened his tie.

'Longer than normal,' she said to herself, cynically. If he followed his routine, Howard would be heading back down the steps to the street in just a few moments.

He didn't disappoint. As she watched, her target leaned towards his companion and muttered something before picking up his umbrella and briefcase.

Toni smiled. In the doorway to the street, a tramp would by now be sprawled on the footway, blocking the exit. Howard would be obliged to climb over the sorry man, being careful not to step on him or cause any unpleasant confrontation. There would be an acrid stench of alcohol and stale urine. Then, if all went as it should, as he stepped clear of the tramp, another man would appear in the doorway: Dave Batey; smartly dressed, a dark wool overcoat covering his blue suit.

With his experience, Howard would, of course, recognise the threat. He would turn quickly to head back up the stairs, but it would be too late. The 'tramp' would have stood up, a 9mm Glock pistol in his hand levelled at Howard's stomach.

Toni cupped her hand over the tiny earpiece that sat in her right ear. Dave Batey's voice reached her.

'Please don't think of running, sir. Just put your hands on your head, link your fingers and relax. We just need a few minutes of your time.'

They had him.

They would search his clothing and body for weapons, making sure that he understood that they knew what they were doing. They would work quickly and methodically, keeping a safe distance from Howard's feet and placing their own bodies in such a way that any attempt to strike would be blocked. He would recognise the experience and professionalism displayed by their method.

'He's clean,' she heard Stuart report.

'Pull around the corner,' she said to her driver.

The black taxi started up. As they came to a halt adjacent to the building stairwell, she saw Stuart was covering Howard from behind. Dave Batey allowed a moment for her driver to climb out of the taxi before stepping forward and opening the rear door.

She was ready. The first thing Howard would see as he stepped inside the passenger compartment would be a figure sitting in the shadow at the far side. In the half-light he would catch a glimpse of a female leg, shiny black shoes, knee-length black dress.

And he would recognise his nemesis.

Chapter 76

As Howard Green sat on the bench seat next to her, Toni looked away from him and out of the window. She remained silent as her Section Head followed him, folded down a bulkhead seat and pulled the door closed behind him.

'Howard Green … meet Dave Batey,' Toni said. 'Dave is my boss, Howard.'

The two men nodded in stony-faced acknowledgement.

'Why the James Bond stuff?' Howard asked.

Toni sensed the anger in his tone. The taxi door next to her opened. Stuart leaned in and handed her a tiny SD card.

It was Batey's turn to speak. 'I'm sure you are fully aware what we have just been videoing, Howard.'

Toni produced the small laptop computer from the seat next to her and was in the process of inserting the SD card when Howard raised his hand.

'I'm sure we don't need to look at the screen to know what it will show, Toni. I just wish it had been you …' Howard transfixed her with his gaze, a thin smile spreading across his lips.

'Not a chance,' Toni replied, 'and certainly not the way you seem to enjoy. We just need your help with some questions.'

'How did you know to find me here?'

'Let's just say that you're a creature of habit, Howard.'

'You've been following me? Rather excessive if all you want is to learn why we've been searching the homes of dead cops for trophy weapons.'

'Don't be too smug, Howard.' Batey continued. 'I know that you copied Toni's security pass before it was used by an operator who killed an IRA prisoner in Belmarsh. We know a lot, Howard. We just need to fill in a few pieces of the jigsaw, so let's cut through the bullshit and make a start...'

Howard scowled and shook his head. 'Not me ... and don't get any ideas. I'm just a small pawn in a great big game. You know how it works ... both of you.'

Batey smiled. 'That's a pity Howard. Especially as I'm quite sure you wouldn't want this evening's recording made public. Just imagine the fuss should it be emailed to your wife, your friends, the newspapers, your workplace ... Not to put you under any pressure, but that will take place in about five minutes if you decide not to cooperate. We'll ruin you, both professionally and personally. And whilst you are trying to rescue your marriage we will have discovered your offshore bank accounts and the cash you've been putting away.'

'Sod off, Batey. You wouldn't bloody dare.'

Dave Batey sat silently.

'Fuck ... you're bloody serious,' said Howard.

'Couldn't be more so, Howard. So ... let's start with the pass. You copied it?'

Blackmailing a fellow security service officer didn't sit comfortably with Toni, but Howard was an exception. By stealing her identity he knew he might be ruining her career; at worst, he could have risked her life. The answer as to how her security pass had been copied had come to her just as she had been finishing off the report breaking down her movements and contacts for the last six months. The only time it had been out of her control had been during that visit to see Howard Green at the MI6 building.

Howard saw sense. Toni's pass had been stolen, he soon admitted.

And then he claimed it was simply because she was the liaison officer looking after the Monaghan enquiry; nothing personal. Anyone else visiting McGlinty would have aroused suspicion. He even attempted an apology. Toni just glared at him. She didn't believe a word of it.

'You warned me away from Chas Collins,' she said.

'For your own good. Collins has rattled some major cages with that bloody book. It was best you didn't get involved.'

'So when Robert Finlay turned up in Romania you weren't best pleased, I presume?' said Batey.

'It was of little consequence,' came the dismissive reply.

'So Toni here had disobeyed you and you had no intention of doing anything about it?'

Howard turned to face her. 'That transgression would have been dealt with,' he said, his face deadpan.

'Some might suggest that using Toni's pass at the prison would discredit her so badly that she would no longer be a problem ... that presumes, of course, that her enquiries into Chas Collins were, in fact, causing a problem.'

Howard twitched his lips slightly.

'What it also tells us is that you were behind McGlinty's death ...'

'... from food poisoning. He died of natural causes, I heard.'

'Were you involved in it?' Batey demanded.

'Like I said ... natural causes.'

Batey just stared at Howard. From the look, Toni guessed that her boss was starting to thoroughly dislike the man. She decided it was time to move on to the murdered SAS soldiers.

'What's your connection to Operation Cyclone in Afghanistan, Howard?' she asked.

'You know I can't speak about that kind of thing.'

'I know you were there,' she pressed. 'I've seen pictures of you with the Increment team.'

'Really? My, my ... you *have* been doing your homework.'

'Yes ... so just fill in some gaps for me,' said Toni, ignoring the attempt to goad her.

'Like I said just now, the *Cyclone* book explains most of it.'

'You're Howard Graham, I guess?'

'Howard Graham, Howard Green. We all had false names on that op. Yes, I was there. That's where I met Bob Finlay. He was in the army then. Good soldier. That's how I recognised him when he turned up at the Red Sea hotel.'

'So, why the interest in him?'

'In those days Finlay was a top operator. I was just being careful, making sure that him turning up really was a coincidence.'

'You're aware that I'm looking into the deaths of the ex-SAS soldiers that were killed recently?'

'Yes, of course I know about it. You asked for authority to view some files, I recall.'

'I think the deaths are all connected. The police conclusion is a vendetta conducted by one of the dead men, Nial Monaghan, but I've found another link ... and the fact that ten out of the twelve men on the Increment team are dead.'

'Do go on.'

'What do you know about "Al Anfal"?'

Howard took a deep breath and relaxed into his seat. 'Well, at least I now know one thing,' he said.

'What is that?' Toni asked.

'It must have been you who typed those words into a public internet search engine, recently. So, let's get back to how you found me this evening – set this up, I mean?' Howard asked.

Toni smiled as she recognised he was trying to veer off subject. 'You're a creature of habit, Howard. Keep coming back and, one day, somebody was bound to spot you.'

'You followed me?'

'You'll never know. Now, shall we get back to the deaths of the ex-soldiers?'

'It's all in that book. The CIA ran a black op to supply the Mujahideen with weapons to fight the Soviet force occupying Afghanistan.'

Toni smiled to herself. Her researcher had done well. She was about to repeat her question about 'Al Anfal' when Howard interrupted her.

'Who else knows about "Al Anfal"?' he asked.

'Outside of this taxi, you mean?' said Toni.

'As a result of your digging.'

'Just us two. We haven't taken it upstairs yet, if that's what you're asking?'

'OK ... Well, you'd best keep it that way. I'll tell you ... for all the good it will do you, but I want some guarantees.'

'That this evening will be forgotten?' said Batey.

'Exactly. I don't for a minute believe your threats but the very existence of the recording you have causes me some discomfort. I would rather it didn't exist.'

'You have my word.'

'The word of one spy to another?'

'Possibly little better than that of a politician ... but it's the best you're going to get, Howard.'

Howard paused for several seconds. Toni guessed he was weighing up his options. His response suggested he had decided to trust them.

'OK ... I'll spell it out for you. But, like I said, it's a poisoned chalice. It's like this: if you think Al Q'aeda are a major problem, think again. Al Q'aeda are the operational side of the threat. A bit like the IRA were in the seventies and eighties.'

'Al Q'aeda didn't exist in the days when those lads were in Afghan,' Toni interrupted.

Howard smiled. 'Al Q'aeda started way before you and I were aware of it. What preceded it was "Al Anfal".'

'You're saying it's another terror group?' asked Batey. 'From what we've been able to deduce, "Al Anfal" seems to be some form of treasure, something valuable.'

Howard laughed. 'Oh, it's valuable alright. But it's *knowledge* of "Al Anfal", not the thing itself that has value. No, "Al Anfal" isn't a treasure, it's ... well ... politics. To quote their doctrine, "I will cast terror into the hearts of those who disbelieve". Al Anfal is the political wing of terror. It's like Sinn Fein for Islam, only much bigger and highly secretive.'

Howard's story was incredible and he clearly knew his subject in great detail. Both Batey and Toni listened with a mixture of horror and fascination.

Al Anfal, he revealed, dated back to medieval times, to '*Sura Al-Anfal*', the 'Spoils of War', which, as he explained, was the eighth chapter of the Qur'an. The chapter detailed military tactics and operations, advocated a base in Afghan and trained its members in the means to spread fundamentalism throughout the world.

Toni understood her error in assessing what 'Al Anfal' was. Her conclusion from the search engine explanation, that the wording meant 'Spoils of War', had been to assume that it was an item of value.

Batey commented that it sounded like a template to spread Islam through the Arabic world and from there, to Europe, Asia and beyond. Howard confirmed the analysis and added that it was a philosophy based on centuries, not years.

Howard related how a patrol of ex-SAS soldiers had stumbled across a document that outlined the Al Anfal plans on how to infiltrate political systems, generate sedition, fester unrest, overthrow governments and install Islamic law in countries across the world. Short-term targets included Iraq, Libya, Egypt, Yemen, Syria and even Saudi Arabia. Other states, such as Oman and Kenya, were also to be targeted. Long-term plans listed European countries, including the UK. The document had been handed to Howard, as MI6 field officer in Afghan. He had forwarded it to London, where it had been translated. The implications were huge and had been taken to the very highest levels. After a great deal of discussion, a decision had been made to use the knowledge gained from the document rather than try to stop the tide in its tracks. When Al Anfal moved people into political positions in the UK, they were monitored, compromised and then turned. Howard seemed proud as he described how MI6 was able to use Al Anfal agents against the organisation and slow the tide of progress.

'It's one of our most closely guarded secrets … for obvious reasons,' Howard said, finally.

'Better to know what your enemy is doing than drive them underground,' commented Batey. 'And better to have them venting their energies fighting each other than uniting against the West as a common enemy?'

'Exactly.' Howard seemed to be enjoying the audience.

Toni was beginning to understand. But so far, it didn't explain why the soldiers had been killed, and it didn't solve the mystery of how Robert Finlay and Kevin Jones had been drawn into it.

'Are you saying there are politicians in the UK who are part of this Al Anfal group?' she asked.

'Yes, all the way through from local councillors, MPs and, until recently, a Government Minister.'

'Who?'

'Don't be naive, Toni. Best you don't know.'

'Does this have anything to do with the Al-Liby enquiry – the so-called 'Manual of Jihad' that the French journalists are planning to expose?'

'You're finally getting it,' Howard sneered. 'That manual is a small part of the document the SAS lads found.'

'Jesus ... those journalists were also warned off. So you're taking steps to stop knowledge of it leaking out.' Toni was aware that the cab was steaming up. She wiped the moisture from the glass and was reassured to see Stuart, the tramp, standing a few yards away. 'How come we don't know about it, in MI5, I mean?'

'At the highest level, you most certainly do. But the security clearance is top flight.'

'So is there a connection between it and the deaths of the ex-SAS soldiers?' asked Toni.

'The Jihad manual is nothing compared to the Al Anfal document. One of the Increment men – Blackwood, we think – photocopied it and kept the copy. A while ago he had it partially translated and, bingo, he realised it was worth a fortune if he could hawk it to a national newspaper.'

'You're not telling me MI6 took him out for that?'

'At that point it wasn't known about. It was only when he actually took it to the papers that one of our agents managed to intercept it. As I understand, an attempt was made to persuade him to stay quiet, but then we found out he'd made more copies, given them to his mates. So, an operation was launched to ensure Al Anfal was kept a complete secret.'

'What kind of operation?' asked Toni.

'Damage limitation. We needed to plug the leak. The plan was to use the same kind of coercion that you've just used on me.'

'I understand,' said Batey. 'But on home soil that would need MI5 involvement.'

Howard smiled, raised his eyebrows, but said nothing. He didn't need to. Both Batey and Toni realised MI5 *had* been involved. In fact, they had taken on the job. Monaghan must have been the officer deputed to do it.

Toni could hardly believe her ears. 'That meant that everybody who knew of it had to be silenced?' she asked.

'Indeed.'

'So the solution was to kill them all ... including McGlinty in Belmarsh? I thought there were rules governing that kind of thing – signed approvals from the Home Secretary ... don't you follow any rules at all?'

'We have rules. Monaghan broke them. He was supposed to just persuade the soldiers to hand over any documents they had and to keep quiet. It should have been a relatively simple job to blackmail them. But, no, he took it upon himself to have them terminated.'

'All of them?'

'Yes, all of them ... and now I'm having to clear up the mess he left behind.'

'Does that include Brian McNeil? He was also one of the other Increment men.'

'Yes, he was one, last heard of in Iraq, I believe.'

'He's alive?'

'To the best of my knowledge, yes. I can confirm he was one of the men that Monaghan was supposed to speak to.'

'And what about the last one, Chris Grady – what's become of him?'

'Grady I can't discuss other than to say that he's also alive.'

'Was Monaghan supposed to *speak* to him, too?' Toni tweaked her first fingers to emulate inverted commas and emphasise the word.

Howard shifted in his seat, seemingly uncomfortable at her inference. 'He was.'

'Is he in hiding or something?'

'Sorry, Toni. I can't discuss Grady.'

'And what about the others? There were a total of twelve men on that patrol – thirteen if the account given by Chas Collins is to be believed. Ten of them are dead. Did Monaghan get rid of all of them?'

'Monaghan had his faults but he was thorough.'

'Jesus. That's wholesale bloody murder.'

'Like I said, the intention was to give them the option to keep quiet. Perhaps Monaghan tried that and failed?'

'OK ... but killing off McGlinty wasn't Monaghan's doing. That was you tidying up any link back to the Security Service?'

'That's about the sum of it. We couldn't take a chance he knew what Monaghan had been doing.'

'What kind of rule is it that allows you to steal my fucking identity card and use it to kill a man in prison?' Toni felt her temper rising.

'I'm sorry, Toni. We needed a way into the prison and your card ... well, it just became available at the right time. Nothing personal ... and, like you said, we needed the option to get you out of the picture in case you got too close.'

Toni became aware of Batey placing a hand on her forearm and squeezing it gently. She forced herself to relax. The time to get even with Howard Green would come later.

Batey resumed the questioning. 'Finlay and Jones ... they had no knowledge of the document, and they weren't on the team that you used in Afghan.'

'Again ... not one of our finest hours, I'm afraid. When Nial Monaghan was given the job, he succumbed to the opportunity to settle some old scores. Those two were added to his hit list. If he hadn't been killed himself, then likely as not, he would have got away with it. He would have just reported that they also knew about Al Anfal and had to be taken out.'

'So who killed Monaghan?'

'We're not sure. One of the terrorists he'd engaged to do his dirty work, we think. Probably the Irishman who had been posing as an Arab. He thought he'd been betrayed by Monaghan, so he had the motive.'

Toni breathed a shallow sigh of relief. Finlay and Jones were in the clear.

Chapter 77

With Howard Green released, Toni and Dave Batey sat for several moments before either of them spoke.

What Howard had said had stunned them, as had his willingness to talk. But now, they began to realise that he wasn't afraid to tell them, because he knew they would dare not tell anyone else. Knowledge gave power but, in this case, it was just as Howard had described: a poisoned chalice. Neither of them could admit to anyone that they knew about Al Anfal, or that they had even heard of it. To do so would place them at risk. The very same risk the former soldiers had exposed themselves to when they had decided to try to sell the story. The soldiers had been silenced. Two more casualties, even MI5 officers, might easily be justified to maintain such a sensitive secret.

As Toni watched Howard march along the pavement towards King's Cross, she understood why he walked so confidently.

The best thing to come out of the meeting was the promise that Howard had made to ensure that the copy of her pass would be sent to Dave Batey the very next day. At least her career was saved.

The tense atmosphere in the rear of the taxi was only broken when Stuart Anderson opened the nearside door.

'Your man has hailed a cab, are we done for the night?'

Toni turned to face the door. 'Yes, thanks. You did a great job. Tell the others to stand down.'

'You OK?' Stuart asked. 'Not being funny, but you look a bit shocked.'

'We're fine ... really. Can you close the door a moment, we need a few more minutes.'

'When is your report on Monaghan due with the Director?' Batey asked, as the door closed.

'Already late with it,' Toni said. 'I'm wondering exactly what to put in it now.'

'Well, you can't mention Al Anfal. Finish the report tomorrow, please.'

'On a Sunday?'

'Yes. I'll be in as well, so you can run it past me. Make your conclusion that Monaghan was acting alone and to his own agenda. Endorse what the police Commander said about it being a jealous husband and a vengeful terrorist.'

'You think Howard is telling the truth?'

'If I'm completely honest with you it explains some other things that have happened in the last few years. Nothing I can share with you, though.'

'What do you want me to tell Finlay and Jones?' Toni asked.

'Again, stick with the initial conclusions. There's no need for them to know any more and no need for any further worry on their part. They don't know about this political Jihad and they need have no idea as to the real reason their mates were killed. Let's leave it that way.'

'They seem to have no idea how many former soldiers have been eliminated.'

'Best it stays that way, I think.'

'Time to mind our own business?'

'Exactly.'

'I just don't understand why Monaghan had to kill all those men. Why not simply blackmail them? They could have used the same kind of leverage we threatened Howard with.'

Batey smiled. 'Think about it Toni. You can't have that many people subject to the same kind of blackmail at the same time and not have one of them leak it ... or maybe some journalist somewhere put two and two together. I wouldn't be too sure that was Monaghan's decision, despite what Howard says. I wonder if it might have been a deniable judgement made at a much higher level. Whatever happened, a decision was made and people like us carried it out.'

'What about Grady and McNeil?'

'Forget about them. In the case of Grady, I'd guess he's not only alive, he's one of us – probably still working for the Security Service. It would seem a likely progression from Increment.'

'Maybe that's why Monaghan didn't find him. What do you think will happen with Collins?' Toni asked.

'At a guess, MI6 will have plans to finish off what Monaghan started.'

'Kill him, you mean?'

'If you want to put it that way. Fear you would discover what was going on is probably the real reason you were warned away from him.'

'And what did you think of the Al Anfal thing, a plan to create some kind of Caliphate in the Middle East?'

Batey thought for a moment. 'I've got no idea. If what they are saying is right then people like Gaddafi are going to be prime targets. We would like that, so would the Americans. Better to have the threat of disorganised fundamentalists than the power of a dictator and, like I said to Howard, better to have them fighting each other.'

'And what about on home turf?'

'At Director level, we must already be aware. There's no way that Six could run an op like that on home soil without the Security Service knowing about it. That means you can't tell your team what Howard told us ... not a soul, in fact.'

'Trust no one?'

'The world of the spy, Toni ... And on the subject of Finlay and Jones, you'd better be careful about what you tell Stuart and Nell about them as well.'

'What about the report on my security card?'

'Leave that with me.'

As Batey opened the rear door to the taxi, Stuart appeared. He was wet, and Toni could see it had started to rain. He looked agitated.

'Nell's been trying to reach you. Green is on the phone; you're not going to believe who he's just called.'

Chapter 78

'Give us a moment, Nell,' said Toni.

They were back at the office and Nell was squirming in her chair, rubbing her hands together and clearly bursting to share what she had heard. Toni flung her wet coat onto the nearest desk and wheeled her chair over to join Nell in front of her screen. Dave Batey and Stuart had just arrived and were in the process of closing the security door.

'Make us a brew, lad,' said Batey.

Stuart frowned, his sense of disappointment apparent. He wasn't going to be close enough to hear the recording Nell was about to play back.

Batey saw his face. 'Sorry Stuart. This is for our ears only.'

Toni understood. Although Stuart was aware that Nell had recorded Howard Green telephoning Dirt, he was in the dark regarding the content of the conversation. As for Nell, it was already too late; she had listened to it live.

'Where exactly did it take place, Nell?' she asked, as her assistant lined up the beginning of the recording.

'Sounded like he was in the back of a cab. It was just a few minutes after he left you.'

Batey raised an eyebrow. 'So he called the Director straight after talking to us?'

'And he wasn't happy,' said Nell.

'Is he out to make trouble?' Toni asked.

Nell rubbed her hands on her thighs and then pressed a key. 'Listen for yourself.'

Toni leaned forward as the voice of Howard Green began:

'Apologies for calling you at this late hour, I have a problem that I need a decision on.'

There was a pause, as if the recipient of the call was trying to decide how best to respond.

'Where are you?'

'In a taxi on the way back into town. It's safe.'

'What's the problem?'

'I'm compromised. Two of your staff have just done a number on me.'

'Really? Am I to presume that one of them was Ms Fellowes?'

Listening to the second voice, Toni was at first uncertain as to Nell's earlier assertion it was Director 'T' Howard had called. But as she heard the way he pronounced 'Ms Fellowes', those doubts disappeared. It was him.

'The bitch tried a fucking honey trap on me. I thought I saw it a mile off but they were clever; set me up with a tart and then filmed it.'

'A *compromat*? Fellowes has the makings of a spy, after all.'

'Yes, a fucking *compromat*. Made it look bad for me and then threatened to send the recording to my wife.'

'That could have been awkward, Howard. I presume this threat didn't actually happen.'

'No. I called their bluff.'

'*Their* bluff? Who was with her?'

'Her Section Head, David Batey.'

Another pause. Toni glanced across. Batey stared intently at the PC screen, beads of sweat forming on his brow.

'So … that rather explains why he has been a little slow in coming up with a report on the misuse of Fellowes' security pass. Am I to conclude they worked out it was you responsible for copying it?'

'Correct. And that the termination of McGlinty was undertaken by Six.'

'Do they know why?'

'They know about Al Anfal. Fellowes thought it was an artefact, some form of treasure, but she had worked out it was the connection between the dead soldiers.'

'They know about Al Anfal? Interesting … and I issued her with specific instructions to keep me informed of any unusual developments in her enquiry. It is most regrettable that she chose to ignore my order.'

'They asked about the searches at the Skinner and Bridges homes as well.'

'What did you tell them?'

'Nothing … but they're not fools. They know it was us.'

Batey leaned across in front of Toni and placed a firm hand on Nell's shoulder. 'Pause it a minute, Nell,' he said, firmly.

Nell tapped a key.

'Nell, I'm going to need to ask you to join Stuart in the tea room while Toni and I talk.'

The researcher squared her shoulders and stood, silently. Without uttering a word, she slid back her chair and walked to join her colleague.

Toni flinched as the tea room door slammed shut. 'Sorry about that,' she said to Batey. 'Nell has her own particular way of expressing herself.'

'I have two daughters, Toni. Trust me when I say I'm quite familiar with door slamming. Now, first things first: are we absolutely sure Howard Green isn't aware his phone conversations are tapped?'

'He isn't. Nell was well aware he uses a secure service device and when she tells me she can hack into it without him knowing, I trust her completely.'

'OK … it's just that it occurred to me that this might be a conversation he knows we are listening to.'

'If he did, would he have let himself get caught shagging a tart on a rooftop in King's Cross?' said Toni.

'I suppose he could have allowed himself to fall into our trap without actually doing that, but what about after he left us? He could have decided to stage this to misdirect us?'

'Do you really think that?'

'No … I'm just trying to cover all possibilities.'

'So, are you suggesting he wanted us to catch him?' It was a development she hadn't anticipated.

'No … I'm just being cautious. That is our Director he is talking to, without doubt.'

'Agreed.'

'So, I also think we need to be prepared for what this recording may reveal. It's already certain the Director knew far more about McGlinty's death than he let on at the post-incident briefing.'

'That's for sure,' said Toni. 'He had me in his office afterwards and asked me to keep him updated on my investigation. Even gave me his private email. He wanted to know what I discovered before anyone else did.'

'And you definitely haven't mentioned Al Anfal to him?'

'No … I was only planning to do so once I was sure what it was.'

'He was using you to test the water, to see if the existence remains a secret or not. And it's my guess Howard is about to tell him we know all about it.'

'Dob me in, you mean?'

'*Us* in. This isn't a school prank we're talking about here, Toni. Men like Howard deal in much higher stakes.'

'Yes, I'm sorry.'

'You realise we may be about to listen to a life-changing conversation.'

'For us, you mean.'

'I do, yes. What Nell already knows – and what we are about to listen to – is a conversation between a Secret Service Director and an MI6 officer who has orchestrated the deaths of an MI6 team of soldiers. The motive for that operation appears to be to prevent them selling top secret information. And that is information we are now party to.'

'You're certain they're behind it, then?'

'Do *you* need any more convincing, Toni?'

'No … I guess not. Nell also heard it, of course.'

'Correct … and, if they say what we're expecting, we have to be prepared to deal with the consequences.'

'Which are?'

'I'm not sure … I just wanted you to be prepared, that's all.'

Toni spun around in her chair to face the tea room. 'I'll get Nell.'

With Stuart still making the most delayed brew in service history, Toni, Nell and Batey huddled around the PC and continued to listen.

'Indeed … as you say, they are not fools. So, what did you decide to tell them about Al Anfal, Howard?'

'Enough to put them in no doubt they could take it no further.'

'You made it perfectly clear this is a matter of national security?'

'And that anyone who compromises the matter will be dealt with.'

'Hmm … very well. So, Fellowes' report will blame Monaghan.'

'I'm certain it will.'

'That's good. Perhaps this hadn't turned out as badly as it might have. And, to be frank, when Monaghan went off track we always knew this might happen. What about the two remaining policemen, Jones and Finlay?'

'According to Fellowes, they are out of the loop, no knowledge of Al Anfal and no reason to think that the deaths of their mates weren't Monaghan pursuing his own agenda.'

'Good. We really didn't need any more loss of life.'

'I'm not entirely sure about Batey, though. He wasn't at all happy that I had used one of his team as a scapegoat.'

'I hope you made it clear that was her own fault. If she'd heeded the warning to steer clear of Collins, it wouldn't have been necessary.'

'My words exactly. I'm just a little wary of Batey's reputation.'

The recording went quiet.

Toni glanced once more at her line manager. He was steely-faced. If he was disturbed at listening to the discussion, it didn't show. For her, though, there was no doubt. Howard Green had intended to end her career in the Service, and the Director had known about it. Batey had been right when he'd warned they needed to be prepared for what the recording would reveal.

It was the Director who spoke next.

'Leave it with me; we'll talk in a day or two. Batey is a good man … due to retire soon and I had thought it likely that Fellowes would replace him. I need to give it some thought.'

'In the meantime, do you still want me to deal with Collins?'

'Yes, have your man on standby.'

'I thought that the TV exposé effectively destroyed him?'

'It did, but his connection with Cristea Publishing worries me. And he knows about Al Anfal, his book makes that clear. The fact that he seems to think it's an artefact doesn't diminish the effect of revealing the name. The whole operation might have been ruined.'

'The damage is done, you mean?'

'Possibly. Eliminating Collins would, to some extent, be shutting the stable door after the horse has bolted.'

'What if he does a second book to cash in on the first?'

'It would all depend on what he wrote. But he's a risk I'm not comfortable with.'

'A problem best sorted, perhaps? It might be tidier if I had Grady terminate his contract.'

'Very well … do what you're good at, Howard. Like you say, it would be tidier. And, I'll let you know as soon as I have Fellowes' report on my desk.'

The call ended. Nell paused the play-back before speaking. 'The next call is to a mobile. He tells someone called Grady to pack his bags for another job. The call ends without a response from the recipient.'

Toni blew out her cheeks. 'Well … that confirms what happened to Chris Grady and why Howard wouldn't talk about him. He *is* an MI6 asset.'

'A hit man,' said Batey. 'No doubt one of the pair that took out McGlinty.'

'So, where does this leave us?'

'The way I see it we are in exactly the same situation we were, except we now know our Director is also part of the operation.'

'You mean we say nothing … do nothing.'

'I think we do exactly what they expect. You finish the Hastings report and blame Monaghan; I'll deal with the issue of your security pass and ensure you are fully exonerated. In normal circumstances the Director might have considered you a security risk, but we now know that's not the case.'

'As he knows full well who was behind the killing?'

'Correct. And, like he says, I'm due to retire soon, so, who knows, he may even decide to promote you.'

Toni half smiled, her fingers digging deep into her neck as she attempted to ease the tension she was now feeling.

'Best you call Robert Finlay,' Nell interjected. 'Put his mind at rest.'

Toni caught the confused look on Batey's face. It was another error she would need to explain. 'I'll do it tomorrow, Nell, thanks.'

Chapter 79

After the girl had been shot, the guards unceremoniously bundled Lynn back to the cell. She counted her way past six similar doors, all locked, all seemingly leading into lock-ups like hers.

A few minutes later, she heard heavy doors being opened and slammed shut. The others were also being returned. After that, she waited, listening in vain at the door for any further sign of voices or movement.

About an hour later, they came for her again.

Any notion to try and spring an ambush was quickly destroyed as soon as the cell door was opened. From behind the torchlight came a narrow torrent of water. She felt its icy blast before she saw it coming. A high pressure hose had been turned on her, the jet knocking her clean off her feet and blasting her body. Torch beams were played on her soaking, struggling form as the hose operator focussed the jet on her head, body and legs. Rolling across the floor, she scrambled to her knees, desperately trying to evade the torrent. But the power of the water was too much. This wasn't a fight she could win. Curled into a ball, shivering and whimpering, she surrendered, begging silently for it to stop.

No sooner had the water been turned off than the order was given for her to remove all her clothing. She ignored the instruction. Don't make this too easy ... show them you aren't beaten, girl, she told herself. It was a pointless gesture. Multiple hands grabbed her roughly from behind. Three men held her down while a fourth ripped her shirt and trousers away. Socks and underwear offered little resistance to the strength of her attackers. Within a minute, the order to strip had been enforced. Then there was silence.

Prostrate on the wet floor and shaking uncontrollably, an awful realisation came to her. Lynn knew her will was already weakened and, with no shoes or clothing, she had been rendered vulnerable. Hunger and isolation had now been followed up by humiliation. Escape was already seeming a forlorn hope.

As the men returned, lifting her bodily from the floor, she experienced an odd sense of relief that, at least, the uncertainty was about to end. A hood was pulled over her head. As it was already dark, she wondered why. Thoughts of a barbaric execution returned.

A few yards from the cell door, the men heaved her upwards and then onto a flat surface. It felt like a table.

Galvanised by a new wave of fear, she fought as best she could. Blinded and desperate, striking out in all directions with arms and legs, even teeth. It was hopeless. Within seconds, both arms were restrained and she was stretched out. Two hands were on each arm, two on each ankle. They stretched her out, facing upwards.

Another man joined in. Five of them, she now counted. This one rested himself across her thighs, his bodyweight pinning her down. The table was smooth, warm. Wood, she thought; remember details. One day, she hoped to be recalling them when these bastards were put away. She stopped fighting. Better not to risk injury until she might have a better chance, when the odds were more even. They were going to take her. For now … accept the inevitable.

The men holding her arms wrenched them downwards, forcing her shoulders into an unnatural angle. It hurt, though only slightly, but she cried as if in agony. They must think her weak, think her unable to fight, then soon, perhaps very soon, she would surprise them. Then a sound reached her. A familiar sound. The ratcheting of cable ties … plastic handcuffs.

Thin plastic was forced over both hands. Lynn heard the sound of the ties being tightened and then felt pressure, tight pressure, as her wrists were firmly clamped to the table legs. The pain increased, agonising this time, the ties were too tight. It had to be for a reason. What were they doing? Cold, wet hands grasped her neck and throat.

'Do not fight this.' A male voice, older than the others.

Fight? she puzzled. And just how could she do that? It was obvious now what was coming. They were going to rape her. The realisation brought understanding, an appreciation of what all rape victims go though at the point where they surrender to the inevitable. As the men continued to bind her, Lynn made herself a promise. One day, they would pay.

But they didn't rape her.

Someone tied a tourniquet around her left arm. It tightened. As Lynn felt a sharp pain in her left forearm, the reason for the hood and the restraints became clear. They had needed to turn lights on to work and had to ensure that she kept still while a needle was pushed into her vein. They were going to sedate her … they wanted to stop her resisting.

Someone leaned close to her. She smelled his sweat. Then a voice in her ear – the same powerful voice from earlier.

'Welcome to paradise, Lynn Wainwright.'

And then, Lynn realised it wasn't a sedative that was coursing through her veins. As the drug started to take effect, as she felt a sense of wellbeing flood her body, the horror of what it was hit home in her mind. She was lost ... even if they found her now she was as good as dead. She prayed for the one chance she might have: the alternative reaction some users described, where their body rejected the chemicals, causing them to experience vomiting and nausea rather than pleasure. Her prayer went unanswered.

The heroin went straight into Lynn's bloodstream. The first sensation was like pins and needles. It started in her chest then moved to her spine. She felt herself smiling. Beneath the pleasure, her brain fought for a short time to resist the effects. The drug quickly won the battle of wills. For a moment, her back arched and then a sensation like a rush of tiny pinpricks spread throughout her whole body. Then came the lights. Bright, flashing, like lightning, then waves, and in all kinds of colours, then combinations of colours.

Within a minute of the needle penetrating her flesh, she relaxed. There was no need to fight ... no need to worry. They'd all be OK, the guys, her parents ... everything would be fine. Everything would be fine.

Chapter 80

The remainder of Saturday was lost to red herrings in the search for Lynn Wainwright.

Lynn's job in SO19 and the recent tension over raised security threat levels inevitably caused the Met senior management to conclude her disappearance might be linked to some form of terror attack. Even at grass roots level, wild theories were in abundance, from an attempt to impersonate Lynn to strike at a sensitive target, through to Lynn having committed suicide or run away to escape the pressure of the shooting enquiry. The truth was, nobody knew.

Whatever the explanation, she needed to be found, and quickly.

I didn't get home until early evening and, as I opened the front door, the smell of cooking reached my nostrils. Jenny had made dinner for just the two of us. It was steak, a favourite of both of us. Luckily for me, I'd remembered the wine.

On the dinner table were candles and as I had walked along the hallway I noticed one of my favourite James Taylor numbers was on the CD player. I'd been expecting some kind of argument, a heated debate, at least. The warm reception was a relief.

Jenny had arranged for her mother to look after Becky overnight. We settled down, enjoyed the food, chatted houses, and other normal things. Although we touched on the subject, I tried to avoid talking about work and the reports on the television concerning the missing WPC. I was slow to raise it, but at some point I knew I was going to have to broach the subject of my need to head down the M4 the following morning.

Marica's email came up as we started our dessert. But it had been put to bed by the time I'd cleared my plate. Jenny told me my assurances were accepted, and, besides, we had more important things to talk about.

I was confident now there wasn't going to be a 'we're separating' speech and, as the wine flowed, I was feeling well and truly relaxed. It was a good moment for my wife to break the news to me.

She was pregnant.

My reaction was also a surprise. I cried. So much so that my chest heaved and my eyes streamed. I figured it was a combination of relief and joy. I never let on that I had been half anticipating a 'Dear John' speech.

Once I had managed to compose myself, we hugged and kissed. I patted Jenny's tum and made a joke about teaching the sprog to play cricket. I've no idea where that came from as cricket had never really been my game.

It was at that point I decided to confide in Jenny about the document. It had crossed my mind to lie – invent a line of enquiry that meant a trip down the M4. I'm glad I didn't. Honesty proved the best policy. As I explained where it had come from, my promise to Bob Bridges' widow and the fact that the translator wanted to see me about it, she mellowed. So long as I promised to be home by the afternoon, she was happy about my going to see Dr Armstrong.

The rest of the evening was a blur. Jenny limited herself to one glass of the wine, which meant that I had to finish the bottle. We went to bed early, made love like teenagers and then drifted off in each other's arms.

Chapter 81

West London to the Black Mountains in Wales turned out to be a long journey in such a small car. I made good progress, though, the motor whining loudly as I maintained a steady seventy. I had to turn the radio up loud to drown out the combined noise of engine and wind. The music helped pass the time and distracted me from the confused thoughts that were still hurtling around my brain. I couldn't work out whether I should feel elated or fearful. I was on an emotional high but still I was left with a nagging sense of impending doom. I figured it wouldn't go away until Toni got back to me with her conclusions over Monaghan.

Dr Armstrong had suggested arriving about ten, so I had set off just before eight. Being a Sunday, there was very little traffic to slow me down and, as an extra blessing, the regular weekend roadworks on the M4 also seemed to have finished. It was only when I pulled into Membury services that I realised I had missed calls on the mobile. There were six; someone really wanted to speak to me.

I cursed as I flicked through the phone menu to identify the callers. Numbers withheld – all six. It could have meant calls from a police switchboard, calls from our temporary MI5 home, or, maybe, from Dr Armstrong. There was no way I could tell. Whoever it was, I noticed that the most recent call had been only four minutes before I had pulled into the services car park.

I decided to grab a coffee and then wait to see if the caller tried again. I wasn't disappointed. My phone rang as I walked into the services. It was DCI Bowler.

'Where are you, Finlay?' he asked, the anger evident in his voice. 'I want everyone in the office. You and Nina are the only people Naomi hasn't been able to get hold of.'

I smiled to myself. Here we go again. I had to be economical with the truth. Where I was and the direction I was heading, I could reveal. The reason, definitely not.

'I'm ... err ... halfway to Wales, I'm afraid.'

'You're where?'

'On my way to Wales.'

I could hear Bowler's tone change completely. 'I'll call you straight back,' he said, and without another word hung up.

I didn't have to wait long before the phone rang again. A lead had come up on Lynn Wainwright. Bowler explained to me that, overnight, a Gloucestershire Constabulary traffic unit had stopped a Mercedes on the M5, near Gloucester. A woman had been found in the boot after two men had decamped from the car. She claimed to have been slave-trafficked, then put to work at a factory.

Importantly, she said she had information about a policewoman who was being held captive.

The local police had contacted the Met incident room that morning.

'It's a bit of luck you're that side of the country. Can you get down to Gloucester and interview this girl?' Bowler asked.

I was a little surprised to be asked, given my lack of CID experience. 'On my own?' I said.

'Yes, on your own, Finlay,' he replied, angrily. 'Have you any idea how many sightings the incident room are following up on in an attempt to find Lynn Wainwright?'

'But this comes from a connection with traffickers,' I protested.

'Which may or may not amount to anything. Look ... I've volunteered your help to assist the team dealing with her disappearance. It's a favour to them as you happen to be in the right place. They've got people in Manchester, Birmingham and even in France following up on leads. If you talk to this girl and you think there's something in it, I'll ask them to send some people down to support you. For now, you're it, OK?'

Just in case, I asked the DCI if Naomi Young could fax Gloucester HQ the photographs of the Relia murder suspects. He promised to do so. I grabbed a scrap of paper from the floor nearby and wrote down their names. We would need to know if the escaped slave girl recognised them.

Bowler also updated me on the reason for the office meeting I was now excused from attending. There had been a breakthrough in the enquiry. Interpol had DNA confirmation the second suspect from the hideaway we'd discovered was definitely Marius Gabor. The dead gunman had been fingerprinted and was now known to be Constantin Macovei. Both men were from Romania and had been confirmed as employees of the Cristea syndicate. DNA from the priest hole had also been matched to the scene of Relia's murder.

We had our suspects.

I was returning to the car, take-away coffee in one hand, when my phone rang again. This time it was Toni Fellowes. I hoped it was better news about Monaghan.

'Hi Finlay ... where are you? I rang Jenny; she said you were headed down to Wales to see a friend.'

'That's right. You didn't tell her what we discussed yesterday?' I felt my heart pound.

'No, of course not.'

I breathed a sigh of relief. 'Good. She accepted my explanation about the Cristeas not being anything to worry about – in this country anyway.'

'Good,' Toni answered. 'Look, why I'm calling – I had a meeting last night to sort out the idea that had come up about why your friends were killed.'

'Not really friends, Toni. There was only one of them I actually knew. And I have to say I'm not sure I agree with you about Monaghan and the others.'

'Well, no matter, now. What I wanted to say is not to worry ... and no need to call Kevin Jones about it. It looks like the alternative idea was a false lead, no basis at all. I'm sorry I even mentioned it to you.'

'You mean that the Anti-Terrorist Squad were right? It was Monaghan behind it?' My voice trembled as I flopped back into the car seat. I briefly closed my eyes.

'Yes ... it looks that way. I mean, well ... it is that way. It's certain now he was behind it.'

'What was the alternative theory?' I asked.

'Oh ... nothing. My researcher had this crazy theory about stolen treasure from Afghanistan.'

'Is that what "Al Anfal" is, some kind of treasure?'

'No ... it turned out to be just another terrorist group. Your friend Bridges was on an operation that took them out. I'm sorry, Finlay. I must have scared you.'

'You did ... just a bit. Do you still want to see the document?'

'No ... I know all about it now. It's a work of fantasy, just an old man's dream of making the world all one under Islam. If I were you, I'd stick it in the confidential waste.'

'That's all it is? So, what Collins said in the book about the Increment men having a fall-out isn't right?'

'No ... just one more thing he made up. There's one other thing.'

'Go on.'

'It's an apology.'

'What for this time?'

'Taking my eye off the ball. It's no excuse, I know, but I've had some distractions of my own lately. I must have rattled you a bit ... I'm sorry.'

'For making me think we'd got it wrong, you mean?'

'Yes. For making you think there was another reason for the deaths of your friends.'

I accepted the apology, and we ended the call. But, in the back of my mind, I was wondering if Julian Armstrong would share Toni's opinion on Al Anfal.

Chapter 82

To describe the road to the Armstrong house as a lane was being generous to its design, its surface and its incline. The 2CV swayed gently over rocks and through the ruts as I made steady progress up the mountain.

'Ty Eira' – Armstrong's house – really did feel like it was on top of the world. The views of the surrounding Black Mountains as I got out of the car were magnificent. Looking west I could see the familiar tip of Pen y Fan poking through the clouds. To the south was Sugar Loaf mountain and to the east, Ysgyryd Fawr, the Skirrid, all names and places I remembered from exercises during my SAS days. The pale-green slopes looked imposing and beautiful from this distance.

'Robert Finlay?' A voice from the door to the house startled me for a moment. I had been away in a world of my own.

I turned to where Julian Armstrong was standing. In his hand he clutched the cardboard document folder I had given to Rupert Reid. I waved. 'Yes ... nice place.' I opened the ironwork garden gate. The rusty hinges squeaked, loudly.

'Do I call you Robert or Finlay?' he asked. 'Rupert Reid tells me most people just use your last name.'

'That's true,' I replied.

My host was one of life's great enthusiasts. Everything about him exuded energy. He spoke quickly, moved hurriedly and did everything at speed. He even seemed able to make the kettle boil faster than anyone I had ever met. In the space of just ten minutes he gave me a guided tour of the house, a description of the outbuildings and a potted history of the local area. He couldn't have been more thorough if he had been an estate agent trying to sell the place.

There was no-one else at home. I saw the doctor's eyes sadden as he described how his wife had died of cancer just two months after they had finished making their home habitable. They had spent their last few weeks together, at the house, enjoying the views and taking ever-shortening walks as Mrs Armstrong's strength had waned. In every room there were photographs of them together, from university days through to her final walk.

I'd noticed the Bob Bridges' document was now lying on a small table just inside the front door. Finally, we returned to the front room and he picked it up.

'I suppose we should talk about this?' he said. 'It is what you drove all this way for.'

'Did you manage to translate it?'

'I'm nearly halfway through it. Wasn't easy, mind. It was written by different people, different languages and several dialects of those languages. Before I explain what it is, I need you to answer me a question, and please be honest. Can you tell me where you got hold of this document?'

I decided, instantly, to tell the truth. If the document was of any significance, I suspected Dr Armstrong would return the compliment.

'A friend of mine died,' I answered. 'He had it amongst his personal effects. It was in a box left over from his time in the army.'

'Special Forces was he, your friend?'

'That's right.'

'Like you, I would guess, Finlay?'

I didn't respond. Not being sure how much Rupert Reid had divulged, I didn't allow myself to be drawn on the suggestion.

'Have you ever heard of "Al Anfal"?' Armstrong continued.

'Rupert Reid asked me the same question.' I said. 'We thought it might be some kind of treasure … or an old terrorist group.' I wondered now if Toni's claim was about to be trashed.

'It's neither, although it would have great value in the right hands. You're quite sure you've never had any contact with Al Anfal?'

'No, none at all. It's not a thing, then?'

'No, it's not a thing.'

'I was planning to look it up on one of the internet search thingies, but I haven't had the chance.'

'Well, I wouldn't do that if I were you. You type that name into a search engine and I guarantee that someone at GCHQ or similar will know about it.'

'GCHQ? Are you telling me this is a document they'd be interested in?'

'Yes ... and no. It's a secret document, yes ... but it's not a UK secret. I wouldn't mind betting that each and every secret service in the world would love to get their hands on this. I'm just surprised it's never surfaced before.'

'Are you sure it's not fiction, a work of fantasy, maybe?' I quoted Toni, already thinking that her explanation was unravelling.

'Definitely not. I could see how it might be mistaken for such but, trust me, it's the real deal.'

'You think the Intelligence Services will be looking for it?'

'If they know about it, yes. That's why I decided not to use the internet to try and validate its authenticity. I prefer to use my reference books, in any event.'

'Is it authentic?'

'Based on what you say was its source, yes it certainly is.'

☩

We talked for nearly an hour. Armstrong's analysis was incredible to hear. It meant that whatever Toni Fellowes said or believed, the Al Anfal document was real.

My host confirmed Rupert's analysis that the document was actually called 'Political Jihad'. It contained guidance, ideas and historical anecdotes explaining how long-term takeover could only really be achieved by political means. Armed action was only justified where such a course supported a strategic aim. It represented an incredible insight into the true plans of people like Osama Bin Laden.

The doctor's interpretation was that Al Anfal was more of a philosophy than an organisation, more of a policy than a plan. One chapter was called 'Al-fath, the One Hundred Year Plan'. Armstrong explained that '*Al-fath*' meant conquest. The chapter detailed an argument for wanting America – the great Satan – to attack Iraq and Iran, Egypt and Syria. And it suggested the same for Libya and the several other African countries.

The aim was to create a power vacuum into which Islam could move and, thereby expand the areas that it covered. In the greater scheme of things, the documents showed that events like 9/11 were a distraction, and sometimes a bait, to entice Western powers into the Middle East.

The document, as a whole, was a very long-term plan to gain control of countries from the inside. It was devilishly straightforward, yet required infinite patience. It also needed to be kept absolutely secret.

'You could call it a guide book on political control,' he explained, 'or to put it in simple terms, a step-by-step manual on how to take over the world.'

I laughed quietly at the 'James Bond' type plot suggestion. 'A mate of mine was thinking of selling it to the newspapers,' I said.

Armstrong held both his hands up in a gesture of horror. 'No ... no, you mustn't do that.'

'Too sensitive?'

'If I were you, I would distance myself from it as quickly as possible. This document has the word "danger" written on every bloody page.'

'Would simple possession of it put someone at risk?' I was starting to think about the searches that had being going on – men in suits checking the homes of my old mates, looking for something.

'Only if it was known you had it. The authors would certainly kill to protect it and, I've no doubt, the Security Services would be prepared to kill to get their hands on it.'

'Or to keep knowledge of its existence a secret?'

'Possibly.'

'So we're now at risk.' I said.

'Only if it is revealed that we know about it.'

'So, what do you suggest?'

'Destroy it ... and then forget you ever saw it.'

'It's that sensitive?' I asked.

'For Christ's sake, Finlay, this is why I needed to discuss this in person rather than over the telephone. If I'm right about this text, and I'm certain I am, then we have to destroy it. If I take it to the Security Services they are going to want to know where it came from, who had it and all the background. You want to be answering those types of questions?'

'I guess not,' I answered.

What Armstrong was saying made perfect sense, but I was too distracted. Toni had said her researcher, Nell, had an alternative theory on the deaths, and Kevin shared the idea. What if they were right? What if the document was the reason for the attacks? Anyone found with a copy would be toast.

'Could we send it to MI5 anonymously?' I asked, thinking – even as I spoke the words – that I was being naive.

Armstrong just stared at me, his eyebrows raised.

'Burn it,' I said.

Chapter 83

Time was pressing. I would have to move quickly if I was to get to Gloucester, do the interview and then get back to London.

As I left, Armstrong was already lighting up his log burner. The more I had listened to what the Doctor said, the more I realised why Bob Bridges had kept the document. If Bridges had managed to get even the smallest part of it translated then he would have known it would be of huge importance to the Security Services and of even greater interest to the press. It had value, if he could find a buyer. Perhaps, like Kevin, Bridges had imagined it was going to be a nice little contribution to his pension.

Flicking the phone menu through to Kevin's number, I tapped the call button. The connection failed. No signal. Kevin wasn't going to be best pleased, but I knew I had made the right decision. I didn't have time to keep calling so I typed him a quick text.

'*Call me ASAP.*'

It took me about an hour to reach Gloucester. The drive through the winding lanes of Monmouthshire and the Forest of Dean was scenic, if not as spectacular as the Black Mountains. Gloucester HQ was a fairly new building just south of the main city in an area called Quedgeley. I found it easily by following the local signs.

After parking the Citroen, I checked my phone. Kevin had replied.

Later OK? Bit busy watching Billy's porn collection. I smiled to myself. If they were still doing that on the morning of the wedding, it was going to be an interesting day in Hereford.

The PC on the front counter at Gloucester was expecting me. No sooner had I introduced myself than I was shown through into an interview room and asked to wait. 'Superintendent Russell wants to speak to you, sir,' he said, before offering to fetch me a tea.

I accepted the offer of a brew and asked about the woman who had been brought in.

'She's being looked after in the rape suite. The Super called in the Domestic Violence team to help you talk to her.'

'Does she need a translator?' I asked.

'No, she's as English as you or me apparently, sir.'

'OK,' I said. 'Your Superintendent? Could you ask him to give me a few minutes while I take a leak?'

'Sure. But it's not a 'him' sir, it's a 'her'.'

A figure appeared in the doorway, just behind the PC. I caught a glimpse of bright red hair, a uniform, and then the faint scent of a vaguely familiar perfume.

'Hello, Robert.'

I knew the voice instantly. Wendy Russell.

Chapter 84

In many ways, policing can be a small world, so bumping in to old colleagues wasn't unusual. But this was a treat; I knew Wendy well from when we had been on the same intake at Hendon Training School.

'Well look who it isn't,' Wendy said, returning my smile.

She turned on her heel and suggested we started in her office.

'Since when were you in CID, Finlay?' she asked, as we climbed a set of stairs. 'I wouldn't have thought it was your type of work.'

'Long story,' I said. 'I left Royalty Protection a few weeks ago and then this job came up. It was too good to turn down. What about you? How have you been? I would have thought you would be a Chief Constable by now?'

'I'm fine. And it's a long story for me as well, mostly to do with quality of life. When I came here it was supposed to be a stepping stone. I found I liked it and decided to stay.'

As we reached the upper landing, Wendy explained that London had been in touch with instructions to keep the slave girl safe until one of their officers would arrive to debrief her. The girl was being looked after in the rape examination suite and any food or drink was brought in to her from the police canteen. There was a PC posted with her at all times and another guarding the outside of the door. Nobody was allowed in to see her without official sanction. Given the nature of the information that the girl claimed to possess, I thought they seemed sensible safeguards.

Wendy was her usual businesslike self. At the second floor, a young woman in a dark-blue suit was waiting for us. Wendy introduced her as DS Fleming and then walked through the open door into her office. Wendy sat down, rearranged some papers on the desk and then indicated that Fleming and I should use the seating opposite her.

'So, how did this girl come to our notice?' I asked.

'She was picked up on the motorway,' said Fleming.

'Hitchhiking?'

'Not exactly,' Wendy said. 'Have you ever noticed those traffic cars that park up and watch the cars going by?'

'Don't we all,' I said. 'Everyone slows down as soon as they see them.'

'Well, picture the scene. Middle of the night, two slightly bored traffic cops, engine running to keep themselves warm, watching the occasional car go by. One of them is paying attention, checking speeds, when a Mercedes goes past travelling just below the speed limit.'

'And something happened?'

'The PC doing the checks watches the tail lights as they disappear into the distance and notices they are flashing, as if they were faulty.'

'So they stop the car?'

'Not at first ... the PC noticed a pattern to the flashing. Three short flashes, three long, three short.'

'Morse code, S.O.S,' I said.

'Exactly. The girl they had slung in the boot had the presence of mind to signal for help by working the tail light wiring loose and then tapping it on and off like a flash light. When the traffic crew attempted a stop, the two men ran off into the darkness and were lost before backup could arrive.'

'Good effort by the girl. They found her locked in the boot, I assume?'

'She was,' said Fleming as she opened a small folder on her lap.

'Have you had a chance to interview her?' I asked.

'We have,' replied Wendy. 'After the two men decamped from the car, the night-duty CID spoke to her. To start with we thought it was an abduction, with the two men holding her prisoner in the boot of the car. It was only when we were able to get her to talk about the sex trafficking and she said she knew about a WPC who had been kept with her that we decided to call your guys. Since then she has been treated as a sex-crime victim. DS Fleming leads our local team.'

I explained that I had been given only the briefest of details from DCI Bowler. Wendy handed over to DS Fleming to take me through what they knew.

The girl's name was Mollie Donoghue. She was a thirty-year-old former waitress from Swindon. Fleming outlined in detail how the girl had been tricked into becoming a sex worker by a drug dealer. Since her abduction, she said she had been kept in some kind of dungeon.

Mollie had described how her normal day was spent making sex videos or providing entertainment for her guards. The DS went on to relate how, rather unusually, Mollie would sometimes be taken from her cell with other girls to burn books on a huge bonfire.

To both Fleming and Wendy, this seemed an unusual combination. But I remembered the words of DS Young, the HOLMES Office Manager in London. To the detective, coincidence is a clue. This time, it led me to one conclusion. The Cristeas – slave traffickers and publishers. It was them.

Mollie had gone on to explain that a girl escaped. Shortly afterwards, a new leader arrived at the dungeon. He brought some other men with him and they went out looking for the missing girl. Mollie had no idea where or how they had found her, but the girl looked bruised and scratched when she came back. It was Mollie's guess that she had been sleeping rough.

The next day, the guards had woken them early. There was an execution. The captured girl had been shot in front of all the women being held. It appeared to have been a lesson to the others on what would happen if they also tried to escape. It was the first time such an event had occurred and the only occasion that Mollie had seen all the others. She had counted nearly thirty women.

I asked if Mollie had been able to learn any names of either her fellow slaves or the guards. I had the names that Bowler had given to me, written down. Fleming reported several girls' first names but nothing for the guards.

'Did my DCI send over the pictures of our murder suspects?' I asked.

'Yes, they arrived a couple of hours ago,' replied Wendy. 'The two traffic cops were on nights and asleep but both were happy to come in and take a look. No luck, I'm afraid. They both said it was too dark to be certain.'

I turned to Fleming. 'What about Mollie. Have you shown them to her?'

'Not yet, no,' she answered.

'OK. We'll do that when we speak to her. Did she manage to tell you anything about the WPC?'

'Yes. When the girl was killed, the leader had a new woman brought in to watch. Mollie knew she was a recent arrival as she was the only one wearing her own clothes. The rest of them are either kept naked or given old clothing if the men decide they like them.'

'So how did Mollie work out the new arrival might be a policewoman?' I asked.

'She was in half-blues. Uniform trousers and boots, white shirt under a light jacket. Mollie has had many dealings with police officers and she recognised the uniform ... and there was something said to her, the policewoman, I mean.'

'What was that?'

'The leader, he said something about her killing one of his men and that he was going to make sure she paid for it.'

For a few moments, I kept my counsel. Outside of the 'need to know' channels, nobody had been told of Lynn's involvement in the shooting of the escaping gangster. Fleming's summary of what Mollie said told me that there was no mistake. The abduction of Lynn Wainwright was connected to that shooting.

I decided to be open with what I knew. 'That fits. The missing officer was involved in an incident a couple of days ago where she shot and killed an armed suspect. Did Mollie manage to tell us where she is being held?'

'No, only that it is within about a couple of hours of where she was found on the M5 motorway. She couldn't be very specific.'

It wasn't good news. A car travelling for an hour or two could mean a search radius of hundreds of square miles. It was no wonder Bowler hadn't been in a rush to send a search team in.

'Did you get a description of the place, any clues at all?' I asked.

'She said it was some kind of factory,' Fleming said, 'with underground vaults and cells. A large redbrick building with a central courtyard that meant they couldn't be seen from the outside. Old bricks, small windows, slate roof with lots of broken slates lying about where they had been blown off by the wind … and it was surrounded by trees.'

'Sounds a bit like an old Victorian place,' said Wendy. 'Maybe an old stately home or a hospital? Perhaps, like Mollie said, an old workhouse or factory?'

'Any ideas?' I asked.

'This is rural Gloucester, sir,' said Fleming. 'We're surrounded by woodland and old buildings.'

'Do you have a map anywhere?'

'Give me a couple of minutes.'

Fleming left the office, leaving me and Wendy alone. 'Mollie seems a lot more helpful than I might have expected.' I said.

'Considering she's been held as a slave for the last few months, you mean?' Wendy answered.

'Exactly. I would have thought she'd be more traumatised … less able to remember things.'

'You'd be surprised, Finlay. I've seen women like Mollie before. The euphoria of rescue from awful situations of abuse can be wonderful for them. The adrenalin flows and they think it's all over. It's only afterwards, when they settle down, that the realisation of what they've been through starts to really hit home.'

'So, her desire to co-operate may be only temporary?'

'You'd better believe it. It's one of the reasons so many victims of abuse change their minds about giving evidence and withdraw their statements. While Mollie is on a high and in our care, she'll be fine. As soon as she returns home to her former life, who knows what other influences will come to bear.'

Fleming re-appeared holding a map which she laid out on the desk. There was a circle drawn on it. She explained it was an estimate to indicate the possible distance the Mercedes could have covered before it was abandoned on the M5. It was a huge area, and included part of Wales.

I asked about forensics. The car had been searched, but nothing useful had been found. It was now sitting in a lockup at the back of the police station, where it would be examined by a CSI investigator the following day. Local CSI people only worked Sundays for murders, it seemed.

Briefing complete, we headed off to the interview suite.

Chapter 85

It was only when I got to speak to Mollie myself that a fuller picture of Lynn's predicament really hit me.

As the custody officer opened the door to the rape suite and I saw Mollie for the first time, I immediately knew she was a druggie. The tight skin and blank eyes were an indication, and then I saw her rubbing her arm, her injection site was itching. It made sense. I had read the briefing notes that Nina Brasov had passed around the office, so I was aware of the methods used by the traffickers to ensure the compliance of their enslaved workers.

We sat down around a circular coffee table, on comfy chairs which, I guessed, were designed to help victims feel at home. Fleming first introduced her Superintendent and then me.

'You're from the Met?' said Mollie. 'My ... even the big boys are interested in what I have to say now then.'

Ignoring the jibe, I explained that I was curious as to why she thought one of her fellow prisoners was a policewoman.

'Know she is ... seen the uniform,' she replied, a hint of a sneer in her tone.

'OK ... perhaps it would help me if you explained a bit about the place where this happened? That OK with you?'

She gave me a mock salute. 'You're the boss.'

The detail in Mollie's description didn't make for easy listening. Housed in a cold, damp building full of leaks and drafts, the girls spent almost all of their time in the dark, locked away in cells.

Normally, the guards only disturbed the women at night for one of their group-sex sessions. Fuelled by lust and alcohol, they would decide which girls were to be the subjects of their attentions by drawing playing cards. Mollie was the ten of spades. In the first weeks following her capture, she had been pulled from the pack on every occasion the men decided to play. Then her popularity waned as new girls arrived. In the last month, her door had remained unopened.

At times, the men left the cell corridors unguarded. The girls would call to each other from behind their doors, ask questions and compare stories. All of them seemed to be from the UK, which Mollie said she thought odd, considering the guards were all foreigners. Some of the girls were runaways, but not all. Others had been lured away from good homes using social media sites and chat rooms. Their stories were startlingly similar. Using the internet, they were seduced by the attentions of a boy who professed to be interested in them. From what Mollie had managed to learn, there seemed to be just three young men who snared the girls, but they were very active.

Some of the slaves did extra work at the factory on the daytime production line. They would pack books into boxes. A few worked in the yard where their job was to burn spoiled books on a huge bonfire. In the evenings, they were taught to dance. The taller girls learned to use the pole and, each week, a woman came down from the city to teach them how to make money from punters in nightclubs. Some of the girls resisted, but not for long.

Within a day of arrival, each girl would receive her first injection of heroin. Mollie estimated, within a week, all new girls were addicted. After that, they were under control. They wouldn't try to escape, they would be compliant and they would not fight off the attentions of the men. They were trapped. The policewoman, she was certain, would meet the same fate.

Mollie said she'd listened at the inside of her own locked door as they had taken the cop from her cell. She had sworn and cursed like a possessed demon as the guards had dragged her to the table where they administered the first heroin injection. From the sounds and grunts of the men, the poor girl had dished out a few kicks as they struggled to keep her under control. I imagined the scene – Lynn fighting like her very life depended on it, which quite possibly it did. She wouldn't have made it easy for them. Inevitably though, they had overpowered her.

'They gave her the queen of hearts,' Mollie said, interrupting my thoughts. 'So she'll soon be doing the groups. I hate cops, don't get me wrong. But that's no fate for any woman.'

She explained how the men would make them promises and suggest, if they were good, a warmer place of work awaited them in the city. At least once a month, a van would arrive, always in the evening, and always after they had been fed. Two or three girls would be taken at a time.

The guards told those remaining that the departed were headed for a new, exciting life, where they would earn well, enjoy freedom and be able to set themselves up for life. A few of the girls fell for it, but not many, and not Mollie. But all went willingly. From the factory there was no escape. From the city, there might be.

Mollie explained how she'd guessed she was being moved on as soon as she heard the unexpected slide of the bolt to her cell door. She estimated it had been about three or four in the morning.

'How many men were in the Mercedes with you?' I asked.

'Two. One of them was the Russian who shot the girl who escaped.'

'Shot the girl?'

'Like I told this lot earlier.' Mollie glanced at Fleming and Wendy. 'She got away somehow. They caught her and made an example of her.'

'Yes, they did tell me. It must have been very frightening, designed to scare the rest of you, probably. And the man that shot her was a Russian?'

'Something like that, yes. All those people sound like Russians to me, even when they were talking in French.'

'They spoke in French?'

'Not all the time, but it sounded like they could all speak it.'

'And these two guys put you in the boot of the Merc?'

'They put cable ties around my wrists and ankles first. I didn't make it easy for 'em.'

'How long were you in the car … I mean when it was on the move? We're trying to work out how far you might have travelled.'

'I'm not sure. There was a smell of petrol and I think I must have passed out. When I woke up we were on what sounded like a motorway. I could see the wires to the lights so I thought, hey, what have I got to lose? I pulled the brake light wire off and started tapping out the SOS signal.'

'That was clever,' said Wendy. 'One of our patrol cars saw it.'

'I know. They told me that straight after releasing me. Like I told them, I learned a few things in school, you know.'

I continued to make notes as I asked Mollie about the guards, what weapons did they carry, how old were they, how many of them? Everything I could possibly think of that would be useful. She was certain, only one of the guards, the leader, had a weapon. She was also certain that she had never seen a gun before the morning of the execution. The others used their fists and a fire hose to keep the women under control.

As we continued to talk, I covered every aspect of Mollie's incarceration I could think of. We talked building layout, smells, impressions, as well as what she had seen and heard.

I was also curious about the girl who'd escaped only to be recaptured and then killed. I asked Mollie why she hadn't gone to the police.

'Are you kidding me?' Mollie replied. 'Some of this lot are in on it.' She nodded her head towards Wendy and DS Fleming.

'How do you mean?' I asked.

'Well, not all of them, obviously, but a few. One was really horrible. He's a regular, and then there's also been a couple of uniformed bobbies who like their freebies.'

I saw Wendy and her DS exchange concerned looks.

'Do you know their names?' I asked.

Mollie laughed and threw her head back. 'Are you serious? They don't tell us their names. The only thing I can tell you is that the horrible one was called 'Buff', you know, as in naked. That made us girls laugh. Whether that was a nickname or his actual name, I have no idea.'

I looked toward Wendy and DS Fleming. They were both silent, but I noticed Fleming had bowed her head and was staring at the floor. 'Mean something to you?' I asked.

'What did he look like, this "Buff" character?' Wendy addressed her question to Mollie.

'Big man ... bald. Bit of a roly-poly. He had to be CID as he'd never get into a uniform.'

Wendy gave me a look that said 'don't press it'. I guessed Mollie had said enough for them to know exactly who Buff was. Finally, I asked Fleming to pull the photographs from her file. She laid the six small prints on the small table. I asked Mollie if she recognised anyone.

Her finger went straight to Marius Gabor. 'Him. It was him who put me in the boot.'

'Was he the one with the gun, the leader?'

'No,' said Mollie. 'This one is the leader. He is the one with the gun.'

I looked down to where the index finger of her right hand had moved to press down on another of the pictures. The hand was sinewy, the skin cracked and wrinkled, the finger nails chewed and broken. Mollie couldn't have been much more than thirty, but the hand I stared at was that of a much older woman. As she pulled away from the coffee table, the face in the picture was revealed.

It was Petre.

Chapter 86

When I phoned in my report, DCI Bowler wasn't pleased.

Not only was I confirming that Lynn Wainwright was in the hands of kidnappers and the reason for the abduction was retribution for the shooting, but I had little to offer by way of a clue as to where she might be being held. We needed a stroke of luck or something more from Mollie to help us narrow down the search.

The anger in Bowler's tone dissipated when I described the softening up process that the traffickers were using. 'You realise what this means?' he said.

I assured him I did, and I understood the urgency. If Lynn was getting the same treatment, she was in deep trouble. If the heroin didn't kill her, she would become addicted to it very quickly, which would likely mean the end of her life as a cop, even if we got to her soon. Whilst we had the good news that she was alive, we were now chasing a fast-burning fuse.

Bowler explained that he was going to have to send the enquiry up the road. I knew what he meant. Investigating a murdered girl in Hampstead could be handled by a small squad. Now that we knew we were dealing with the kidnap of a police officer, it took the enquiry into a whole new arena. The moment I put the receiver down I knew that phone calls would be made to senior officers, plans would be mobilised and specialists called into work. By that evening the Commissioner would have been briefed and the operation would be placed under the command of AC 'SO', Assistant Commissioner 'Specialist Operations', or someone of similar authority.

With an instruction for me to head back to London as soon as I could, he ended the call. Very soon, Nina and I would be debriefed and then told to return to our normal duties. Our contribution to helping find Lynn would be at an end.

But as I put down my phone, I decided I wasn't about to let that happen. Not just yet. Not while I was close and not while I could try. The Met had incredible resources but they would take time to swing into action. By then, it might be too late for Lynn. There was one chance. Since discovering the extent of the Cristea interests, Toni Fellowes had mentioned tasking her assistant to do some research on them. It was time to call in a promise.

I made my apologies to Wendy, excused myself, and headed back to my car. Only once I was there did I dare phone Toni. She picked up straightaway. I was halfway through explaining the background – what Mollie had told me and the need to find Lynn soon, when she interrupted me.

'It's the Cristeas.'

'That's what I thought,' I replied. 'The books, the heroin, the slaves ... it all adds up.'

'I agree ... can you give me a few minutes? Nell did me a report on the family. There was something in it about a factory in the West Country. I'll find it and ring you right back.'

Toni Fellowes was reading my thoughts, and doing just what I'd hoped. I hung up, and decided that my next call better be to Jenny. I sat with the phone on my lap for several minutes while I thought about how I was going to explain I was going to be away from home a lot longer than I had promised. I expected her reaction to the news wouldn't be good. I was right. Explanations about the demands of the job and the fact that a WPC was in danger fell on deaf ears.

As the line went dead, I felt a momentary surge of anger. I slammed the phone down onto the passenger seat of the car. For one crazy moment, I nearly dropped everything to head home. But the phone rang again, almost immediately. It was Toni. She had the address and a grid reference for the Cristea factory. Apparently Nell had found out about it through a building planning application made to the local authority. There was some irony at the prospect of compliance with such a simple law proving to be the Cristeas' undoing. I just hoped it turned out to be what we were looking for. I jotted the details down and promised to let Toni know what I found.

Back in Wendy's office, I brandished the grid reference.

'I've had a suggestion from a contact in London. Someone I know I can trust. It's a possible lead on where the factory might be.'

'You'll need help. I'll start a call-out procedure. How many people will you want? I think we should have armed officers ...'

'Hold on,' I said. 'You heard what Mollie said. Some of your lads have been going to the factory. I don't think they were buying books.'

'What are you saying?'

'I'm saying that we can't let this out until I'm sure it's the right place. Then, no disrespect Wendy, but I'm going to have to call London for help. I can't take the chance someone local might tip off the traffickers. If Lynn is still alive, they might decide she is too much of a risk and dispose of her.'

Wendy slowly nodded her acknowledgement. 'You're right; I can't be sure who to trust. But by God I will find out. Why not call London now?'

'On a hunch? If the building matches Mollie's description, I'll call London then.'

'So I'll come with you,' Wendy said.

'I'll be fine,' I answered. 'I'm best on my own.'

'Look, Finlay. I can't let you do that. And, if what Mollie is saying is correct, I can't be sure who to trust to send with you. Besides, do you have any idea where you're heading?'

'Not really,' I answered, honestly. 'I was going to buy a local map.'

'That settles it. And anyway, you might be an old friend, but if you're up to something on my patch, I want to know what it is.'

The argument was lost.

Ten minutes later, Wendy and I were in her car speeding towards the Forest of Dean.

Chapter 87

I did my best to follow an Ordnance Survey map Wendy's DS found in their main CID office. She estimated it would take us about forty minutes to get to the area.

Wendy knew the roads so we made fast progress, but I still wasn't sure about having her along. As we travelled, I raised the subject again. She reiterated the somewhat valid point that this was her area and she was the ranking officer.

We were heading for a large woodland area outside a town called Coleford. The afternoon light was fading as we pulled into the small town. I did my best with the map and, after half an hour or so, we found the entrance to the factory site. But that's as far as we got.

Surrounded by woodland, it was gated and enclosed by a high, brick wall. Wendy stopped the car, and I got out and walked up to the entrance. It was padlocked. In front of me a long, narrow dirt track ran for about two hundred yards through woodland and then turned left, presumably to the buildings.

There were tyre tracks, but no vehicles to be seen and no people. If it hadn't been for the fact that the padlock looked new, I would have guessed the place to be deserted.

'I need to get inside,' I said to Wendy through the open car window.

She pointed to the barbed wire that topped the redbrick wall. 'Won't be easy. Shall I park the car? We can have a look around the side; see if there's a place we can get over?'

'Not we, Wendy. Thanks, but I prefer to have someone on the outside, in case I hit problems.'

Wendy scowled. 'Not a chance, Finlay. You're not going alone, with no backup.'

She was right. On my own, I would be vulnerable.

Wendy found another track about a hundred yards from the wall where she was able to park the car far enough from the road so that it wouldn't be seen by a casual passerby, and then she rejoined me and we began to walk along the wall. I wasn't sure what we were looking for, or exactly what I was going to do, but I promised myself there were going to be no heroics.

Soon, we found a section where the barbed wire was missing.

Climbing a wall requires a lot of upper-body strength. With an apex about ten feet from the ground, the obstacle that faced us wouldn't have been too much of a problem when I was in my twenties. Now, it might as well have been thirty feet high. There was no way I was going to be able to climb it.

I tried. It must have looked ridiculous to Wendy, standing behind me. As I jumped, my hands barely reached the top and, with no grip to find, I fell backwards onto the dirt, winded.

Wendy laughed quietly. 'Want me to try?' she asked. I smirked and gestured for her to make me a foothold. She shrugged as if to say 'I'll give you this one', leaned back against the wall and cupped her hands.

I stepped up and pushed upwards. My less-than-willing assistant strained to hold me as I scrambled onto the flat surface above and then sat with my legs astride the wall. I stopped for a moment to get my breath. Gazing into the woodland, I could now see a lot further. There was still no sign of any buildings.

From behind me, Wendy pulled on my dangling leg. 'Given any thought as to how you're gonna get back?' She was right. I reached down. She grabbed my wrist and, in an instant, was sat beside me.

'You made that look easy,' I whispered.

'I was always fitter than you, Finlay.'

I smiled. She was right; on my own I would have had more joy digging a tunnel.

Chapter 88

The woodland floor was wet. I moved carefully and slowly but I hadn't gone far before my feet started to feel cold. My shoes were good for normal use but for tramping around a forest, they were pretty useless.

I managed to find some harder ground by sticking close to the larger trees. The soil was drier where roots had drawn moisture from the earth. It also meant the surface was firmer and I was less likely to leave a clear foot mark.

I moved slowly. Wendy had agreed she would stay on top of the wall, where she would be able to hear if I got into difficulties. If I did, or if she hadn't heard from me after an hour, she would call for help from the Met. It was a bit of a rushed idea, but if both Lynn and I were missing, it seemed a decent enough backup plan. We also agreed I would high-tail it back to the wall if there was any indication of an approaching dog.

I wasn't sure about the time, but I reckoned I had about half an hour of daylight before dusk set in. As any soldier will tell you, the best time to move around is the twilight period, either just before dawn or just as sunlight fades from the sky. Human eyes need a while to adjust to the changing brightness, to detect movement and to see detail clearly. But there is more than enough light to move by.

That time was approaching. Twilight was also a time when sentries tended to be at their least observant. It was something to do with the human body clock. I didn't understand why, but it suited me perfectly. I needed no more than a few minutes with enough light to check out the buildings and discover if they matched the description that Mollie had given.

The wood was quiet. As I stopped to work out a direction in which to head, I listened. There was very little bird song. About a hundred yards ahead I heard a car door slam, then a human voice. I couldn't make out what was said but it sounded like someone giving orders. I waited, in case it was a reaction to my presence.

Several minutes passed and the wood remained calm. I knew from experience that, if anybody had entered the trees to search, my first clue would have come from the movements of songbirds. By keeping still, it wouldn't be me that they reacted to. Blackbirds, in particular, would give off an alarm call as they took off through the wood, away from the perceived danger. If they flew past me, I would know from where the danger threatened. But what worked for me might also work against me, and if the guards – the 'French speaking' guards – were the ex-military types I thought they could be, they would also know about bird behaviour.

I had to find a place from where I might observe the buildings, listen to voices and write down the details of any cars I could see. If I moved too quickly, the birds would be spooked and, to the trained observer, my presence might be revealed.

✠

Fortune favoured me and I reached the edge of the trees, just as daylight was fading to night. There was just one building that I could see. It was as Mollie had described: three floors, red brick and a slate roof. With bars on the inside of the windows and what looked like the remnants of ancient flower beds, it did indeed look like it might have been an old Victorian hospital.

My foot touched something solid. I glanced down to see the remains of an old wooden sign, discarded in the undergrowth. I crouched down and cleared away the dirt that covered it. A name was revealed.

'Clearwell Asylum'. I sensed this was the right place. To the traffickers, a former mental hospital would be perfect. Mollie had described a central staircase which led to the dungeons where she had been held. The way she had depicted them seemed a bit incongruous when compared to my picture of a redbrick Victorian hospital. But, an asylum. That answered many questions. I wondered if the three floors I could see hid other levels beneath the ground where the slave girls were kept, safe from prying eyes or from being overheard, and where the poor insane folk of a long-forgotten past had also been incarcerated.

Moving along the edge of the wood, I was careful to mask my movements by keeping the shadows of the dark trees behind me. I hadn't gone far when I came across what looked like a car park. There were several dark-coloured minibuses, all with their back ends parked against the building walls. Behind them I spotted a Range Rover. It looked new. Very clean ... very expensive.

Two men were stood next to it, chatting. They seemed relaxed, their demeanour reassuring. A heightened state of tension might have indicated awareness of a prowler.

I checked the walls for any sign of CCTV or sensor lights. There were none. The building looked run down. Loose slates, dislodged from the roof, lay broken on the drive. The windows were all grey with dirt. It didn't look like the place had seen any repair work for many years.

I inched closer, trying to hear what the men were saying. Risking leaving the cover of the trees, I edged forward and pressed myself up against one of the minibuses. The effort proved to be pointless. Close proximity only revealed words being spoken in a foreign tongue. It sounded Eastern European, but I wasn't sure. I could tell that it wasn't German and I was fairly confident that I would recognise Russian, but most of the languages from the Baltic States sounded the same to me.

It was as I moved back to start my return to find Wendy that I spotted a small sports car near to what looked like an entrance to the building. The sight of the car stunned me to the very core.

It was a small, silver sports car. Two doors, very distinctive.

I had ridden in the passenger seat only two days previously.

It was Nina Brasov's.

Chapter 89

I returned to the wall, trying to make sense of what I had seen. Was it Nina's car? Was I mistaken? Could there be an innocent explanation? Had she been taken as well? My thoughts returned to the door at the Hampstead flat where we had discovered Relia's body. Ever since I had learned that somebody had cleaned off the footmark, something had niggled me. At the time, I'd put it down to the actions of someone who had been covering up their neglect.

But, if Nina was a spy in the camp, the removal of the mark would have been easy for her. She'd had the opportunity. And she was also one of very few people who knew where Relia was staying. I wondered now if she had taken me along simply to give her a cover story when we found the body. I also remembered that she hadn't been too keen to look for which route the killers had taken.

Then there was Lynn Wainwright's abduction. On the day we had gone to Old Street to take Lynn's statement, Nina hadn't wanted me to go with her. Afterwards, she had been looking over Lynn's car. She'd had plenty of time to jot down the details.

Finally, I recalled that DCI Bowler had mentioned he couldn't get hold of Nina when everyone else on the Murder Squad had been called into work. I stopped for a moment to check my phone. No signal. If Nina was here, was she also out of reach of the network?

It all added up. Mollie had mentioned a woman from the city. A woman who came to give the girls dance lessons. I quickly discounted Nina having been abducted, too. If she had been, why would her car be here? Why not leave it like they had left Lynn's?

But none of this, told me why. Why was Nina here and why now? If they were holding Lynn here, was she helping them in some way? So many questions.

Wendy immediately sensed that there was something wrong. And, with my thoughts going around in circles, I needed help to resolve them. She was the ideal person; she knew me and she was practical.

So, as we sat together in her car, I opened up. Once I'd released the floodgate, I couldn't stop. I wasn't sure quite where to begin, so I started with the London attacks and the crazy campaign of my former CO as he tried to kill off anyone he suspected of having slept with his late wife. I didn't hold back, telling Wendy how Kevin and I had foiled the threat, how I had nearly lost Jenny to a vengeful terrorist and how I had only ended up on a CID squad as the police didn't know what else to do with me.

She didn't interrupt me as I went on to tell her about what was important right now: about Toni Fellowes, the trip to Romania and the mistake that had brought me into contact with the Cristeas. I finished with the murder of Relia, the shooting at the house in Ealing, what I'd seen, and my suspicions about Nina now that I had spotted her car.

It was cathartic. As if a lake of confusion that had been held behind a dam was, finally, being released. After I had finished, we sat for a minute in silence before Wendy spoke.

'Jesus ... you are a dark horse. I thought I knew you pretty well. Better than most I would have said. But you're ex-SAS ... and you were at the Iranian embassy siege?'

'Sort of ... I was in a house down the street with the negotiation team.'

'So, maybe I'm not fitter than you after all?'

'Maybe not when we first met ... but you manage pretty well now.'

'Yeah, OK ... so, this old Commanding Officer of yours tried to kill you and the others?'

'That's about the sum of it, plus the kid from Ireland who hooked up with him to have a go as well.'

Wendy took a deep breath. 'We all thought those bombings in London were just random Real IRA attacks. If it's this much of a surprise to me, I wonder how your wife is coping.'

'I'm not sure, to be honest. It's something I need to dedicate some time to … as soon as I can get back to normality.'

'Normality? And what might that be, I wonder?' Wendy moved her left hand from the gear stick and squeezed my forearm.

I responded by patting her hand. 'I wonder too, sometimes … so, do you have any bright ideas what we do here and now?'

'You knew these Cristea people might be here, didn't you?'

'From what Mollie said, yes, I knew. I just wasn't sure how much I should share with you.'

'Which is why you didn't want me coming with you?'

'Correct.'

'OK … not that I don't understand … I do. But maybe you need to learn to trust people sometimes. So, let's think who we can turn to. Does your MI5 contact have access to any help?'

'What kind of help?'

'Well … like you said, we can't really ask my people to help and now it looks like you can't ring back to the Met either. If Nina is a lone-wolf, fine. But if there is anyone else involved, then as soon as the word gets out that we've found where they're holding Lynn, the bad guys will get a call and spirit her away before we can stop them.'

'Or worse … I never thought there might be more than just Nina.'

'I'm not saying there is, it's just you can't take the risk she's the only one involved. It just takes one person to make a call and what we've found is no longer a secret. Seems to me, the best source of help is your MI5 liaison officer.'

I agreed.

✢

We had to drive for nearly half a mile before I had a good enough signal to make a call. As usual, Toni answered immediately. She agreed with Wendy's conclusions. Going through the usual channels would be a risk. MI5 did have a response team; however, it would take a few hours to get them together and on their way to our location.

Despite the problems it might cause, Toni agreed to call them, and, in the meantime, I would work on a plan to stop anyone leaving the former hospital.

I also asked Toni if she could try and source a plan of the former hospital especially if it included the underground cell area that Mollie had described. Once on scene, the Operational Commander would need it before planning an entry. She promised to try.

As I finished the call, Wendy interrupted my thoughts. 'I've had an idea,' she said.

'Try me.'

'I was doing some thinking of my own while you were inside the wall. I was wondering what an old factory would be doing with underground cells.'

'It's actually an old mental hospital but go on ...'

'Well, it made me think about my childhood. What Mollie described sounded like the cell she was kept in was created by bricking up some form of a cave complex. When I was a kid; we used to go into some nearby caves with my pops. He knew the local freeminers and they used to allow us to go underground.'

'What are freeminers?' I asked.

'Local men who have the rights to dig for iron ore and ochre beneath the forest. A bit like commoners grazing rights for livestock but under the ground.'

'So what's that got to do with us?'

Wendy explained. The Forest of Dean freeminers had created a warren of underground passageways that connected huge caverns – now abandoned. One or two were used as film sets for programmes like Dr Who, but the majority didn't see a human visitor from one year to the next. Her theory was that the cells being used to house the slave girls were most likely former miners' passageways, now bricked up.

It sounded plausible. And, as she went on to suggest, it might just provide a covert entry into the underground areas of the former hospital.

The miners favoured one of the local pubs, near Clearwell. Wendy was confident that, with her family connections, they might be persuaded to help us have a look.

We had the beginnings of a plan.

Chapter 90

At the pub, it didn't take Wendy long to make her move. In an alcove away from the bar, two old-timers had just finished their pints. They accepted her offer of a drink and, as she set the two ciders down in front of them, they invited her to sit down.

'Copper ain't y'a?' said the older-looking man.

Wendy just smiled.

'Needing summat, I guess?'

'A favour, if you can oblige,' said Wendy. 'Something that only a miner would be up for. Let me explain.'

As soon as Wendy mentioned who her father was and that a young girl might be being held against her will, the two men stopped drinking. They both had daughters, and they both read the papers.

The men knew exactly where we wanted to go. As soon as Wendy started talking about a cavern beneath the hospital, they nodded in unison. They knew of it. They also knew that it had been walled off many decades ago when the hospital had been used to house mentally ill patients. It all seemed to fit. We struck a deal. They agreed to show us the tunnels provided that afterwards, Wendy agreed to buy their cider for the rest of the evening.

Their pints of cider drained, we headed out to the car park.

Half an hour later, in the company of two rather ancient and slightly tipsy free miners, wearing hastily donned and tatty overalls, wellington boots, lamps and helmets they had borrowed from a supply kept for sightseers, the four of us entered the Coleford mine system.

✢

Despite the ciders, our guides moved confidently, seemingly familiar with every nook and cranny of the tunnels. Wendy and I simply followed the beams from their helmet lamps. I had no doubt both men were over the drink-drive limit and I'd said something along those lines as we followed them in Wendy's car to the mine entrance. She'd simply shrugged and said nothing. I guessed why. The roads in this area were dark and completely deserted, meaning it was pretty unlikely we were going to bump into any uniformed patrols.

I lost count of the number of times I hit my helmet on the roof of the passageways. I was also grateful for the protection given by the boiler suit I'd squeezed into. My elbows crunched against spurs of rock that were hidden by the darkness. Ahead, the helmet lights of our guides gave little indication of what dangers surrounded us. They simply moved forward at a clip that belied their age.

The caves were warmer than I had expected, and less stuffy. The walls were powdery and, in the glimpses of light, I saw rich veins of colour that I guessed was the ochre that had been mined.

After twenty minutes, the lights in front stopped moving. I was breathing heavily. Wendy, who had been just ahead of me, seemed to be doing better. One of the miners was carrying a large hessian bag across his shoulder. He reached into it and produced a flashlight.

A large concrete wall faced us – eight feet wide and six feet high. With the help of the additional light, I could see there was no sign of any gaps, despite the uneven nature of the rock against which the blocks had been laid.

I tried the wall surface. It was dry. I had hoped that years exposed to a damp atmosphere might have caused it to start decaying. It looked old, but the blocks were dense, the mortar between them dry. I tapped the blockwork. It felt solid – too solid to break through easily.

'Want to make a hole, see if there's anything to see?' the older of the two men asked.

I looked across to him. In his hand he held a small, cordless power drill. I wondered what other goodies he had in the bag.

Wendy raised her hand. 'What if they hear us? We need to keep surprise on our side.'

It was a good point. But Mollie had been adamant the only blockwork she had seen had been the back wall of her cell. I had the beginnings of an idea forming in my brain, but for it to work we were going to need to get through the wall.

'Can you drill through slowly, without using a hammer drill?' I asked.

A huge, grimy hand tapped the end of the bit. 'Diamond tip, mate. So quiet, you wouldn't hear it in a church. Name's Albert, by the way.'

I decided to chance it. If Lynn was behind the wall, we might even be able to rescue her immediately.

Penetrating the wall took no more than a few minutes. Once the drill was pulled clear, I tried to look through the hole. There was nothing, only darkness, and no sense of any air movement on my eye.

Albert whispered in my ear. 'Let me try.'

I stood to one side as he pushed a long, thin drill bit into the hole. It penetrated to a depth of about six inches and then stopped.

'Second skin,' he declared. 'There's another wall behind the first one.'

I swore.

'Gimme a few minutes. There's an even longer bit in me bag.'

A few tense minutes later, and Albert announced he had broken through the second skin. He was listening at the hole.

'All quiet,' he whispered.

As he stepped to one side, I leaned against the wall and looked into the small hole.

There was no light, but I could feel the faintest of breezes against my eyeball. I stared into the darkness in the hope that, as my eyes adjusted,

I might be able to see something. Nothing. Turning my head, I put my ear close to the drill hole. I waved my hand to indicate to the others to stay silent. I could hear something. It sounded like a child … a soft whimpering sound. Crying.

It stopped. Then I picked up a faint voice … a whisper, dry and croaky. Not a child … a woman. She spoke.

'Is there someone there?'

Chapter 91

I stepped away from the wall, turned, and raised my finger to my lips. There was just enough light for the others to see the signal for silence.

Praying, silently, that it would be Lynn's voice I heard, I whispered into the drill hole. 'Can you hear me?'

Several seconds passed without a response.

Then I heard the voice again. This time clearer, the speaker closer to the opening. 'Who's there?' The voice was weak but clear.

I had to think quickly. If I said it was the police or hinted we were rescuers then the reaction of the woman on the other side of the wall might give us away.

'Miners,' I said. 'Who are you?'

'Please … help me.'

'Are you trapped?' I asked.

'Not trapped … prisoners. Please get help.'

'What's your name?' Again, I hoped it would be Lynn.

'Angie.' The woman said a surname but I couldn't make it out.

I turned to Wendy and gently shook my head.

'Not her?' she said, softly.

'A girl called Angie.'

'Talk to her, Finlay. She's our only insight into what's going on behind that wall.'

Whispering a conversation into a narrow hole that cut through two concrete block walls would have been hard enough at the best of times. Trying to talk to a woman who was both excited and extremely frightened was a real challenge. At first, either we both spoke at the same time or we both tried to listen at the tiny aperture. It took several attempts before we were able to slow down and take it in turns to speak.

I was able to learn that Angie was alone in a small, dark cell with no lights and with a wooden door. The guards would only open it when she was to be allowed out to work or when they brought food. Several times, all went quiet when she became fearful of being overheard.

I kept up the pretence that we were simple miners who had stumbled across her. In response to a question about other prisoners, she confirmed what Mollie had said: there were perhaps thirty to forty girls, all held in separate, locked cells.

In an effort to learn about Lynn, I asked if any new girls had come in during the last few days. Angie confirmed there had been just one. The men seemed to be giving her special treatment.

'What do you mean "special"?'

'They've been hosing her down a lot and beating her up. She's a fighter.'

It was just as Mollie had described. The power hose used to ensure compliance. I asked if she knew where the new girl was.

After a few seconds, Angie simply replied, 'It's too late for her, mate.'

My heart sank. 'Why?' I asked.

'They've started on her. She's had her jabs, just like the rest of us. I heard 'em talking. Tonight they're gonna rape her. They got a table, they'll tie her to it ... set up their cameras and video themselves having her.'

Angie's accent was East London, suggesting she was a long way from home. I wanted to reassure her, to tell her that we were going to save them all, but I knew I had to be patient. We were close; this was no time to panic or accidentally warn the traffickers before we were ready.

'That's awful,' I said, as I sought to control the anger that surged through me. 'We'll be back later. I'd best call the law...'

'No, don't,' she said, immediately. 'Can't ring the feds; they're part of it.'

'What do you mean?' I asked. 'I know the local coppers; no way they're a part of something like this.' I wanted – needed – to know if Nina was part of it. If Angie knew Nina was a cop, it would confirm my fears.

The whispered response was insistent. 'They are, they are,' she repeated. 'That's how they catch the ones who escape. They even come here in uniform. The guards get us out to entertain them.'

I wanted more detail to help put together a plan. Mollie had been helpful but this new girl was right here. I needed as much as she could tell me about the guards, any firearms or other weapons, the inside layout of the building, how the cell doors operated, and anything else she could tell me.

I was just about to start probing Angie further, when she interrupted me. 'Shhh ...'

I held off from speaking and raised up my hand for the others to keep silent. For a moment, all went quiet. Then I heard male voices, muffled and indistinct. They seemed angry, one voice becoming louder. I heard the word 'move' and the sound of heavy doors slamming. Several minutes passed before Angie returned to speak to me.

'You still there?' she asked.

'Yes,' I replied.

'You'd better be quick. They're moving us.'

The minibuses. The ones I had seen in the car park. 'What's happened?' I asked.

'I dunno. They're panicking. Some of the girls been taken out of their cells to do some packing.'

I'd learned enough. I ended the conversation with the promise that we would be going for help. In the light from Albert's torch I relayed what Angie had told me and then indicated to the others that we should leave.

As we marched quickly towards the surface, Wendy grabbed my arm. 'Did I just hear what I thought I heard?' she whispered between breaths.

'About the cops, you mean?'

'Yes. Local uniform lads. It's what Mollie said about Buff ... unbelievable.'

In the darkness, I couldn't see Wendy, but her voice gave away her disgust. Angie had confirmed the potential risk if we went to the local police for help. So calling MI5 had been the right decision.

But, there was another, more pressing problem. How would we prevent the traffickers from escaping while we waited for help?

There was one chance, one person I could turn to. He was less than an hour away by car.

Kevin Jones.

Chapter 92

After pressing some cash into Albert's powerful hand, we said goodbye and Wendy led the way back to her car. As soon as we shut the doors, I put my idea to her.

'And he's close enough to help?' she said.

'He should be. And if he can persuade a few of the lads to spend a night off-base, we can isolate the building until MI5 arrive.'

'Well, I can't think of anything better for now, so go ahead. Make the call.'

Unfortunately, not only was my friend not expecting my call, he was drunk. Not falling-down drunk, but still too drunk to be of much help to me, and way too drunk to drive. Plan A hit the buffers.

Noise from the wedding reception made conversation difficult. I waited a few moments while Kevin found a quiet place to speak. When he came back to the phone, his voice sounded like he was in an echo chamber.

'Where are you?' I asked. 'Can you speak?'

'I'm in the head. There's nobody here. What's up? Any more news on those papers we got from Bob's missus? You sent me a text ... is my pension sorted?'

'The translator's nearly done.' I was careful. Wendy could hear what Kevin was saying. 'I'll fill you in on it soon.'

Explaining to an inebriated mate that I needed him and a few of the Regiment lads to head down to the Forest of Dean for an off-the-radar operation proved difficult. Not surprisingly, Kevin wasn't keen, especially when I explained why we couldn't get local help or call in the Met. Finally, after several attempts, some odd discussions about slaves, miners, bent coppers and the hospital, I seemed to get through to him.

'No good, boss. All the CRW team are on half-hour call. Most everyone else is here at the do ... and we're all pissed.'

The Counter Revolutionary Warfare team were on permanent standby in case of an incident anywhere in the UK. They all carried pagers and all had strict orders to stay off the grog and keep within travelling distance of the new Regimental Base. Those that had families further away tended to either live on base or share digs in the local town. It wasn't looking good.

'There must be somebody,' I demanded.

'There's only three people around here that are sober. Superpig, but he's an officer; Cochrane the armourer, cos he's behind the bar ... and a lad called 'Danny' who drew the short straw and is on the door. He's just back from Belize ... just been badged.' Kevin slurred his words. It was going to take a few mugs of black coffee before he would be in a fit state to be any help.

'Who's Superpig?' I asked.

'The 'A' squadron commander. He's making sure we don't wreck the bar.'

'Christ,' I exclaimed. 'You can't ask him. What about the other two – could you ask them? I just need them to do a containment until help arrives and we might then have to break down a wall.' Even just two additional lads would be better than nothing, I thought.

'Gimme a minute,' said Kevin.

I waited. After what seemed an eternity, I heard his voice once more.

'You're in luck,' he said. 'Cochrane seems to think he owes you and said to pass on that it's because you're the only fuckin' Rupert who would have thought to lay on beers for the lads after the Embassy.'

I grinned. Over twenty years later, and Cochrane still remembered.

'There's an armoured Landie from the Northern Ireland police here on trial,' Kevin continued. 'Cochrane's gone to get a couple of lads from Goon troop to look after the bar. He says, if we can get back here before dawn, Superpig won't even notice.'

Briefly, I outlined to Kevin what we were facing and the kind of kit we needed. To break in to the armoured windows at the Embassy, we had used frame charges. I explained about the double-skinned wall and asked if Cochrane could dig out something similar we could use to break through and, hopefully, not harm the girl in the cell beyond.

We arranged to meet in the pub car park. It wasn't the most discreet of locations, but I figured it would be an easy place to find.

Then I settled down with Wendy to wait.

+

The pub was still busy, which helped as we were able to tuck Wendy's car in amongst all the others that were in the adjacent car park. From the side, it would be impossible to tell if our car was occupied, but we could see people coming and going and, as an extra benefit, we could watch the main route from the former hospital to the nearest motorway.

In the other direction, the road led into the forest. If the minibuses left before Kevin arrived, we would see them. That would mean implementing plan B. Problem was I didn't yet have a plan B, which was why I sat with fingers crossed, hoping that no effort would be made to move the slaves before we were ready.

We sat in silence while I went through our options in my mind. I reckoned I could get us into the underground complex, now that we had found the block wall. But what might happen after that was worrying me. If things went wrong before MI5 arrived, we were going to have to handle it ourselves.

Cochrane, the Regiment Quartermaster, and the new lad were soldiers. This wasn't an operation like anything they would have done before. Mollie had said one girl had been killed with a pistol, but that was the first and only time she had ever seen a gun of any kind. I wasn't sure if the guards were going to be armed.

Kevin and I were cops and, despite the way Grahamslaw and MI5 had covered for us after the incidents in London, there was only so far we could push our luck. Down here, away from the Met, a lot of questions would be asked if we had to open fire. If someone was shot then the Police Complaints Authority was bound to be called in. I'd seen and heard several tales of how police firearms officers had been hung out to dry for doing their job. I didn't plan to join them. I was going to have to make sure that the two serving soldiers understood the implications for the two ex-soldiers they were about to team up with. It was going to have to be police rules: 'Only fire to prevent your own death or the death of another.' That meant giving the bad guys the edge. Not something a trained soldier was going to be happy with.

My thoughts were disturbed by Wendy. 'You look troubled, Finlay,' she said.

'What makes you say that?' I asked.

'You've got that furrowed-brow look you've always had when you're stressed. And you keeping rubbing the back of your neck. They should have taught you about nervous signs on your CID course.'

I laughed again. 'So far as I know, I'm the only DI in the Met to have never done the course. Like I said, the Commander at SO13 sorted me a place on the slave-trafficking squad. It's a detective job ... so they made me a DI.'

'Is that where you met the girl who drives the sports car you saw at the hospital?'

'Yes ... Nina ... she's a DS. Bloody good one, or so I thought. I would never have guessed she was bent.'

'I've been thinking about that since you told me. Maybe she's not? It's not impossible that she's been abducted as well.'

'That's clutching at straws. Nope ... it adds up. Flash car – I don't imagine she has the cash for that. And she was an ideal way to get to the slave girl that was murdered … and to Lynn Wainwright as well.'

Wendy simply grunted. She knew I was right. A few minutes later any notion that Nina was a prisoner was dispelled. Along the main road, not thirty yards from where we sat parked; a familiar silver sports car drove past, heading away from the hospital.

In the driving seat sat Detective Sergeant Nina Brasov.

Chapter 93

'Talk of the bloody devil,' I said, pointing towards the road. 'There she goes now. See if you can pull out behind her.'

'What if she sees us?'

'Just make sure she doesn't.'

Wendy edged the nose of her car out onto the road. About a hundred yards away, I saw the brake lights of the sports car come on. It was pulling in outside a parade of shops.

I held my breath for a moment, wondering if Nina had seen us. We hung back and, after a few seconds, she got out of her car and walked into a takeaway food shop.

'See if you can find somewhere we can watch her,' I said.

Wendy quickly parked up between two cars so we would be hidden. It looked like Nina was ordering fish and chips. I checked my watch. It would be about an hour before Kevin arrived with the others.

'Wind down the windows a bit,' I suggested. I didn't want a simple mistake such as condensation to reveal our presence.

After about ten minutes, the door to the takeaway opened and Nina appeared. She was carrying two plastic bags. Nina was no kidnapping victim. She opened the passenger door to the sports car, dropped the bags onto the seat and then started to walk around the front towards the driver's side. Next thing, she stopped … her body seemingly tense.

Once again, I feared we had been spotted, but then I realised she was reaching into her coat pocket. She pulled out a mobile phone.

I watched carefully as Nina spoke to somebody.

'Have you got a phone signal here?' I asked Wendy.

Wendy pulled a phone from her pocket. 'Yes ... three bars,' she replied.

I didn't take my eyes from where my DS stood talking. I could not believe it of her. Her briefings on slave trafficking had been so good; she seemed so keen on doing her bit to stop the trade. Now, it looked like she was one of them. As good a bluff as I had ever seen.

After a few moments, Nina appeared to write something onto a small piece of paper. Immediately afterwards, she ended the call and opened the driver's door of her car. The leisurely way in which she had left the takeaway was now changed. The car door slammed shut, and she jerked the vehicle around and headed back in the direction from whence she had come. The tyres span on the tarmac as she accelerated away, Wendy and I ducking down to avoid being seen.

'Give me a couple of minutes,' I said.

I climbed out and walked quickly over to the fish-and-chip shop. It was empty, save for two women behind the counter. As I approached, they both turned to face me. I took a gamble.

'Sorry,' I said. 'I'm supposed to be collecting some food. I'm late. Can you tell me if they've already been in?'

'You just missed them,' one of the women laughed. 'It was a lady tonight. She just left.'

'Did she get enough for all of us?' I asked.

'Six fish and chips, one with a sausage. She settled the account as well ... better late than never.'

'Settled the account?'

'You lot had run up a bill of nearly a hundred quid over the last fortnight.'

I smiled. 'Sorry about that.'

I said goodnight and headed back to where Wendy was waiting. As I climbed back in the car, she started the engine.

'Learn anything?' she asked.

'Yes, she ordered six meals. They're not feeding the slaves, so I reckon there are now only six guards, including Nina. Mollie said there were at least eight before. I just hope it doesn't mean that some of them have already left and taken Lynn with them.'

Chapter 94

An hour later, an armoured Land Rover Tangi drove in from the main road. I realised then I could have suggested somewhere better than a pub car park to meet. With its Police Service of Northern Ireland livery, it stuck out like a sore thumb.

Quickly, I asked Wendy if she could lead us to somewhere quiet where we could talk. We moved off and, just outside the village, pulled into a small petrol station. It was closed, and behind it Wendy showed us a small yard that was hidden from the road. It was an ideal spot. Kevin climbed slowly out of the Land Rover, closely followed by Cochran and a young, blond lad wearing full black counter-revolutionary warfare kit. Kevin looked stiff. The bullet wounds were taking a while to heal, it seemed.

We shook hands and I introduced Wendy. Kevin and Cochrane were polite but I noticed them both give her the once-over.

For someone who, just an hour earlier, had seemed to be very drunk, my friend was now pretty steady on his feet. I asked him if he was OK. From the passenger well of the Land Rover, he pulled out a thermos flask.

'I met my old buddies Hughie and Ralph over the bowl in the bog,' he belched. 'Then a few ProPlus washed down with a couple of mugs of the Quartermaster's best black coffee. Now … right as rain.'

I grimaced, his breath smelled foul. Kevin had made himself vomit to get rid of the alcohol that was sitting in his stomach. The coffee would help counter what had already made it into his bloodstream. If he felt better, he certainly didn't look it.

The blond lad, introduced as 'Danny', was an infantry sergeant and had just finished selection. He looked fit and confident, just as he ought to be after having recently completed such a tough course. Fortunately for us, Danny was also an expert in using the latest Regiment MOE, the specialist 'method of entry' techniques.

I suggested we sat in the back of the Landie to run through my plan. As Danny opened the rear door, he and Cochrane laughed at my reaction. The object they had brought resembled a medieval cannon.

'What the hell is that?' I asked. Large, black and about five feet long, the device resembled a double-barrelled howitzer. It wouldn't have looked out of place had it been mounted on wheels and dragged about the countryside behind a team of horses.

Cochrane laughed again. 'It's called the Harvey Wallbanger, boss.'

I stood looking at it as I thought. The Wallbanger seemed to be a huge, heavy piece of equipment. It was going to be tough to move. I couldn't see any way of getting it down the mine, and, if we could, it would surely kill anyone on the other side of the wall.

Danny seemed to sense my uncertainty. 'Trust me boss, I can operate this on my own. It's surprisingly light and the wheels make it very manoeuvrable.'

'How does it work?' I asked.

'It uses a stored water charge and compressed air rather than explosive so it's much safer than the frame charges you guys used to use. The pressure wave it creates will take down a wall and anyone behind it.'

I looked Danny straight in the eye and made him promise me that it worked. He smiled and nodded. 'Trust me, it's sound.'

'Have you got anything else for cutting blockwork?' I asked.

'Thermic Lance. It'll cut anything but it's a lot slower,' was the disappointing reply.

A new idea came to me. If the Wallbanger was as effective as Danny described, then we could use it both as a weapon and a means of entry. And if not? Well, there wasn't a lot of choice. As if to demonstrate just how easily it could be moved, Danny and Cochrane lifted the Wallbanger from the rear of the Land Rover and onto the ground. It looked surprisingly light. With the space cleared, we climbed in, pulled the door to, and then started to talk through my plans.

For nearly fifteen minutes, we debated, discussed and decided what we would do if we needed 'immediate action', and what containment plans to implement before the MI5 response team turned up.

I wanted to hand the entry over to MI5 so they could handle any inquest if anyone got hurt. Danny and Cochrane were off-books and didn't want to get caught up in a witch hunt if things went wrong. We also agreed, before any plan could work, we had to stop the traffickers from leaving.

But we needed a contingency solution in case we had to go in early. Surprise would be essential, together with overwhelming firepower. Cochrane suggested what the Americans called 'shock and awe'; what I called 'rapid dominance'. It relies on a spectacular display of force to overcome an enemy quickly and to destroy his will to fight. Cochrane's proposal relied on a rapid entry, and surprise and fear amongst the slavers. If Mollie was right and Petre had the only weapon, then the remaining guards would be unarmed. We would have superior firepower and the element of surprise.

To start with, I suggested, we should secure the escape routes, get the entry equipment into place and then wait for help. Once Toni Fellowes came through with the MI5 response team, we would be good to go.

Wendy agreed to drive the Landie. Originally my plan had been to take Kevin into the mine with me. As he was still suffering and Danny was clearly the expert in using the method of entry equipment, we came to a group decision that the young trooper would come with me. It was agreed that the two of us would get the Wallbanger into place and then make ready for MI5. I would maintain contact with Angie in the cell to try and gauge if the minibuses were likely to depart before help arrived. Cochrane and Kevin would insert through the woodland to maintain eyeball on the buses in case they looked like leaving before we were ready. Wendy would position herself at the main road near the hospital so that, if the guards did try to leave before we were ready, she could block the exit.

If my new plan 'A' went as intended, Wendy would bring part of the MI5 entry team into the mine, to where we would be waiting at the wall. We would then break through the cell wall and have another team enter the main gate to trap all the occupants between us. Up top, they would also mop up any potential escapers.

The 'immediate action' plan would be to rush the building from above and below. That was the only part of the plan that troubled me. Down in the tunnels, I wasn't confident that the slave girl we had established communication with would be able to warn us if things kicked off up top.

The stickiest part of my plan, however, was when I came to the rules under which we could open fire. Cochrane, as the oldest hand, was understandably reluctant, but it didn't take long for him to appreciate the implications if we fired first. Danny, with his selection course just behind him, was far more aware of the rules of engagement. Success was going to depend on speed, timing and shock.

As we climbed out of the Landie, Cochrane handed me a set of overalls and some boots. 'Size ten, according to my records,' he said.

I grinned wryly. As I slid my shoes off and pulled the heavy-duty suit over my trousers, I couldn't help but wonder how the hell I had gotten myself into this kind of situation again.

Chapter 95

As mobile phone communication near the former hospital was impossible, I was immensely pleased to discover that the Land Rover was fitted with a satellite phone.

I called Toni for an update just before we headed off to carry the

Wallbanger into the mine. Her news wasn't good. She'd been trying to call me on the mobile to tell me that MI5 wouldn't rustle up an entry team for an operation that wasn't under Security Service control. After trying every means she knew to get us some help, nobody had been willing or able to take a chance and help us.

The others saw me on the phone, clocked my reaction and guessed. We were on our own.

Kevin was for going in with just the four of us. He had a point. We had to get to Lynn Wainwright quickly. If we made enough noise, put in some smoke and threw a few flash-bangs, we could create enough of a panic to overcome whoever was inside.

I guessed it could work, but only if I was right about there being just five or six traffickers. If there were many more, we could end up with a serious problem.

'How long do you need to get the Wallbanger into position, boss?' Kevin asked.

'An hour, at least,' I explained.

'OK, how about this ...' He outlined his idea.

We would agree a time and, at that moment, he and Cochrane would slash the tyres on the minibuses. If the people inside tried to leave early, they would fire a few warning shots to act as a deterrent.

Inside the mine, Kevin suggested we should fire the Wallbanger and go in through Angie's cell. Plenty of smoke, a few flash-bangs, and it will be all over in minutes. If, however, the people inside didn't try to leave, we should still fire the Wallbanger at an agreed time. The resultant furore would be heard at the surface, so those up top would know when to come in and help.

I admired Kevin's confidence, and Cochrane and Danny nodded approvingly. Wendy also appeared content. I smiled at my old colleague but she didn't react. She was keeping quiet, seemingly happy to allow experience to lead.

Kevin's plan seemed sound. We subdued the bad guys, stopped the slaves from getting hurt and then called in the local cavalry. And by going in before calling for help, we avoided the fear the traffickers might be warned of our presence. I liked it. At my suggestion, we set a time of midnight for the Wallbanger to be fired.

It all looked sorted … until a solitary hand was raised. It was Wendy. She didn't look happy.

We all fell silent.

Wendy cleared her throat. 'Look … I'm sorry if this doesn't sit comfortably with your plans, boys, but I think we're forgetting that I'm the ranking officer here and if the shit hits the fan it'll end up in my lap.'

The three lads just looked at me.

Cochrane broke the embarrassing silence. 'I thought we had an agreement?'

'You don't like my plan?' asked Kevin.

'I appreciate you guys know what you're doing … and if this was an official SAS hostage rescue, then I'm sure it would be fine. But it isn't.'

Nobody answered. Kevin sat up and braced his back against the inside of the Landie. He looked uncomfortable. I said nothing and from what I could read on the faces of Danny and Cochrane, they didn't plan on opening their mouths either.

After a few tense moments, I decided to break the ice. 'It's what these guys do, Wendy. They train for this kind of scenario, day in day out.'

'I just want you to hold fire before we rush into something that gets way out of control … and with no backup plan.'

'But we don't have the luxury of time. There's a WPC in that building who needs our help, now.'

'I know that, Finlay. But we're only five people. Only four of you are going to try and rescue the girl and you have no real idea of what you are going to find in there. What are you going to do if all hell breaks loose? You don't have a contingency plan.'

'We have to go in,' I said, again. 'Lynn Wainwright is relying on us.'

'I know … I know,' Wendy replied, quietly. 'So … if you'll just listen to me for a minute, I'll tell you what I have in mind.

So we listened for five minutes as she briefly analysed, assessed and debated the options to rescue all the women that were being held in the old hospital. And she made one very, very good point. The strength of Angie's cell door. What if we couldn't breach it?

It was impossible to not be impressed. The plan changed.

As soon as we were in a position to contain the escape routes from the hospital, Wendy would put in a call for assistance from her own force. She would route the request through her Territorial Support Group so as to reduce the possibility of a local officer tipping off the traffickers. And, even if someone did – as she correctly pointed out – the escape routes would be sealed off.

The TSG could muster three personnel carriers, each carrying twelve officers and were always ready to be deployed to any disturbance. In addition, Wendy would call in a firearms-trained dog unit to work with an Armed Response Vehicle on the initial entry. That way, she said, the operation would be undertaken speedily and lawfully. And she was confident they could be with us before midnight.

Kevin and Tom Cochrane would slash the tyres of the vehicles in the hospital car park as outlined in Kevin's plan. I was to set up below ground, with Danny to listen through the block wall for any evidence that the slavers were about to depart early. If an escape started, then, and only then, would we go in hard.

If everything went to plan, there would be no need for the SAS lads to get involved. And she had a good plan to get us through the cell door should it prove necessary. We were convinced. Plan 'C' went to the top of the list.

Chapter 96

Getting the Wallbanger through the mine wasn't straightforward, even though it was on wheels.

The first part was relatively easy. Albert had left the gates unlocked and, to start with, as we wheeled the heavy device along the dusty tracks, we made good progress. But, as we headed deeper, the tunnels narrowed and the uneven surface sloped so steeply that we struggled to stop the cannon from running away from us. Then, just as we regained control, the slope would change as we came across rocks and small uphill sections that were a real struggle. In my forties and out of condition, I found it as tough as any training run I had ever done. Danny hardly broke sweat. I envied him his youth.

Cochrane had given me a Diemaco rifle, which I had slung across my back. Although it dug into my skin, the unfamiliar weapon was surprisingly light. Using the headlights from the Landie, Danny had given me a quick run through on how to use it. I was surprised at how comfortable it felt in my hands.

Danny wore black kit; coveralls, boots, body armour and helmet. On his back, a small bergen held smoke canisters, flash-bangs, two sets of night-vision goggles and some plasticuffs. A holster strapped to his thigh contained a SIG P226 pistol with a small Streamlight torch attached to it.

From what Mollie had said, there would be very little lighting once we broke through into the cell complex. If we needed to break in before the police arrived, the NVG goggles also provided by Cochrane would enable us both to operate in the dark. Although they restricted peripheral vision, they would give us an advantage over the occupants.

Danny and I talked about how we would handle an emergency entry. We agreed that, after entry, he would take point. My role would be to use an ASP. The small telescopic steel baton was very effective at close quarters. Danny had handed one to me along with the Diemaco. It was the same type as the official police issue baton that I had drawn several times over the years without ever having the need to use it. The simple act of racking it into the open position was normally enough. Danny suggested that he would take down any guards we came across, I should then disable them with the ASP and plasticuff them around the wrists and ankles. He would also handle the smoke canisters and flash-bangs. Although I might be able to do a decent job as number two, to ask me to take point wasn't a good idea. Danny was fitter and recently trained, so he would lead. I readily agreed to his ideas.

Once the police officers were with us, Kevin and Cochrane would bring in their team from the car park about thirty seconds after we made our first entry. From their position outside, they would hear the flash-bangs going off and, in that way, I also hoped any guards on the upper floor would race downstairs to investigate the commotion. With armed police all around and with the confusion caused by the noise and smoke, I hoped the hospital would be taken without too much difficulty.

Like most operations, though, it all depended on timing, and a bit of luck.

☩

An hour and a half later, Danny and I had finished heaving and shoving the Wallbanger into position. Behind the wall, a petrified slave girl was going to prove key to the whole attack.

While Danny set the Wallbanger ready to fire, I spent the next few minutes with my lips pressed to the drill hole, whispering instructions to Angie. I reassured her that rescue was on its way. She was to listen at her cell door and let me know what was happening outside. We needed to know if the evacuation started early and, for that situation, I had to explain Wendy's backup plan. I prayed that Angie understood me. If the shit hit the fan, I needed her to scream blue murder until the guards came to find out what was going on.

I gave her a key word to yell as the cell door was opened. Whatever happened, she was not to use the word until the guards actually entered the cell. Opening the door wasn't enough. Mollie had told me how they liked to use a powerful hose to subdue the girls. If the local police chose to do a two-pronged attack and come through the mine, they wouldn't want to be facing a powerful jet of water as they went through the wall.

I told Angie that, after screaming the command word, she should dive into a corner of the cell, keep her eyes tightly closed and stick her fingers in her ears. She was then to wait and keep still until we came back for her.

Her voice trembled as she relayed the instructions back to me. She sounded terrified. I checked my watch. An hour and twenty minutes to go.

Chapter 97

Every so often, I listened through the wall for any sounds of disturbance or movement. There was none.

It seemed likely to me they would move the girls in daylight. A fleet of minibuses on the road, late at night, was bound to draw the attention of any patrolling police car. Provided they took steps to prevent the girls shouting or waving for help, it would be far more anonymous if they travelled amongst the rush-hour traffic. Nina would know that. She would know how to move and how to avoid getting noticed.

Likely as not, they would be planning to take the girls somewhere temporary until the heat died down. With Mollie having escaped, they wouldn't want to take the chance that she might lead the authorities back to the hospital. If Nina now knew I had been sent to interview Mollie, then it was likely she had warned the slavers we were getting close. They would play safe, hide the evidence, and only move back to the former hospital if she was sure it was going to remain undiscovered.

I'd had no choice but to include my knowledge of Nina's presence in the brief I had given to Kevin and the two soldiers. Nina wasn't to get any special treatment. If the smoke did its job, she would be taken down with the others. The priority was, however, to get to Lynn Wainwright before it was too late.

The wait gave me a chance to try the NVGs. I hadn't used a set of night-vision goggles for nearly two decades. The set Danny handed to me was much lighter than I had experienced. With two image-intensifying tubes that strapped around my head, a small chin strap held them securely in place. Flicking a switch at the side of the headset, all around me, the tunnel complex was bathed in differing shades of green as the infrared turned on.

My watch beeped. Midnight. An hour to go.

I pulled the goggles away from my face to make it possible to whisper into the drill hole through the walls. There was no response.

Shit, I thought, she's fallen asleep. I whispered again, louder this time, trying to inject some urgency into my voice. Still, nothing.

'Shut up,' came a hissed voice.

'All OK?' I asked.

'Quiet ... something's happening.'

I waited. A moment later, Angie returned to the wall. She seemed petrified.

'You'd better get the coppers here now. There's a hell of a fight going on with the new girl. They're either killing her or raping her.'

'Are we ready?' I asked Danny. It was just the situation we didn't want, but the one we had planned for. We had to go in immediately.

'Good to go, boss.'

'OK. It looks like we're gonna have to go without the local cops. They've started attacking Lynn.' In the darkness, I could just make out a faint, green glow from Danny's NVGs.

'Great,' he replied. 'Let's get this over with, then. Just make sure you're crouched behind me when I fire this thing off.'

I called through the wall again, this time louder. Angie was crying. I managed to get her to calm down.

'You want me to start screaming now?' she asked.

'Yes,' I replied. 'As if your life depended on it.'

Angie started. She screamed. Even through the double-skinned wall, I could hear it. Slow and deep at first, within a few breaths she was at fever pitch.

'Fuck me, that girl's got some lungs,' said Danny.

I listened at the drill hole. It must have been at least a minute before there was any response to Angie's efforts. A male voice, angry. 'Shut up, shut up...'

Angie kept screaming. 'Leave her alone,' she cried. 'Leave her alone, you bastards.'

It wasn't working. For Wendy's idea to succeed, I needed the guards to open her door. They were simply ignoring her.

'Tell them you've got a man in there,' I shouted through the wall as Angie stopped for breath.

'Help me, help me,' she shouted. 'Someone's attacking me...'

It did the trick. I heard the cell door open and a moment later the roar of water. Just as Wendy thought would happen, they were hosing Angie down. We were nearly ready. My heart raced ... just a few more moments.

The sound of water stopped. Male voices ... two of them.

Angie screamed. 'GO.'

The key word. The guards were in the cell.

I pulled the NVG goggles over my eyes, backed away from the wall and crouched behind Danny.

'Ready,' I whispered.

The narrow passage erupted. Shock and awe.

Chapter 98

First came the noise.

It roared into my ears, dominated all senses and even hurt my eyes. Then, before I had time to register, came the pressure wave – like standing in front of a steam train as it entered a narrow tunnel; huge and all-powerful. Finally came the water, the dust and the rocks, which seemed to be flung at us from all directions, bouncing off the sides and roof of the tunnel. For a moment I feared we were about to be buried as the cave roof gave way.

It was no wonder Danny had suggested I duck behind him, he knew what was coming, but I'm sure even he had made no allowance for the tunnel effect.

'You OK, boss?'

The voice came from above me ... familiar. I opened my eyes. I was on my back. Everywhere was green. Feeling returned slowly, and with it, understanding. I knew where I was. I mumbled something, tried to speak. My mouth was full of dirt.

'Fuck ...' It was the best I could manage. I moved my arms, sluggishly at first, not even sure they were still attached to me.

Danny must have sensed what I was looking for as I ran my hands over my chest and legs. 'Don't worry ... you're in one piece.'

A gloved hand rubbed across my face. My skin felt rough, like sandpaper. I tried to speak again but nothing was happening, and I could taste blood, warm and salty. I tried to lick my lips.

'Try this.' The voice calm, reassuring. Cool water, dribbling into my mouth, clearing the dirt, my tongue now free to check my teeth – all there – and to try and form a word. Then, just as I determined to speak, more water, this time up my nose, into my throat. Not sure if I was about to cough or retch, I rolled onto my side, catching a glimpse, as I turned, of Danny holding a small plastic water bottle. Slime and spit ran from my nose and mouth as I struggled for breath. In the background I heard the sound of crying ... a woman ... Angie.

It brought me quickly back to my senses. 'I'm OK,' I coughed.

Danny thrust the ASP into my hand and wrapped my fingers around it. 'Here ... take this. We need to move now.'

I scrambled to my feet, still unsteady but getting better by the second. Both knees felt sore. Around me, the floor was littered with debris from the wall. My peripheral vision limited by the NVG goggles, I turned my head back toward where I expected to see the remains of the block wall. It wasn't there. All that remained was a pale-green mass of swirling dust.

From my left, I heard the sound of Danny starting to move. Remembering our agreed plan, I once again tucked in behind him. In his gloved hand I saw that he held a black flash-bang.

I tapped his arm to signal I was ready and, a half-second later, watched as the stun grenade flew forward into the dust cloud. I'd warned Angie to close her eyes tight and stick her fingers in her ears. I just hoped she'd remembered.

The light emission was immediately followed by two explosions, not the single effect I was used to. Danny flicked on his torch, the narrow beam struggling to penetrate the dust. We moved forward cautiously. I saw a bed, and beneath it what looked like the bare limbs of a woman. Then there was a hand, the fingers trembling but clasped in a 'thumbs-up' sign. I smiled to myself ... good girl, Angie. She was safe.

Two more prostrate figures lay just inside an open doorway ahead of us. The guards. What with the combination of the Wallbanger and the grenade, I could see they were now out of the game. One was moving slightly, groaning as if in pain. The other lay still and silent. Both were soaking wet and covered in a layer of pale-coloured dust. As Danny covered the doorway, I crawled forward, snapped plasticuffs around ankles and wrists and pulled them tight.

Returning to the bed, I felt beneath it. 'It's us Angie, you're safe,' I called.

A hand reached out, touching my goggles and the mat of drying dirt that now caked my hair. 'Thought you said you were miners?' Angie said, her voice trembling with fear.

'Something like that. Can you keep an eye on these two while we deal with the others?' I asked.

Angie popped her head out from under the bed, but it was clear she was too petrified to do anything more for us.

'Ready?' said Danny.

'She's too scared to keep these two covered.'

Danny crept back to where I was crouched next to Angie. 'OK ... let's give her a little help then.' He prised the ASP from my grip, leaned over the guard showing signs of coming round and then brought it down hard on the man's exposed thigh muscle. I cringed as his unfortunate victim cried out in pain.

'Move and we'll be back,' Danny screamed in the man's ear as he handed the baton back to me.

Seconds later, another grenade flew away from his grip and through the door. This one was smoke. As the corridor filled, we waited two, three, four seconds. A second grenade followed. Another flash-bang. Two explosions – same as before.

Danny moved fast as the grenade took out the lightbulb and plunged us into darkness. He was through the door and into the cover of some nearby crates before I knew it.

'Clear,' he called.

We moved on. Danny progressed so quickly that I struggled to keep pace with him. Smoke – flash-bang – room entry – clearance.

The smoke slowed us down but it was something we'd agreed on to minimise the risk of needing to go loud – to engage in a fire-fight. Every time we found a new area, Danny would enter first, scan for danger and then call me in behind him to apply the plasticuffs as he located and disabled the guards. He was a top-level operator, swift and efficient. We were a pretty decent team.

The three remaining guards were overpowered very quickly and, to my relief, with no gunfire.

Just as Kevin had predicted, the noise of grenades was heard outside. There was an almost comical moment when, as Danny and I searched for the final man, he made a break for freedom up some wooden steps. Reaching the top, with little thought other than escape, he ran straight into the solid frame of Tom Cochrane. The Quartermaster barely flinched as the guard bounced backwards, his nose having smashed itself very forcefully into a heavily tattooed forearm.

✠

The doors in the hospital basement proved easy to open: no keys, just bolts that slid across to make them secure. It was Kevin who first found Lynn. As I reached her cell, she was standing naked with her arms wrapped tight around his neck. The cell was soaked, suggesting that she had recently been hosed down.

I stood in the doorway as Lynn glanced in my direction. There was no sign of recognition in her eyes. I felt a surge of anger. The woman before me looked nothing like the young WPC I had seen demonstrate such bravery and skill when facing an armed gunman. Skin bruised and filthy, her eyes scared me. They looked vacant and lost, the brain behind them spaced-out on the drugs the traffickers had been feeding her. Behind, in the dim light, I noticed a tiny cot. There was no bedding, save for a soiled, tatty blanket, and no sign of her personal clothing.

And there was no sign of Nina. I had prepared what I was going to say to her and had even mulled over the idea of locking her in a cell with Lynn so they could have a little chat. As we were releasing the girls from their cells, Kevin told me that Nina's car was also missing. She'd slipped out before we arrived.

It mattered little. First chance I got, I would be exposing Nina Brasov to the unpleasant reality of arrest and life in a cell.

Chapter 99

We'd done it.

The traffickers were face-down on the ground, wrists and ankles cuffed, near the front entrance to the old hospital. Danny and Tom Cochrane had taken them outside first, to make sure they were out of the way before we led the girls up the steps and away from their cells.

We counted thirty-four slaves, including Lynn. They were all scared and weak from hunger. As we'd encouraged them outside, they had all moved hesitantly, seemingly afraid this rescue was some kind of trick. Kevin got the generator working, and the light made moving around easier, but it also illuminated the scale of what we had uncovered. It was a factory dedicated to the production of pornography. Two cells had been set up as recording studios, with expensive looking cameras and lighting equipment, and a third as a dressing room. In a room upstairs we found computers to transfer recordings onto DVD, and, in an alcove near the stairs, piles of cardboard boxes containing DVDs ready for dispatch to whatever market they were destined for.

Kevin had found some blankets and organised the slave girls into a huddle to try and keep them warm.

The two SAS lads were standing away from us, in the darkness, so they could observe everyone without being seen themselves. I'd noticed that both of them were surprisingly subdued as we'd secured the male prisoners and then mustered the women into the open air. As Kevin joined me while we waited for Wendy, I asked him what was up.

'The porn stuff,' he said. 'At the stag do before the wedding, there were a few porn films shown. What we've just seen makes you realise ... well, let's just say we always assume the women are willing and are well paid for what they do. We never thought they might be forced to do it.'

'Easy mistake, Kev.'

'Kind of makes you wonder, though, doesn't it?' He paused. 'Any news on the documents?'

'Sorry, mate. The translator went through them. It was interesting stuff but old hat ... and it certainly wasn't a treasure map.'

'No extra pension then?'

'Not this week, old son.'

He shrugged. 'There are a lot stories going around that the Increment team found something valuable out in Afghan, though.'

'Something that got a few of them killed, you mean?'

'You said that, not me.'

'Well, if they did, that document wasn't it ... and maybe for us it's just as well. It was a Jihadist Manual and, apparently, MI5 have known about it for years. Toni Fellowes rang me only yesterday to confirm that Monaghan was definitely behind the murders. I say we leave it at that.'

I left Kevin to check over the prisoners. He now looked fully sober, any lasting effect from the wedding party having passed. I found Wendy and asked her to bring the Land Rover closer to the hospital building so we could use the lights to help watch the prisoners. She had made contact with her force HQ as soon as Cochrane radioed to report the flash-bang explosions and say that he and Kevin were going in. She wasn't best pleased we'd gone in early – until I explained to her what had actually happened underground.

'But there's some unexpected news,' she said, her anger dissipated. 'An SO19 Armed Response Team from the Met is only fifteen minutes away.'

I was both reassured and surprised. I guessed Toni had managed to call them in after all.

Moving on to the prisoners, I checked they were secure and, by the time I returned, I found Kevin had carried Lynn from the building and lifted her onto the Land Rover passenger seat. Wendy had given her a clean blanket and a jacket but, even with the car heater at full blast, they were struggling to get warmth back into her shivering frame.

She could talk though, and, between tears and bouts of uncontrolled shaking, she told us what had happened. The screaming Angie heard had been Lynn desperately fighting off two traffickers. I guessed it was the same two that Danny had taken out with the Wallbanger. Temporarily distracted by their anger, the two men had broken off their attempt to rape Lynn in order to silence Angie.

I left Kevin next to the Land Rover talking to Lynn and Wendy. I needed a few moments alone. We had been just in time, and I wondered what might have happened had my old friend not put her foot down and taken charge.

✢

The familiar beating-rotor sound of approaching helicopters brought my thoughts back to the here and now. As I sat down on the grass near to the slave girls, Wendy turned on the Land Rover blue lights to let the approaching cops know we were friendlies. They made a fast approach, the powerful helicopter landing lights flickering across us as the pilots searched for a safe place to set down.

There were two aircraft, the first of them landing on the grass not fifty yards from where I was sitting. Immediately after touching down, I saw a side door slide open and dark figures jumping to the ground.

They adopted a crouched style, small carbines pointed forwards as they advanced. I lay back and made sure the Diemaco wasn't easily seen. I didn't want to get shot accidentally.

To the rear of the approaching firearms officers I saw a familiar figure, tall and slender. In the harsh light from the Landie, I thought at first that I was mistaken. Then I realised, I was staring at someone I hadn't anticipated seeing quite so soon.

Nina Brasov.

Chapter 100

As Nina walked towards the Land Rover, I leaned up on my elbow and watched her.

I was the last person Nina was expecting to see, and, as I was still wearing the CRW kit, she walked right past without giving me as much as a glance. She seemed confident. Either I'd missed something or she was acting out an incredible bluff.

As I turned to face the glare from the car headlights I could see she was talking to Kevin and Wendy. The apparent friendliness of the conversation confused me. Then it occurred to me they might not realise who Nina was. Wendy turned towards me and pointed. Nina looked over, surprise on her face. The expression turned to one of confusion as she appeared to recognise me. She walked across.

'What the hell are you doing here, Finlay?' There was anger in her voice as she looked me up and down. 'And what's that gear you're wearing?'

'I might ask the same question,' I replied.

'I asked first.'

'And I'm the one asking the questions,' I said firmly. 'I don't know what exactly you're up to *Sergeant* and it won't be for me to work out. Nobody likes a bent cop...'

'What the fuck are you on about, Finlay?'

'You, Nina. We saw you.'

'How long have you been here?'

'We found the place early yesterday evening.'

'You've been here since yesterday? ... I see.'

She crouched down and leaned in close to me. As she started to speak, she kept her voice low, but the menace was crystal clear. She was livid and it looked like I was the cause.

'I think you'd better listen to me, Finlay ... I've put up with a lot from you recently. Now, I don't quite understand what you're doing here or how you found this place, but you are not getting away with calling me bent. You owe me in more ways than you might imagine.'

'Really, how's that?' I asked.

'You remember in Hampstead, when that gunman had you cold?'

'Hardly likely to forget it.'

'His name is Marius—'

'I know who he is,' I blurted.

'... If you'd let me finish, Marius recognised you from Romania. At that moment he figured you were a police spy. I'm sure you can imagine what Romanian gangsters do to spies. The only reason he didn't shoot right then was because he also recognised me. That saved your life.'

'I already knew he'd recognised me,' I replied. 'I told you that at the time. You're saying he knew you as well?'

'That's right. How do you imagine I know so much about the Cristeas? I've been undercover for months. While you were swanning around, guarding the Royals and playing happy families, people like me were doing the dirty work. Marius didn't know what to think when he saw me with you, but when I shook my head, he knew enough not to kill you.'

'I suppose I should thank you?'

'You don't owe me anything. Did Youldon tell you I was only going to be on the trafficking squad for a short while?'

I remembered the conversation that I had with our Superintendent on my first day at Scotland Yard. 'Yes, he said you were off to the National Crime Squad, I think.'

'Exactly, NCS is my real job. We've been working on the slave-trafficking ring; I've been our way into them.'

'While working with us as well?'

'Our little squad was only created to gain the Cristeas' confidence. It was Grahamslaw's idea. The Cristeas wanted to be sure I was useful. They were made to think I was a disillusioned cop who could be paid to keep them one step ahead of the police. Having me on a temporary posting to a new trafficking squad was perfect. They thought I applied for the job to help them.'

'You said, "for months"?' I probed. 'I thought the squad only started a few weeks ago?'

'Do you have any idea how long it takes to place someone in a crime syndicate like the Cristeas?'

'I guess not.'

I took a moment to absorb what Nina had said. When I had first spotted her car, the idea of her being corrupt seemed to answer a lot of questions. It explained how the traffickers had found Relia and how they had managed to abduct Lynn Wainwright. It also meant that the removal of the footprint from the door to Relia's flat was probably an accident after all. 'How did you get inside their organisation?' I asked.

Nina's quiet laugh sounded cynical. 'Internet dating, would you believe? We set up a fake profile and one of their men took the bait. They constantly trawl for vulnerable girls and they thought I was an even better catch.'

I looked back to where the slave girls were now being led by uniformed officers along the entrance drive to waiting personnel carriers. 'So, we've messed things up for you somewhat? I guess I owe you another apology.'

Nina shrugged. Her temper had waned, her voice now less threatening. 'The operation was over as soon as they snatched Lynn. I couldn't let her suffer the same fate as Relia. Once I'd located her, I just needed to find the right moment to call in help.'

'So, what happened with Relia? I figured you'd given her up to them.'

'Do you remember, when we got back to the office, I was called in to see Youldon? He'd worked it out. The Cristeas had to have had me followed and I led them to Relia. It was my fault.'

'And what about Lynn? Did you accidentally lead them to her as well?' I could see Nina bite her tongue. I'd struck a nerve.

'I don't know. I didn't ... like I said, as soon as they snatched Lynn, she became my priority. I came down here with one of their goons to see if this was where they were hiding her. When we got here, one of the slave girls escaped ...'

'I know. It's thanks to her that I found this place.'

'Well, her escape caused a panic. They got word she was talking to the local police. They were about to pull out.'

'So why didn't you call for help as soon as you knew Lynn was here?'

'You think you were the only one making plans, Finlay? How did you think SO19 got here so quickly? They've been on standby at a local RAF base, waiting for my call. I volunteered to get the guards some takeaway food to give me a chance to signal them. The plan was to do an armed stop on the minibuses as the men transported the girls away from the factory.'

'Safer than a raid on the factory?'

'Exactly. We'd have had them in the open and it might have given me a chance to escape without blowing my cover.'

'They'd have guessed it was you had tipped off the police.'

'Maybe ... or maybe we'd have made them think the escaped girl had led us to them.'

'So, what changed things?'

'I was trying to delay things because we wanted the leader – the one called Petre – and we wanted Marius, of course. They were due back here to organise the departure. Last night, while I was getting the final meal, Petre called me. He'd been trying to get through to the others but he couldn't get a connection. He rang me and gave me some orders for the rest of the men. He dictated it in Romanian thinking I wouldn't understand what he was ordering them to do. Either he forgot or he didn't know that my father is Romanian. I could understand it. I knew then they were going to kill most of the slave girls and finish off Lynn as soon as he arrived.'

I thought back. The phone call outside the chip shop. 'Is that when you called for help?' I asked.

'Just after that, yes.'

'Any idea where Petre might be now?'

'He was definitely on his way back here when he rang me. Marius should have been with him. Where did you park that Land Rover?'

'Outside the main gate – to stop any escape.'

'They probably saw it as they were arriving. Just lucky that mobile phones don't work here, otherwise they would have tipped off the people inside. Now, I guess they will have gone to ground or be heading back to Romania. I don't understand why you didn't call SO19 for help?'

'We were planning to, but, as it looked like you were on their side, we opted to call in the local lads. The Superintendent over there, she was supposed to call them after we'd made sure the traffickers couldn't escape. The timing of things got complicated when we found that some local cops had been using the girls' services. In any event, you'd have been too late. We were underground when we heard they had started attacking Lynn.'

'Underground?'

'We found some tunnels that led from a local mine to the outside of the cell walls.'

'Who's "we"?'

'See those lads over there?' I pointed to where Danny and Cochrane were standing. 'Those two lads are from 22 Regiment. They brought a thing called a Wallbanger. It blew out the wall and took some of the bad guys with it.'

'So the SAS helped you?'

'Yes … unofficially.'

'Anyone killed?' Nina asked.

'Not a single person, just a few cuts and bruises. In fact, we didn't fire a shot. Can you ask the SO19 boys to give them a hand to bring the Wallbanger up from the basement?'

'No worries, but how did you manage to get the SAS involved?'

I sighed. 'It's complicated, they really shouldn't be here. They're off-books, doing me a favour. When I saw your car I didn't know who to trust so I went to the only people I could.'

'Well, it's lucky you did' she said, the harsh tone fading from her voice. 'It looks like I wouldn't have got SO19 here in time. You saved Lynn ... you saved them all.'

'Just lucky, Nina. Right place, right time.'

'What about you? How are we going to explain you sitting here with a bloody machine gun resting in your arms?'

'I have an idea,' I said, as I got to my feet. 'Just don't tell the SO19 Inspector that I'm in the job ... And there's one other thing.'

'Another favour? You already owe me big time.'

No ... not a favour, an apology. For not believing in you.'

☩

To implement my plan I needed both the help of Nina and the co-operation of Wendy. I managed to secure both. Nina was keen to keep things simple and Wendy seemed too tired to argue.

After a short discussion, we agreed Kevin would return to Hereford with Danny and Cochrane. I would make my way home and Wendy would be given the credit for leading the rescue of the slave girls.

As no shots had been fired and nobody had been killed there would be no need for a coroner's inquest or Police Complaints Authority enquiry. SO19 could take the glory for the arrests and the press could be given a story of how local cops had foiled an international slave trafficking ring. As for me, I would head back to London.

Chapter 101

The SO19 lads had brought a medic who took Lynn off to the local Accident and Emergency. It was too early to assess the effect of the heroin but she was as well as could be hoped for.

Within an hour, Cochrane and Danny had packed the military kit into the back of the Land Rover and were on their way back to Hereford, Kevin with them. Nina fed the SO19 Senior Inspector a story about a highly sensitive Security Service operation that required the military lads to be written out of any involvement in the rescue. As I'd hoped, with no shots fired, he agreed to keep quiet.

Wendy offered to lend me her car to return to Gloucester and collect my 2CV. As I took her car keys, she moved close to me. 'I've been talking to Kevin, he's worried about you.'

'I know … he's been onto me a fair bit lately. What did he say this time?'

'That you're not sleeping well, having nightmares … that you check under your car every time you go near it.'

'Can you blame me? I had a bomb under my last car, remember?'

'Of course I do, Finlay. Just keep an eye on yourself. The kind of things that have happened to you can play tricks on the mind, make you paranoid.'

'I know. I'll be fine, I promise.'

Wendy placed her hand on my forearm and squeezed, gently. 'Don't be too proud to ask for help.' She showed me a folded piece of paper in her hand.

'What's that?' I asked.

'The woman you thought was working with the traffickers? She gave it to me. It's the names of the three local officers that have been visiting the factory.'

'Recognise any of the names?'

'Yes, all three. One of them is Paul Travers, a DS at one of our smaller CID offices … he's the one they call Buff.'

'A nickname?'

'Bald ugly fat fucker … suits him down to the ground. He's a bully, a lazy bastard who draws his pay and does nothing to earn it. '

'So, you knew who he was when Mollie mentioned the name?'

'I didn't … but Fleming did. She filled me in afterwards.'

'Can she be trusted not to warn him?'

There was irony in Wendy's laugh. 'There's no love lost between her and Paul Travers, believe me. She's looking forward to seeing him exposed.'

'Be careful,' I said. 'People like that think they're untouchable. What will you do with him and the others?'

'I'll deal with it, don't you worry. Now, what about this?' Wendy pointed towards the hospital. 'I'm still wondering exactly what happened here tonight.'

'Wish I could say it was all in a day's work,' I answered. 'We were bloody lucky, that's all.'

'Luck you call it? I hardly think so, and I still can't believe just the two of you took out five guys who are supposed to be ex-legionnaires? Are you telling me SAS lads are that good?'

'A combination of talent and practice,' I smiled. 'It was one reason I was happy to allow them to plan the entry to the building.'

'Well I'm amazed that no one got hurt and I still have a career.'

I smiled. 'Let's hope I do as well.'

'Leave that with me. I'll call your DCI in the morning and tell him what a fantastic job you did locating the missing WPC. He'll probably commend you.'

I laughed. 'Somehow, I doubt that and, if you remember, I was only here to help you. Plus, the two main suspects seem to have got away again. Nina reckons they'll already be on their way back to Romania.'

'That will be a job for the lawyers to sort out, to see if they can be arrested and then extradited.'

'I guess so.'

We exchanged a hug and a promise to keep in touch.

'You stink, Finlay. If you're going straight home to Jenny, I suggest you have a shower before you get too close to her.'

We said our goodbyes as I turned the ignition key and started the engine. As I was about to pull off, I realised the conversation with Wendy had distracted me. I hadn't checked her car. I gripped the steering wheel and edged forward.

Nothing happened.

Chapter 102

Dawn was breaking as I pulled up outside the safe house.

A light was on in the main bedroom. I let myself in through the front door and crept as quietly as I could up the stairs. All was quiet.

In the half-light I could see the door to Becky's room was slightly ajar. Gently, I pushed it open and leaned in to look in on my daughter. A small night-light cast a soft glow across the bed. I stood, silent, so as not to disturb her. It was a wonderful experience, listening to my own flesh and blood breathing, gently and steadily. She was deeply asleep, her tiny fingers wrapped around a small bear wearing a familiar blue uniform. I took a deep breath, stepped backward, closed the door and then walked into the main bedroom.

Jenny was awake. I dropped my clothes onto the floor and, as I climbed into bed, she rolled toward me and extended her arms. I moved closer, pressing up against her skin. She felt warm, her skin soft and sensual. Her hands stroked the back of my head and neck. 'You smell of fireworks,' she said, softly

'It's been quite a night,' I replied, only then remembering Wendy's advice to take a shower.

'I know. Toni Fellowes rang – she wants you to call her in the morning, by the way – she told me to check the news updates. I was still listening in as I heard you open the front door.'

'What did it say?'

'That the missing policewoman had been rescued following a joint operation between the Met and Gloucester police. It was you, wasn't it? That's what you were doing down there.'

'Yes, I was there. Sorry it took so long.'

'I was worried, and if I'm honest, a bit angry ... but then I thought. That girl is someone's daughter. If it were my daughter ... well, I'm just glad it was my husband that was looking for her, my husband that helped find her. Was she alright?'

'We were just in time.'

Jenny pulled me tight. 'I'm so proud of you Robert Finlay. I want you to always remember that...'

The words faded as I closed my eyes. In the darkness, I smiled. Exhaustion released my mind from all thoughts, both conscious and uncontrolled. Sleep, irresistible and comforting, drew me in.

I welcomed it with open arms.

Chapter 103

Grahamslaw studied his companion as she ordered a second round of coffees.

He now understood why she had insisted they meet privately, and away from the Yard. What he had yet to work out was why she had chosen to confide such sensitive information in him.

He allowed his focus to switch to the window. Outside, along Strutton Ground, shoppers and commuters wandered past, blissfully unaware as to the content of a conversation that had been taking place just yards from them. In many ways, he envied their ignorance.

Toni Fellowes paid the barista and, with her purse tucked under her arm, she held his gaze as she returned to their table.

He slid the Hastings file to one side. 'Best not get coffee stains on it, eh?' he said.

Fellowes sat opposite him, the scent of her perfume wafting gently in his direction; Rive Gauche, if he wasn't mistaken.

'What happened to the WPC that was rescued?' she asked.

'She's OK we think. Time will tell. She's in a convalescent home in Brighton for now.'

'And the outstanding traffickers? I heard two of them got away.'

'One of them did, for sure. We found the other one dead on a railway line a couple of days ago. He was in a real mess and might not have been identified very easily, except for the fact we found Relia Stanga's severed hand in his jacket pocket.'

'Nasty.'

'We think the main suspect has headed back to the continent, but we'll catch up with him soon enough, I'm sure. Now ... what about this file here?'

'Have you finished reading the official version?' she asked.

'Yes ... if what you're saying is true in this alternative – and I'm not inferring it isn't – that official report is sanitised.'

'For obvious reasons ... that you now understand.'

'Indeed. You're quite certain of your evidence to implicate MI6 in the killing of the Increment men?'

'Absolutely.'

'Well, at least I got one part right; it was Colonel Monaghan behind it.'

'And it was only due to his belief that Finlay and Jones both had an affair with his wife that he decided to include them as part of his brief.'

'How did Finlay take it when you told him?' asked Grahamslaw.

'Surprisingly pragmatic. To be honest, I think he had an inkling there was more to it. He's happy it's forgotten about.'

'He's no fool. So, if the news didn't cause upset, I'd figure you're right – he probably knew something. Why did you choose to tell him?'

'For the same reason I'm telling you. If something happens to me, I want someone to know why; someone who might be able to see justice done.'

'You're confident Finlay won't go after this Green character?'

'He won't ... and we've agreed he will keep it from Kevin Jones. Jones would want to get even, I suspect.'

'Yes, I think he probably would. So, telling Finlay and me is a kind of insurance?'

'With a difference. The people I'm insuring against won't know this policy exists.'

'It might be useful if you remind Green you have a means to expose him, just in case? Without mentioning me or Finlay, of course.'

'Fair point. I'll give that some thought.'

'And you think that also having me know about this Al Anfal organisation will help you? It might have the opposite effect – add me to the list of those at risk.'

'Not if you keep it to yourself.'

'It's useful. And I wouldn't be surprised if their existence becomes public knowledge one day.'

The barista was closer now, cleaning tables. Grahamslaw waited until he had collected the crockery from their previous drinks before continuing. 'You know ... when I first started this job I was given a bit of advice by my predecessor: beware the men in suits.'

'He was telling you not to trust people like me?' said Toni.

'That's what I took it to mean, at first. But then, as time wore on, I came to understand what he was really referring to. Yes, it applies to spooks, but it can also refer to bureaucracy – the system, the old boy's network or simply the established way of doing things.'

'Anything that wears a suit?'

'Exactly. In your case, it would suggest you'd be wise not to rock the boat.'

'To heed the warning, you mean?'

'That would be my suggestion, yes. What do you intend to do, now that this report is finished?'

'I've been giving it a lot of thought lately. For a while I thought of quitting.'

'Yours isn't an easy profession to move on from.'

'True. And I've just learned that I'm up for a promotion to Section Head.'

'Is it a shoe-in?'

'Not exactly … but let's just say my information comes from a good source.'

'Will you take it?'

'I think so, yes. I've had an education in the last couple of weeks, an introduction to the real world, you might say.'

'The world of the spy?'

'The world of dishonesty and subterfuge. I've discovered I can hold my own in a world of hidden agendas, where using people to fulfil your duty to your country is acceptable, but also where it's OK to use people to fulfil personal ambitions.'

Grahamslaw noticed Toni's smile transform into a wicked grin, like that of a naughty boy who had just performed some fiendish practical joke. He wondered what thoughts it revealed. 'And that's somewhere you want to stay?' he asked.

'Not only that, I think it's something I'm quite suited to … now that I know the rules of the game.'

'Was it Le Carré who called it a "deadly game"?'

'Quite possibly …'

The Anti-Terrorist Commander drained his coffee in one. He understood only too well how Toni had now come to terms with using people. She had done it with Finlay and got away with it. Maybe now might be a good time to tell her he knew, or maybe not. He leant back in his seat, slowly came to a decision and met her eyes.

'We should talk again, Toni,' he said. 'Maybe over dinner one evening? We could talk about things other than work for a change.'

Returning his gaze, with a hint of a playful smile, Toni said 'I was thinking the same thing. In fact, I have a black dress in the office I think would be perfect.'

I bet you have, he thought. And I bet you know a lot about many subjects we haven't yet discussed. As he stood to leave, he paused for a moment, wondering how best to leave things. In the event, he just smiled, and headed out into the fresh air.

It could wait.

Chapter 104

Julian Armstrong leaned back in his leather chair.

The frame creaked. It was late. The fire had long since burned out as he worked. So absorbed was he in discovering the wording of the document, he had forgotten to add extra logs and then hardly noticed as the house started to chill.

The script was a mixture of ancient and more modern language, as if it stemmed from an original plan that had been modified and adapted to meet changing circumstances. From what he had deduced, Al Anfal was already over a hundred and fifty years old.

A half-empty tumbler of Penderyn sat next to the computer screen. He hadn't touched it for several hours.

Outside the house, the mountain was bathed in low cloud. All around, the early-morning light was grey, every surface damp and chilled. Reaching for the whisky, Armstrong took a large swig and then swept his spectacles onto his head. With his free hand, he rubbed the bridge of his nose. He had promised himself he would destroy the Al Anfal file as soon as Finlay left. Temptation had proved too strong. Now, he was beginning to wonder if he had done the right thing. He had suspected all along that the document was far more than he had revealed to the curious policeman. It was. Al Anfal was a veritable Pandora's Box.

Possessing it – even simply having knowledge of its content – was a curse. As if knowledge of the Jihadist political agenda wasn't enough, the document revealed the incredible plans to lure Western powers into conflict with Middle East dictatorships, creating power vacuums that represented opportunities to seize power. How it had ever come to be in the possession of a former SAS soldier, he could only guess.

Armstrong reassured himself. He knew if he had destroyed the document without finishing the translation, he would always have wondered. The academic in him cried out to retain it. The survivor warned otherwise ... and reminded him that he had made a promise.

He placed the half-empty glass to one side, opened the doors to the log burner and lit a small fuel block. Topping the burner up with kindling, he waited as the flames grew. Doubts remained.

There would be no turning back. If he lived to be a hundred, he would never see the likes of the document again.

Slowly, he lifted the top sheet from the pile, studied it for a moment then started to crush it into a small ball. The fire was now growing. The welcome heat, comforting.

The survivor prevailed. This is going to take a while, he thought. But it was the best thing to do. The first sheet started to burn. Soon it was joined by a second and then, a third. And then he stopped. What was he doing?

Turning to face the sideboard, he sought out the only source of independent advice he had. 'What would you do, Mary?' he asked of the photograph.

His wife didn't react, didn't move or even register the question but still, she gave him the answer he sought. 'Be brave, Julian, be brave.'

He sat back, pulling away from the growing heat, drained the whisky glass, stood … and stretched his aching frame.

'Yes,' he said. 'Be brave.'

Acknowledgements

To my agent, James Wills of Watson-Little Ltd, I extend my thanks. Not simply for your counsel, but for your friendship. For taking the time to listen to me when all was not well and for saying the right thing at the right time.

To my editor, West Camel, I save a huge hug. You have taught me so much in the last couple of years. I cannot thank you enough.

To my inspirational publisher, Karen Sullivan, thanks for having faith in me and for providing the opportunity to realise this ambition.

To my good friend Danny and to Roddy Llewellyn, I extend a thanks for your time and generous advice. I hope the result does it justice.

And a special mention to my friend, Sian Phillips (@_Sians) who proofreads with such skill and looks after my blog with such creativity.

At home, my partner Heather who has read, checked, commented and made incredible suggestions as I worked. Without her, *Deadly Game* would never have been written. Finally, to Harry, Xhosa and Buddy, my four-legged companions. My little mates who listen to me and help me unwind as we walk the Welsh Hills together and make plans for book three. And to Harley, who sadly passed before this work was complete.

If you enjoyed Deadly Game, you'll love ...